The Mercy

of

Snowmelt

A human-authored, indie-published work

Fiction under the pen name JoJo Riley

The Mercy of Snowmelt

Yellow Moon Rising (Book One)
Yellow Moon Justice (Book Two)

Nonfiction under the pen name Pjo Riley

Atheist in Church – on heaven and other mysteries

Postcards from Planet Eldercare – the final frontier

More info at www.pjoriley.com

Cover design by the fabulous Lynne Pierce (says the author)

*For my part, I know nothing with any certainty,
but the sight of stars makes me dream.*
Vincent Van Gogh

One

L ater, details of their fight would sharpen and fall into sequence, but just now Lolly's mind seemed filled with jumbled images— the knife in Russell's hand, the long wait for daybreak, his cry of pain, the fireplace poker, the blood on her blouse.

She had made it to Salt Lake City, where the driver of the Greyhound bus announced a stop for the night. Passengers could travel north in the morning, or continue west. Back in Gilleon, she'd faced that old dilemma of choosing safety versus doing what the nuns had taught: *Turn the other cheek.* This time she had chosen safety, thus her flight by Greyhound. Hopefully, Utah was far enough removed from Oklahoma that Russell could not intercept her in the morning when she reboarded. She rechecked the locks on her motel door then washed at the sink, leaving her bra in place with its extra layer of medical cotton inside the right cup. Only a little blood had seeped through.

Taking up her trusty pint of Old Grand-Dad, she knelt beside the double bed and swallowed a mouthful. A calming, golden heat flared in the core of her and worked its way outward as she concentrated on a habit learned in childhood. During truly rocky times she practiced simple prayers grounded in those early years of Catholicism and a bit of her own Bible study. She'd never had a prayer directly answered, but the notion of God remained attractive for its suggestion that events seemingly beyond control were actually part of some greater plan.

Plenty of subjects deserved prayer, for instance President Kennedy's quest for an answer to the threat of communism, and for America to win the space race. Plus, children were always starving somewhere in the world. But in the cone of light spilling from the motel bathroom, Lolly asked forgiveness for detouring from the *till death do us part* portion of her wedding vows. There was no death because he hadn't killed her and she hadn't killed him, but their fight had damaged her dedication to keeping her marriage intact, and that itself felt like a type of death.

Switching prayer gears, she once more acknowledged having failed her childhood friend Norma Jeane Baker, a subject as familiar as the moon. It had been a winter's night when Lolly scrambled through the orphanage to save herself instead of summoning help for Norma Jeane. A child's innocent mistake, but weighted with such gravity that she carried it to this day, thinking of it often and ... and ... a detail mentioned by the bus driver penetrated her thoughts. He'd said that tomorrow's route would pass through Reno, the location of Norma Jeane's last movie, *The Misfits*.

That movie had capped her old friend's unsettled march through marriages and divorces, triumphs and failures. Through the haze of shock surrounding her current situation, Lolly's hopes rose a little. She had harbored no particular plan when boarding the Greyhound out of Gilleon; lacking her own vehicle, it seemed the best way to put some distance between herself and Russell. Now, though, she saw that she needn't only remove herself from her husband's violence, she could seek out the last location linked to the one person who had loved her like a sister. And whom she had loved the exact same way.

Norma Jeane's death last year, in August of '62, had rocked the world and dashed forever the slim-to-none odds of Lolly reconnecting with her, a daydream Lolly had nurtured for years. What remained was her hope that Norma Jeane had found a final resting place worthy of her gentle soul. Now she dared to imagine that if heaven was indeed eternal, clues about those who reached it might leave a trail of starry crumbs to be noticed by someone searching for them. She could be that searcher and finding that trail would ease the guilt she had carried all these years. With nothing much to lose and so much to gain, what harm could there be in spending a little effort on following the remains of a daydream that had once seemed plausible? She made up her mind. *Call me crazy, but Reno, here I come.*

Warmed by her newfound purpose, she stashed her bourbon and crawled beneath the faded sheets and tufted bedspread. When she lay back, her pillow flattened with a sigh, as if it too had waited a long, long time.

After sleeping fitfully through all the highway noises and voices on the street, Lolly rose early to stand outside Salt Lake City's interstate bus depot until it opened to admit passengers. At the black-and-white counter, she paid for a day's transport to Nevada.

Taking her ticket from the agent, she felt a prick of pleasure that her goal was a town famous for its "Harolds Club or Bust" highway signs dotting Middle America. She opened her mind to the notion that Reno held an answer to her old friend's ultimate fate. Optimism and a twenty-dollar fare would get her there.

Her journey west resumed, Lolly dozed, largely oblivious to various stops and starts and a light snow falling along Nevada's eastern border. Outside, miles of sagebrush and greasewood lay buried beneath a thick white crust. Along came the majestic Ruby Mountains, and later, frosty alkali flats in the middle of what looked a lot like nowhere.

After a couple of stops in small desert towns, the bus topped a low hill and descended into the open palm of snow-capped mountains. Dead ahead, under a blue-black sky, lay the jeweled valley that was Reno. From its center stretched threads of twinkling lights that made it look not too large nor too small. Perhaps just the right size for people to conduct a bit of personal business without anyone paying them much mind. Lolly sure hoped so.

The mud-spattered coach swung wide through a series of streets before shuddering to a stop alongside a cinderblock building. A bit wobbly from the extended confinement, Lolly stepped down into the chilly night air. Cases in hand, she hailed a taxi and asked the driver to show her the main drag on the way to the closest bargain motel.

Circling round to Virginia Street, the cabby mentioned recent rains falling on high-elevation snowpack and a day's worth of flooding around town. Then he cruised past a slew of buildings sporting neon signs that glittered like multicolored stars tethered to the streets. Lolly had always viewed stars as mysterious, hopeful objects blinking across distances too deep to fathom, yet here was a place that captured their likenesses in its plate-glass windows.

Catching her eye in his mirror the driver spoke. "How about them apples?"

Lolly nodded. She could count on two fingers the things she knew about Reno—its reputation for fast living and the thousands of divorces granted each year. That last detail had not escaped her, but she was reluctant to examine the state of her marriage. She wasn't proud about her flight from Gilleon and the reasons for it, but she shoved thoughts about that episode into a corner of her mind. She had crossed three states for a cause more heartwarming than the current state of her marriage, a cause connected to the gentlest person of her life—Norma Jeane. Her old friend's effervescent spirit seemed apparent among these flickering, dancing lights. The effect steadied her. "Is it always like this?" she asked the cabby. "Always lit up like there's no tomorrow?"

"You bet," came the reply. "The better to see what you're after."

Lolly allowed herself a smile. She had come to the right place.

Two

L olly had extracted half of the money in her and Russell's checking account the same morning she fled Oklahoma. That cash would run out before month's end, so she spent the next few days strolling Reno's downtown zone to study every casino, restaurant, and retail business from inside and out and applying for work at a half dozen of them. She would need funds to last her through her search for potential signposts pointing to a heaven for Norma Jeane. Such a search could consume a few weeks, and she couldn't exactly call Russell and ask him to send her more money with which to keep her distance from him. Plus, then he'd know exactly where she was.

The first job she was offered was as hostess in the Paradise Club's coffee shop. It was listed as permanent but she figured that revealing her commitment as temporary would get her exactly nowhere so she kept her temporary intentions a secret. With her job confirmation in hand, she secured a room in a women-only boarding house where the landlady posed no awkward questions.

A week later, finished with her fourth shift at her new job, Lolly zigzagged through the narrow rows of clinking, clanging slot machines lining the casino floor. It was 8:10 p.m. and the Saturday evening action was getting underway.

Approaching the club's Hideout bar, she detected the distinctive sound of guitar music layered atop the clatter of slot machines ingesting and regurgitating coins. This wasn't jukebox tunes or a recorded soundtrack, but real music that called her closer. She shouldered her tote bag and stepped past the L-shaped bar and through the narrow entrance of its adjacent lounge, pausing to let her eyes adjust.

In the far corner, a Negro musician strummed an instrumental version of one of Sinatra's signature songs. Much-beloved Hollywood royalty, Sinatra. Maybe one of Norma Jeane's favorites too, during her quest for ... What was it her old friend—by then an adult and going by the name Marilyn—had sought? Only love, surely, and respect, the same as people everywhere.

The guitar man was dressed like a beat poet, in a dark turtleneck sweater and pants, with dark glasses set on his face. The sight of him cast her back to 1956 in Los Angeles when she would go with roommates to a barbecue joint that let local musicians play for free meals on Friday nights. Some of them were pretty good but you never knew who would show up to play. One musician might try his hand at covering Little Richard's rock 'n roll. Another might regale diners with folk music, or country and western. Since country music was almost all she'd heard while in Oklahoma with Russell, she found herself grateful that this lounge musician played something else, anything else. At the end of his current ballad, he segued into a number made famous by Dean Martin. No singing, just the music.

Lolly surveyed the scene. A tipsy couple sat snuggling behind circlets of smoke rising from an ashtray on their table. To her right, a half-dozen drinkers watched each other in the mirror above the bar. The coffee shop where she spent her shifts sported well-lit linoleum and Formica-topped tables, the better to see your meal when it arrived, but this low-lit lounge was built for flights of song and romance. She wasn't in the market for romance, but music seemed a nice way to cap an evening.

Few of the lounge's occupants applauded when the guitar man finished each number. He might have been invisible, just a pair of hands and an instrument, as noteworthy as the flocked wallpaper or the carpet underfoot. Heat rose in her at the apparent dismissal of one of her fellow employees and when the musician finished another Dean Martin number, Lolly applauded. Some other time she would settle in to listen longer. Stepping back to leave, her tote bumped against someone standing close behind her. "Oh," she said, turning, "pardon me."

The person she'd practically stepped on broke into a smile, saying, "Did I startle you?" He stood his ground, a bulky man in a tailored suit. "My apologies, my fault entirely. I hope you'll let me make it up to you. With a cocktail perhaps? I'm Ben Caldwell, casino manager. It's a pleasure to meet you … um?"

Lolly's hand went automatically to her name badge. "Luella, but I go by Lolly."

They shook hands as he said with mock-reproach, "If you're on duty, no booze."

Lolly unpinned her badge and motioned in the direction of the coffee shop. "I'm done for tonight. It's the end of my first week. Well, half-week."

"I *thought* you looked new. I've been away or we might have met sooner." He stepped toward the closest lounge table and gestured for her to take a seat.

"Wait a minute," said Lolly. She really shouldn't accept, not in her new place of employment and with someone essentially a stranger, even if he ran the place. "Why the offer?"

He shrugged. "You work here and I work here. It's just a way to say 'Welcome.'"

Lolly *was* thirsty, and obviously, she could leave at any point. But first— "Do managers drink on duty?"

Crinkles formed around his eyes as he signaled the bartender. "Managers do almost anything they please."

When a cocktail waitress appeared beside them Caldwell said, "Cara. My regular, please, and for this young lady ..."

Lolly paused. She had only meant to look around and absorb a few details. Besides, back at her boarding house room she had her Old Grand-Dad.

The casino boss spoke up. "I know. A 'Grasshopper.' All the ladies like them."

The waitress left and returned promptly with a frothy green concoction for Lolly and a highball glass of something dark for the casino boss, who signed the register slip. As the waitress left, the boss lifted his glass and clinked it with Lolly's. "To new faces that brighten our landscape."

"Cheers," said Lolly. She thought it improbable that a casino executive would befriend a lowly hostess, except that most men would want to size up the new girl. She didn't mind; they all did it. Besides, she hadn't any place more compelling to waste an hour. At her boarding house she kept mostly to her room, dodging the other boarders in order to avoid swapping personal details. Her room there was pleasant enough, though rather silent.

She wouldn't have chosen this sweet, girly drink, but now she bobbed her foot to the guitar music as she savored how the crème de menthe and crème de cacao produced the beginnings of that familiar warm glow inside her.

The boss made small talk, eventually asking what had brought her to Reno. Having come from a place where everyone seemed to know everyone else's business she simply said, "It's complicated," and agreed to a second cocktail.

At one point the boss motioned to her ring finger, saying, "Happily married?"

She gave her plain gold band a turn. Ten days ago she might have answered, "As happy as anyone," but the two cocktails, mild as they were, had diluted her usual restraint. Instead, she shrugged. Let him think whatever he wanted.

He studied her for a moment, then drew out a business card and offered it, saying, "It's been a pleasure, but I'd better get back to the casino."

Lolly dropped the card into the zippered pocket of her canvas tote, drained the last drop from her glass, and stood. "Thanks a lot. You know, for the hospitality." She meant it. Even small kindnesses were better than none at all.

Nodding, he moved to help her with her coat.

"Not just yet," she said. "You go ahead." That's when she noticed the guitar man was gone, leaving behind a tan-colored amplifier but taking with him a measure of the sophistication she always credited to people with talent. "Wait," she said to the casino boss. "Who was that playing the guitar?"

He glanced toward the corner where a trio of performers were now setting up additional microphone stands. "That first one was the warm-up. These next ones, they're the prime-time entertainment." With that, he left.

In spite of the boss man's words, Lolly felt she'd missed something about that first musician, who had exuded a certain controlled energy behind his playing. In her experience, reserved people often had interesting things to say.

She made her way out of the lounge and crossed through the noise and smoke of the casino to the Virginia Street exit. Outside, the din of machines gave way to the *shush* of cars rolling slowly past. Her breath rose pale around her face as she buttoned her wool coat. From her tote she pulled on gloves and weatherproof overshoes before turning in the direction of the boarding house and away from a pair of spotlights set up to sweep the night sky.

A block beyond the glow of the brightest lights, she paused before a telephone booth. She had half a dozen times imagined phoning

Russell to let him know ... what exactly? That she had lied? Old news. No doubt he was reveling in the chance to call her a thief all over town for taking money that was his though it was actually theirs. The sympathy elicited from his drinking buddies would ease his outrage, a little. If she called and he answered, he would insist that she had wronged him, and she would counter that he had wronged her. Their conversation would go nowhere. She couldn't do it.

Pulling a dinner roll from her pocket, she took a bite and stepped past the booth. Chewing slowly, she walked south.

At the boarding house, Mrs. Ruddle, the owner, and her other boarders, Shirley and Doris, sat watching a television variety show through a scrim of grainy patterns. It looked a lot like listening and not much like watching. Lolly gave them a wave as she headed for the stairs.

In the upstairs hall bathroom, she steeled herself for a task she had been dreading. For a week she had worn her Maidenform bra all day and night, cushioning its seams with a layer of cotton in the right-hand cup. The constant throb and the pull of her stitches had eased, but the threads were still with her. In the mirrored medicine cabinet above the sink, she studied the row of black sutures in a pattern resembling railroad ties running beneath her right nipple. Had Russell needed stitches too?

The bathroom's pink porcelain fixtures receded as she mentally replayed her hurried dash to the country clinic, the concerned physician, her one-syllable answers, and fatigue as deep as the ocean. Stitched up, but numb and confused, she had left before the clinic staff could summon the deputy sheriff from the next town over. Other wives might press charges, but so might other husbands.

Now she assumed the roles of doctor *and* patient. With a dab of rubbing alcohol, she sterilized the tweezers from her travel kit and the blades of her sewing snips. Gritting her teeth she clipped the center of each stitch, tugging each heavy thread from its bed of flesh. With each release, a pinch of pain.

Her extractions left tiny puncture marks. The clinic doctor had called the slash "superficial" and the damage cosmetic, but the scar it had left was red and raised, a tribute to Russell's anger that night. Wincing at her own touch, she massaged the raised line with petroleum jelly then pulled on her flannel pajamas. "Follow up in a week," the doctor had instructed. Well, nine days had passed and she had followed-up with herself.

Within minutes Lolly knelt on her room's oval bedside rug. Once again, a swig, a request for guidance, then sleep.

Three

The start of Lolly's search for clues to Norma Jeane's heaven came on her second Sunday, when she rose early to use the shared hallway bathroom before the other boarders climbed out from under their quilts. She thought about making a breakfast of the pear she had bought at a neighborhood market, but all she could stomach was a dinner roll she'd brought home from work.

Though any trail of Norma Jeane's would be faint, this was the town that might hold evidence of Lolly's old friend. So many years had passed—more than twenty—since Norma Jeane turned fifteen and began planning her escape from their southern California orphanage by marrying a boy she hardly knew. Now Norma Jeane was truly gone, her sudden death by overdose carried last summer by nearly every newspaper, television network, and magazine.

If Norma Jeane's manner of death might have pointed her toward purgatory, could her life before death have earned her access to heaven? And what sort of heaven would have welcomed her? To Lolly, the notion of heaven included contradictions: a warm welcome, eternal happiness, and the likelihood of being cast out for not meeting certain standards. The nuns she'd known would have derided the adult Norma Jeane for her sexy calendar and racy movies, but to Lolly's mind, her friend was more qualified than most for heavenly relief.

Norma Jeane's religious practices had included a variety of jig-sawed pieces cut from multiple traditions (Lolly had learned this from Hollywood fan magazines and the occasional gossip column). But had Norma Jeane ever settled on one religion? For her third marriage, the actress had wed a Jew, and it stood to reason that through some type of human gravitational effect, that religion might have stuck, even though the marriage eventually fizzled. Judaism might hold answers to Norma Jeane's final reward.

Quite some time had passed since Lolly herself had attended any worship service. Her serial absences began shortly after that night in the orphanage when the day man showed up at the church she and the others attended. As if to signal that having witnessed her cowardice, he was watching to see that she kept her mouth shut. Since then, she struggled with a nameless anxiety about Catholic houses of worship not being entirely safe. A Jewish house, though, was probably benign.

She brushed her one-and-only dress skirt, donned a sweater set, and dabbed clear nail polish on a tiny hole up high in her last good pair of stockings. In the kitchen she greeted the lady of the house who gestured toward Lolly's upswept curls.

"Don't you look nice," said Mrs. Ruddle. "And your hair … Are you off to church?"

"Synagogue, actually. I looked in the phone book and there's one downtown."

"Are they open today? I didn't know you were—"

"Oh, I'm not." Lolly couldn't very well say that she was looking for clues to a heaven for a deceased friend she hadn't seen for twenty-plus years. When you put it that way it sounded a little crazy. She said, "I'm … gathering information."

The landlady narrowed her eyes. "If you're not Jewish, will they let you in?"

Lolly thought a moment. "I hope so. They have the same Old Testament as everyone else. I think."

"Well," said Mrs. Ruddle, "when you put it that way."

"Anyway, I figure if I take the bus, I can keep my good shoes dry."

"You'll need twenty cents."

Lolly patted her pocketbook.

Mrs. Ruddle tipped her chin toward the women at the dining table. "I'll go to Mass later, myself. Some can't be bothered to fix their own toast." But she didn't look unhappy about a simple meal she could charge extra for. "Mine is Trinity Episcopal. You could go with me at 11:00. Our choir is the best in town."

"I'm sure you're right," said Lolly, "but this one's on my list."

"You have a list?" She looked perplexed. "Will you need a hat?"

"For Jewish?"

Mrs. Ruddle shrugged. "Even the Episcopalians have that rule."

This stumped Lolly. She'd only arrived in town with the basics. "I know about the Catholics."

"Let me get you one," said Mrs. Ruddle, "just in case."

Carrying her landlady's cloche, Lolly rode the orange and yellow downtown bus, which took her slightly north and west of the casinos, whose neon signs looked positively dull in the light of day. The No. 5 bus let her out at Fourth and Sierra streets, within one block of the two-story brick and granite synagogue. Arriving at the building, she noted a single white sedan parked at the sidewalk.

Lolly could count on one finger what she knew about Jewishness— just the part she'd heard about the Old Testament—but the sight of a lone car on the street and not a single one in the side lot seemed a poor omen. Even if she was early in arriving for service, there ought to be signs of preparation.

She climbed the east-facing steps and knocked on the double door. After a full minute of waiting she knocked again then retreated to the street and studied the upper windows, which stared back blankly. The place was closed up tight. Already a setback and she'd only just begun her quest.

The air held a chill, but the sun shone warm on the sidewalk. Lolly's boarding house lay south so she started walking in that direction, circumventing puddles of meltwater and admiring the fronts of businesses and shops that were closed for the day. Eventually, the street she was on terminated at a brick building. Glimpsing snippets of bare trees to the right, she turned that direction. Soon, the deep brass tones of a church bell reached her from beyond a bridge and a small, frosty-looking park. Lolly followed the sound.

Within half a block she passed a telephone booth without slowing her steps. She still had not called Russell. Just the act of leaving Gilleon had loosened her thoughts about whether she had wed the right man. She was supposed to have loved him, and he her. But, how could someone who loved a woman force her into sex, and how could someone who loved a man feel so willing to leave him, leave town, leave the state? Her early life had been nearly empty of examples of love. She'd had no family life. The nuns hadn't loved her or the other children. They'd been more like wardens. Now she wondered if she'd really loved him. Beyond the sisterly love of Norma Jeane, did she really know what love was? She hated to be a quitter, but she and Russell probably didn't belong together because the day that Greyhound bus deposited her in Reno, a deep relief washed through her like a cleansing rain.

She halted before a flower shop whose sign read "Closed" though she could see people inside. Russell had always deemed cut flowers a waste of money for how quickly they faded and died. The thought of his inflexibility prompted Lolly to try the shop door, which opened with a jangle. Inside, harried-looking workers were busy making last-minute displays for an evening event, but sold her a single thorn-less rose. Returning to the sidewalk, she sent a silent message toward Gilleon: *Take that.*

She had been pondering lately what had gone wrong between Russell and her. She could name any number of false pretenses and obstructions each one of them had created for the other. For instance, he had sold her a story about being a rodeo professional, and while it was true that he knew his way around a saddle bronc and rode every chance he got, that's not how he made his living, which was in a tire store. New tires, retreads, balancing, and alignment. Russell's association with grease and vulcanized rubber would not have bothered Lolly if it hadn't seemed to plague him so. He seemed to think he ought to be a star of the horseback circuit, as if he somehow deserved it. His view was that the world conspired against his stardom. There was also the matter of her waitressing, which with tips sometimes rivaled Russel's wages, further feeding his prickliness.

Catching herself, Lolly shoved thoughts of Russell aside and turned her ear to the sound of the nearby river splitting in two beneath a wide bridge. A walkway led to the far side, where, as if Mrs. Ruddle had led her to it, she made out the sign in front of Trinity Episcopal Church. Episcopal wasn't one of Norma Jeane's religions, but Lolly figured she might as well glance in.

The early service was well underway as Lolly dropped into a pew at the back. There she loosened her shoes and bent to rub one stockinged foot. Catching a sharp look from a woman at her far right, she sat a little straighter, grateful for Mrs. Ruddle's hat.

For the balance of the hour, she followed the flow of hymns and prayers, one beat behind the movements of everyone else who knew when to sit or stand. Mrs. R, as Lolly thought of her now, had been dead right about the service containing rituals cribbed from Catholic traditions. At least it was in English.

Along came another hymn. Lolly stood, concentrating on the beautiful woodwork and vaulted ceiling and sent a personal message to God: *I know I haven't been exactly regular at showing up in person, but I could use some help. The worst part is how I watch and wait when I should act. I would like to be braver, really. I'd like to be ... worthy, and ... anyhow, I hope it's not too late.*

When the service concluded, Lolly pulled her hat on more firmly and walked forward against the flow of parishioners for a closer look at the ornate stained-glass panels positioned above the sanctuary. As she stood gazing up, a clergyman arrived. Not the young one who had conducted the service, but an older one who had assisted.

Lolly bade him a good morning.

He presented a pleasant, weathered face as he pushed his spectacles higher on his nose. "Hello. I see you've discovered our windows. We try not to be too proud of them but they are rather grand. These two you probably know—Matthew and Mark. The others are Saint Gregory and Saint Cecilia, both patron saints of musicians. They benefit our choir."

"They're terrific," said Lolly. "Like windows you'd see in heaven. I know, that's not what the Bible says. It says pearls and streets of gold and lions lying down with lambs. I know that, but when I think of heaven I think of bright colors and everything moving slow and easy. No fights, no weapons, just peace."

The clergyman touched a hand to his chin. "You've given considerable thought to the subject."

"I think about it all the time. But still I wonder, how hard is it *really*, to get there? The Bible makes it sound possible, but then there's all sorts of rules and requirements and all that talk of sin, how sinful everyone is, and, I don't know, it seems like maybe the odds aren't very good."

"I don't suppose it was meant to be easy. Keeping faith can take a fair amount of effort."

"Don't I know it?" Lolly's eyes began to water. "I have this worry ... about someone finding life too hard, and maybe they give up. But for years before they give up, they truly search for something to believe in. Would a person like that make it into heaven?"

The clergyman looked thoughtful. "You sound discouraged."

"Me? No! I'm ... I'm asking because of a friend."

"I see, *a friend*." His eyes creased to match his smile. "Well, reaching heaven isn't promised, but we might say a good end follows from the way a person lives. Whether theirs has been a heartfelt belief in the Lord, and a relinquishing of sin."

Sin was the element that concerned Lolly most. It seemed there was always some sin or other waiting around the corner. If a person believed the nuns' teachings, sins were a dime a dozen, in fact, people came into the world as sinners. How then, could any person truly measure up to all the expectations?

Lolly wondered now whether her old friend, having worked for a while in Reno, had also stood before these same colorful glass panels. She asked, "Have you been preaching here long, Father, um ..."

"Father Gerard or even just Gerard. I am semi-retired, mostly assisting our young priest. I led Trinity's services for more than a decade."

"I'm thinking that you've seen a lot of worshippers. Would you remember most of them?"

"I would know all our regulars, but we also receive a fair number of visitors. It's the nature of this town. If someone came for only one visit ... well, I would not vouch for my recall."

Lolly's own recollections rose like the morning sun. Norma Jeane's sun-kissed hair and ready smile. The way she rarely protested when the orphanage staff ordered them around or brandished a switch. She had an easy spirit for someone whose mother regularly disappeared for long stretches. If not exactly religious, Norma Jeane had at some point heeded a call to faith, but in adulthood she hadn't been all innocence and purity. And if she'd been turned away from a heavenly outcome, some of the fault would surely lie with the way Lolly had once failed to protect her from the sexual attentions of a creep.

"I'd better go," she told the Father. "Thanks for letting me take up your time."

He spread his arms in a gesture that encompassed everything around them—altar, pulpit, carved railings, and pews. "This will be here whenever you need fellowship and worship." He looked directly at her. "Peace be with you."

"Thanks," she replied, "and with you too."

At the back, in the vestibule, Lolly placed the rose, wilted but still fragrant, on the table that held the church's guest book. A white rose in memory of her friend, gone but not forgotten.

Outside, she turned toward Virginia Street, wondering if Sunday night would find those with cleansed spirits out on the town. Perhaps the morning's hymns, sermons, and prayers bestowed good luck upon Sabbath gamblers. Maybe those with clean consciences could count on coming out ahead.

Back at the boarding house, Lolly greeted Mrs. R, now dressed in church finery, and the other two boarders, who were reading magazines at the kitchen table, then went upstairs to soak her feet and change into her uniform—black skirt, bright pink blouse. She walked to work and by noon was at her hostess station, greeting coffee shop guests and escorting them to their tables. At 3:00 p.m. she clocked out and ordered the free meal that came with the job, sitting at the counter to nibble at a grilled cheese sandwich. Then she took her paycheck to the casino cashier who examined her Oklahoma driver's license and gave her folding money in exchange. Her own fair-and-square earnings to supplement her declining funds.

Russell would still be cursing her for taking money that had been theirs together. She'd had no choice. She would not have left Gilleon without paying their landlord, and it wasn't as if the bus lines handed out tickets for free. You couldn't rent a motel room using charm or buy groceries with a lick and a promise. No, that money was as much hers as his, maybe more so, given how they'd parted.

In the casino lavatory she unpinned the back of her hair and shed her name badge before heading to the Hideout lounge where she found the music corner empty. Only the distant noise of slot machines filtered in. Too bad. The place seemed less interesting without the guitar man's live music.

The bartender caught her eye and beckoned her over.

"You're the new girl," he said. "I'll pour you a Grasshopper."

Lolly recoiled a little. "Those aren't my kind of drink ..." She squinted at the name badge pinned above his shirt pocket ... "Roger."

His crooked smile was sincere. "Since the boss favors you, the first one's on me. What'll you have?"

"It *is* a cold walk home."

"Below freezing maybe."

"I'm getting goose bumps just talking about it."

"So, what can I pour for you?"

"How about bourbon and water, hold the ice."

Roger nodded and reached for a glass.

Lolly took her drink to the far end of the bar where she sat in relative darkness, watching people flow past the lounge entrance. In due time, Roger approached with the booze bottle and brandished it as if posing a silent question.

Lolly shook her head. "My first paycheck had only three days on it, and this week's pay goes to my rent."

"Some other time then."

"Roger that," she said with a smile.

He shook his head as if he'd heard similar jokes a thousand times. Then his eyes lit up. "I should have asked. What's your name, new girl?"

"A long-ago friend gave me the name Lolly, so that's what I go by."

"Lolly it is." He raised his bar towel and she raised her empty glass. "To friends," he said.

Lolly's days off were Monday and Tuesday. In her free time, she bought clear nail polish at the Woolworth's five-and-dime, stockings at Lerner's ladies' shop, and soda crackers at the market just north of the tracks. At the boarding house she asked Mrs. R for directions to a cheap shoe repair. She held up her best pair. "They need heel caps and maybe soles, and I can't put it off any longer. Where do you take yours?"

The woman looked down at her own scuffed black flats. "I've been wearing these for two years straight. Guess I'll wear them till they give out. Say, I don't mean to pry, but I saw you've been leaving a light on at night."

"That little one on the dresser." Lolly looked away and back. "I hope it's all right."

"Of course. I was only asking, and also, I'm wondering if you'll be staying in town after you've met the residency requirements. You might want to stick around. A girl like you could be a secretary, or an assistant to a banker or some type of executive." Mrs. R planted her feet a little wider, as if settling into the conversation. "Take my niece Linda over in Sacramento. She got herself a great secretary's job with an insurance company. Regular hours, regular pay. She meets a lot of people."

Lolly resisted glancing down at ring still on her finger. "Is there a shoe repair I can walk to?"

"I've got two textbooks Linda left behind. One of them tells you how to make a proper letter and organize files, how to book travel arrangements and a hundred other things. You'll be wanting a better job, one where you might meet another Mister. There aren't good prospects in a casino."

Lolly's face grew warm. Nothing she was any good at had come from the little she'd learned from books. Still, she didn't want to hurt the woman's feelings. She said, "Okay. I'll look at them, but about my shoes ..."

The landlady's smile widened. "Try Nevada Shoe Factory over on Sierra Street, south of First."

Walking back from the shoe repair, Lolly lingered before a pawn shop window displaying two clarinets and a trombone waiting to be rescued. She wondered who had pawned their instruments in order to pay the bills or skip town or whatever. She had never played an instrument, never had the chance, but there was something special about a person who could.

Funny. Thoughts of music didn't dredge up the worst of her years with Russell, even though during one of their disagreements in early January he had stomped on the 45 rpm records she'd carried with her from California. Bill Haley, Sam Cook, Patti Page. More and more he took offense at the smallest slights and worked out his frustration on the closest objects. She would never have been so cavalier with his possessions, his saddle or boots or riata, so instead of coming undone over her lost records, she had acted unbroken-up about them, depriving him of any satisfaction he might have gotten from her tears. She had not replaced them either. The fewer her personal effects, the fewer Russell could command.

To Lolly's mind, music represented the serene days and nights when Russell was away on the circuit. With a record on by The Kingston Trio, for instance, she had sometimes daydreamed about what her life might hold if only things were different. Not different as in the happy endings and popsicle-colored sunsets of the movies. Not rosy in their material aspects either—mansions and yachts and strolls along some foreign boardwalk—but different as in the infinitely varied ways that people approached love and friendship. She needed to stop falling for people who ended up leaving, or were dangerous, or dead: parents, Norma Jeane, boyfriends, husband. Maybe spending some time in this gambling town would change her luck.

After a Wednesday shift as hostess, Lolly slalomed through the familiar banks of slot machines to reach the Hideout. A handful of people occupied tables in the lounge, but once again the performance corner sat quiet. Her spirits drooped a little. By being absent, the mysterious guitar player grew more significant in her thoughts. Not for the famous instrumentals he played, you could hear the popular versions on many radio stations, but for the way he held himself, like someone entirely certain of what he was doing. She'd love to feel like he looked—confident and in control.

In the back corner of the performance floor, the tan amplifier sat like a solitary place holder for the black-skinned man who dressed in black. She walked to it and skimmed a hand over its tweed-like surface and the name plate reading Fender. Though it now sat lifeless, she could imagine it humming with heat while he played. She hoped its presence signified the musician's eventual return, the better to watch him make music.

Lolly reversed course and took a table where the casino's glow penetrated the lounge's low light. From her tote bag she pulled one of her landlady's offerings: Rowe Typing, Second Edition.

A cocktail waitress in a sparkly dress appeared. "What can I bring you?"

Lolly considered her financial situation. "How much for a bourbon and water?"

"If you want to call your brand, it's one-ten. Otherwise, a dollar."

"How much for a plain Coke?"

"Two bits."

Lolly ordered a Coke then waited until her drink arrived before she opened the red, canvas-covered book that hinged at the top. Inside was a diagram of a typewriter with arrows pointing to its thirty-eight parts. She turned randomly to the page that held Lesson 15. One of the lines read: d3# y6_ f4$ k8' t5% j7& s2" 19(;) d#e ;-* d3# t5% ;p* k,/.

At a glance she added the numbers, which equaled sixty-two, but nearby paragraphs of solid text joined hands to make blobs that squirmed and jiggled. That same old problem of her brain's trouble with blocks of words.

Back in high school she had been allowed to substitute study hall for the requisite typing class, for the reason that when pressured to perform on cue, she could not focus beyond her heart's panic at letters that shimmied in place or lined up wrong. Labeled "unteachable" by some of her instructors, she took an extra round of summer school to graduate. As her school life ended, she closed the door on her years of being instructed and shaped by orphanage workers who meant for her to behave without question. Afterwards, for nearly four years, she made ends meet by waitressing and cooking for an east-LA diner, attending to diner customers and the occasional suitor until one fall day, along came her husband-to-be. Different and seemingly full of promise.

Now she flipped through the typing book. One set of images showed the proper posture for a typist followed by pages and pages of timed exercises and lists, diagrams of typed letters and envelopes, "corrective drills," and "alphabetic paragraph drills." More than three hundred pages worth. Imagine!

A voice broke through her swirling thoughts. "Ah, Lolly, I thought I might find you here." It was the casino boss.

Lolly snapped her book closed. "Mr. Caldwell."

"Call me Ben, won't you? Or Caldwell. No 'Mister' needed. Studying for a typing class?"

She laid one hand atop the red cover. "Not really."

Caldwell sat himself at her table and raised a hand to signal the cocktail waitress. "I see you've switched to ... rum and Coke maybe?"

"No, it's plain." She slipped the book back into her tote.

"If you're thinking about jobs, there are plenty that pay pretty well. Running cocktails for instance, or dealing blackjack or roulette. This is a swank place. You'd look great in a cocktail outfit."

The waitress arrived and set a drink in front of him and a fresh cola in front of Lolly. "See here?" he said, pointing to the hem at knee height on the waitress. "These are made nice, to show off a girl's ... figure." He signaled the waitress to pivot slowly, which she did. "Good from all sides."

The waitress left as Caldwell continued. "Clearly, you're thinking about work that pays better. That shows ambition. We train our cocktail waitresses. Dealers take classes."

Classes. All that frenzied activity. All that competition to see who could come out on top. Lolly didn't know how to describe what was wrong about Caldwell's suggestions. Or, not *wrong* exactly, just not right for her. Wasn't it the case that every town needed people of all talents, some of whom would build businesses, invent marvelous contraptions, or conquer diseases, and others who would get up in the morning, put on a uniform, and go to work? If you could believe news reports, a diversified workforce helped the country prosper.

Of course, Caldwell couldn't know that she had chosen Reno not for its casino jobs, but for Norma Jeane's history and her own concerns of a heavenly nature. She wasn't about to share such personal details, which meant she might not easily dissuade him from making a project of her work status. She said, "If you're going to talk jobs, I'll need a stronger drink. Just none of those green things."

Caldwell grinned. "No more sissy drinks, I promise. You can name your own poison."

Four

During the next few days, Lolly spent her spare time exploring the streets beyond the casino zone. Reno was not as big as a person might think from all the night-lit businesses and the stream of cars crossing slowly beneath the Reno arch with its Biggest Little City slogan. It was, though, a bustling place, with most of the action contained within a half-mile of the casinos.

Harolds Club's gigantic mural added a certain western flair to its position north of the Paradise Club. The colorful panels arrayed above its front doors showed a wagon train, cowboys, and gold miners from pioneer days. There weren't cowboys on every corner, not the way the movies sometimes made out. When you looked past all those clanking one-armed bandits and high-stakes card games cloaked in smoke, you found ordinary folks out for a day or a night. There were well-heeled audiences, too. Lolly had seen some of those nightclub customers strolling along Virginia Street, fur coats snugged tight against the frosty air and diamonds glittering at their throats. Norma Jeane would have been right at home among them. Oh, how she wished her childhood friend was among them now.

One day before work, Lolly walked south on Virginia Street and pushed through the doors of the Mapes Hotel. Talk about a swank place, all red and gold and plush seating, and a full twelve stories of casino and hotel spaces.

The female elevator attendant resembled someone's mother dressed for business at the bank. She delivered Lolly to the Sky Room on the twelfth floor, a posh setting for dinner, drinks, and floor shows, said to have the best view around. Workers looked to be setting up for the lunch crowd as Lolly crossed the carpeted expanse to look down from the bank of windows upon the hatted heads of people below. She could picture Norma Jeane stepping carefully from a limousine, one shapely calf appearing first, then a slit up to there, a gloved hand, a fur jacket, the dazzle of her smile and that bewitching walk. A scene like that might have played out within view of these very windows. It could have, back in 1960.

The view through the wall of glass encompassed the city's southward run along a snowy mountain range that from this vantage looked like it touched the sky. The town nestled short of the mountains, its distant-most houses looking dwarfed by the long stretch of tawny foothills. South across Virginia Street stood the Riverside Hotel, opposite the same river she crossed each day on her way to work—the narrow Truckee River, recipient of all those wedding rings cast with relief into its waters. Lolly wondered what happened to all the declarations of "good-riddance" spoken aloud as the slate-colored water erased all evidence of marital mistakes. Caught on the wind, such oaths and prayers might drift upon Nevada's ever-present breeze across prairies and oceans to arrive, eventually, in some faraway country.

"Help you with anything?" asked a worker who was wiping windows.

"Just picturing what it would have been like," she said. *To feel on top of the world, for a day, or a minute.* In Reno, Lolly's sense had deepened that she had missed out on insights her old friend would have shared once they were past childhood. Given the chance she might have learned a thing or two from Norma Jeane.

"The bar's always open, of course, and lunch service will start in half an hour. If you don't mind, I'll finish this glass pane in front of you before the boss comes 'round to inspect."

Lolly moved away, wondering if she might be wrong-side-out in searching for Norma Jeane's heaven among the town's worship halls. Perhaps Norma Jeane's fate had been forged from time spent in places like this, with a rare and glorious view of a valley filled with ranchers and dreamers, con men and seekers of wealth. Inside this very building were shops full of expensive shoes, seventeen-jewel watches, and people employed to serve a customer's every whim, any of which might point to Norma Jeane and her time spent hereabouts. Such worldly things were only inferences of course, but even inferences counted; they were all she had to go on.

On another day Lolly walked back to the pawn shop. The notion of self-improvement had taken hold of her after she'd skimmed the textbooks provided by Mrs. R. If she could just latch onto the right subject she could smarten up. There were things she was plenty sharp about, just not refined, educated things.

Inside the shop, rows of objects sparkled in the glass-front counter; rings mostly, but watches too. In one aisle, a shelf held a mishmash of pocket books. She had thought she might find a book more instructive than a Perry Mason murder mystery or a story about Wyatt Earp, but then again, such slim volumes seemed approachable. You could fit four of them in the same space as one of those secretarial tomes of Mrs. R's. She fingered the sweet, Christmassy cover of *Miracle on 34th Street* by Valentine Davies. Twice she'd watched the motion picture when it first came out. Handsome John Payne had played the Fred Bailey character opposite Maureen O'Hara. She just knew Fred would prove a good father to that little girl.

Of course, that was only a story, only some writer's imagination at work, but how satisfying it felt to rejoice with little Susan when Kris Kringle's promise came true. Susan had prayed and wished and hoped like heck, and sure enough, there was the yellow house she longed for. It was enough to make a person think that prayers could come true. "How much for these?" Lolly asked the white-haired shop man.

He paused, a gold watch in hand. "Let's see. Some of them were two bits or more when they were new. How about ten cents each."

What was she doing, thinking about buying books? She liked the idea of reading, but school books had left her with a sour taste. The nice thing about these was their unassuming size. That plus how they weren't textbooks. "I don't have much to spend," she said, "and there's twelve of them. Would you take a dollar?"

"It's a deal," the man said, taking the money she pulled from her pocketbook. She tucked the books into her tote and stepped out into the winter breeze, feeling as if she'd embarked on some brave new mission.

After turning up the collar of her coat and tying a scarf over her hair, she set out for Sinclair Street. The other pedestrians she passed nodded in greeting and at first, she wondered what made them so friendly. Eventually she realized that it was probably the smile of satisfaction on her own face.

Back in her room, she dusted the pocket-sized books and set them up on the pine bureau, her own little library made from stories, paper, and paste. Then she went to ask Mrs. R for directions to certain other churches in town. While at the Mapes she had felt a connection with Norma Jeane and the sort of high life she'd had, glamour and risk and certain types of earthbound pleasures. But heaven didn't stem from lavish casino details, did it? Wouldn't entry require accomplishments beyond movie scripts and skirt lengths, dinner menus and publicity photos? Lolly needed to keep her sights set on loftier clues. She needed to keep searching in places where preachers pointed the way.

On Friday night, Lolly's shift was almost over when Ben Caldwell stepped into the coffee shop. "Oh, hello," she said before she checked her table diagram. "How many in your party?"

"No party. I'm here to take you upstairs."

Lolly glanced left and right. "What do you mean?"

"You're coming with me."

"It's only 7:45. My shift's not done."

"I spoke to your supervisor. They can spare you for the last fifteen minutes."

Lolly stood her ground until he said, "For Pete's sake, it's company business." At that she unlocked the hostess cabinet, took out her coat and bag, and accompanied him to the second floor and down a linoleum-clad hallway to the wardrobe department. There, on duty, was the same woman who had provided Lolly's hostess uniform. She seemed to be expecting them.

"Mela," he said. "This is Miss Cooper."

"Mrs. Cooper," said Lolly.

"I remember," said the petite Filipina. "She work the coffee shop."

"I'd like to see her in a cocktail uniform." He turned to Lolly as Mela retrieved a garment of the same style worn by cocktail waitresses throughout the property. "This is your chance to step up to a position that pays better."

Mela said, "I think this be close your size."

So, the other night hadn't been a fluke. Caldwell really was going to suggest she change jobs to one that paid better when you counted tips. Apparently, she had not properly explained that she didn't long to serve drinks or deal cards but to find an occupation where she *belonged*, where she felt like a contributor of something meaningful. She had sipped cocktails while he'd described the virtues of various options, so she'd been at fault for not speaking up when she should have. That old failure of courage.

Glancing at Mela's open expression, Lolly realized that the woman before her didn't know about her checkered history as an orphan or her weaknesses as a friend and wife. She could accept Lolly at face value, just a woman in need of a fitting.

And then there was Caldwell, who had taken the time to arrange a fitting for her. At this point she might as well comply. With the uniform in hand, she entered one of the fitting rooms.

After a moment, Mela knocked then joined Lolly. "Ah," she said quietly, reaching to fasten the top of the neckline. "You taller than most girls. Most need me take up hem, but not you." She reached up to tuck out of sight a stray wisp of the cotton Lolly still wore inside her bra.

Lolly waited for a question or comment about the cotton, but Mela simply walked around her, pinching the fabric this way and that. "Wrong bra," she said, gazing up at Lolly's shoulders. 'Need bra with straps no show, and give you this—" She pantomimed an upswept bosom.

"This was *his* idea," said Lolly, caring little about whether Caldwell could hear them from his post in the outer room. Admittedly, the costume made her feel a little like an actress, or a chanteuse. Where else on a daily basis would someone wear a low-cut dress shot through with metallic threads?

"Ah, bosses," said Mela with a shrug. "But everyone hope for job with tips. Good as office."

For a moment Lolly studied the guileless woman. "You have the prettiest eyes," she told Mela. She wasn't just trying to postpone the inevitable—displaying herself before Caldwell. She meant it. Mela's almond-shaped eyes were the deeply calming color of chocolate.

Mela opened the dressing room door and called out to Caldwell. "You look now." She led Lolly into the open space fronting the wardrobe counter where Caldwell squinted at her in concentration.

"Give a slow turn ... Very nice," he said. "They'll expect you to wear more makeup. And about your hair ..."

"What about it?" Lolly said, lifting a hand to her upswept curls.

"It's, ah ... kind of old-fashioned. A lot of girls are wearing their hair shorter." He held a hand up to his own brow. "It could swoop."

Suddenly Caldwell's intentions seemed entirely counter to Lolly's view of herself. She narrowed her eyes. "Clearly everything about me is wrong. Someone unhook me."

"Don't get mad," said Caldwell. "I'm telling you straight. This is about expectations, about the Paradise keeping up with the casinos that have floorshows and showgirls. We don't have a showroom but we've got good-looking waitresses and decent dealers and we serve full shots of booze in our drinks. That's how we compete."

His pronouncements stung. Lolly recalled the other evening when he'd made the cocktail waitress show off her uniform. She said, "You make it sound like employees are ... whatchamacallits."

"Commodities?" said Caldwell. "That's one way of looking at it. Our good-looking people are the same as new felts on the gaming tables and slot machines that pull smooth, and forty-nine cent ham and eggs. Everything, every person, every uniform serves a purpose. It's smart business."

Lolly wondered if he knew that money wasn't everything. That people counted for more than cash. She opened her mouth to protest but he continued.

"Here's how it works," he said. "Happy customers spend more loot. Happy, lubricated customers spend even more. That cash flow pays the overhead and the payroll and ..." He looked pointedly at Lolly, "sometimes comps the bar tab."

Lolly snapped her mouth shut. They weren't even cogs. She, Mela, Roger, and all the rest were but a handful of the many teeth circling the cogs powering the Paradise. Even Caldwell was just a wheel in the machinery that was larger than all of them. That last thought tempered the sinking feeling that had come over her. Yes, she needed a better-paying job, and yes, a place like this provided jobs that paid a person's bills and maybe a little extra to put aside. But the way he described it—it sounded so impersonal. It was one thing to frequent the Hideout, but another thing entirely to sashay around in costume, knowing that while you did so you were also a tool in someone else's get-rich plan. That clinched it.

To Caldwell she said, "I'm not in the market to cut my hair, or to wear this."

Caldwell glanced at Mela, who simply shrugged. He sighed as he looked back at Lolly. "Then we'll have to think of something else."

Back downstairs, Lolly went to the closest end of the Hideout's L-shaped bar, which faced the casino. Caldwell's pronouncements had made her feel as if the only way to advance herself was with a sparkly dress and a push-up bra, but there had to be better options. She hadn't any grand idea of a fruitful future; there hadn't ever been much reason to expect one, but maybe, if she kept her eyes open, some choice would present itself. She wasn't certain how Russell figured in such a future.

This had become no night to pinch pennies on cola; Lolly wanted the real deal. At the first open bar stool she leaned in close and ordered a bourbon and water, hold the ice. Roger took her money with a smile that made her feel welcome. She was sliding a tip across the bar when through her thoughts came the sound of guitar music.

Her heart bumped. That musician was back. Drink in hand, she hurried to the lounge entrance and stood just inside to let her eyes adjust. It was him, all right. She moved halfway in and claimed a chair at an empty table. The lounge audience seemed distracted by other interests, perhaps which roulette wheel to try next, or where they'd gamble tomorrow night. She was the only one not paired up but she didn't mind sitting by herself. There wasn't anyone's company she wished for. In fact, left to herself she might identify why she'd been making up names and scenarios for a musician's life in a casino town. All of which was speculation, but that's the effect he'd had on her.

She had known a few Negroes, though none well, not even in her California days. She'd gone to school with all races, and of course restaurant work attracted all types, including Mexicans and Negroes, none of them flinching from the dirty work. One of her roommates back then had been Puerto Rican; a hard worker, that girl. Then, too, there had been that one gentle Negro man at the orphanage all those years ago. He had treated her, a desperate, lost kid, with respect.

Through instrumental ballads and snazzier numbers, the musician kept his dark glasses on and seemed to perform as if for some internal audience of his own making. He didn't banter between numbers with those sitting closest and didn't sing along with any of the songs. She wondered whether he noticed that she was one of the few paying attention.

Fortified with a second cocktail, she screwed up her courage and crossed to the corner where between songs the guitar player sipped from a drink containing a wedge of lime. "Hello," she said. "Do you take requests?"

He set his drink down on a three-legged stool and swiveled slowly in her direction, leveling his dark glasses at her. Up close a faint line of stubble showed on his chin. "I know a lot of numbers but I don't sing. What's on your mind?"

The song she'd meant to propose flew out of her head. All the numbers he'd been playing were famous fifties ballads and love songs for the over-forty set. She said, "A Chet Atkins number, or Patsy Cline? Or, wait—maybe Elvis?"

He grinned, white teeth gleaming, and nodded a little as he strummed a few chords.

Lolly held up a folded dollar bill, a generous amount given her circumstances. "Where's your tip jar?" she asked.

"Don't have one." He turned his attention to tuning his guitar and she returned to her table.

As she retook her seat, the musician fingered an intro then broke into an Elvis ballad from recent times. She'd heard it plenty on the radio back in Oklahoma because Elvis was just hillbilly enough to fit in alongside the country and western tunes Okies favored. Silently she sang along with him ... *Are you lonesome tonight, do you miss me tonight? Are you sorry we drifted apart* ... until tears welled up from somewhere inside her. She blinked hard and smoothed invisible wrinkles from her work skirt. Drat. She needed another drink.

She stepped over to the bar and waited to catch Roger's attention. Behind her, the guitar man segued into a number that she didn't recognize. It had a slower, sadder tempo. She stood watching Roger pour eight drinks for the cocktail waitress to arrange upon her tray before heading back into the casino. By the time Lolly had paid for her highball and returned to her table, the guitar player was gone. Tears threatened to rise again, but she fought them into obedience. Her encounter with Caldwell had made her tense, all that talk of self-improvement. She had flaws, all right, as anyone paying attention would notice, but her past failings were heavier to carry. Those needed to remain her secret.

The next evening after work, Lolly again went to the lounge with a plan to watch the guitar player. This time she kept her distance and made no requests, simply watching the way the musician's guitar strings gleamed as his dark hands passed over them. The man could probably make music in his sleep.

At 8:30, Caldwell came in. "I'm beginning to think you're a person in need of company," he said, helping himself to a seat at her table.

"Guess mine will have to do, though I can't stay. Big crowd tonight at the tables."

She gave him a halfhearted smile. "I'm trying to figure out this musician."

"That's not the answer I hoped for."

"He's different. It's like he's playing for the crowd, but not exactly *to* them, you know? It feels like the rest of us, the audience, we're outside of what he's doing." She looked at the guitar player then back at Caldwell. "He's good though. I've listened to a lot of records and he's as good as any of them."

Caldwell shook his head. "If he was that good, he'd be making records, wouldn't he?" He gestured with one hand. "Lots of people play guitar. He's actually, well ... a charity case."

Lolly blinked against the unfairness of Caldwell's words. "How can you say that? Playing music is work. It takes, I don't know, natural talent, plus tons of practice. I can't play any kind of instrument, can you?"

When Caldwell shook his head, Lolly continued. "See? Not everyone can. And, if this place didn't want people who could actually make music, you could just turn on a tape player, right? Music goes with the lounge and the club and all. It must be one of those ingredients feeding the casino's money-making machinery." Her words sounded sharp, even to her.

The boss man frowned. "Okay, I get your point. You're right about the music. We've got to have it, but that musician, he's not what you think, not what you'd call ... regular."

She looked again at the guitar player on the flat stage, handling his instrument with ease. Even though she hadn't heard him play a Chet Atkins number or some others she could name, she would bet he could. She said, "There's no reason to look down on a person for doing their job. Besides, you must have important customers and their loot needing your attention."

An annoyed look crossed Caldwell's face. He shoved his chair back and stood. "All I'm saying is you don't want to—you should keep your distance from ... musicians like him." If he spoke any other words they disappeared as he turned toward the casino.

Lolly felt fueled by her resistance to Caldwell's influence. He might be one of the casino bosses but he wasn't the boss of her life. She would choose her own off-duty interests and make friends as she pleased. *And* she would choose the type of work she would do. She'd had her fill of cowboy types and might befriend a musician next, without anyone else's approval. She knew next to nothing about musicians, just how certain songs, certain music, improved the air in a room, and the company of whoever sat nearby. Music improved just about everything. If Caldwell didn't appreciate people who made music, that was his problem, not hers.

Nine o'clock was the guitar man's witching hour. As other performers arrived and prepared to set up, he methodically unplugged his guitar and fitted his gear into a worn black case, his movements verging on mechanical. Lolly's curiosity ticked up a notch. When he reached behind him and took up a white cane with a red tip, her breath caught in her throat—*That explains things*—and when he tapped his way out of the bar, she couldn't help herself. She followed him through the casino and to the exit doors to Lincoln Alley. There he paused to button his coat. With his instrument case once more in hand, he pushed carefully through the right-hand door and stepped into the slick, cobbled passageway between the club and the back entrances to other casinos and bars.

Lolly followed at a distance, curious about how the man would manage to find his way out from between the buildings. What if he fell? What if someone accosted him? What if he needed help and no one came to his aid? But none of those things happened, in fact no one seemed to pay him any mind. Now he kept to the left side, ticking his cane against the concrete footing, moving with a measured gait and stepping right through patches of dirty slush and water. Where Douglas Alley crossed Lincoln Alley, he paused before advancing to where the alley ended at the sidewalk. There he seemed to be listening for pedestrians. After advancing, he stopped just shy of the curb.

Lolly stood in the shelter of the alley, standing approximately where the getaway occurred in that Reno heist movie starring Kim Novak. In a few minutes there came the sound of an auto's horn just before an old sedan pulled to a stop at the curb next to the musician. The guitar man felt for the passenger door handle and pulled it open. He handed his guitar case in, then climbed in after it, closing the door with a bang.

As the car drove away, Lolly stood dumbstruck. She'd been mildly curious before but now she felt magnetized by the dark man dressed like a Negro Johnny Cash. To flip Caldwell's words, this man wasn't "regular." Not at all. She found herself moved by the recollection of how he conjured music from his guitar, and how in spite of the audience's indifference he flavored each number with a dollop of extra character. Caldwell had warned her away from "musicians like him." As Lolly stood in the lee of the building, her breath rising in clouds of steam, she knew she needn't avoid musicians like him because there'd be no others like him. He was one of a kind, and he would be someone special to know.

Five

L olly returned to searching out clues about Norma Jeane's heavenly resting place in the most likely places. Her old friend had searched for a spiritual home. Back at the orphanage, children's attendance at church was required, but the older girl had seemed to treasure her Bible, and would randomly read aloud from it to Lolly. Added together, those snatches of time wouldn't amount to much, but each moment remained a tiny treasure secreted away in Lolly's cache of memories.

On Saturday evening, Mrs. R identified locations of other churches on Lolly's list. Some were too far for walking in her dress shoes so Lolly put on a brave face and asked to borrow Mrs. R's creased city map and her automobile. The woman wouldn't hear of it; she had once lent her automobile to a boarder who wrecked it during a night of revelry.

"What do you need more churches for?" asked Mrs. R. "You said you liked Trinity fine."

"It's not about me. Well, it is, in a way, but ... I just *have to*, that's all."

For years Lolly had imagined reuniting with Norma Jeane for a day, or even an hour, long enough to apologize for her part in the event that seemed to have launched all manner of troubles for her old friend. Lolly had been young then, much younger than Norma Jeane, so there were people who would absolve her of having skirted her responsibility. But she knew what she'd done was cowardly, just plain wrong, so she had passed judgement on herself.

Nothing had come of her wishful thinking about once more speaking with Norma Jeane. Years had passed, and then—the unthinkable. Earlier this year, her old friend had died. The flickering light she had watched from a distance and all her daydreams about conversations and a hug vanished like smoke. A twist on her question insinuated itself into her thoughts: Was there actually a heaven for someone like Norma Jeane? So many obstacles likely littered her possible admittance—affairs, divorces, drinking, drugs. Rumors about abortions too. Lolly's regret over things left unsaid and undone dredged up that old ache. Her eyes began to well.

"Aw, hon," said Mrs. R. "What do you have to go and cry for? Now I feel awful."

Lolly sniffed. "Never mind me. I'm just out of sorts about being here at all."

Mrs. R patted her shoulder. "No matter how much you want it, it's still emotional. I've seen a lot of girls get worked up the closer it gets."

Lolly had missed a cue. "The closer what gets?"

"Your divorce." The woman nodded sagely as she took up a dishtowel. "It packs a punch but you'll be better off."

"I didn't say—"

"You don't have to. I understand. I've seen a hundred heartbreaks just like yours. Tell you what. How about you fix my hair the way you do yours, and I'll become your taxi to and from the churches too far for walking to. It'll be a trade between us." She flicked her bangs out of her eyes. "I've been thinking I could use a new look."

Lolly blinked and nodded. Something had just happened but she wasn't sure what. All that mattered was her objective regarding heaven, and now it seemed that Mrs. R was offering to help.

Mrs. R gathered towels, shampoo, and cider vinegar while Lolly ripped a soft old pillow case into strips for tying up curls. In short order, Mrs. R let Lolly trim her split ends with the shears from the kitchen junk drawer, and by bedtime the woman locked like a rag-headed doll.

Morning revealed the night's dusting of snow. Lolly combed Mrs. R's soft waves and pinned them off her face. The result didn't quite resemble her own head of natural curls but Mrs. R seemed satisfied. With Lolly's tote and uniform set on the back seat, they set off in Mrs. R's Dodge for a 9 a.m. service.

The First Church of Jesus Christ, Scientist occupied a statuesque, pillared building on Riverside Drive. Mrs. R pulled up close to the curb so that Lolly could avoid the gutter filled with slush. "I'll come back at 10:30," she said. "Then I can drop you at work."

"Won't you miss your own Mass?"

"I'll say my prayers at home. Besides," she added conspiratorially, "I've never been inside this church, and you'll tell me all about it."

Lolly's shoes crunched along the freshly swept and sanded sidewalk. Like supplicants, nearby cottonwood trees lifted bare branches skyward. At the front door, an older man doffed his hat as he welcomed her into a shallow foyer. Her insides grew queasy at the thought of yet another foreign church; she was already up to her chin in new experiences. Casino work, a casino boss, and that musician she couldn't get out of her head.

Ahead of her, the tall, airy space was filled with honey-colored pews, slowly filling with adults and a smattering of children. The interior lacked any adornment by carved crucifixes and stained-glass panels, rather like the Baptist church back in Gilleon. In this case, there was no altar, just a podium and a lectern. The simple furnishings calmed her but still she pulled a hankie from her tote to have it at the ready. For some reason, she tended towards tears during church services.

Worship proceeded sedately from one element to the next without drama or anyone shouting "Amen!" At the front, a man and woman took turns reading bits of Bible verse followed by explanations. The congregation stood for traditional-sounding hymns. When the organ music swelled, Lolly wiped a tear away as her heart lifted. In this simple place she could picture Norma Jeane's radiant smile and in the contemplative calm, a response to her friend's hunger for personal peace. Maybe Norma Jeane had been onto something.

After the service, Lolly pocketed her hankie and lingered until the crowd had largely cleared out. A woman approached her with a magazine in hand. "Is this your first visit?" she asked. "If it is, you might like one of our publications."

Lolly took the glossy piece in hand. "I haven't been to a Christ Scientist church before. I've only been in town three weeks."

"And are you finding Reno very different from ... wherever you're from?"

"It's not at all like California. Well, that's not right. I grew up in California, but since then I'm from Oklahoma. It's nothing like that at all." She held a hand to her gurgling tummy.

"Does your husband attend? He's welcome too."

Lolly fingered the gold band she wore. How could she put it? "His people are Southern Baptists, so that's his preference. When he has one." She glanced around. "I was hoping I could talk to your priest, if he's available."

The woman smiled. "We have no priest. Maybe I can help you."

"You haven't a priest? How about a reverend?"

"That's one of the things that makes us different. We don't employ a church leader but many of us have studied and trained to counsel others in the ways of the Mother Church. During the service we are readers and such, and at other times we work as a committee of church trustees. During the service today you saw two of our readers."

"I just thought that your ... he ..." She glanced around. People were visible through an open doorway in the far side of the main space. "Does that mean there's no one in charge? Someone to answer questions?"

The woman clasped her hands before her. "Not in the way you're thinking. Here we are all individuals on a path to a personal understanding of the Lord and His work on Earth. We look to the Bible and our own books of teachings to lead us in knowing ourselves, and therefore God."

Lolly felt the grip of disappointment. This faith was one that Norma Jeane had actually practiced for a while, at least if she could believe what the magazines reported. Before she posed her next question, she had a sinking feeling that the answer she hoped for would not be coming. She said, "Could you tell me about your heaven?"

"I suppose so." The woman looked to be choosing her words. "I'll explain the basics, as best I can, but it's usually a matter for study." She looked into the distance and then back at Lolly. "We believe that upon death, all people pass into another state of consciousness, into a spiritual state that is one with God."

Absentmindedly, Lolly pulled a soda cracker from her coat pocket and took a bite as she pondered what another state of consciousness might mean. "So, all people become spirits and are somewhere together?" she asked at last.

"Not in a place, per se, but a state of being. A state of love."

That sounded a little better. "Would that mean God is there?"

"That's right."

"But no pearled gates?"

"Right again, because a state of love does not require any physical structure." The woman motioned to the foyer they stood in. "Humans desire a place for worship, but after this life we'll have no such need."

"Does God take believers to his side? Do they sit at his right hand?"

"In our teachings, God is simply *love*. There's no need for hands because in death, we take a different form than our present, physical state, becoming kindred to the spirit of love."

Lolly was having trouble picturing this different version of an afterlife with love but not an actual entity in charge, so she tried a different tack. "I've got this old friend who was once a Christian Scientist. I'm trying to figure out if she could have made it to God's side."

"All of us while alive and also after death, are at God's side, at *love's* side. Always."

Lolly perked up. "For real? You don't even know—I don't even know, whether she was a true believer."

"Everyone makes it to the other side. All of us."

"You mean it? Everyone?"

"Absolutely."

"Me for example? I'm not even a Scientist."

"You, too. Everyone. All of God's children."

That sounded better, except ... there must be exclusions. There always were. "What about sinners? What about flubbing your choices, maybe a whole string of them? Do those people still go?"

"They do."

Such details seemed hopeful. Lolly's thoughts swirled out into a wispy place at the edge of nothingness, beyond trees and casinos, churches and rodeos, fishing with her imagination for evidence of spirits meeting each other after two decades apart. Could spirits even *meet*? "Are you saying that somehow everyone is there? All people who have died?"

"We believe they're there in spirit."

A terrible thought came to Lolly. "What about people who harm others? What about—" she could hardly speak the words— "men who ... who ..."

"Everyone, if they relinquish earthly anger and hate. Of course, our bodies remain behind. All that remains after death is love."

Lolly wondered how any person could know with certainty that this astonishing version of heaven actually existed, especially since you couldn't go to see for yourself and come back to report on what you'd found. Most of the things she herself knew for certain were decidedly not of a heavenly nature. Quite the opposite, they were all human in nature—violence, fear, uncertainty, and the anticipation of the next loss. Also human was the adoration for another person such as Norma Jeane.

The woman reached out a hand. "Are you okay Miss? You look a little pale."

Lolly's head had filled with feathers. She dropped the remainder of her cracker into her pocket and handed the magazine back to the woman. "I think I'd better wait outside."

Out on the front walk, the late morning chill cooled Lolly's hot face, but the weather held no answers for her growing concerns. How could Norma Jeane have gone to an afterlife that included everyone? Every. Single. Human. Even that dangerous man from the orphanage. Lolly wouldn't hear of it. No, these Scientists surely had it wrong. She would just have to keep looking and asking questions until she found an answer that made more sense. An answer she could live with.

That night her dreams held images of spirits, in the shape of unformed fog, floating around in search of God. In search of love. The spirits, which all resembled the same wisp of fog shape, passed through one another and filled up the universe, though it was a universe without stars or planets. Somehow, she was there with the spirits, worried about which of them might cause harm to one of the others. How could you know a spirit's intent when you couldn't look it in the eye?

She woke with a vague urge to call Russell. She really ought to call because she was growing accustomed to her distance from him, which felt like a betrayal of how she had always treated their marriage—fair and square—even when he had not. She had not telephoned on previous mornings when her equilibrium felt off, and by the time most work shifts had ended, she could only imagine him battering her with words about having skipped town without notice. Perhaps she should have stayed in Gilleon to argue everything with him, but it was too late now to rethink the choices already made, so she pushed thoughts of Russell into a corner of her mind and went downstairs in search of tea.

In the kitchen she found Shirley and Doris conspiring to catch a movie called *Days of Wine and Roses*. "That Jack Lemmon," said Shirley. "He can act. I'd watch him any day."

Lolly was invited to join them but she declined. Her inclination was to climb back into bed, but Mrs. R asked for a permanent wave, paying Lolly five dollars for the hour and a half it took. The next day, at Mrs. R's invitation, a lady from down the street was coming for a perm, and just like that, Lolly began earning extra cash.

The boarder named Shirley, a fallen-away Catholic, had traveled to Reno as a "New Year's gift" to herself. On Wednesday, the same day the papers reported Jayne Mansfield's passage through Reno on her way to South Lake Tahoe, Shirley dressed in a skirt suit and left for the courthouse. She looked joyful, as if severing her matrimonial tie would prove more happily-ever-after than her marriage. Lolly knew that Catholics couldn't divorce without feeling the pinch of guilt she'd been taught to practice in her early years. Suppose the Church wouldn't recognize their divorces, which it wouldn't, and supposing they wanted to marry again—and who wouldn't? Then what would they do? Under those circumstances, Shirley looked pretty darn happy.

Lolly took one of the pawn shop books to work with her, and on each of her breaks applied herself to reading a paragraph or more. It was slow going, but eventually she worked her way through a handful of pages. There were certain letters and combinations that proved troublesome no matter what, but she found that by reading them multiple times she could discern the thread of the story.

During one break, a busboy asked what she was reading. She was only on page five so she explained that the story was a mystery by Erle Stanley Gardner involving a hit-and-run car accident, a dead baby, and a hardboiled district attorney. The pimply-faced kid looked impressed. After that, the book seemed less an obstacle to overcome and more like a lucky charm. Simply tucking it into her tote alongside her overshoes and face powder made everything she carried seem more substantial.

On Thursday, Shirley announced that she'd been granted her divorce and it was time for a night on the town. She wanted Lolly and Doris to join her for a steak dinner and celebratory martinis. Even Mrs. R was invited, but she shook her head. "That late night stuff isn't for me." Turning to Lolly, she said, "Why don't you go out with Doris to send her off right? One of these weeks you'll be the one celebrating."

The landlady had read her wrong. Lolly had never said she was working toward a divorce, just that she had business in Reno that would take some time. She didn't know why she had obscured her intentions because it had turned out that Mrs. R was a good egg. "I don't get off work until eight," she told Doris. "You'll have to go without me."

By the time Lolly left for work, the two young women were nowhere to be seen, and in the Paradise coffee shop she filled the hours with hostess work.

A half-hour before shift change, the cashier noticed how one of the newer girls had goofed at totaling her tickets. The head waitress huddled with them near the cash register, talking low, until Karen, the offender, began to hiccup. "I don't know, I don't know," she sobbed, hiding her face behind her hands.

The lead waitress banged the pencil down hard as her words came out a hiss. "Go back and refigure them all. You'll have to make good on the ones that are off."

The younger girl was shaking so hard she collapsed against the cashier counter. In a half-dozen steps Lolly was beside her with a hand on her shoulder. "Karen, shhh," she said, speaking low. "Take a breath." She glanced at the cashier, who scowled and turned away.

"I'm usually okay but I had a whole lot of big parties today. Six-tops and eights," said Karen. Her eyes were rimmed with red.

Lolly sifted through the stack of order tickets. "A bunch of these look fine," she said, "but others have mistakes. You want me to help?"

The girl nodded, so Lolly took her pencil and reworked the columns of figures for M Loaf dinners and M Cristo sandwiches, Fr Chick and A-Pie, all variations on the shorthand used by waitresses everywhere. She said, "You just got your columns crooked." In a few minutes she had the new totals penciled alongside the old ones. None of the tickets totaled more than nineteen dollars and most were much less. "There," she said. "Eight of them underpaid, but four paid a little too much." She leaned close to Karen. "Seems to me you could pay the difference between the overs and the unders. It comes to seven dollars, fourteen cents."

Karen flinched. "Oh, God. So much?"

"Afraid so," said Lolly.

"What'll I do? I can't afford to lose my job and now Sheila knows I messed up."

Lolly thought a moment. "I know what. Ask Sheila to call for Mr. Caldwell to come and okay it. She won't argue with him."

Karen looked ready to dissolve. "What if he fires me?"

"Tell him that you don't have a way to make it right to the customers who overpaid, but maybe they won a little in the casino. Count up your tip money, and here—" She pulled two dollars from her pocket. "Take this in case you don't have enough. Tell him it won't happen again and hand over the exact amount."

Karen half-choked on her next words. "What if it doesn't work?"

"Be sure to say that I helped you, and that I'll check your tickets tomorrow."

"Is there some other way?"

"Can you think of one?"

The waitress frowned.

"Then you might as well try."

Lolly spotted two customers on the approach. Scooping up menus she lowered her voice to Karen. "Did this happen before? What went wrong?"

"I guess I got rattled," Karen whispered. "This morning ... I found out I'm ... pregnant."

Suddenly, Lolly felt too warm. She beckoned the customers forward and seated them before going to get a sip of cold water. Poor Karen, unmarried and in trouble.

After her shift, Lolly considered going to the bar to wait for Caldwell. She assumed he was on duty—he always seemed to be there—and she might as well take her licks for meddling in personnel matters. It wasn't like she was trying to assume a boss's role, but really, what would have been a better outcome? It was no use firing a good employee and no use siphoning the total of all errors from Karen's pocket when God only knew she'd be needing every penny soon enough.

Lolly held her coat and stood behind the seated players at one of the blackjack tables. Cards flew from the dealer's hands to land smoothly before each gambler. The man seated directly in front of her held an ace and a six. He called for another card, then another, bobbing his head as he silently counted the spots on each. "Twenty," said Lolly softly. She could tell by the set of his shoulders that he'd heard. He slid his cards, face down, under his stack of silver dollars.

The dealer turned up a seven to go with her own four, then a two, then a king. "Twenty-three," murmured Lolly as the gamblers beamed at their good luck.

"Smooth counting," said a voice at her left shoulder. Caldwell, as expected.

Lolly took a silent breath. "I'm fine with numbers," she said at last, watching the dealer shuffle the deck and change a gambler's ten-dollar bill for stacks of silver.

"A good thing to be strong at."

The next hand was dealt before Lolly glanced at Caldwell. He was a full head taller than her and dressed in a smart suit. His rusty-red hair looked freshly trimmed. He'd spoken calmly, so far. She said, "Some days just go wrong."

He turned his attention back to the table game. "It cost her."

Lolly looked again at the gamblers, two of them calling for more cards and the others sitting tight on what they'd been dealt. "Seven-fourteen?" she asked.

He left the question hanging for a moment between them. Then he said, "Yep."

Her smile was a flicker that Caldwell couldn't see. "I'm glad to hear that. Not that it cost her, but that it wasn't any worse."

"That's part of the job, you know, being able to add."

"Waitressing is tough enough without paying to keep your job."

"You say that like you know waitressing."

"I do."

They were both silent as more cards flew and stacks of silver changed hands. The dealer shuffled and dealt again. Lolly quietly called out the card totals she could see from where she stood. As the dealer turned over her own hole card and began to deal herself more cards, Lolly counted the growing total aloud. This time the dealer had five cards to equal twenty-one. The gamblers groaned and the dealer looked appropriately chagrined.

"You *are* good with numbers," said Caldwell as female laughter erupted behind them. Shirley and Doris had arrived.

"We found you!" they cried. "You missed dinner but we came to get you." Shirley had buttoned a fur collar to her coat and wore earrings that flashed light. Both of them wore plenty of lipstick and a bit of rouge.

Lolly started to protest, but they slid their arms through hers. Shirley looked up at Caldwell. "We've come to take her out on the town. She never does that kind of stuff." She was slurring her words.

He gave them a broad smile as the casino noise rose and fell around them. "Is that right? Never?"

"Nothing but work, work, work. But tonight, we celebrate."

Caldwell dipped his head a little toward Lolly. "Sounds like you'd better join the fun."

"I'm wearing my uniform."

"Doesn't matter," said Doris. "We're not going very far."

"Just far enough," said Shirley with a giggle. "Say," she continued. "Anyone got a cigarette?"

Caldwell produced a pack of Salems and held a lighter to the one she took.

"You smoke?" Lolly asked Shirley.

"I do now," Shirley said with a little cough. "I'm a free woman. Until, you know, next time."

Doris plucked at Lolly's coat sleeve. "Let's go," she said. "Shirley heard about a place."

The two young women led Lolly toward the double doors leading out. When Lolly shot a look back at Caldwell, he was standing where they'd left him, faintly smiling as he watched them go.

Six

Arms linked, Lolly joined Shirley and Doris as they strolled north on Virginia Street from the Paradise Club. She had maneuvered Shirley into the middle position but somehow the woman kept listing to one side. They passed under the Biggest Little City arch, walking along the lit fronts of small shops until Shirley turned them onto a side street where the glow of casinos seemed to fall away in favor of streetlights.

"Are you sure you know where we're going?" asked Lolly.

"I heard about it downtown," said Shirley.

"Who told you?"

"This good-looking guy. Italian, maybe."

"Someone you know?"

Shirley gestured with one hand. "We were just talking. He's here for a divorce too." She pulled up short. "I hope he wasn't Greek. I just got unhitched from a Greek." She shook her head as if to clear it. "He said it's two blocks this way, then over." She pointed in a vaguely northern direction.

They walked on, the two in high heels trying to avoid cracks in the sidewalk. At each cross street and alley, Lolly peered into the shadows. She didn't know anything about this neighborhood; their boarding house was many blocks the other way. Not that she expected trouble. She'd not encountered any so far, and a group of three ought to be safe enough.

Finally, at an intersection of two streets, all of them looked north. "There," said Doris, peering up the block. "Isn't that a sign? What's it say?"

"Should be Polka Dot," said Shirley.

"A sign with dots?" asked Lolly.

"No, silly," said Shirley. "You'll see.

From a car rolling the opposite direction came the sound of catcalls. Shirley nudged Lolly.

"Don't look," said Doris. "It just gives them ideas." She tucked in closer to Shirley.

"Fellas like pretty girls. Nothing new about that," said Shirley, throwing a glance over her shoulder in a way that made her lean into Lolly to keep her balance.

"That's the club up ahead," said Lolly, redirecting Shirley's attention. "See the sign?"

A large Negro man stood in front of the club beneath a backlit sign, hands in his coat pocket, surveying the sidewalk and street. A bouncer. The approaching women were close enough now that every time the club door swung open, a snatch of music could be heard. "We don't know anyone here," said Lolly, speaking low.

"Doesn't matter," said Shirley. "This is a jazz club. All the big cities have 'em and everyone goes. I mean people who like music. Besides, that cute Italian might show. Gordo, or Guido, or whoever."

There was a sound of a car door closing behind them and a male voice that seemed to be calling to them. Suddenly, the man at the doorway pointed at the threesome. "Hey!" he shouted, bringing the women to a halt. His face contorted in fury, he launched himself toward them, long strides gobbling up the distance, his fist a pointed hammer. "Get back!" he shouted as the women peeled away from each other, shrinking from the madman and drawing into themselves. He barreled through the space between them, voice booming as he passed down the sidewalk. "Get your ass back in that car before I put it there, y'hear me?"

Lolly and the others turned toward the scene unfolding behind them. The big man's fist was almost in another Negro's face, punctuation for his threat. "I said it before, don't you come 'round here. That's the last time I tell you. It's gonna be me or the cops, and you don't want it to be me."

The smaller man shook himself as he backed off. There was the sound of muttered swear words as he turned back toward a tan car parked at the curb. The women, mouths agape, watched the offender climb into his auto, which started with a roar. Engine revving, it screeched away from the curb.

Lolly stepped over to Doris, who looked shaken, and Shirley, who appeared to study the scene. The big man approached their little group and stopped a few feet away.

"Sorry 'bout that," he offered. "We don't take kindly to his type."

"He was right behind us?" asked Doris, her voice shaky.

The bouncer nodded. "He was gonna try to slink in with you and then talk you into buying him drinks." He shrugged, "Or try something. He's been kicked outta here before."

Doris spoke low to Lolly and Shirley behind the shield of her hand. "I don't feel so good about this now."

Shirley replied, "Well, first of all, that's what men do, follow women around, and second of all, the bouncer took care of him."

The bouncer glanced around. "Don't be put off by that dude. Y'all are welcome."

Shirley looked at her companions as she spoke in full voice, "We came all this way. Let's finish what we started."

The tall man consulted his watch. "It's jam night. Nothin' formal, just some cats trying out some blues, some jazz. 'Bout time for them to break but another group'll get going soon." He motioned toward the club and led the way to hold the door open for them.

"Come on," said Shirley as she swayed through the entrance and into the dark, smoky place. Lolly and Doris fell in behind her.

The shock of the sidewalk incident fled as the last, extended note from a saxophone met Lolly's ears. Whistles and applause rose from the audience, mostly Negro with the rest white. The musicians from the elevated stage stepped down into the mixed audience, the volume of voices and laughter rising accordingly. Someone had opened a side door so that a drift of clean, cold air sluiced the crowd. She felt herself relax. The Polka Dot jazz club was okay after all.

At the bar along the closest wall, a Negro bartender glided from one end to the other, placing beers and mixed drinks in front of customers. Shirley sashayed up to the bar where a man in a sport coat moved over one spot so the three women could take adjacent stools. "I need a strong drink," she declared.

"Let me buy," said Lolly. "It'll be your going away."

"I've got money from hocking my ring. Wasn't going to drop it in the river."

Lolly thought about the jewelry and loan man who'd sold books, but there likely were a half-dozen other shops who might have paid Shirley for her wedding band. She said, "Won't you need some money when you get home?"

"I hope not. I've got a job with my daddy's business."

"Aren't you the lucky one?" said Doris, who seemed to have decided that she was in no danger.

"Here's to March—Hey! That's next week," said Shirley. "And to getting on with life." She took a big swig of her martini before the three clinked glasses. "I felt so stuck, didn't you?" she asked.

Doris nodded knowingly.

"How long were you married?" Shirley asked Lolly. "I never even asked."

"I still am," said Lolly.

"Well, for now. But how long?"

"Six years last June."

"Ten," said Doris.

Shirley broke into laughter. "Ten! Me, I got that seven-year itch, like in that movie."

Lolly blinked hard. Shirley's reference brought Norma Jeane to mind. This close press of bodies in this kind of nightclub might have aligned with her old friend's tastes; she *was* known for being race-blind (just another reason to love her). And the out-of-the-way location might have yielded an evening's privacy for a person weary of the limelight.

Shirley continued. "Well, the problems started years before, but I never thought ... you know. It seems like maybe there's more chances now. To be happy." She turned to Lolly. "Don't you feel like you want something other than being married?" Lifting her drink, she slopped some on the bar.

"I guess, maybe," said Lolly. She did want more than she'd had so far, but expressing any what-if, perhaps-in-the-future imaginings seemed a great way to jinx everything.

"At some point in your life you must have wanted something different—thought it was out there if only you could find it. Else you wouldn't be here now." Shirley licked her lips. "You know what I mean," she continued, poking Lolly with one red fingernail. "You didn't actually move here to open a dress shop or whatever. This is just a stopover, a temporary kinda station on the way to somewhere else." She looked blearily around. "You left wherever—where'd you leave from?"

"A place called Gilleon."

"You left because of a reason. People don't leave without a reason."

Lolly had her reasons, all right. She said, "You make it sound so ... desperate."

Shirley wagged her head and narrowed her eyes. "I'd call it

desperate when you go through all that wedding stuff and marriage stuff and ... and find out it's rigged. So that only certain people get what they want." She swiveled her head toward Doris. "Don'tcha think?"

Tears began a slow descent down both of Doris's cheeks. "I don't know what I'm going to do when this is over. You've got somewhere to go and a job. But I'm going back to—" She shook her head a little. "Starting over. Plus, I even borrowed money to come here."

As Shirley polished off her martini, her words became more slurred. "There. Y'see?" she said to Lolly. "That's a sad thing. We either hafta catch a man, or know someone who can open doors. We can't just go along with everything, we've gotta look out for ourselves ..." She set a clumsy hand on Doris's shoulder. "You'll think of something. You'll be okay."

While the women talked, four musicians assembled on stage with a mix of instruments. When they began tuning up, the room's energy grew. Soon the drummer started tapping out a rhythm against the side of his snare drum and in a moment the others broke into a soulful number that Lolly had never before heard. The crowd telegraphed its approval with snapping fingers and nodding heads. Lolly watched the stage, transfixed, the music pushing away all thoughts of jobs and Oklahoma and desperation. Her heart seemed to know the brand-new old-sounding music before it reached her ears. Music to make you hungry while it filled all the empty places, or at least called them out into the light. The riffs and grooves washed her with colors that hung in the air.

Three long songs passed while Lolly sat deaf to what the other girls said. There was only the music and the crowd alive to it. When at last she looked over, Shirley had her forehead on the bar and Doris was stroking her hair. Doris spoke but Lolly couldn't make out her words. The girl leaned closer to say, "We'd better take her home."

Lolly had six dollars of the cash she'd earned fixing hair. She asked the bartender to call for a taxi and left him a tip from Shirley's stack of change, plus a half-dollar of her own. She and Doris wrestled Shirley back into her coat and guided her out past the tall man still lounging against the front entrance who lifted his chin in farewell. The two propped Shirley between them at roughly the same time that a dark sedan rolled by. The vehicle might have looked familiar to Lolly if she hadn't been occupied with flagging down a taxi approaching from the south.

Back at the boarding house, Mrs. R buzzed about them as they eased Shirley up the stairs and into her bed fully dressed except for her shoes. As Lolly pulled the quilts up, Shirley gripped one of her hands. "There's places to see, and I just want to ... I just want ..." she mumbled as she nodded off.

Lolly could think of a half-dozen ways to complete the unfinished sentence. Wasn't it just like life to be riddled with things left unsaid or undone, like those spaces in the night sky that you sense are full of stars if only you could see far enough? She stepped into the hall and closed Shirley's door. In a handful of hours, Shirley would catch a train headed east.

Ready for bed, Lolly took a swig from her bottle and then a second one for good measure. She'd had just one highball at the Polka Dot. That familiar warm glow ushered her to the brink of sleep and in the moments before it overtook her, she realized that the jazz club had made her think of the blind guitar player. He'd been playing songs written for orchestras or big bands while he was just one guy with a guitar, reducing those arrangements to their simplest recognizable versions. She began to think that perhaps what made him different wasn't the music she had heard him play, but the music he had not yet played.

On Friday, Lolly double-checked Karen's arithmetic as promised and asked to trade one of her breaks for leaving a little early, what they called an "early out." At 7:45 she hurried to the employee locker room. Her work skirt would do but she changed her bright pink uniform top for an everyday blouse she'd brought from home, for no other reason than to look more like a regular Friday night customer.

She arrived in the Hideout lounge as the guitar player struck up a familiar pop song. Cara was working the room and before too long she delivered an iced drink to the musician. When he paused for a breather between songs, Lolly went to stand before him. She waited until he sipped from his drink and was facing forward again. "Hello," she said.

He swiveled a little more in her direction. "Is that the Elvis fan?"

"How'd you know?"

He shrugged. "Your voice. Got another request?"

Lolly smiled. This time she was ready. "I was thinking Johnny Cash."

The way one corner of his mouth turned up sent a little ping of pleasure through her. She was back at her table by the time he launched into "Ring of Fire." He leaned into the song, his lower lip caught between his teeth, his head swaying to the rhythm. Beads of sweat appeared on his brow. She'd been right. The songs he played for Paradise Club clientele were different from the music that moved him. She was so pleased with this discovery that when Caldwell stopped by her table, she didn't mind that he might have hatched another scheme to talk her into a different job. Nothing he could say would ruin the evening for her. As it happened, he asked her out for Sunday dinner.

His invitation so took her aback that she said, "I thought you worked every night."

"It seems that way, doesn't it?" He glanced around the lounge. "I am perpetually on call, even when I'm not here, but I do take some time off."

Various thoughts were competing for Lolly's attention. She was trying to listen for whether the musician, without a request, would play a number that stretched the boundaries of what the Paradise management seemed to expect. Distractedly, she said, "I work on Sunday."

Caldwell spoke evenly. "We could go afterwards. Or if it's too late to go after, we'll make it another day."

At last Lolly said, "You know I'm married."

"So you've said. But you don't speak the way a wife might if her husband was waiting for her after work, or about anything that leads me to think that he's on your mind."

He was right. Lolly had avoided the subject of Russell. Not only because of how she had fled him, injured and confused, but also because of how much time had since elapsed. Three whole weeks, and somehow, the wide-open sky, the peaceful boarding house, and the coffee shop staff grown friendlier over time had made her feel as if she might belong in a place that embraced longing and dreams, bright lights and high desert skies.

Caldwell said, "I apologize. That was unfair, but could we at least dine as friends?"

Lolly knew that she had not acted as if she pined for home or for how unpleasant Russell could be when he was on a losing streak at the rodeo. For their rundown rental house and that dusty little prairie town, or the honkytonk on a Friday night, husbands playing pool while the wives sat to one side like trophies on display. Come to think of it, that Johnny Cash song went right to the heart of her Gilleon days. She had shoved Gilleon and its associations into a mental room with a door shut tight as possible against her indecision and now she wondered how Caldwell had read her situation so clearly. Or was he just guessing how long it had been since she'd been asked out to dinner, and that she'd welcome the invitation? Still, there was an air about him that suggested he often got his way. She glanced toward the guitar player. "What's his name?" she asked.

"What?"

"That guy playing guitar. What's his name?"

"What's that got to do with anything? I warned you about musicians."

 "Okay then, what's the bartender's name?"

Caldwell glanced toward the bar. "That's Roger."

"And the cocktail waitress?"

"Cara. You met her."

Lolly wasn't sure where she got off being so direct, except that this town seemed to bring out the boldness in her. She'd even followed the musician into the alley that night and watched him get into a car. This desire to command a moment was new to her. It felt kind of special. She said, "You know Roger and Cara, and probably everyone dealing cards tonight, and most of the regular gamblers, but you don't know the name of someone who plays music in the only lounge in this place? I guess my answer to dinner is no."

Caldwell shook his head. "Now, wait a minute. Why would you— That's not—" He stood. "All I'm doing is asking you to dinner."

"And all I'm doing is asking someone's name."

The big man's mouth became a straight line as he stood and looked around the lounge, which had grown more crowded while they'd been talking. Then he turned and stalked away, and Lolly thought that she may have fractured his will to spend time with her. She didn't know what to make of her own behavior. It seemed now that the longer she spent away from Russell's influence, the blurrier the dots connecting what other people expected of her and her inclination to please them.

A minute passed, then two, then two more. She wondered at

Caldwell's reluctance to tell her the musician's name. He either didn't like her asking about another man, or he truly didn't know the names of Negroes who worked for the Paradise. She didn't like the sound of the latter, too much like Russell and his cronies, bigots, most of them, along with being anti-Negro. She hoped that wasn't the case with Caldwell because her opinion of him was not the least bit sour.

The musician was playing a number recorded by Nat King Cole when Caldwell reappeared next to Lolly's chair. She felt his presence, the way he took up space and blocked the backdrop of casino noise filtering into the place, but she kept her attention on the guitar man. Finally, Caldwell took a seat on her left and she turned toward him.

He said, "I concede your right to ask the question. His name is Jackson."

"Just Jackson?"

He sighed. "Jackson Mayberry." He looked as if he'd been subdued by her stubbornness, but she knew that before long he would expect to retake command of the conversation.

"I don't have a dinner dress, and any restaurant has to be close enough for walking after work," said Lolly.

A look of relief came over Caldwell's face. He said, "I'll pick you up."

"I'd rather meet you. I have a landlady, and ... well, you know."

He didn't argue. "There's a little Basque place called Sarratea's down Virginia Street, just south of California Avenue. How about eight-thirty?"

Lolly nodded as the casino operator's voice reached them from a distance, paging Caldwell to one of the craps tables. After he left, she watched the guitar man finish his set and leave with his case in hand. Roger had actually provided the man's name to her a week ago. Wasn't that how it usually went? The working stiffs all knew each other because they mostly all held the same rank, but the bosses chose who they wanted to acknowledge.

She rolled the musician's name around her mouth, speaking it softly to herself. *Jackson Mayberry, Jackson Mayberry*. She was pretty sure he had been named for someone special. A father, an uncle. His name sounded strong and good and she thought he must be a good son, too. For some reason she could not begin to explain, her acceptance of Caldwell's dinner invitation felt a bit like she was cheating on Jackson. She couldn't say that she actually knew Jackson, but it seemed she was sort of letting him down.

Seven

On Sunday, Lolly slept through her alarm and arrived in the kitchen after ten. She was still in her robe while Mrs. R was dressed for Mass.

"Do you need a ride today?"

"I've got to call that synagogue," said Lolly. "They were listed in the book. Why would they be listed if they're closed?"

"Oh, I forgot to say that I asked one of the girls from a bridge club I used to play with. She said that Jews worship on Saturdays." She tapped her chin with a finger. "I'm not sure if I used to know that. Of course, I've never been to one of their services."

"They go on Saturdays."

"Right. But besides that, why are you shopping at churches?"

"I'm not shopping."

Mrs. R poured herself a mug of steaming tea water. "You could have fooled me."

"I'm just looking for answers I can't get anywhere else. I'm going to look them up and call them."

"Aw, hon, you can find answers at Trinity. They've got tons of answers."

"I know, but I *have* to do this." Lolly stepped into the hall and looked up the number. When she dialed, her call went unanswered.

"I don't mean to pry," said Mrs. R as Lolly returned to the kitchen to make toast, "but when you went to that Scientist church you came back looking all dragged out, so maybe whatever you're doing doesn't sit well with you."

"Oh, that. I told you about the service. I guess what threw me was afterwards. I had a conversation with a woman about, oh, heaven being full of...everyone."

"Everyone? You mean all those Scientists?"

"No, they said *everyone*. Believers, non-believers, even criminals."

"That can't be right. I mean, heaven—it's a big place, but it can't let everyone in." Mrs. R squinted a little as she dunked her tea bag.

"Me, I've got generous feelings toward all types, but as far as I'm concerned, you've got to earn your way in. Otherwise, what's all this for?"

Lolly had no answers, all she had were questions. Not only about extraordinary things like what kind of people made it to Saint Peter's gates, though that had been on her mind at some point in every day, but about ordinary things too. Everyday things, like why Caldwell had acted put out over her interest in the guitar man when what he really wanted was for her to join him for dinner. Her desire to know someone's name didn't seem worth his getting all puffed up about, even if the person in question was a Negro.

She told herself that Caldwell was simply lonely from working so many hours around people who were always out on the town for some fun. He couldn't very well take a break from casino work by going to a casino, and dinner out was not much fun by yourself, she knew that. He *had* been generous so far, and a gentleman, buying drinks and holding out her chair. And nothing but polite, even when explaining to her that most people don't recognize their own potential and need someone to be their champion and "shine a light on their talents." All she knew was he had better not think there was anything more to their dinner tonight but dinner.

Mrs. R went out through the back door. From the kitchen window, Lolly watched her car pull into the alley and head for downtown. With a start she realized that the trees at the back of the lot looked ready to bloom. She'd been in Reno just shy of a month without any progress in her search for Norma Jeane's fate. She had expected to find traces of Norma Jeane all over. Not monuments or statues, nothing so permanent, but more evidence than simply the view she'd absorbed from the top of the Mapes.

Perhaps she'd been wrong. Maybe Reno had been nothing special to her old friend. For the first time, she began to worry that maybe there were no proper clues to be found. Perhaps because Norma Jeane had lacked sufficient commitment to a way of believing. It wasn't as if heaven would offer a door for each different religion, where you could knock until one of them opened and allowed you in before it snapped shut to keep out the people who believed some other way. What kind of heaven would that be?

All she had to look forward to was work, and dinner with a casino boss at a place she'd never been to. The thought of going to dinner with a man who wasn't her husband made her return to the telephone nook in the hall and ask the long-distance operator to ring her home number back in Gilleon. Or maybe she should call it Russell's number, or the number they used to share; she wasn't sure it qualified as "home" any longer.

She hadn't practiced what to say to Russell, had been avoiding thoughts of him. Every time his name came to her, she felt the wrought-iron bar in her hand and his blade slashing her. During her first few nights in Reno, she worried that come morning she would find him waiting outside her motel room door. No soft winter sun beyond the auto court's entrance, just one angry Oklahoman. Her unease had receded when she secured a place at the boarding house, but for all she knew Russell could still appear at any moment primed with vindictiveness.

The ringing on the other end echoed down the line and her pulse ratcheted up a notch with each repeat. The thought that he was about to answer siphoned her breath away. Within moments the hallway, built to hold two or three people abreast, felt too narrow for her alone. Dazed by the racing of her heart, she hung up.

At work, Lolly went through the familiar motions of ushering customers to tables and assisting waitresses. Originally, the waitresses had acted leery about her propensity to help but she had won them over by making clear that she wasn't angling for their jobs or their tips. Now they rewarded her with appreciative nods and small talk whenever a lull broke over the steady stream of customers.

During her first break, Lolly tried to master a few more pages of "The Sun Bather's Diary," one of her Perry Mason mysteries, but her comprehension flagged like it had in the days when her inability to decipher words had earned her ruler slaps from elementary teachers. "Stupid," they had called her. "Lazy. Dumb." Then Norma had come along. For almost two sweet years the older girl sat with her, poring over her beginning readers. Never once did she make fun of Lolly's struggles. That's all it took to make Norma her hero, just a bit of kindness and the occasional hand to hold. For those two years they had been like sisters.

Lolly had just returned from break when a middle-aged Reno police officer approached her hostess stand. Something about his uniform and the purposeful way he glanced around gave him an air of business. He wasn't there for lunch. "Can I help you?" she asked.

"I'm Officer Dorning of the Reno Police Department." His heavy leather belt creaked in protest as he set a hand on one hip and consulted his notepad. "I'm looking for Luella Marie Cooper. The Paradise business office said she'd be here today."

Lolly's hand went to her name badge and her heart jumped. Her full name, used by orphanage staff and the Baptist minister officiating at her marriage. "That's me," she said, frozen to the spot.

A trio of businessmen stepped up behind the officer. They seemed to be debating some story in the morning paper. The officer glanced back then stepped aside. He motioned them forward so that Lolly, with shaking hands, could seat them. Various concerns flitted through her mind as she poured water for the party of three. Was there a problem at the boarding house? Was Doris okay? Mrs. R? On wobbly legs she stepped back to her podium. "What's wrong?" she asked the officer.

The policeman's mouth turned down a little, as if he hated to be the bearer of bad news. "It's a report we've had, an inquiry out of Oklahoma. The Woods County Sheriff's office." He glanced around. "I need to speak with you but not while you're trying to work. Can an officer come around to your residence? That would do."

Lolly swallowed hard. "How did you know to find me here?"

"When we're not sure where a person is we start with the biggest employers, casinos first."

Lolly would not invite the police to Mrs. R's house, not if she could help it. "Did something happen to my husband?" she asked.

The officer smiled wanly. "It appears so. That's what I need to ask you some questions about."

Concern overtook Lolly's thoughts. The way saddle broncs stamped and snorted behind the chute gate, sometimes trying to crush the rider climbing on against the boards. Turned loose they became frantic, rocketing beasts. As a rider fell off, frantic hooves might hammer their skull or split some ribs, puncture a lung, bruise their liver. Those were regular injuries on the circuit, but even worse could occur. She asked, "Is it bad?"

The officer caught her worried gaze and held it. "Don't you know? Seems you ought to know."

"What? He rides rodeo, where he could get hurt, and he fights sometimes when he's drunk."

Sheila, the lead waitress, wandered into Lolly's peripheral view. Standing up straighter, Lolly said, "Can we talk outside?"

At the officer's nod, Lolly crossed to Sheila and explained that she needed to take care of some personal business away from work.

"Now?" said the waitress.

"Family emergency," said Lolly. "I'll come back and finish my shift. If I can."

The waitress glanced at the waiting officer. "All right. I'll clock you out. You can't be paid for the time you're gone."

Lolly retrieved her coat and pulled it on. Her tote held her casino ID card and her Oklahoma license.

The officer's city vehicle was parked at the mouth of Douglas Alley. His breath a bloom of fog, he suggested they take advantage of the relative privacy it offered. They climbed in. There was a shotgun banked between the seats. Keying the radio, Officer Dorning reported that he'd located Mrs. Cooper. Then, with his torso turned toward her, he said, "We called around to locate you because we take this kind of thing serious. This report we got is out of Oklahoma. It asks for verification that you're here. Says you fled after assaulting one—" here he paused to consult his notepad— "Russell Eugene Cooper, with a heavy object, resulting in broken bones. That's called 'battery.'"

Lolly's mouth fell open. Her heart thumped behind her ribs. "He said *I* attacked *him*?"

"That's the report."

A bubble of outrage broke free from the room inside her that she kept shut against Russell. From a distance he was still throwing jabs. "Are you here to arrest me?" she asked.

"There's no warrant, but my instructions are to ascertain what I can." He paused as he drew out a pen and turned to a clean page. "I take it you're the Luella Cooper that this report names. How long have you been in Reno?"

Lolly's breath was coming too fast and too loud inside her head, overriding staccato sounds issuing from the police radio. She calculated the days since she'd climbed down from the Greyhound bus and told him.

Officer Dorning looked out through his windshield before he spoke again. "So, you left after injuring your husband."

A half-dozen fictions ran through her mind. She could claim to have been somewhere other than Gilleon when Russell's hand was broken, but if the authorities asked around the town, they could find any number of people who knew that she'd been at work earlier in the day that Russell was injured. That she was injured. She decided to describe a part of what had happened.

"He was, um, chasing me, and I swung the fireplace poker to stop him."

"Did it connect with him?"

Lolly bit her bottom lip. "Yes, it did."

"Were your actions intentional?"

How unfair this line of questioning sounded! Did she mean to hit him? She meant to stop him from fulfilling *his* intentions. The full memory of that night washed across her. Russell in a drunken temper, and growing fouler as she refused his advances. The previous night he had forced himself on her, wrestling her to the bed and pinning her hands while wrenching her skirt up. After he was done with her, he'd said, "There. Your duty is done."

The next night, the one in question, she was ready for him, watching his expressions and sideways glances. When he came for her, she resisted with all her might. Twisting out of his grasp she stumbled into the living room with him scrambling after, the stink of bourbon, anger, and fear filling all the spaces. Overriding his shouts came a sound she hadn't heard before, the keening of an animal. It was coming from her.

At the fireplace she grabbed the cast-iron poker and spun hard to face him down. The heavy, forked end met his outstretched hand with a sickening crunch. Stunned by the snapping of bones and his outraged howl, Lolly dropped the weapon as he drew his knife and swiped it at her, shouting, "Get away!"

When Lolly cried out in pain, Russell's mouth fell open at the sight of blood welling through her slashed blouse. He glanced down at his knife. Wide-eyed, he backed up, spun away, and ran out into night.

And now he had reported her to authorities. She thought for a moment about what else she might tell the officer. Women's stories were often about strangers down back alleys or the criminal parts of towns. Gilleon, a typical small town, was in many ways the least likely place for that sort of danger. She had never given a second thought to strolling down any of its streets or roadways. It was only this year that she had discovered how her own husband posed a danger.

Should she explain to this policeman that a violent husband hadn't any right to sexual relations with a wife? That Russell deserved what she had done and had unfairly struck back at her. But what man would concede that point? Anger rose up in her at Russell's half-truth. Flush-faced, she said, "I meant to stop him."

"Sounds like you accomplished that."

Lolly slumped against the seat. "He didn't tell the whole thing. Didn't he say anything else?"

Officer Dorning flipped to another page in his spiral pad. He wagged his head a little. "That was the gist of it. Also, that he loved you."

Lolly let out a puff of breath. She knew Russell well enough to interpret the meaning behind his complaint against her and that past tense of "love." He had exploited his ties with one of the Woods County deputies to send her the message that he could reach her even from three states away. She could think of only one response. She said, "There's more to it than what his report tells."

"Like what?"

"Like how he injured me too."

The officer studied her a moment as she waited. Finally, he said, "I'm listening."

Lolly realized that she hadn't a prayer about the first part of what had happened that night. She couldn't prove that Russell had previously forced himself upon her and had been trying to force her again. Besides, the police officer might sympathize with what husbands expected of wives. She said, "There's physical evidence."

"Bruises from weeks ago don't help. Broken bones, maybe. If you've got X-rays you can bring them to the station and we'll make a report."

"It's not like that. It's more … personal."

She could see her words sinking in.

"Well, certain claims can't be attributed to one person or another so that might not …"

Lolly offered what seemed like her only option. "I could show a doctor except I haven't been here long enough to have one." Then she thought of a detail that might strike a chord. "Another thing you can put in your report is that Russell Cooper's hunting knife has a carved bone handle."

The officer's eyebrow rose. "Are you saying he used a knife against you?"

"I can't prove it was him and his knife any more than he can prove I swung that poker."

The officer didn't look convinced. "Except you told me you did." He thought a moment. "But okay, let's get a verification of your claim. The closest place is the E.R. at Saint Mary's Hospital. There's a nurse on each shift who attends to the women we bring in. We'll see what she says."

At the hospital's ER reception, Officer Dorning explained that he hadn't brought a patient for admission but needed corroboration of a recent injury to a Mrs. Cooper, who was present.

A few minutes later a petite blonde appeared. Nurse Duncan. The officer said, "Mrs. Duncan, I'd appreciate it if you could verify what Mrs. Cooper has to show you."

Lolly followed the nurse back to one of the examination rooms where she put aside her coat and unbuttoned her blouse. She was still using a bit of cotton to cushion where her bra's seams rubbed her wrong. Now she peeled away bra and cotton from the long stripe of raised red scar beneath her right nipple.

Their conversation was muted and the walk back to Officer Dorning silent. The nurse motioned for Lolly to join her and the officer to one side, out of hearing range of other emergency room patients.

"Well?" he said, notebook and pen at the ready.

The nurse spoke slowly as the officer scribbled. "Her injury appears to match her account of a knife wound, slightly deeper than superficial. Its location should not interfere with future functioning, such as breast feeding."

The officer chewed on his bottom lip as if processing the nurse's words. Nurse Duncan narrowed her eyes as she added, "No woman would do that to herself, if that's what you're wondering. In my book, whoever did this deserves to be strung up." She placed a slender hand on Lolly's arm and gave her a nod, then she turned on her heel and left.

Officer Dorning's mouth softened. "All right then. I guess the next question is do you want to make a complaint against Mr. Cooper? I can ask Mrs. Duncan for a formal report."

Lolly took a breath. "You'll take the nurse's word?"

"I will. She's my sergeant's wife."

The clock on the emergency room wall read 3:15. Lolly had missed almost half her shift. "Did you see the actual report from Oklahoma?" she asked.

"I saw it."

"Did it say that Russell, I mean Mr. Cooper, will lose the use of his injured hand? Anything like that?"

"It indicated multiple broken bones but it didn't predict an outcome, if that's what you're asking."

"Did they mean for you to arrest me?"

"Not necessarily. The Chief likes to be responsive to other jurisdictions. There's all kinds of people come through this town. Some of them are dangerous—even women—and we like to know who they are." He glanced at his notebook. "You can understand how this looks. You injure someone and then leave town. It's usually guilty people who leave. People with something to hide."

Lolly's mind skipped back to how far she was from Gilleon. She had boarded that westbound Greyhound without giving notice, with hardly a look back. It had felt like the only sensible choice.

The officer spoke again. "In this case, we can let Woods County know what we found. That there's evidence in your favor."

"Will that be the end of it?"

"I'd say yes, unless you decide otherwise."

Lolly shouldered her tote. Her fight with Russell was no longer secret. Others now knew what he had done and what she had done. She wasn't exactly proud of either of them. "I'd like to just be done with it."

The officer slipped his notebook into his jacket pocket. 'That's it then. I'll give you a lift back to work. Or home."

They returned to the squad car with its squawking radio and drove back downtown without further conversation. Lolly asked to be let off at Douglas Alley so she could hustle back to finish her shift at the Paradise coffee shop. There she told the lead waitress that everything was settled; family matters were firmly in hand. Which was nearly true because she knew that you could not lock away the past so that it never surfaced again. The past always left ripples in the present.

There was work to be done, though, so Lolly set her mind to it. Throughout the rest of the shift, Karen asked Lolly to review her tickets. At a safe remove from the incident of mathematics gone awry, they could chuckle over Karen's brain blip at the pregnancy news a thousand other U.S. women must have heard that same day. Maybe more than a thousand, if you could believe the projections that America's population would reach two hundred and twenty million within the decade.

At 8:00, Lolly clocked out and changed her bright pink blouse for her royal blue sweater set, the nicest clothing she owned besides her good skirt. The night sky was overcast as she left the casino beneath low clouds turned pink from the city lights and headed for the restaurant where she was to meet Caldwell.

At First Street she crossed beneath the neon cowboy whose bowed legs formed the capital M in the Mapes sign. At Hilp's Rx, the window display held cold medicines and throat lozenges. Where California Avenue met Virginia Street, she crossed to the west side and waited at the traffic signal.

A downslope in the street indicated the secondary business district, and there in the next block, Sarratea's neon sign glowed red and green. A few minutes later she paused before the front door to pull off her gloves and brush a hand across her coat. Then she went in to meet Caldwell.

Later, in the boarding house kitchen, Lolly would submit to direct examination by Mrs. R, with Doris listening from behind an old copy of Cosmopolitan, a literary magazine kept handy for the place's more sophisticated guests. Doris nursed a cup of hot tea and seemed stuck on a page that she never once turned while Mrs. R plied Lolly with questions.

Yes, the dinner had been good. No, Lolly had not previously tasted stewed beef tongue, but she had found it good and spicy, fixed in tomato sauce with garlic. Lolly said, "I'm willing to try new things. You just have to not think about them too hard." Dinner had included bean soup and French fries, green salad and fragrant loaves of bread, and in a million years she could not have eaten that much food at one sitting. Caldwell tried some of everything while Lolly picked at what she took from the bowls and platters passed down the long table. She sampled a picon punch made with bitters but switched to the red table wine poured from heavy glass carafes.

The small establishment rang with conversation, but not so they couldn't talk a little. And yes, Caldwell had offered to drive her home in his Oldsmobile, but she had taken a taxi instead, the uphill walk seeming a bit much to contemplate on such a day as she'd had.

What she didn't tell Mrs. R and allow Doris to overhear, was how Caldwell had acted downright solicitous, never mentioning her job prospects or repeating what he'd once intoned—that with the right mindset, casino work could grow on you. He had asked about where she had lived, and complimented the weather in southern California. He wondered whether she knew any cattle ranchers in Oklahoma and what sorts of television shows she liked to watch. Even though They laughed together over the way Jack Parr's show made fun of New York City. Neither had ever witnessed the Big Apple's skyscrapers, traffic gridlock, or the sheer magnitude of the place. Lolly didn't say so, but she did like the idea of a world of immigrants cohabiting one major city, all those people of various shapes, sizes, and colors looking for a place to start over. In a city like that it was commonplace to be different. Being different was a trait most everyone shared.

Lolly expressly did not mention the perfume Caldwell had pressed upon her as a thank-you for joining him for dinner and being the most interesting—and yes, challenging—woman he'd met in a long time. Though her heart had jumped a little at the tiny red box edged in gold, she at first refused. Though not her direct supervisor, he was a boss—one of the big bosses—and accepting his gift didn't seem right. She was married, after all, and a hostess, and temporarily in town, not a girlfriend, certainly not his girlfriend—all thoughts that whirled through her head. But in the end he said, "I know what you're thinking, but it doesn't have to symbolize anything. It made me feel good to choose it for you, and you'll make my night if you accept it."

With that, he had pressed the gift into her hand. She opened it carefully and gave it a sniff and thanked him, and tucked it into her tote, where it rested, untested, while back in the boarding house kitchen Mrs. R fished for more details and shook her head over the parts that displeased her.

"Basque, though," said Mrs. R. "That's the kind of place you take someone you know, not a first date."

"It wasn't a date," said Lolly. "It was just dinner."

"That's the sort of place you go with people you know well, or when you're married. Everyone at those long tables like one big family. You don't court someone over Basque food."

"Well, that's good."

Doris stretched and yawned. "A casino boss?" she asked a little wistfully. "I suppose he has a nice car."

Exhausted by sharing so many carefully-edited details, Lolly stood. "It's been a long day, so I'll say good night."

Once she was ready, Lolly knelt on the rag rug and opened the little red box again to look more closely at the tiny perfume bottle. Its label looked foreign, French maybe. She should not have accepted a gift from Caldwell and she ought not to keep it. There was no telling what he really meant by giving her such a thing, and yet it was her first ever real perfume. She tipped the stopper against her index finger to release one rich, heady drop, which she pressed between her breasts. The fragrance registered as roses, earth, and sunshine, a perfume Audrey Hepburn might wear in one of those movies where she's pursued around Rome or becomes a fashion model in Paris. Russell's gifts had been watches or sweaters, and once, a silver belt buckle he had won for saddle bronc riding. This, though, was a gift for no reason but for being herself, and Caldwell had chosen it to suit her.

She pulled her bourbon bottle from beneath her bed's box springs and, taking a swig, told herself again that Caldwell's gift didn't mean anything. She maintained what she'd said and he had agreed to—they could simply be friends. Now she wondered, could they really?

Eight

A pattern had formed around Lolly's days off. If the weather allowed, she would walk the downtown area, looping up one side street and down the other, gazing at store displays and purchasing necessary items, always small things. Mrs. R seemed to know neighborhood women who wanted their hair fixed or trimmed or colored. Woolworth's carried Lady Clairol options that were easy to apply at home, and with Mrs. R reading the instructions and Lolly performing the hands-on duties, Lolly found herself with a side job tending to women's hair. On those days off she wore one drop of perfume, thinking it might go unnoticed. Mrs. R and the other women boarders, perceptive about such things, noticed though, so she told them she had brought it from home but forgotten to wear it until now.

On Wednesday she found herself looking forward to having a couple of drinks after work. It seemed like Caldwell appeared less often midweek; perhaps he did take an occasional day off. Should he appear, he would likely try to discern whether she was making use of his gift, but she didn't want to give him the wrong idea or any reason to think she treasured the elegant bottle and how just possessing it brightened her days.

Caldwell. Lolly still wasn't sure quite what to make of him. During their dinner together he hadn't said much about his home life, just that his was a bachelor's existence and that he filled most of his hours with work for the Paradise. He mentioned having once worked for a San Francisco hotel. Mostly he had posed questions about her that she avoided answering completely, instead making small talk about safer subjects. President Kennedy's Camelot life, for instance, and the Life magazine photos showing Jack and Jackie Kennedy sailing, or strolling with their children on the White House lawn.

One evening after work, Lolly stood watching the blackjack table closest to the bar. A dealer whose name tag read Marvelle seemed to be losing a lot of hands to the two gamblers at her table. The cash dollars Lolly had earned fixing hair seemed to weigh her purse down.

She thought of those bonus dollars as lucky money, and lucky money might bring her luck if she put her numbers skills to work. One hand of blackjack couldn't hurt, could it? Just one hand to say she had tried it.

She fished a silver dollar from her purse and set it in one of the circles printed on the table's green felt. Marvelle gave her a smile as she shuffled the deck of cards and offered it to one of the other players to cut. On the first deal, Marvelle had a nine showing while Lolly was dealt a ten and a queen. She had watched the game enough to sense a good hand, so she put her cards down and waited for the other gamblers to play their hands.

The dealer's hole card gave her nineteen. One of the other gamblers at the table lost his bet, but Lolly and another player each won, and just like that, money that had belonged to the casino or some other gambler was now hers. She scooped up her original bet and left the winning dollar in place for the next hand as a circulating cocktail waitress took her order for a free drink. She won another dollar. After two more winning hands, she bet two dollars and promptly lost them, which felt like a blow to the stomach. Those two dollars could have gone into the pot of cash she was trying to build up, money for paying her rent and perhaps, just maybe, after her quest was complete, for returning to Gilleon to settle things regarding Russell. It bothered her that every one of their friends back in Gilleon knew by now how she'd up and disappeared. Russell's version of it. No one would know her version unless she went back to tell it around. Fat chance.

Lolly switched back to making one-dollar bets and won again. After half an hour and one free cocktail, she had thirteen dollars in winnings and quit the table, pushing a dollar tip to the dealer, who tapped it on the table's edge and stacked it with a few others to one side. Now Lolly understood why people got hooked on gambling—for the thrill of it, that uptick of energy with each win that overrode the kick in the teeth at each loss. The key to surviving even a short session would be controlling your heart rate.

Thursday after work she tried her hand at blackjack again, losing three dollars before her luck turned. She walked away satisfied at breaking even, deciding that perhaps once per week would be often enough to risk a few of her hard-earned dollars.

Friday loomed as bright as spring and Lolly hoped that the coming weekend would yield more information through her visits to Reno churches. What she had learned thus far suggested that various Christians held differing views about heaven, what it looked like, and whether it even existed. Also, which people could earn entry. She had a sneaking suspicion that Jewish believers would hold yet another view. Had Norma Jeane, who had tried all these approaches, understood those differences? Had she been searching for heaven, salvation, or simply inspiration?

Lolly's own early upbringing had been Catholic, at first, and then a blank period, and later she married Russell, who said things like "I like my whiskey neat and my religion straight up." His mother subscribed to the fundamentalist teachings of Christ the Redeemer where everything was black and white. You were either a sinner or not, had given yourself over to Christ or not, and with the second coming you would meet your maker. Or not. That sort of background might explain why Russell never seemed to understand the shades of gray that clouded her mind about religion.

At the house, Lolly stood close to the telephone nook and dialed the synagogue number again and this time a woman answered. "I'm so glad to reach you," said Lolly. "I'm wondering if you'll be open this weekend for worship. I'm not trying to join, I just thought I'd see how your service works."

The voice on the other end hesitated, then answered. "Our worship is on Saturday at ten."

Lolly paused to calculate how much time she had available before work on Saturday. She had already committed to helping another of Mrs. R's friends with matters involving hair. "I guess maybe I'll visit another time."

When she had cleared her call, she went to tell Mrs. R about what she'd learned. "You were right about Jewish worship. I went on the wrong day. Have you been to that synagogue?"

"Me? Heavens no. Nothing against them, but no. I've had Jewish girls stay here, but none of them went to worship while they were here." She folded her hands across her ample stomach.

Lolly thought a moment. "Christian Science was a bust. It didn't help me at all. It sort of made things worse, so I'm hoping you know someone who would talk to me about being Jewish. You know a lot of people, right?" Mrs. R picked up a dishtowel as Lolly pressed her case. "Maybe someone you trade with, in a shop or a bank or somewhere?

Someone who, because they know you and like you, would talk with one of your boarders."

Mrs. R wagged her head. "Let me think about it," she said. "Couldn't you just skip to Catholic next? You showed me your list, and Catholic is on it."

Lolly gave a shiver at the mention of Catholicism. She wasn't ready for it yet. She had attended Mass as required by the nuns and learned the Our Father and Hail Mary. The older girls often practiced aloud when memorizing the Creed. Lolly had absorbed a basic understanding before things went awry.

Soon after the shower incident she had gone with the others to Mass and *he* had been there. That man. Throughout the service he sat two rows behind their little group, his flinty gaze boring a hole in the back of her head. She had imagined all manner of troubles for Norma Jeane if the truth came out. The nuns had taught that a girl would be at fault, and come to think of it, Evangelicals were the same. The fairer sex was always at risk of sinning. Thus, she had never told a soul about what had happened and had never again ventured to Catholic mass.

Mrs. R continued. "I don't make any promises I can find you a Jew. Maybe you should plan to go back to the synagogue."

"I suppose," said Lolly, wrestling her thoughts back to the present. "But if I wait until next weekend that would mean more weeks here— not that I don't like it here, you've been great—but I didn't mean things to take this long."

Mrs. R's smile turned sympathetic. "I know exactly. Haven't hundreds of girls been in your shoes? It's the waiting that's hardest. Tell you what. I'll make a couple of calls and see if I know someone who knows someone."

"Someone for what?" asked Doris, entering the kitchen in robe and slippers.

Mrs. R considered Doris thoughtfully. "I guess we'll let Lolly explain. I don't think I can."

Both women turned toward Lolly, but Lolly was already headed for the staircase.

Jackson was plying his music that night when Lolly arrived in the cocktail lounge. She did not herself understand why his presence exerted such a pull on her. She admired his deft playing—who wouldn't? —but also how he performed while blind to the audience and the boldly patterned carpeting and the bustle of folks arriving and departing. Except for noticing the smattering of distracted applause at each song's conclusion, he couldn't know if people were paying him much mind. Yet he played on, conducting himself with grace. She herself could use a little grace.

Lolly went straight to the bar and purchased a gin and tonic. She told the waitress—not Cara this time, but someone new—that she'd take it to the musician, and she did, setting it down on the fixed-leg stool near his swivel seat. "There's a drink right here beside you," she said.

He glanced up, his guitar resting across his lap. "Hello again. You got good timing."

"Also, I thought of another request."

His face softened. "I been wondering what you'll ask for next. You're the only one who does."

Lolly had perused Doris's Hollywood magazines in search of news about the music scene and the names of Negro musicians and such. Those gossip rags provided titillating bits about which actors and actresses had appeared at lavish galas or beside name-brand hotel pools, but they didn't exactly promote music. Lolly's last six years had been spent in a place where country and western music reigned. She had pondered the music she'd heard at the Polka Dot, the combination of musicians and instruments and the way some of the songs sounded mournful and hopeful. That was the most jazz she'd ever heard at one time.

In Mrs. R's front room, she had dialed up various frequencies on the Farnsworth console radio-turntable, a lovely old piece of furniture with a golden veneer, all rounded corners and wood grain. Fishing about, she had found a big band performance, plenty of news reports and local gossip, a bit of network comedy piped in from Los Angeles, some western tunes—Marty Robbins and the like—and a smattering of classical music. Then she'd done the next best thing, which was to ask around at work, which had netted the trumpet player Louis Armstrong. Famous as he was, he could not serve her scheme. Another name was one she'd never heard before. That was the one to try.

"What'll it be?" Jackson said, feeling for the drink she'd delivered. He took a long pull on it then shook his head and blew out a breath.

"What's wrong?" asked Lolly. "You'd rather have vodka? I was guessing, because of the lime."

He set the drink aside, saying, "That explains it. You have a song in mind?"

Now she felt dumb. "There's a musician, actually, and I don't even know what he plays. Or his group, or whatever."

He resettled his guitar and said, "That's all right. Lay it on me."

"Do you know someone named King, with initials B.B.?"

"Blues Boy?" he asked, eyebrows lifting above his dark glasses. "He's a mad player. You heard his stuff?"

The way he asked made Lolly nervous. There was so much she didn't know that she wanted to know, and clearly this was one of those subjects that she had been missing out on. "I—I don't, exactly. I heard his name mentioned."

"I see," said Jackson. "He plays electric and I play acoustic. There's a big difference, but since you asked, I'll try a different kind of number that might suit you."

He extended a hand the color of coffee for her to shake, saying, "It's the thought that counts."

They shook and when their hands parted company, he lit into a number that ranged far from what he played on other nights, and not at all like the Johnny Cash and Elvis songs Lolly had previously requested. This one sounded more like the music being played at the jazz club. This song was new to her, which meant there were likely a hundred others she didn't know. Or a thousand. Her thoughts buzzed with the realization that she'd taken a leap about a thing that in other circumstances she might have shied from.

Her mind also stirred with a memory connected to the orphanage. A white shirt sleeve rolled back along a muscled black forearm and a large black hand, callused but clean, grasping her child-sized hand to lead her to safety. Recalling her gratitude for that particular dark hand, she walked back to her Hideout table.

As she reached her seat, she encountered Caldwell arriving to join her. "Is that your kind of music?" he asked.

Coming out of her reverie, she said, "I asked for it. I thought I knew what music I liked, but now I'm not so sure."

He looked at her oddly, but the cocktail waitress arrived right then and he turned to place an order for them both. An instant later, the hotel operator paged him. He said, "They've got me running tonight." He excused himself and went to the bar to sign the slip. When the drinks came, Lolly tipped the waitress though she knew Caldwell would have done so. She left his drink sitting on its napkin until it was clear he wouldn't be back anytime soon. When her own was gone, she took a sip of his scotch and water, thin tasting from the melted ice.

During his second set, Jackson played a bunch of standard songs which were pleasant enough, but now that she knew he could cut songs from bands and musicians other than Andy Williams and Roger Miller, she began to think of his true music as originating from a world apart. She applauded after each song, which prompted some others to join in. A musician ought to know that listeners appreciated his efforts.

At 9:00, Jackson ended his set as the next combo rolled their gear into place. His instrument at his feet, he patted his coat pockets and felt around the swivel stool and the stool holding the melted cocktail she'd bought for him that he hadn't drunk. No one sitting closer offered to help so Lolly shouldered her tote bag and crossed the lounge to find out what was wrong.

"I'm missing a glove," he said. "It must have fallen loose."

Lolly peered about before finding it behind the amplifier. "Here it is," she said, scooping it up.

He took it from her, saying, "That's nice of you. I hate to lose things."

"Me too, and listen, I'm sorry about that drink being wrong."

"Nothing wrong in principle. Operating in the dark is tough but it gets worse if I'm tipsy. That's all."

Lolly put a hand to her mouth. "Gee, I never thought..."

"No harm, Miss, but if you don't mind, I've got to get going." He loaded his guitar and started toward the lounge entrance, his cane silently tapping a path on the carpet before him.

Keeping pace, she said, "My name's Lolly." In the background, the next group was tuning up. "Do you want to stay a minute," she asked, "and listen to the combo that's coming on?"

One corner of Jackson's mouth turned up. He set his guitar down and pulled on his gloves. "You from around here?" he asked.

"I've been here about ... four weeks. Why?"

He tapped his cane silently against the carpet. "See any Negroes in this here lounge?"

Lolly felt her face go warm. Instinctively she knew without looking. "Only you," she said.

He moved two steps toward the racket of the casino and she followed. He said, "Are there any Negroes playing at the tables? In the four weeks you been here, you ever seen any gamblers the same color as me?"

The way he asked the question, she could tell he knew the answer, but she told him anyway. "I guess not, no." On any given night, a person would find ranchers in Stetson hats, city slickers with their hair glistening and shoes polished, pale people, tan people, thin and fat, Italians, Irish, Germans, but no Negroes gambling in the casino. Orientals and Negroes worked behind the scenes.

"There's a reason for that," he said. "Just the same, it's hospitable of you to ask, and I thank you." With that, he stepped across the gap leading to the casino.

Her face burning, she said, "Jackson."

He turned slowly at the sound of his name.

She shrugged a little, though he couldn't see her. "I'm sorry. About … well … I'm just sorry, that's all."

He didn't reply, just tipped his chin in her direction and turned to go, his posture upright. In a moment he had disappeared beyond the lounge entrance. Lolly pictured his cane sweeping a path before him until he reached the curb where a dark sedan would be waiting.

No longer interested in the trio on stage, Lolly went back for her coat and made to leave. Where the lounge met the casino, she paused to button up, glancing distractedly across the gambling scene before her, a kaleidoscope of people in motion around concentrated shapes and colors and lights. Take away the visuals and you'd be left with layers of conversation and laughter, the metallic click of silver dollars, the clank of slot machines, and the invisible operator paging guests to the house phones.

She closed her eyes briefly and tried to recall the cushioned stools pulled up to table games. Were they red vinyl with button-backs? She felt certain the dark carpet was patterned with some overall geometric design, but its particulars eluded her. The physical manifestations of the Paradise Club had become almost too familiar. Over the last few weeks, she had learned to navigate through the casino without any longer seeing the details. She'd be quick to say she knew it well, but were she instantly struck sightless, she would collide with every object and person between where she now stood and the doors leading out. And from there, how would she manage?

She opened her eyes and let her gaze sweep to the craps tables on the far side. There, Caldwell stood speaking with a pit boss, but his eyes flickered to her position in the lounge entrance and his posture telegraphed his interest in what she was doing. She kept her gaze moving so that she wouldn't have to acknowledge him. No reason, really. She just didn't want to read anything into the look on his face.

Nine

During mornings, Lolly felt torn between her old world of Oklahoma and Russell and this new world of Reno. Since arriving in town, she'd had vague stomach troubles and lost most of her appetite. The only time she could shed thoughts of Norma Jeane was when she was working, or when Jackson played a new-to-her song. Even then, it was like her memories of Norma Jeane somehow inhabited the songs that seemed strung together out of longing and loss. She was turning more to alcohol but couldn't seem to stop, having already sprung for two more half-pints to keep in her room. This morning, she had awakened tired and a bit hung over, but also needing to prepare for the arrival of one of Mrs. R's friends. In her room, Lolly downed a cup of tea and dabbed a bit of perfume on her throat to cover any stink of casino smoke clinging to her hair.

After Russell sent the police, she had given up imagining that she could return to him without negotiating some sort of truce. She knew what he meant by reporting her for assault. His pride wouldn't accept her absence from Gilleon without the need to impress upon her the significance of his loss of reputation with rodeo chums and drinking buddies. So many people had said, "Get married! Start a family," but she wondered now if that was a joke people played on each other. She had meant her marriage vows, but could see now that perhaps she and Russell had not really known each other. Should they ever attempt a reconciliation, Russell would expect a contrite, submissive wife, which would prove a sticking point because she could feel herself changing. She'd begun listening for her own voice among the many others around her.

Having been the one to escape without giving notice, she should at least attempt to speak with him. She *should*, but every time she passed the boarding house phone, her brain jumped to some other subject of lesser import, such as which of the landlady's friends might next need a five-dollar permanent wave or a dose of hair color.

Then there was Jackson. Unsettling as her conversation had been with the guitar man, he'd responded graciously to her ignorance about a place that employed him to entertain customers while refusing him access to its casino and lounge. He had kept his cool but she had heard the heat in his voice and understood his disappointment. Suddenly she wondered whether the same was true at other casinos in town. She had a feeling that the Paradise Club, an imitator regarding menus and uniforms, also mirrored the others when it came to race.

Those were her thoughts as she added the last pink plastic curler to the damp hair of Mrs. Shelton, who now sat at Mrs. R's kitchen table. Lolly pinned a dry towel around the woman's substantial neck as Mrs. R came through the back door, discarding her coat.

"Aren't I the one?" said the landlady. "I wasn't sure it would work, but Mrs. Overburke, who works for the city, says her son married a Jewish girl even though they tried to convince him that blending religions makes it hard to keep a happy home—and what about the children someday? She said they seem to be getting along fine and the girl is smart and all, and what's to be done if young people don't listen to their parents? Anyway, she'll come over—the daughter-in-law—for a talk tomorrow before you leave for work." She brushed her palms together as if dispersing dust. "I told Mrs. Overburke how you're good with hair and cheaper than the parlors, so you might want to see if the daughter-in-law needs anything done." She glanced toward the woman in curlers. "Hello, Ginny. I guess you'll have a new spring look."

Mrs. Shelton sat silent and wide-eyed as the conversation unspooled around her. Lolly ignored the woman's quizzical looks and opened a bottle of curling solution. "That's terrific," she told Mrs. R, blinking against the cloud of ammonia. She leaned toward the seated woman and said, "Hold that towel up close. This will feel cold."

When she had doused Mrs. Shelton's curlers, Lolly set the stove's timer and handed the woman a damp cloth for blotting errant drips. She motioned Mrs. R into the hallway so that they could speak in whispers. "What's the daughter-in-law's name? Am I supposed to do her hair?"

"No, no, it's a favor for her mother-in-law, but suppose she doesn't have the money for getting her hair trimmed regularly. You could ask her, that's all I'm saying. She might want to do a little business. Her name's Rachel. Used to be a Levine, but now she's an Overburke."

"I'd really like to speak with her but I'll have to leave on time for work."

"She'll come at about 10:00. Why don't I make a nice coffee cake and you can be dressed for work so you can skedaddle when you need to."

Questioning Rachel wouldn't be the same as speaking with a rabbi, but second best could sometimes be as good as the first choice. Lolly gave Mrs. R's pear-shaped frame a hug before turning back to her customer.

Mrs. R smiled. "I still don't know what you're so intent upon," she said, "but if you're satisfied, I am too."

The Hideout lounge was busy when Lolly arrived after her shift, every table holding one customer or more, so she took an open spot at the bar. Jackson, in that same black outfit and dark glasses, was playing songs that Lolly recognized, which meant they weren't particularly special. Roger was on duty and when she nodded at his unspoken signal, he delivered a bourbon and water to a napkin he set before her.

"What's up?" he asked, taking her money to the closest register.

"Nothing. I guess this has become my regular hangout."

"Why not? The music's pretty good, and the company's even better."

"Does that line work on all the girls?"

He winked. "Not often, but I keep trying."

"Oh, hey," said Lolly. "Do you know what that musician drinks?"

"Jackson? Club soda with a lime. I usually send him one at the break. Why?"

Lolly nodded to herself. "I thought it was booze."

"Musicians have that rep, for booze and all."

"Really?"

"Oh, sure. Drugs, too. A lot of 'em. Some even play better when they're a little 'tight,' others when they're sober." He pivoted toward a customer down the bar holding a finger up.

Lolly left her coat to hold her place and stepped across the lounge to stand before Jackson. As he finished the last bar of the number he was playing, he paused and said, "Yes?"

"How'd you know I was standing here?"

"Ah, Miss Lolly, or is it missus? You're blocking a bit of the sounds from the bar and the casino. That gives you away."

Lolly noticed this time how his guitar's face was golden, with darker wood curving around its sides. She paused long enough that Jackson said, "Did you come for a song?"

Lolly realized that she had arrived unprepared, stepping forward to stand near Jackson with no clear excuse, just the desire to observe his hands on the strings and his calm countenance. Standing close to this musical man obscured the concern she felt about the attentions being paid her by Caldwell, and the clock ticking in the background of her time away from Russell. So much around her seemed in flux. She had begun lately to wonder if the universe was dealing her a hand independent from her needs. If that was the case, she would have to either play it, or fold. "I could use a song," she confessed, "but I don't know which one."

"That's all right. I can tell you been putting effort into thinking them up."

"I guess not today."

"Tell you what. You act like you're requesting a song and I'll fill in the blank." At Lolly's pause, he added, "Just smile and nod your head like I agreed to play a song you've asked me for, and I'll play you a song that's not on the boss's list. It'll look like I'm taking care of the customers."

"I get it," said Lolly, nodding. "In that case, will you play two?"

A grin lit up his ordinarily sober face. "Sure will." He cocked an ear to his guitar, adjusting one string and then another, and Lolly went back to her seat at the bar. When Jackson broke into a hard-driving number, she took a long pull on her drink and tried to imagine the sphere in which the composers of such music laid down long runs of notes meant to communicate joy. And grief. Music supposedly spoke a language of emotion. If that was true, the emotion she heard clearest was...desire.

Mrs. R proved good as her word, with a sour cream coffee cake that Lolly served to Rachel Overburke when she came to visit in the morning.

"Aren't you going to have some?" Rachel asked Lolly as she took a bite.

"I've had tea," said Lolly. "And they feed us at work."

The newly minted Mrs. Overburke was darkly beautiful, with full lips and chestnut-colored hair, some of the curliest that Lolly had ever seen.

"I know this will seem strange," began Lolly. "Someone like me fishing for information about being Jewish. Oh, I'm saying that wrong. What I mean is, I have questions about certain aspects of Jewishness, of Jewish faith."

Rachel touched her napkin to her mouth. "It *is* kind of...unusual. Not very many gentiles ask about Judaism." The woman was so very young, she looked barely twenty.

Though Lolly wondered what someone this young could know about matters of life after death, she figured she had nothing to lose by asking. Aware of Mrs. R and Doris in the nearby living room, magazines in their laps and the radio turned low, she formed her query carefully. "I'm trying to learn about what people believe comes after death. For instance, is there a heaven, and what would it take for a Jewish believer to make it there?"

Rachel studied Lolly for a moment. "I guess I'm a little confused. You're not Jewish but you want to know about a Jew's afterlife?"

"I know it sounds strange, but it's about a friend of mine."

"Who is Jewish ...?"

"Not quite. She married a Jew and studied the faith. And then they divorced so I suspect she may have given it up."

"Why don't you just ask your friend?"

"I didn't ever get the chance, and now...well, she died rather recently, so I'm too late."

Rachel took a breath before she spoke. "The rabbis and teachers are better equipped to explain things like this, but even they would say that two Jews will be of three opinions, which could apply to understanding the afterlife. Yes. No. Maybe." She smiled wryly. "Just so you know, marrying doesn't make someone Jewish."

She explained about how conservative Jews would say that when a person dies, they're gone, with no heaven to take them in. They simply live on in the memories of those they leave behind. But also, she'd heard about a more mystical perspective on the afterlife, in which karma plays a roll, one's actions during life circling back around to influence one's future.

Lolly asked a few questions and mostly listened. This was not going the way she needed. Then Rachel mentioned reincarnation.

"A person comes back?" asked Lolly.

"Not everyone believes that. I guess the mystics do, and I'm no mystic but I kind of like the idea. Of course it doesn't mean the person returns, but the soul. Perhaps. But if you asked my mother, actually both my parents, they'd say that's nonsense. There's a lot of debate about how to think about these things."

"So it's not for sure? Then how would you know—or, how would I know if a person's soul had somehow returned. After death."

Rachel glanced around the kitchen, as if verifying she would not be overheard by anyone who could take her to task later. "Say you have a feeling about your friend, like she's nearby. You know she's not, but it feels like it to you. That could be her soul returning."

The notion astonished Lolly. Had she been haunted by more than the worries and thoughts that followed her about that night gone wrong in the orphanage? Could Norma Jeane's spirit have guided her to Reno? She gave a shiver.

Rachel continued. "There's no way to know if there is such a thing but just supposing there is, then there would be no reason to fear those lost souls or ghosts because God watches over us all. There's not much debate about that part."

The only thing Lolly was certain about was that Norma Jeane had married a Jewish man, but that didn't make her Jewish or a ghost, did it? She asked, "Do you suppose someone could die without particular beliefs but not be actually forsaken?"

Rachel looked thoughtful. "I guess so. If God's watching over everyone, then no one is forsaken. That could make sense."

"I learned about virtuous pagans in limbo and sinners gone to Catholic purgatory. Your way sounds better." Lolly glanced around. It was hard to tell if Mrs. R and Doris were eavesdropping. Maybe that didn't matter. She asked, "Have you ever been to Catholic Mass?"

"No. Jews and Christians don't really mix."

"But wasn't Jesus a Jew?"

Rachel just shrugged so Lolly figured she'd crossed a limit. After a bit more conversation, Lolly had to conclude the visit. She walked Rachel to her car under a light spring snow and watched her drive away. Then, wearing a plastic hair bonnet and her overshoes, she walked to work without truly seeing the flakes falling fast and soft along the sidewalks and gutters and into the dark waters of the Truckee, or the cars turning the snow to gray slush. Her head was full of the differences between what Rachel had described and the answers she had gathered during church visits.

The bottom line was: nothing matched. The sin-free dead went to heaven, or else their sinning didn't matter one iota. The believers were welcomed to the golden city on the hill, or else all humans knew God, also known as *Love*, and knew him after death. Or the spiritual life after the bodily life was a matter left to God and what mattered was how each day, the here and now, was lived. A person's soul might get lost on the way, but don't worry over that because it might return somehow in a different body. Or without a body. Take to your knees to pray, or ask God's forgiveness in private prayers and seek atonement from the person you have wronged.

Lolly had thought that knowing what Norma Jeane believed, or wanted to believe, would provide her with proof that a girl wronged in life could still enjoy peace in the afterlife, forever safe from those who had hurt her. Such an outcome would give Lolly peace that she herself through her cowardice pointed Norma Jeane toward purgatory or hell.

If Lolly had ever confessed her own sin of omission, perhaps Norma Jeane would have been absolved too, and being contrite, if in fact she was, end up welcomed to the Catholic heaven. Or, if Lolly had somehow atoned during Norma Jeane's Jewish phase, Norma Jeane might have remained Jewish after divorcing that playwright. Or maybe not, since after the fact Lolly was never able to undo having once been seven years old, arriving in the second-floor shower room with Norma Jeane already in a booth about to start the water when the man in charge of the building's daytime maintenance suddenly appeared. He was a smallish, sturdy man who always seemed to be around the next corner, tinkering with equipment and checking locks, ever observant.

The man leaned close enough for Lolly to smell his sour breath and register his flinty gaze. "Get out," he growled.

She looked at the tuft of hair showing at the throat of his shirt and then at his eyes, and pulled her ratty sweater back on. She said, "But—" as she threw a glance toward the stall holding Norma Jeane.

He snarled, "You don't want to stay," which chased all rational thought from her.

Norma Jeane's head appeared between the two halves of shower curtain. When she saw the man there, her expression changed to one of resignation. Casting a sad glance at Lolly, she said, "Go on."

Red-faced, the man added, "You heard her!"

Lolly fled blindly into the stairwell between the second and first floors where she tripped, catching her saddle shoe between two shelf-like steps. That's where the Negro man found her, hyperventilating and with tears in her eyes. The Negro was the one who cleaned the kitchen and mopped the hallways at night, which left him smelling of lemons and lye. With hands the color of ripe plums he loosened her foot and rescued her shoe. When she wouldn't tell how she'd come to be trapped, he walked her down to the first-floor kitchen where a radio played old-timey race music. There he fixed her a cup of hot milk to stop her shivering before escorting her back upstairs to the entrance of her dormitory hallway.

She had crawled fully dressed into her bed across from Norma Jeane's, which stood empty, the other beds empty too, because it was early yet and those girls were in the dining hall playing Monopoly. She was shivering again beneath the covers when the day man came in, the one who had bullied his way in after Norma Jeane, but before she could cry out, he pulled a flask from his pocket and put it to her lips. "Drink," he said as she choked down a mouthful of sharp-tasting liquid. He poured another mouthful into her then turned away. Almost immediately she fell hard asleep and, in the morning, wondered if what she recalled about the night before had been a dream. Of course, it had not.

In the Paradise coffee shop, Lolly automatically seated customers and assisted the waitresses. When Caldwell stopped in at 7:30 to ask if she would join him for a simple meal after her shift, she accepted because it was once again Sunday and there would be no music in the Hideout lounge.

Forty-five minutes later, she met Caldwell at the Ground Cow, a burger joint across the main drag that smelled of frying potatoes. She had no appetite but Caldwell ordered for her anyway, the smallest hamburger combo with fries and a milk shake. When their orders came, she sat picking at hers, the echoes of Rachel Overburke's words still in her head.

"You seem preoccupied," said Caldwell.

"Do I? I guess I am."

Caldwell dipped a small bouquet of fries into his tomato catsup and chewed thoughtfully. "Like you're somewhere other than here."

Lolly roused from her swirling thoughts. "I know what. I need a drink."

"Not the shake?"

"A drink from the bar, a double please."

He looked down at his hands then signaled their waiter. They both sat silent until her drink came and she took two big swigs. "Tough day?" he asked.

Had it been tough? Yes and no. Her interview with Rachel had been enlightening to the point of incredulity. It seemed now that nothing was what she had thought. The world, its people, its many versions of God. How could there be so little consensus about God and his promises? How could a person be sure what was real and right, and know in their hearts what they should pray for? Or whether they should pray at all?

"I spoke to a Jewish woman today about heaven."

Caldwell cocked his head and started to speak, then paused as if reconsidering. Finally, he said, "I didn't realize you were Jewish, working on Saturday and all."

"Oh, I'm not. We were just talking."

"A friend of yours."

"Not that either. A stranger, really, but she told me things I'd never heard before."

With one of his fries, Caldwell drew a circle in the catsup on his plate. For the first time since they'd met, he seemed at a loss for words.

Lolly continued. "The conversation kind of confused me when I thought it might—" She looked sharply at Caldwell. "Are you a Christian? Or a Jew, or a ... Christian Scientist, any of those?"

"No."

"One of the others, then."

He looked uncomfortable, as if forming and re-forming his thoughts. "I have this feeling you need a certain answer from me, and I don't know what that answer is. Religion is not—"

Lolly broke in. "It's okay, whatever you believe. It seems like there's too many versions of God to keep straight unless you never think at all about how there could be more than one."

Caldwell blew out a breath. "You might as well know. I don't believe. Not the way you're asking."

His words broke through Lolly's mental fog. "Is there some other way to ask?"

He reached out to cover one of her hands with his but she moved her hand away. He inhaled deeply. "Ordinarily I pride myself on marching to a different drummer than others do, not falling for political propaganda, not following the most obvious path the way so many would. I can do it though, follow others, when it seems a reasonable compromise. But in this one thing it's not possible to conform because none of the religions make sense to me. I don't understand people's attraction to the notion of an invisible, supernatural creator who doesn't communicate directly and whose existence cannot be proved. The stories about God and all those biblical figures sound like fairy tales. I could say the same about the Hindu gods, and witches, and leprechauns. Which leaves me with no other choice but to stand outside of it all." He motioned skyward. "It's not like I could ask and ... presto, the spark of religion would be in me. It doesn't work that way. For me it's not a choice."

Lolly snapped her mouth shut. What did he mean by religions being irrational, or not having a choice? Didn't everyone get to choose? And what about heaven? Didn't he hope for a heavenly afterlife, some place to end up? If he didn't, he was miles apart from most other people. She sat back in her chair. So, this is what it meant to know Caldwell better. This is what she got for asking.

His voice broke through to her again, earnest and hopeful. "It's not the believing or disbelieving that makes a person worth knowing. It's how they conduct their lives. It's about keeping your word, being reliable."

"Kindness," she said.

"That too."

She drained her drink. "How about conducting a profitable business? How does that fit with reliability and kindness?"

He glanced around as if to buy a little time before answering.

"Never mind," said Lolly. "I'd better be going." She stood unsteadily.

"Are you sure?"

"I am."

"Let me drop you home."

"No thanks."

"Please. I'm sure it's still snowing."

"I have money," she said, raking a hand through her tote. But she knew without looking that because Sunday wasn't her blackjack night, she only carried a dollar in change; walking home from work cost nothing.

Caldwell held her coat for her. "A taxi will deliver you home safely before dropping me at my car over on Center Street. I insist."

"You insist," said Lolly, shaking her head. But she let him signal a taxi for them to share, and she gave the boarding house address. Suddenly she was so very tired, the day's confusion merging with the evening's impasse. She had been curious about Caldwell's life beyond the Paradise. A natural curiosity about someone who seemed generous and attentive. But somehow this new disclosure of his felt unhelpful. He was one hundred eighty degrees from anyone else she'd known. She wanted to allow him his differences; wasn't that what she wanted from others? But people didn't admit to what he had disclosed. She didn't know of anyone else confessing such a thing.

It was one thing to doubt—didn't she herself wonder whether longing for happiness was futile?—but Caldwell's words only added to her disquiet. He had not looked the slightest bit embarrassed to tell her, more like wary about her reaction. And another thing—he never talked about his family. He wore no ring, so was probably unmarried. Then again, she knew from experience that under certain circumstances some men went without their rings. Russell for instance, who said wearing a ring while riding rodeo could cost him a finger.

But didn't Caldwell have parents to mention or siblings to grouse about? Maybe even children. This *was* the divorce capital of the world, which meant he could easily live a bachelor's existence by being divorced with children. Heck, by this point she knew quite a bit about Mrs. R and the husband she came to Reno to divorce. Bill Ruddle, who'd been a gunner on a war ship, went missing before she'd filed her papers. Consequently, she'd received his life insurance payout and some widow's benefits with which she'd purchased the boarding house. To Lolly, even knowing those few details seemed plenty.

It was Caldwell whom she couldn't get a handle on, a man both pushy and polite, who until tonight had explained many nuances about how the Paradise worked and mentioned certain businesses to be found in town, but next to nothing about his personal life.

This new knowledge only made it clearer to Lolly that she and

Caldwell were on different paths. With his lack of belief, he would end up nowhere with all those departed conservative Jews who ended up nowhere while she meant to land somewhere golden. Of course, the Scientists' God might take him in. They took everyone.

That was her final thought as she crawled into bed and fell to sleep.

Ten

A fter a restless night, Lolly woke determined to put thoughts of Caldwell and his unorthodox non-beliefs aside in order to concentrate on obtaining more songs to request from Jackson. Feeding Jackson opportunities to play bluesy music was feeding her in some unnamable way.

She drank a cup of tea while deflecting Mrs. R's questions about how she'd gotten home through the previous night's snowfall.

"You look peaked, hon," said Mrs. R. "How about a little breakfast. Eggs maybe, scrambled, or do you like them runny?"

As an image of runny eggs appeared in Lolly's mind, she tasted bile. She set her cup down with a clatter and hurried to the first-floor bathroom where she hugged the throne and vomited noisily. With her stomach empty and her head clearer, she emerged to find Mrs. R in the hall, waiting to comfort her.

The woman's hands fussed at the air around Lolly. "Aw, now. You've been doing too much, working plus fixing hair. How about going back to bed for a little longer?"

"I'm sorry to have done that, but now I feel better," said Lolly, and she meant it. "I'll just brush my teeth. I have an errand to run."

"In the snow? Walking to work is one thing, but can't your extras wait for another day?"

"The sun is out and there's something I should have thought of before."

In the upper hallway, Lolly found Doris. "Oh," said Lolly. "You're dressed up."

"For court," said Doris, smoothing the front of her fine wool dress. "Do I look all right? I know it doesn't matter much at this point but I kind of want to look good when everything gets wrapped up. I feel like I'm applying for a job, you know? A job as a divorcee."

Doris had been friendly, always handing hot drinks around the kitchen, and they'd had that one night on the town. "Does this mean you'll be leaving?" Lolly asked her.

"Sure. I've got to return home and start over."

"Listen," said Lolly. "I didn't ever ask this. How much did it cost you, your divorce?"

"Too much. I make my last payment today, before we go in front of the judge." She patted her purse. "Three hundred is a lot when you don't have much to start with, plus room and board and all."

"Three hundred—that's a whole month's pay!"

Doris looked dubious. "Didn't you pay that much?"

Lolly swallowed hard. "I didn't ... I haven't."

"You haven't what, paid your lawyer? How'd you file then? How'd you get a date on the court calendar?"

Lolly looked away, shaking her head.

"Wait a minute." Doris took a step back and put one hand against the hallway's striped wallpaper as if for balance. "I thought you came here for—Then why'd you come? You let us think—"

"Well, I—I had reasons for coming. There's a reason. I just didn't ever explain it, exactly."

Doris narrowed her eyes. "But you didn't ever say you weren't. I mean, you kept to yourself, but me and Shirley, we thought that we were all of us in this together." She pulled herself up taller. "I know some people are bound to keep secrets, but you could have at least told us."

Lolly stepped aside to let Doris push past. It wasn't that the others ought not know how she had not come to Reno for a divorce but was slowly favoring that very thing. She couldn't even say when her intentions had changed. Like slow-moving lava, the realization had come gradually over her that too much time had passed for returning to Russell as the same woman he had married. Surely his temper had acted as one force upon her thoughts about wifely matters, but so had her walks to work and back, those quiet half-hours spent pondering the meaning of what made a happy partnering between men and women. Factored in—Caldwell, the lifeforce of Jackson's music, and the nearby mountains lined up like elephants on parade. It seemed like the local townspeople accommodated other people's pursuits without voicing judgement, except for when they disallowed Negroes. That lack of mercy was as bad as Oklahoma's and ten times worse than California's.

Lolly brushed her teeth and dressed in haste, then hurried downstairs to skip out before Mrs. R noticed.

It was not to be. Mrs. Ruddle stepped into the entryway as Lolly was pulling on her coat. "Mrs. Cooper," she said. "I know you haven't set an exact schedule, but now I'm wondering how many more weeks you'll be wanting your room."

So, Doris had spilled the beans and Mrs. R had retreated to formalities. Lolly asked, "Do I need to tell you now?"

"I have placed a newspaper advertisement so there will soon be more tenants wanting to board here. Were you to leave me in haste that room might sit empty until I can fill it, which wouldn't be fair."

Lolly bit her lip. "Haven't I paid my rent on time and kept my room neat? Have I made any trouble?"

Mrs. R wavered. "I'm not saying you're trouble. But the question is, how temporary are you going to be? That's what I need to know. I've got a house to run. And I introduced you to my friends." Her look said she would not brook one false move.

"I wish I could tell you what I'm going to do," said Lolly. "I wish I knew. All I can say is I'm not done in Reno, but I'll know reasonably soon."

"How soon? I've been soft on you because you seemed ... well, you seemed lost. But now I want a commitment for how many weeks you'll be staying."

Lolly blinked, wishing she had a crystal ball. Mrs. R did not know about Norma Jeane, but she was right that Lolly could not continue waffling about her own future. She said, "Two more weeks, this week and next. By then I'll know enough to stay on, or I'll pack my bags and you'll have your room back."

Mrs. R nodded and smoothed her hands across her checked apron, appeased for the moment, and Lolly breathed a sigh of relief. She had not meant to antagonize the woman who powered the household.

Outside, the air hung heavy with moisture and smelled as clean as snow on a mountaintop. Lolly smiled at her own silly thought. She *was* on a mountaintop, after a fashion. She and the whole town.

Setting aside concerns about Mrs. R's displeasure—surely there would be other boarding houses to take her in—and strode north on Sinclair to where it became Lake Street, crossing the river near First, the early spring sunshine making glitter of the previous night's snow. Some of the sidewalks were cleared, like those near the corner barbershop, and along the front of the New China Club in the two-hundred block. Then the streets narrowed as she neared the mixed residential/business zone she'd visited with Shirley and Doris. The fronts of buildings looked different in the daylight, each one finished in cinder block or redbrick, shingles or painted siding. She passed an ironworks and when she'd walked far enough north, she turned east and walked on.

After a time, she decided she'd gone too far and doubled back, looping south on a trajectory toward downtown. Then she found it, the Polka Dot, made of boxy gray cinderblock, its neon sign blank in the daylight. She drew closer and stopped to gather her thoughts.

She had set out with the notion that someone here could suggest jazz and blues artists or song titles she could request of Jackson, but she hadn't thought about how the place might be closed at this hour. In fact, it looked downright unoccupied, the graveled parking areas standing empty. She approached for a closer look.

The heavy front door was painted black with large, overlapping royal-blue dots, which had not registered on that other night. The entry alcove held an overhead fixture. On the street-facing wall was one small window embedded with wire. Lolly pulled her gloves off and rapped on the black-and-blue door. The sound echoed in the nook where she stood but no one answered. That figured. Why had she thought the club would double as a lunch place or house a daytime business of some kind? Why had she imagined herself a music sleuth when she'd been positively rotten at navigating the mysteries of her own quest? In her hands, mysteries seemed to multiply.

She rapped harder on the door. There was still no answer, but from inside the building came a sound. Recalling the interior, Lolly visualized a side door open to the wintery air. Around the building she went, to its north side, where she found a strip of trampled weeds bordering a metal door. Again, she knocked and again got no answer. She tried the knob and the door gave way. She pushed open the door so that a wedge of daylight spilled onto a small platform. As she sniffed air laced with stale smoke, her eye went to the dim square of frosted glass in the wall behind the bar. She stepped toward the half-railing before her, which held a black overcoat. The balance of the space was cast in a thick gloom so she stood, letting her eyes adjust as she got her bearings. She and the other girls had drunk cocktails at the bar, which from this vantage sat to her left. The sunken seating area was splayed out three steps below her and the stage was a bulky shape to her right. From the railing she called into the semi-darkness.

Her throat was dry and her voice came out a squeak. "Hello ... Anyone here?"

"Not open," came a man's voice, the words reverberating strangely in the boxy space.

Lolly coughed to clear her throat. "I'm sorry to bother you. Do you have a minute?"

"What is it?" spoke the voice, almost familiar, though not quite. "I kind of got my hands full."

After a moment, she made out the back of a dark figure squatting between the backs of chairs upended on tables. For some reason she said, "Can I help?"

"No thanks." After a pause came, "Oh hell, why not. There's glass broken right beneath me. If you mean to help, find the dust pan to the left of the bar. And the broom."

Lolly settled her tote bag straps on her shoulder and half-felt her way down the steps to her left and up the steps leading to the bar and the front cocktail area. In the glow of the rectangular window, she found what he had asked for. As she approached him, the man unfolded from his crouch and turned to face her, one cupped hand holding shards of dully gleaming glass.

Up close she recognized the features she had studied so intently in the Paradise lounge. She said, "Jackson. It's me, Lolly, from the Hideout." She blinked against the vertigo induced by her thoughts having somehow made Jackson appear.

"What's that?" he said, cocking his head. "What are you doing here?"

"I've got the pan."

He felt for the leading edge of the dustpan and dropped his handful of broken bits into it, flinching as he did. "Yeow. Feels like there's a piece in my left palm, and ... my right thumb too."

"Is there something I can do?" asked Lolly.

"Can you see them?" He held his left palm outward.

"Not really. It's pretty dark in here."

At that Jackson threw back his head and laughed.

"What's so funny?"

"Of course. You need lights."

Lolly cracked a smile. "I could turn some on."

"I've got to clean up whatever I've missed because I'll never find this exact spot again if I walk away. How about if you go to the door you came in and find the switch nearby. I think there's dimmer switches somewhere behind the bar but try the one by the door first."

The room's shapes sprang to life when Lolly turned the overhead lights on, small round tables set with jars holding candles and chairs with their legs in the air. She returned to Jackson and swept the floor for five or six feet in each direction, saying, "Do you think we need to mop?"

"Already did. That was a glass got left on the stage and I dropped it."

"You mopped?" asked Lolly, headed for the trash bin behind the bar.

Jackson followed slowly, touching tables and the backs of upturned chairs as he passed between them. He crossed almost perfectly to the front corner of the bar. "People always think that blind folks got no talent for everyday things. But they do. Of course, it figures I'd be clumsy today when you're here to see it."

"I was only thinking that the room looks bigger in the light, and then there's all the tables and the stairs too."

"I dig. Years ago I'd have thought the same. Doesn't take too long before you realize that people who *can* see underestimate those who can't. Happens all the time so don't feel bad." Jackson placed his left palm face-up on the bar. "Will you look back by the register for a drawer? Should be a First Aid kit."

Lolly left her effects on a bar stool and fetched the plastic first aid box. "I don't see tweezers. Let me look at your hand." She peered at the palm he proffered. "It's barely sticking out. Oh—my sewing kit. It's got a needle." She brought her tote bag to the bar and dug through it for the tool she was after. "We'll need more light," she said, spinning away to search for other switch plates. When she found them, she turned them all on. "Better," she said. "Do you want me to try to get it out?"

Jackson nodded as if thinking to himself. "Might as well."

"I'm going to sterilize it with a match from one of those folding packs and pick at it so I can get hold of the end." Lolly pulled a barstool close and perched upon it for a view to the glittery shard in Jackson's hand. "Be still," she cautioned, flattening his palm so she could widen the opening with her needle. "It's in the fleshy part."

When he jerked, she steadied his hand and worked her needle as fresh beads of blood began to appear around the jagged opening.

Until this moment she'd felt calm and collected. Now, though, her heart began to pound. Taking her thread clippers, she pinched the glass and lifted it slowly into the light. "My God, it's hair thin but it must be a quarter inch long," she said, beginning to feel shaky. "I'll drop it in the trash. No. I'll wash it down the sink."

When she returned to Jackson's side of the bar, he had not moved. A spot of blood had pooled in the palm of his hand. "Look at my thumb on this other hand, will you?"

"Okay," said Lolly, concentrating.

Jackson leaned closer and inhaled. "You smell nice," he said, speaking low. "You always wear that?"

Lolly made an effort to steady herself. "I can't see the one in your thumb. If it's that small it would be better to use tape. There's some in the first aid kit."

By the time she cut a length of tape she felt steadier. What was the matter with her? For weeks she'd been thinking about the guitar man and how to engage him in conversation so that she might study the shape and texture of him, his voice, his mannerisms. She had fictionalized a darkly romantic life for him, playing fabulous music on a stage lit with colored spotlights. In another scenario he composed music on a wintry night at home before a fire in the hearth, and a pet—she hadn't thought that part through—a cat, maybe, which would require little care. Come to find out, he did ordinary things like anyone else.

"Here," she said. "I'll roll this across the spot." She did just that, without success, then again, each time Jackson testing his thumb against his fingers.

After the fourth try, Jackson's face lit up. "That's it," he said. "I think so ... yes." He flexed his playing hand as if it were free from some demonic spell then made his way to the bar sink and running the water to get it hot, washed up with dish soap. He dried his hands on a bar towel then licked his left palm. "Still bleeding a little. I'd better cover it."

The kit was still on the bar and he felt around in it to pull out a gauze bandage and asked for the roll of tape.

"Want help?" asked Lolly.

Jackson lifted his face toward the sound of her voice. "I'll do this part, but thanks." When he was done bandaging, he held the results out for her to inspect. The tape and gauze glowed white against his skin.

"Good enough," she said.

Jackson's palm remained outstretched. "Now let me see yours," he said.

Lolly glanced around. Though they were alone she felt a stab of alarm at the thought of laying her hand atop his taped palm. She calmed her thoughts and placed her right hand into his. With coffee-colored fingers he traced her digits and palm, then circled her wrist. Her breath caught as little sparks ran through her. She couldn't take her eyes off his hands. There were two small scars on the back of one. He smelled of peppermint and Palmolive.

"Are you some kind of nurse?" he asked.

"No," she squeaked.

"You didn't slip once while you were picking out that glass." When she didn't answer he said, "How'd you find this place? You didn't say."

His serene voice and slow movements were calming. She could sense no harm in being truthful with a fellow casino employee. "Your music," she said. "Not the regular songs, but the others. I heard something like them here one night and I wanted to ask some questions."

Jackson tipped his head. "That's pretty bold of you."

Bold? Lolly smiled at his choice of words. Jackson couldn't know how meek she'd been for years until Russell forced her hand. How his guitar music buoyed her, brightening her day. "If you say so," she said.

He still cradled her hand. Now he began tracing her wrist to the cuff of her blue striped shirt before running three fingers along her sleeve and up her forearm to the knob of her shoulder. She drew back a little but didn't pull away, her heart thumping madly like a bird trying to escape the cage of her ribs. To focus her thoughts, she studied his face as his fingers drew a path along her shirt collar to her neckline. A tendril of her hair hung down and he swept it aside as his fingers drew a line upward, past her right ear then across her temple to the peak of her hairline in front. She thought he must surely feel her blood beating through her skin.

"You okay with this?" he asked belatedly.

All she could do was nod.

A triangular scar notched Jackson's forehead above his left eye. The panes of his dark glasses reflected her face as with one finger of his bandaged hand he drew a soft line down to the tip of her nose. With both hands he traced the line of her jaw, from her chin upward to the outer corners of her eyes. At last, he straightened. Mere minutes had stretched like hours. "Delicate bones," he said, "and fine hair. Is it pale?"

Lolly roused herself. "Kind of."

He nodded as if cataloguing her features on an index card destined for some mental filing cabinet stocked with observations about the world. "You don't know how bad you'll miss the sight of things," he said, "and people, till everything goes dark. Later it's only handshakes and voices. Impressions. Nothing solid. Now I have a better sense of you."

Unspoken thoughts hung in the air. Admonitions about how people who were unalike might do well to keep their distance. How the races ought not to mix. Rules made by people whose lives ran like that. It occurred to Lolly that Jackson wouldn't notice whether her hair was fixed in a modern way because he wouldn't concern himself with fashion advice for women. He would see her differently because her looks would matter less than her personality. She was a good listener; he might learn that about her.

She moved to close up the First Aid kit. Taking it to its drawer behind the counter, she asked, "How'd you end up doing this kind of work? I would have thought you'd be playing in one of the bands."

"I have a better question," said Jackson. "How'd you learn to like the music in clubs like this?"

Turning back, Lolly's eye caught movement behind Jackson, a figure in the open doorway on the far side.

"You got me wondering," he continued.

Lolly spoke, keeping her voice low. "There's someone watching us."

"Huh? Oh. What time do you have?"

Lolly checked her watch. "Just shy of one."

"Then it's my mom, come to get me and I'm not done." He called out, "Over here."

The woman's voice carried across the room. "I see you. Who's that with you?"

"Just a friend giving me a hand."

"You got a girl in here."

Jackson started for the stairs that led up to the exit landing. "A work friend." Over his shoulder, he said to Lolly. "Shut off those bar lights, will you?"

Lolly did as he asked and scooped up her coat and bag and followed Jackson around the perimeter and up the three steps leading to the side door. The Negro woman at the door stood as tall as Lolly, only an inch or two shorter than Jackson. A handsome woman with a streak of silver in her hair. She said, "The chairs aren't even set proper."

Jackson lifted the palm wrapped with tape. "Got sidetracked. Lolly, this here's my mother, Mrs. Ruby Truth Mayberry. Mother, this is Lolly, uh—"

"Cooper," said Lolly, unsure whether to offer a handshake. "It's nice to meet you."

The woman gave Lolly a hard look. "You don't work here."

"No ma'am, but I have come at night for music." Which might recommend her, or not.

Jackson remained silent as his mother drew herself up. "Well, I need to ask, why're you here now?"

Jackson broke in. "Let me say how glad I am that she pulled broken glass out of my hand. No one else here, and she helped me." He turned toward Lolly. "I do thank you for that."

Mrs. Mayberry studied Jackson then said, "I'll have a word with my son."

As Lolly stepped outside, the woman pulled the door shut though it didn't quite latch. Her voice carried through the crack. "I have told you this before. You don't belong nowhere alone with no white girl. You hear me? Doesn't matter what your story is. It will not stand up."

Jackson's voice again. "You don't know her, and you don't know what—"

"I don't have to know," Mrs. Mayberry broke in. "All that has to happen is for some white girl to make a claim against you."

"Hush," he told her. "She'll hear."

"Don't you act like you don't know what I'm saying. You *know* what I'm saying."

There was a pause, then the door creaked opened. Lolly cut her eyes toward the street, as if to make note of its interesting attributes. She wanted to assert that she was not the type to *make a claim*, but one look at Mrs. Mayberry as she emerged followed by Jackson, left her wordless.

Jackson, now with his coat on, took a key and locked the exit door. "Lolly," he said.

When she answered, "Right here," he turned toward her.

"We'll be happy to give you a lift."

Mrs. Mayberry cleared her throat and started for the sedan that was parked against the outside wall. Getting in, she closed her door with a bang.

"I walked here," Lolly told Jackson. "I can make it home."

"I suppose you know the way. Of course you do."

"Reno's not as small as the town I moved from, but it's easy to get around."

He shoved his hands into his coat pockets. "I thank you for … today."

"Anyone would have helped." Perhaps an overstatement.

"Well. See you around."

"Sure."

Pea gravel crunched under Lolly's feet as she walked away. Behind her there was another slam of a car door and a motor turning over and the sound of tires on gravel as the car pulled out into the street, headed the opposite direction.

On the walk home Lolly tried to figure out what the morning had meant, if anything—her random discovery of Jackson at the Polka Dot and his mother's intervention in their innocent encounter. Innocent enough, the cleaning up of broken glass and a cut hand, but intimate too, in an indescribable way. Mrs. Jackson clearly opposed Lolly's proximity to her son, substantiating Jackson's earlier reference to how whites and Negroes didn't mix. Even his mother was opposed, and yet, white jazz musicians shared the stage with Negroes, and the Polka Dot's audience had been mixed, full of appreciative listeners called to music that was not black or white, but the color of night, all possible colors at once.

Mrs. Mayberry's objections seemed specific to Lolly being female, over which Lolly had no control, and Lolly's skin color, of all things. It was one thing for mothers to protect their young, but Lolly figured Jackson for someone capable of choosing his own friends. Lolly had hoped in Reno to uncover Norma Jeane's ultimate fate, but so far her greatest discovery had been music with a different kind of heartbeat and a black-skinned man somehow connected to that music.

She could do worse than befriending Jackson. First there was all his talent, plus unlike her, he was sure of himself. And his touch was gentle yet firm. Caldwell hadn't even held her hand, though he'd taken her by the elbow to escort her into a taxi and had touched her on the shoulder more than once. Of course, with him she'd emphasized her marital status, a technicality, because since coming to town she hadn't entirely acted the part of a married woman, and that bothered her. A little.

Eleven

B ack at the house, Lolly sought Mrs. R's good graces by offering to shell peas for dinner, which she had asked to join. To save money, she usually didn't take her evening meal with the others, but she was tired of eating canned peaches and cold soup in her room on her days off. Also, this was Doris's next-to-last night.

During dinner, Mrs. R painted a cheerful outlook for Doris's future in the town where Doris had grown up, with people all around who looked out for each other—and yes, intruded some and offered advice, solicited or not—if a person fit in.

Mrs. R knew about such well-meaning, nosy folks because she herself had grown up in rural Missouri and knew the pleasures and perils of generations sprung up one after the other like weeds along the lanes, every family's children in plain view. She even sounded wistful as she capped her reminiscences with the old saw about how people say you can never go back again, though in her view you could and lots of people did.

Dinner dishes had been cleared and they were sprinkling nutmeg on their bowls of warm tapioca pudding when the doorbell chimed. "A visitor," said Mrs. R, "at this time of night?" She rose from the dining table which they'd set with proper linens and two lighted candlesticks in honor of Doris and her new lease on life.

Mrs. R's voice carried from the front entry. "Well, I'll be," she said. "I'm the landlady so I'll sign."

She came back to the table carrying a flat package wrapped in plain brown paper.

"What'd you get?" asked Doris.

"It's a special delivery for 'Mrs. Cooper, care of 103 State Street.'"

Lolly's eyes grew wide. Her mind first raced to the delivery of documents, as in divorce petitions, but that would suggest a willingness in Russell to plug money into anything other than rodeo fun. Besides, the package was the wrong shape and too heavy for a batch of papers.

"Open it!" cried Doris. "Did you order it?"

Lolly shook her head.

"Here," said Mrs. R, returning from the kitchen with a pair of scissors. "Who do you know in San Francisco?"

"It says 1420 Market Street," said Lolly.

Doris chimed in, "If that's a store address, you must have ordered it."

Lolly cut the brown paper open and carefully folded it back. Inside were layers of corrugated board with another slice separating two records that looked like long-playing singles.

"Music?" said Mrs. R. "Where in the world ..."

"Isn't there a card?" asked Doris. "Did you order them or not?"

"I did not order them," said Lolly, her thoughts swirling. She had spent time today, though not musical time, with a guitar musician, then lo and behold, into her hands came music. In the Hideout lounge she had requested Jackson play songs of his choosing, and like a gift, he'd played them for her. For himself, too, judging by what she'd seen and heard, and now here was more music. She didn't even recognize the artists' names—Barney Kessel and Nina Simone—but she ran her fingers over the paper labels of each record. The vinyl felt powerful in her hands, each like a window onto another place or time.

"Dreamy," said Doris. "Aren't you gonna put 'em on?"

Mrs. R looked from Doris to Lolly to the 45s. "Go ahead," she said. "You might check for dust on the turntable."

Lolly moved two stacks of old Life and Look magazines from atop the radio-record console and set her gifts in their place. First, she listened to Kessel, whom she knew nothing about, but playing it just the once, she had to concede that Jackson was not polished enough to make a recording like this. Still, she would encourage him, because people needed to hear from other people that they could rise to almost any occasion.

Lolly knew nothing about making music. Listening was one thing but making it was entirely different. Tommy Dorsey's big band sprang to mind, with dozens of stringed instruments and brass. A band like that produced a multi-layered sound to fill a dance hall, whereas with Kessel's band, the lead guitarist was distinguishable from the instruments completing the arrangement. This sounded like music for smaller spaces.

Later, after Mrs. R and Doris had retired to bed, Lolly put on pajamas and a robe and brought her Old Grand-Dad from her room. She turned the lights down low and played both records. Earlier she had played only the one because Doris had listened a while and said she didn't understand the attraction and besides, she needed her sleep for getting up early to fetch her final papers from the courthouse. Mrs. R had listened to that first one but declined to linger for the other, saying she preferred music that you could sing along to.

Lolly felt just the opposite. She liked the power of these songs. Nina Simone's plaintive vocals sounded real and raw, reminding her a little of spiked gospel music. She pictured a smoky nightclub crowded with people. A pianist, a horn player, a guitarist, a bass player, the mix of smoke and the conversations of lovers leaning close to one another, whispering, laughing, knowing how the night could end.

That woman sure could sing. Lolly took a swig of bourbon and played both records again. Once more she checked the package's return address, smoothing the stiff brown paper then folding it neatly. Unfolding, folding. Who could have sent these? She wasn't sure if she should be concerned about the surprise appearance of a package addressed to her in care of the boarding house. Music was not the sort of thing you could draw any conclusions from. If the sender was Jackson, which was highly unlikely, he might be trying to encourage her interest in an area where he obviously excelled. He probably detected her need for schooling in order to talk intelligently about music styles like jazz and rhythm and blues. She'd grown up with big band music playing on the Zenith transistor radio the children were allowed in the orphanage, and jukebox songs by Patti Page, Sam Cook, and others in her restaurant days. One set of foster parents had been fond of polka music. But the music world was clearly broader and deeper than she'd experienced.

Without thinking, she smoothed the fingers of one hand along the line of her jaw. What an inspired gift this turned out to be. Perfect for her. She kept trying to assign this lovely surprise to Jackson, a natural progression from that half-hour of, well, tenderness—if it wasn't wrong to call it that—to this hour of transformative music. A part of her wanted Jackson to be signaling the contents of his soul, just for her. The problem was, he couldn't easily have ordered a gift from San Francisco, nor would he know her boarding house address.

The air crackled crisply around Lolly the next morning as she skirted the eastern perimeter of downtown to arrive a little earlier at the Polka Dot. She didn't exactly fear being discovered there again by Mrs. Mayberry, but avoiding the woman seemed a smart choice. To that end she carried with her a kitchen timer.

Inside the club she found Jackson working. This time she helped him turn the chairs up onto the tabletops. While he took a damp cloth to the bottles behind the bar, she ran the dry mop around the floor to corral its accumulation of fluff and cigarette ends.

"I know," he joked, gin bottle in hand. "Nobody should trust me again with glass objects, but that was a fluke."

"Sure," she answered playfully, "whatever you say."

In the hour they spent working, they didn't talk enough to fill a teapot, but after a period of companionable quiet, Lolly felt she could pose a question or two. She started by asking how he came to be working in the Polka Dot.

"It belongs to my uncle on my mother's side."

"I was so sure you must be a musician here. In one of the bands."

Jackson chuckled. "I'm not that good."

"You sound fine to me." Lolly dampened a towel for wiping bar stools.

He paused at his work. "You said you've been here for music. Who'd you hear?"

Lolly shook her head. "I don't even know. It was a Thursday jam night."

"You catch anyone's name?"

"I, well … there were three of us and we were … celebrating."

Jackson cocked his head to one side, then nodded slightly, and resumed his work. "So, besides jazz clubs, what do you do when you're not working? Or not sitting in the Hideout."

"Well, there's my restaurant shifts. I fix ladies' hair, sometimes, and I like looking through Hollywood magazines." She didn't explain that she paged through the handful of Hollywood Story and Screen Story back issues she'd carried with her, the ones with Marilyn in them, her own Norma Jeane. "Say," she said to change the subject. "Have you ever heard of Barney Kessel?"

"Kessel? Sure. He's a white cat plays jazz. I've only heard a little bit of his original stuff, but it's pretty good. This mean you gave up on Elvis?"

Lolly laughed. "Why, don't you like him?"

"'Course I do. Negroes like him. All I ever hear about him, he's cordial toward black folk. And then there's his music. He comes right out and says his style comes from what came before, which is race music. The blues. Know what I mean?"

"Um," said Lolly, not quite sure.

Jackson continued. "Some music claims no color. Lots of it does, but some doesn't. Elvis. He gives credit where it's due."

Jackson had not confessed to being the mystery giver of the Kessel record, which solidified in Lolly's mind who had sent it. Caldwell. She switched subjects again. "So, are you studying to be a band musician?"

"Not me. I'm okay at it, and I could be better, maybe even good enough, but that's not my aim."

Lolly put down her cleaning rag. "What then?"

"At the university I was a sprinter. Had my eye on the Olympics. Then all hell exploded and that was the end of that. No blind athlete competes for colleges or anywhere else. No such thing."

He didn't sound shaken, but Lolly felt like she'd been punched in the stomach. Somehow, all of Jackson's dreams had been sidelined. She was about to ask him to tell her more when the kitchen timer she'd brought along began to ring.

He said, "Cinderella, that's for you."

"I told you we'd better set an alarm." She shut off the timer and grabbed her coat.

He held up a hand in salute. "Till you're better paid, thanks for the help."

Lolly went out the side door and circled around the back of the building, her shoes crunching on the gravel lot. When she came out on the front side of the club, she looked intently south so that anyone watching would see a person with business somewhere in that direction. The only business she had was, first—avoiding Mrs. Mayberry, and second—hitting the market for soda crackers and bourbon.

On Wednesday, Lolly stopped in at the Hideout after her shift. The lounge held little appeal when Jackson wasn't there to play his guitar, and the Paradise itself felt empty somehow. She hadn't seen Caldwell in days. Either he'd been ordering music from San Francisco for her, or he'd left for California (the state where she was born but had years ago departed). She had decided not to fret about his unorthodox slant on religion. He marched to a different drummer. So what? A person with her history ought not to cast stones.

After sipping her highball dry, she went to what she thought of as her lucky table and played a few hands of blackjack with Marvelle, winning eight-fifty before her luck turned. During that time she drank a free cocktail, tipped the employees, and pocketed six silver smackaroos. When she finally checked her watch, it was almost ten, so she looked a little harder around the casino. Another of the suited men who supervised table games was circulating among dealers and customers. The club seemed light on substance, missing not an object but a *someone*, the person who had given no sign that he would disappear without a warning.

Feeling a little let down, she walked home, her breath steaming out around her, and spent an hour snuggled under a quilt on Mrs. R's floral couch, her Simone record playing just loud enough to soothe the empty space inside her.

Like Christmas delayed, another package arrived on Thursday. This one held a Mercury record by Sarah Vaughan.

Lolly thought back as far as she could, to recall any other time when a surprise had come to her from anywhere. A valentine, once, in her high school days, delivered to the foster home where she then resided. Sweet as that red paper heart looked, embossed with pink and white lettering, it was the sort of message that a million other people received that same week. Innocuous, benign. Be mine. It had come from one of the less popular boys she went to school with. He knew a fellow misfit when he saw one.

This gift, though, felt as welcome as a warm breeze. She could flip the switch on the Farnsworth turntable and be transported to some other, exotic-sounding place. This newest package, like the last one, held no card or signature but she was certain that it came from the man without whom the Paradise lost a bit of its luster.

When Caldwell proved absent from the casino that next Friday, Lolly's thoughts began to solidify around the notion that he'd moved away, leaving the other bosses to run the place. And the owner, too, of course, the one he called Old Man Byrne. She felt a pang of regret that Caldwell hadn't acted like the friend he said he'd be. She'd believed him at the time, but real friends would take the time to say goodbye.

Twelve

After her Friday shift, Lolly went to the lounge and sure enough, Jackson was there, playing the old standards. At the half-hour she went to the bar to order a plain soda water with a squeeze of lime for him. Roger was on duty. "That for Jackson?" he asked.

"I thought I'd buy him one."

"You don't need to pay for a soda for him. Entertainers can have a hard drink on the house or two plain ones."

"Really?"

"Sure. Cara's on. She'll take him one."

"Okay." Lolly thought a moment. "If I write out a song request, will she take that too?"

"I guess so. Why don't you just go ask him?"

"I don't know. I just thought I'd sit and watch."

"Go ahead and write it out."

A few minutes later, Cara delivered the iced drink to Jackson along with the paper bar napkin that Lolly had written on. From across the room, Lolly watched their exchange. Then Cara used the pen on her cocktail tray to write on the napkin before progressing around the room taking drink orders and collecting dirty glassware. At the bar she handed everything back to Roger. When Cara left the bar with a fresh tray of drinks, Roger signaled Lolly with the napkin. He wore a sly grin.

"What?" she asked, taking the hand-off.

"Nothing," said Roger. "Did I say anything?"

"What's that look mean?"

"I'm just teasing, but you ought to know that the old man doesn't much go for ... um ... fraternizations between inmates—I mean races."

At least he could joke about it. Lolly thought back to Caldwell's warning for her to steer clear of the Negro guitar player. Or did he mean *musicians*, like he'd said? "How about Mr. Caldwell, is he particular too?"

Roger shrugged. "Can't say I've noticed. He's close with the old man so that's why I mention it."

"Have you seen him around?"

"Mr. Caldwell? Someone said he's gone to California on family business."

"Did they say when he'll be back? Or *if* he'll be back?"

"I don't think they'd tell me."

"Men," said Lolly. "Thanks, I guess." Lolly took the napkin back to her table and unfolded it. Newly penned was "9:00." That was all— nine o'clock. When Jackson broke into Elvis's "Blue Suede Shoes," she smiled to herself. He knew she was there.

As the hour signaling the end of Jackson's performance drew near, Lolly felt herself growing jittery. Roger's information suggested that Caldwell had for some reason taken leave of the Paradise, but that could be temporary. It didn't mean he'd never return. He might appear tonight, perhaps at the exact wrong moment. If he did so, she would have to choose between his company and responding to Jackson's message, which she had deciphered.

At last, the next group of musicians came bumping in and Jackson played his final number then unplugged his pick-up from the amplifier and packed up to leave. When he pulled on his coat Lolly rose and left the relative calm of the lounge to cross through the casino and exit out into Lincoln Alley. There, she waited.

In a few minutes, Jackson came through the glass doors with his guitar case, feeling with his cane for the outer wall. She watched him briefly before falling in beside him as he headed toward Commercial Row. "Hey there," she said, her words making fog in the air.

At the intersection where Douglas Alley met Lincoln, the foot traffic grew thicker with bunches of people cutting east toward Center Street or heading for alley entrances to various neighboring establishments.

Jackson paused to listen to the sound of footfalls approaching from the left and right then proceeded cautiously enough that other pedestrians could either let him through or skirt around him. Near the Wine House on the opposite side, he located the building's foundation and resumed his rolling gait. At that point he quoted her song request. "Somethin' blue? Is that how you're feeling?"

"Not especially. I just meant for you to know I was in the crowd."

Jackson nodded. "It sounds like what a person would say when they're down."

"Well then, maybe." Lolly found Jackson easy to talk with. He hadn't ever pressed her for personal details or recommended how she might improve herself to suit him.

When they arrived at Commercial Row, Jackson said, "I've got a half hour extra before my ride tonight."

This was new. "Can we go somewhere for coffee?"

He gave a wry smile. "You *are* bold. Only a couple of places would serve us at the same table. Neither is close by. How 'bout we walk a bit."

Lolly scanned left and right. No one seemed to be paying them any mind. "To the right maybe, toward Center Street? Looks like plenty of people out tonight."

He started that direction, his white cane sweeping a path before him. "It'll help if you warn that I'm 'bout to run into anyone."

They walked a few minutes in silence, passing under the glow of signs beckoning customers into turf clubs, bars, and eateries. Jackson pulled a peppermint from his pocket and offered it to her. Lolly declined, saying, "I'm more a lemon drop person."

After a minute he said, "So I guess you like working at the Paradise."

"Don't you?"

"It's okay."

The way he said it made her ask, "But you'd rather be somewhere else?"

"I sure would."

"Why's that?"

"I got plans that don't include this place."

"You mean the Paradise, or Reno?"

"I mean that someday I'm going to take part in something that counts."

Lolly turned his words over in her mind as they ambled past a tangle of people exiting the Hotel Golden, indoor noises spilling out with them. They passed a backside entrance to the construction zone of Bill Harrah's new casino. She wasn't sure what Jackson meant by "something that counts" and she was hesitant to ask. Eventually they arrived at the corner where Second Street ran west past the Grand Hotel. Lolly said, "Turn right here," which they did.

"Tell me, do you drive?" asked Jackson.

"I know how."

"So, you could go anywhere."

"I guess so."

"Across the country."

"If I had a car."

As they cleared the south end of Lincoln Alley, Jackson's voice took on an urgency. "You could drive to Chicago, or D.C."

"If I had a reason to."

"There's all kinds of reasons to go places. Take Washington. A person could maybe talk to the president, if only they could get there."

Lolly touched the sleeve of Jackson's coat and he stopped in his tracks. "You mean President Kennedy?" she said. "People don't get to just show up and shake his hand, do they? I never heard of that."

"He's everyone's president, isn't he?" asked Jackson. "I mean, my people helped get him elected, that's what the news said. All those Negro people going to vote. He won because of people like me."

Lolly could picture blind people casting votes, crippled people, Negroes and most everyone, but a blind person taking off for distant places where it wasn't about voting … that could get a person hurt. It wasn't like the world was wide open for people who couldn't see the same as everyone else. "Okay," she said. "Say you could get close enough to shake his hand. Then what? You'd still be in a big city, way bigger than here. How would you get around? Do you have people there?"

Jackson wagged his head. "My family's here, most of them, but *my people* … my people are everywhere, every Negro in every town from here to the deep blue sea. And those big cities, that's where things are happening." He began moving forward again.

They progressed to the corner of Virginia Street without any mishap. "You want to circle back toward the Paradise?" she asked. He nodded.

The traffic was busier on the main drag, with cars cruising slowly enough for their passengers to admire half-lit storefronts and blinking casino lights; teenagers waving at each other from car windows. Briefly tugging his sleeve, Lolly directed Jackson around a grate in the sidewalk. He shook his guitar case for emphasis. "Isn't nothing going to happen here to change things for people. In Las Vegas, they got up a big strike and forced opportunities for better jobs. But they got a lot of Negroes there so they could really make a point."

A couple dressed in evening finery cut a wide path around them as Lolly asked, "Don't people do that here?"

Now a few other pedestrians were giving Lolly and Jackson looks, but of course Jackson carried on, his frozen breath punctuating each word. "This town's the Mississippi of the West. There's hardly any Negroes here, and they're far outnumbered for making change. Go down south, way deep, and you got all those great-great-grandchildren of plantation slaves. Still treated like slaves, mostly. That's where the action's going to be."

They had come back around to the short stretch where the Paradise Club sign cast a blue and red glow in all directions. Then they reached the much larger Harolds Club beneath orange and yellow lightbulbs.

Jackson's enthusiasm held such energy that Lolly couldn't help but admire his passion for a cause meant to benefit not only himself but thousands of others held back by threat or worse. He sounded like even though it might be dangerous, he meant to rally for the poor and downtrodden, which enlarged her esteem for him. He seemed to emphasize an improved life for his people, but Lolly thought that his cause could apply to others too. There had to be a million people who only wanted the same chance as the next guy. "You're set on joining some action, even when you don't know if it's dangerous until you get there?"

"It's a big unknown, parts of it. But what will ever get accomplished by people staying put with what they know? There isn't anything more important than working toward making things better. Which takes more than one person at a time. Takes more like a thousand people, or ten thousand."

Lolly could feel the ache in Jackson's words. A thought came to her. "If there *was* a way you could get there, what do you think you'd do?"

They came to a halt at Commercial Row, the rumble of slow-rolling cars all around them. Jackson stopped and lowered his voice. "Well, I would join a march or picket a lunch counter. That's peaceful resistance. It worked in Las Vegas because the people in charge, all those businesses, none of them wanted a fight. But that's not true everywhere. Peaceable change would be nice. It would be best, but in some places they don't want change, and peace don't suit 'em. Won't stay that way, though, mark my words."

"The other Negro people here. Do they talk about crossing the country to join protests?"

"A few, I guess. But most of them are not for giving up what little they got in order to go somewhere and maybe get hit by some cop with a nightstick. They got too much to lose."

"And you don't."

"Not as much."

Lolly wanted to challenge that last assertion but she didn't exactly have the right to say what Jackson had to gain or lose. Instead, she said, "It seems to me that other people would have an advantage, if it comes to a fight."

"True enough. I can't see a punch comin'. Here's the thing. Back when I could see, I ran track and I was good at it. Good enough to get invited to the university, but they wanted my legs. To get in because you want to better yourself or get a good job? It happens, but not often. For a college education to be an everyday thing for my people, that's worth marching for. And fighting for. But it will take changing minds, thousands of minds. I can't run track anymore but I still got a voice. If we don't speak out—all of us that can—then no one's got to listen."

Lolly hadn't given much thought to the specific struggles of colored people. It had always seemed to her that most people ran up against obstacles standing in their way. To keep a roof over their heads and food on the table, a little respect. She'd known plenty of white people struggling to make ends meet but she never much thought about whether they'd put their safety on the line for an education or a job. She asked, "What does your mother think about you going all that way to join the protests?"

Jackson tossed his head. "Let's not talk about her. She's ... she's the reason I'm not there already." He abruptly swiveled right and proceeded to complete the rectangle they'd walked.

Lolly wondered if he was counting steps in his head because when they got close to where the north-south alley met the sidewalk, he edged toward the curb and halted. "This about right?" he asked.

"There's a parking meter on your left."

He nodded. "Supposed to be my cousin driving me tonight. Little George. But might be my mama."

Lolly read that as a warning. "In that case, I'll go. It was nice walking with you."

"Same here. Listen, I don't mean to put you off, or scare you with how I get on my box sometimes. I don't know any other way to be about things that are important."

"Don't worry," said Lolly. "You won't get rid of me that easily." The subjects he spoke about were far more interesting than the "stupid fuckers down at the shop" that Russell had regularly groused about. That kind of talk made her thoughts go blurry. But this. This talk of Jackson's made her think about the nature of people and who held the power.

She paused to allow him time to either assert how he didn't mean to get rid of her, or else ask her to come by the Polka Dot again, but he didn't. He stood upright with his cane in one hand and his guitar case in the other, seemingly intent on the night sounds sparking around them, the cars accelerating through nearby intersections and people calling to one another. Dark man on a dark night listening for his ride.

Lolly had a sudden urge to gamble, which she'd only practiced during the relative quiet of certain midweek evenings. She bade Jackson goodbye and left him at the curb, returning to the Paradise through the alley doors and glancing around until she found Marvelle's blackjack table. She draped her coat over one of two available swivel stools and took a seat as Marvelle opened a new deck of cards and shuffled. When offered the deck to cut, Lolly waved it away. She didn't feel lucky so much as determined. Other people had plans and ideas, sometimes big ones. Even Jackson, who couldn't drive, couldn't eat in white people's casinos, who worked part-time jobs that probably paid poorly, even *he* was better at what she'd been timid about for most of her life—speaking up for himself. She was only beginning to assert herself. Reno seemed to be having that effect on her.

Five weeks had passed since she'd arrived at the bus depot on Center Street and ended up at the motor hotel just north of the arch, and what did she have to show for them? The nebulous attentions of a casino boss, now disappeared, and what felt like a growing fascination with a Negro musician. Oh, and nothing solid about a spiritual resting place for Norma Jeane.

Lolly's plan regarding Norma Jeane, such as it was, had produced no discernible results. All those religions and not two of them could you rub together to produce a clear picture of heaven, or what it took to get there. Or if there was even a *there* there. She didn't even know what exact beliefs, if any, Norma Jeane had held on the day she suddenly died from what news reports intimated was a combination of alcohol and drugs, uppers probably, but possibly downers too. Under the circumstances of such a messy end, did religious beliefs flicker clearly enough through a person's mind to prompt a renouncing of sin? Or did the world simply turn into a vapor that final thoughts couldn't penetrate?

How would the average person know what portion of celebrity stories was gossip designed to feed the appetites of readers, bad news for one person making others feel better about their own lives? Had she a clearer picture of Norma Jeane's inner thoughts while alive, she might better grasp which version of God her old friend had most identified with. Then Norma Jeane's heaven might identify itself.

These were the concerns running through her head as she checked her cards and watched Marvelle respond to each player as they refused more cards or called for hits. Marvelle paid winning hands and swept losing bets into the table's waist-high tray of silver dollars and gambling tokens. Lolly's mind was only half on the game, but before too long she had run her winnings up to twenty dollars. A cocktail waitress came by and Lolly ordered her usual, adding "Have him make it strong, will you?" Maybe a stiff drink would turn her into a bigger winner and double her money.

After another hour, Lolly had indeed boosted her stack of silver to twenty-eight dollars but time had fled. Deciding to quit while she was ahead, she tipped the dealer who had taken Marvelle's spot at the table. When she rose, she felt herself listing and thought, *What?* Then it hit her—she had skipped dinner. Unsteady as she felt, there was no use walking back to the boarding house. Whittlesea Checker taxis often idled in the loading zone out front, so getting home would be no problem.

It was almost midnight when Lolly let herself into the house. At the sound of the front door, Mrs. R came from the kitchen in her nightgown and robe.

"You're up late," said Lolly.

"So are you."

Lolly wasn't sure if the woman was displeased or simply tired. "I was talking with a friend," she said. Partly true.

The woman studied Lolly a moment. She said, "I stayed up to tell you that an envelope came from Oklahoma today. I thought it might be important."

Lolly's pleasure over having beaten the casino imploded. *Oh, God, Russell's police report.* She'd given the boarding house address when countering his accusations, so now he knew where to find her. She put a steadying hand on the coat rack and told herself to calm down. Perhaps he was sending a divorce notice, or a threat of some kind. If it was a threat she could go to the police—no she couldn't—unless she wanted to fuel more speculation about her marital dramas. *Think.* Russell could not spring bodily from an envelope carried all this way by the postal service. Paper only conveyed words; it couldn't draw blood. With a sigh, she hung her coat then followed Mrs. R to the kitchen.

"You look a little green," said the landlady. "How about a cup of tea or some warm milk?"

"Tea, please," said Lolly, her gaze fastened on the breakfast table, where a thin white envelope lay. She approached the table slowly, not entirely convinced that mail couldn't strike like a rattler. The familiar scrawl set out her name and the boarding house address. He *did* know where she was.

Mrs. R put the kettle on and pulled a mug from the cupboard. "For your information, I've got another boarder coming next week. Her name's Anna. She'll take Shirley's room."

Mrs. R offered Lolly a letter opener. The kettle began to sing as Lolly, hands shaking, slit the envelope and extracted two wrinkled pages bearing the ragged margins of spiral notebook paper. They were folded separately. The first one read, "It's been long enough I know what you're up to. Me and Chester are headed north to Browning. I boxed up your stuff."

Three sentences and no signature. How like him. With her he had never expressed anything of substance, said anything that seemed to come from the deepest place at the center of him. Like what had happened to his father, or if he had dreams that took him places beyond the rodeo circuit. Another city, another country, another life. Their marriage resembled one of those red and white bobbers on the surface of a trout pond, bound to a single spot, waiting. She had clung to the notion that no one was perfect, no marriage was perfect. A couple could work through any rough patches, if only they tried hard enough. Russell was imperfect, as was she. Truly flawed, the both of them.

The second page held even fewer scrawls. It read, "I don't know why you had to do that. You probably think you're fooling me." Not a word about the extent of his injuries. Not one word about hers. Anyone ignorant of Russell's ways might think this a casual communication, no more menacing than a note declaring *Going for beer*. Lolly knew better. The lack of substance simply signaled Russell's disregard for her position. Also, that he could reach out from a distance and turn her day upside down.

Lolly's cup of tea sat cooling on the table. Distant sounds from down the hall suggested that Mrs. R was readying for bed.

When Lolly reached at last for the tea and took a sip her stomach rebelled. She dropped the mug with a clatter and stumbled for the hallway bathroom adjacent to Mrs. R's bedroom. The door was not quite latched, so Lolly pushed it open and lunged for the toilet. Mrs. R spun from the sink and reached for Lolly as she flipped the seat up and folded to the floor.

It was over in less than a minute. After Lolly had exhausted the meager contents of her stomach, she sat back on her haunches.

"What in the world?" asked Mrs. R.

Lolly just shook her head.

"Hon. This isn't the first time."

"I know."

Mrs. R shifted to wet a cloth and bring it to Lolly, who remained upon the floor. "It doesn't act like influenza or you wouldn't be able to work. I've seen a lot of young women in my day. Mrs. Ernstrom's daughter, for instance, had the same symptoms. I could be wrong, Lord knows my husband used to say so, but you seem to be ill the same way Elizabeth was, and she turned out to be pregnant."

The landlady's words hung in the air like smoke above a fire. Lolly thought back to the last time her monthly cycle had come. Best she could recall it had started three weeks prior to her arrival in Reno. She'd been busy since then with the concerns that brought her here and the ones that had arisen after that. She knew that stressful events could cause a change so she'd been glad to imagine a temporary respite from her monthly. Was she pregnant? The timing seemed plausible. Pregnancy would explain her nausea and ready tears.

Slumped upon the lavatory's checkered tiles, Lolly felt a silent clock power up inside her, the type of clock that metered not hours, but days marching toward a deadline. A great sorrow welled up inside her. She gave in and wept until she was flat wrung out, then told herself she would cry no more over anything related to Russell. She had physically left Gilleon and Russell behind, but clearly, he had not left her. A fragment of him was now lodged inside her.

Thirteen

The notion of pregnancy was like a gut punch. It signaled more trouble on the way. She had already abandoned her Gilleon home, and if she'd abandoned her home, she'd abandoned her marriage to the man who lived there. She did not want the child of a man who could do what he'd done to her, plus she knew what it was like to be an unwanted child, untethered from a parent's love. That type of child carried certain vulnerabilities and a sense of unworthiness through all its pursuits, even when it donned an exterior of competence. She would not do that to someone else, certainly not to a child. From her seat on the black and white tiled floor she turned to Mrs. R. "We won't tell anyone."

The landlady looked surprised. "But hon—"

"Neither of us. Not a soul. Promise me."

Mrs. R studied Lolly. "I wish you wouldn't think that way."

"But I do. It's my private business."

"Haven't you kept enough secrets? And, besides, you're one of my boarders. I'm at least partly responsible for your wellbeing."

Lolly calculated the odds of her talkative landlady keeping such a secret. She needed privacy until she could formulate a plan. "Let's keep it between you and me. Please? Until I know what I'm going to do."

Mrs. R blinked hard. "Well, I suppose it is your affair." Her hands fluttered as she talked. "But I insist that you get proper attention from a doctor. Will you promise me that?"

Lolly nodded. "I'll see a doctor. Yes."

She declined Mrs. R's help in preparing for bed. Exhausted, she dozed fitfully and came full awake when the bulb in her dresser lamp burned out. After that she lay in the dark, waiting for daylight. Funny. Since that night in the orphanage and throughout her single years, she had slept with a light nearby, steeling herself against a particular type of threat appearing at her bedside in the night. None had ever arrived. Instead, betrayal had come to her in the form of her husband.

Russell had not been trying to start a family with her when he stormed into their bedroom after her. She had felt his fear. Fear that his mastery over her was slipping away. It seemed now that similar to the way stags and bears marked their territory, scraping trees and leaving scat, Russell had marked her so that the world would know she'd once been his and so she would be reminded of him for a long, long time. Possibly forever, a thought flared red. Even if Russell hadn't planned this outcome, he had known it was possible.

Now she realized that in recent weeks she'd had a peculiar feeling that days were slipping through her fingers, a sensation she'd attributed to her unsuccessful search for Norma Jeane's heaven. If she'd known that sleuthing could take so long, would she have started down this path? And now, this new calculation of time counted in weeks and trimesters. There would be a limit to making certain choices.

Suddenly she realized that she'd fallen into bed without executing her bedtime prayers. Not that prayers had been all that helpful. As always, they seemed simply one-way conversations. Perhaps expecting an answer to prayers was folly (there was no good way to know for certain). Or maybe only the most devout and studious believers could count on receiving answers, which would leave her out. Still, she liked the singular comfort of praying about any and all subjects without fear of recrimination. She would not forsake that comfort.

She wondered now if Norma Jeane had ever faced a delicate decision about a pregnancy? As far as Lolly knew Norma Jeane had never borne a child. As an adult she'd had mountains of money, of course, and plenty of Hollywood contacts, resources for handling almost any quandary. Lolly had neither. What she did share with Norma Jeane, though, was determination coupled with resourcefulness—minimum traits for attracting lady luck. If Lolly wanted out of her predicament, she would have to put those traits to work.

In the morning, Mrs. R rapped on Lolly's bedroom door. "I've brought you some warm milk with a little bit of coffee."

"Come in," called Lolly from beneath her quilts.

Mrs. R crossed the small room to set a tray atop the crocheted dresser scarf. "I got worried when you didn't come down." She motioned to the mug. "This seemed the sort of thing you might go for. 'Coffee-milk,' my mother called it. I've brought soda crackers too."

Lolly gave a wan smile. She'd been living on soda crackers she sometimes carried in her tote bag.

Mrs. R glanced around then continued. "It's a nice day. Sunny looking. The crocuses by the front steps are open. The yellow ones I planted, oh, twelve years ago now. Don't know what's keeping the purple ones." When Lolly lay silent, Mrs. R wiped her hands on her apron and took a deep breath. "I know I'm not your kin. I haven't even raised a girl of my own. But I was your age once, and there were times that I thought there was no good way forward, that life had let me down. But somehow, I muddled through, and if things didn't come out perfect ... well, what's ever perfect, right? So, I carried on, and you might be surprised—maybe you're too young to realize this—but life goes on, no matter what." She handed the warm mug to Lolly, who took a sip. "Of course, maybe I was wrong about your condition," she continued. "I got to thinking about that and I might have been."

"You weren't," said Lolly. Last night in the bathroom, Lolly had recognized Mrs. R's declaration as truth. She'd been so busy with her search for her old friend's heaven and her curiosity about the new people she'd met, that the last thing on her mind was the timing of her cycle. As recently as two years ago she had imagined she might cherish a child someday. Since then, though, Russell's firecracker anger had grown worse. She told Mrs. R, "I do appreciate your kindness."

"I suppose you'll go home now."

Lolly had totaled the pros and cons of her situation. "Actually, this has made up my mind for me. I'll divorce him if you let me room with you a little longer."

"Oh?" The woman looked taken aback.

"I guess I've established residency, but from what I've learned it will take a few more weeks for filing paperwork and going to court and all."

Mrs. R seemed to marshal her composure. "Of course you'll stay. You are still welcome here, and you'll need someone to look out for you. Are you sure though?"

Lolly nodded sadly. "I've got a little money saved, but I'll need more. For the ..."

"Lawyer. I understand. If you bought yourself a new pair of hair scissors, could you cut hair?"

Lolly thought a moment. "Nothing fancy."

"Bangs, maybe. Or a little shaping to go with perms and colors."

"People better not want anything professional."

Mrs. R wagged one hand. "They can pay more at the El Cortez or The Beauty Mark. It's when they want a better price they can come to you."

A couple of regular hair care customers might pad Lolly's savings, but there was still the problem of the baby she was carrying. Not an actual baby, but the start of one. And of course, once started, babies had a tendency to grow. The situation she now found herself in called for action of a kind she wouldn't wish on anyone, herself included.

She could not ask Mrs. R, a clearly religious woman, about which doctors, if any, there were for addressing her situation, but she figured Reno for a thoroughly modern town, capable of arranging a thousand divorces a month in its heyday. Surely there would exist a doctor who catered to unwanted pregnancies, either some merciful soul, or else the type who could profit from that which ailed others. That's what her predicament felt like now, an ailment.

"I suppose you'll want to take a little better care of yourself," said Mrs. R.

"I will?" asked Lolly.

Now the woman looked flustered. "Well I was going to say—oh, never mind. It's none of my business." She wiped her hands on her apron and caught Lolly's gaze. "You look a little perkier," she continued. "Did the warm drink help?"

"That and your advice about earning extra money," said Lolly. "Maybe after my shift tonight I'll write out notices to post around the neighborhood. You know, with prices for a trim or a permanent wave, that sort of thing." With that, she pushed back the covers and climbed out of bed. There was work to be done and she knew that silent as it was, her internal clock was now counting the days.

At work, Lolly went through the motions. She could handle most restaurant jobs blindfolded and this night her thoughts kept returning to the previous six or seven weeks. How time seemed to sprint when you needed it to crawl. She had been saving a little of her unspent weekly pay plus some of her casino winnings but what she needed was the inside scoop regarding a certain kind of doctoring.

Availing herself of such measures would be a sin, of course. Along with simply thinking about such options or asking for advice. She didn't need church lessons to know that life was meant to be cherished, but what about life begat by violence? Surely, that was an exception, wasn't it? At least it ought to be.

As the evening drew to a close, Lolly worked up her courage to speak with Karen. The waitress had regained her senses about tallying tickets. She no longer needed Lolly's help, but they remained friendly. In fact, having once intervened to clear the waitress's good name, Lolly counted the woman an ally. When she gauged a lull in the restaurant's action, she took Karen aside and asked her if she had debated at all about continuing her pregnancy.

"What makes you ask that?" said Karen.

"It's just I have a friend who's ... trying to figure it out. Keep or not keep. Become a mother, or not."

Karen looked around warily. "But why are you asking *me*?"

Lolly maintained a steady gaze. This was just like gambling, where success required a calm demeanor. "It's only that you've lived here longer than me. I'm trying to find a doctor to ... send her to. For advice."

Karen's face grew rosy. "Well, I don't—I can't—" Tears sprang to her eyes. She wiped at them with one hand then turned away, leaving Lolly staring after her.

After her shift, Lolly ate chicken soup and crackers at the coffee shop counter before changing her blouse and heading for the Hideout lounge. She had a request for Jackson. Once there, a quick glance told her that there was no sign of Caldwell. She had to admit that she missed his subtle attentions. She appreciated his benevolence but clearly, they were opposites, from entirely different worlds. Jackson, though, was more like her, both of them operating with what was left over after life had dealt them harsh hands.

She crossed over to Jackson's corner stage and waited for him to finish playing "King of the Road." Leaning close she said, "Jackson, it's me. Will you bring your guitar to the Polka Dot on Monday?"

He swiveled toward the sound of her voice. "My guitar? What for?"

"I'm going to stop by. If that's okay."

He gave a small smile. "You sure? You know I like your company fine, but—"

Before he could refuse, she said, "Good. I'll see you then."

Lolly headed directly to find Marvelle's table, but the woman was nowhere in sight. The dealers took hourly breaks, which was probably as much about breaking the spell of a cold dealer or a hot gambler as it was about giving employees a reprieve from hours of standing on their feet. Still, dealing cards looked like it paid well. At any time of day, at any table, there seemed always to be a few silver dollars stacked to one side—the dealer's tips.

She had brought along ten dollars for the purpose of enhancing her meager pot of savings by winning at blackjack. She needed to somehow accumulate enough money for both a divorce and a doctor. Winning a few dollars here and there would boost her funds. She had earned a little bit from giving perms and after paying for her room with Mrs. R had a bit left over with which to gamble. Pity the poor people who cashed their paychecks only to lose all their money at the tables. Not that people didn't lose their dough in other ways. They did. Betting on the horses, for instance, or riding rodeo. She could not afford to be one of them.

Lolly gambled for a while but her luck of the other night had fled. It was a good thing she had not brought more because she lost all ten dollars in the space of half an hour and one complimentary cocktail. She'd have been smarter to spend the money on flyers for promoting her side business of fixing hair (ten dollars being enough for printing flyers for half the town). Gambling had one thing going for it, though. It beat the hair business hands down for the speed with which you could make a little money. Not with one-dollar bets, the way she played, but perhaps playing for bigger stakes. Five dollars per hand, or ten. The maximum was $100 and there were probably plenty of die-hard risk takers who could stomach such a bet. Clark Gable and those types were probably big betters. The director John Huston. The Rat Pack. All of them had spent time in Reno and she could feature them betting large.

Out of money, she gave up on blackjack and walked home to the boarding house. After getting Mrs. R's permission, she clipped likenesses of fashionable women from back issues of Mrs. R's magazines and pasted them onto leftover paper once used by Mrs. R's niece for typing practice. Soon she was showing her finished flyers to the landlady, who overnight seemed to have grown more watchful.

"Eat a few bites, please," said Mrs. R, offering slices of biscuit and a square of American cheese.

"Cheese? Do I look like a mouse?" Lolly teased.

"Eat it. It's good for you."

Lolly acquiesced. It felt good to count Mrs. R as someone who cared about her. She wouldn't want to lose that support.

Sunday arrived. It was a day Lolly should have spent canvassing another church for clues about Norma Jeane's spiritual resting place. But the only religion left on her list was Catholic, the very type she had purposely avoided for the last twenty years. The orphanage kids had attended Our Lady of the Mountains. Lolly, too, for two years. Those early lessons and rituals felt etched into her brain. Along with the knowledge of danger.

Instead of dressing for church, Lolly dressed for work and left the house extra early to tack a few of her flyers on utility poles around Mrs. R's immediate neighborhood. As she walked, one topic kept making loops in her mind: Last night, Karen had found Lolly at a blackjack table and slipped her a folded napkin with the name of a doctor and his address.

Posting flyers served more than one purpose. It might bring a few more ladies to Lolly's side business but it also made the perfect cover for taking a walk before work. A walk that would allow her a look at the special doctor's office while the streets were quiet.

She walked up Lake Street, crossing over the Truckee, which resembled gleaming, shadowy serpent scrolling eastward, as if seeking the sun. The air flowing over the bridge held odors of damp ground and mountain sky. At Second Street she turned west, then north again at Virginia, headed for Third.

Her shoes thudded solidly as she walked the now-familiar downtown streets. There had been no significant snowfall for a week or more though Mrs. R swore that in every month of the calendar, Reno had at some point seen a snowfall. Even July! Lolly smiled at the thought of all those people on their way to work and kids kicking balls around deserted schoolyards under a gathering dome of clouds. Next thing they knew, here came a veil of crystalline flakes blanketing the city.

The summer storms of Oklahoma were a different sort. Not only thunderstorms, which in their Midwestern incarnation could turn cattle into bawling bunches of water-riven cowhide. The worst were devil storms—dense walls of dust rising up in clouds tall enough to dirty the shoes of angels—sweeping straight across the plains to plaster everything with a thick layer of red-brown grime.

Half a block beyond where Ralston crossed Third, Lolly slowed her steps as her stomach knotted at the sight of a 1930s clapboard house-turned-office standing at the address that Karen had provided. Its front walk looked recently swept and the planter boxes affixed to the front porch rail held the green shoots of flowers yet to bloom. Somewhere in the distance a dog barked and from a block away on Second came the intermittent sound of sluggish Sunday traffic. Lolly stood rooted to the sidewalk. She could just make out the block letters of a sign to the right of the front door: Dr. Malcom Hall – Obstetrics and Gynecology. This was it.

Lolly's hand moved involuntarily to her waist. Such a conventional façade for a place offering the extraordinary. Behind those shuttered windows and that brown door lay a refuge for women with certain female needs. Reproduction. Sexuality. Subjects discussed in the same hushed tones as mental deficiencies or child abuse.

Lolly had been a waitress, an occupation second only to hairdresser as a receptacle of gossip and breaking news. Women might not talk publicly about their needs, but they talked among themselves, from behind cups of coffee and plates of eggs-over-easy. Even more personal in nature were the subjects discussed within the walls of places where men never ventured, places where hairdryers blew hot and tongues debated topics rarely covered on the six-o'clock news. Men might imagine women as creatures who didn't think about sex and didn't desire it. But women *were* sexual precisely because men existed. When you mixed the two, sex was what resulted.

A distant blast of sound signaled an incoming train on the tracks that ran adjacent to Third. Lolly looked west toward mountains pressing upward against a deep blue sky. The range's upper reaches were mottled with the dark green of pine forests deep in snow. Not an inch of snow on the streets in town, but plenty on the humped-up mountains ringing three sides of the valley. A deep cleft pointed in the direction of the last Winter Olympics village, but also where a brutal winter had once killed almost all of those poor Donner Party pioneers; those history lessons courtesy of Mrs. R.

The train's horn grew closer, accompanied by a rumbling in the air. Soon a Southern Pacific engine lumbered past, its steel wheels hammering the rails, sending vibrations up Lolly's legs and spine, its air brakes hissing in advance of the downtown passenger depot. Gleaming silver cars glided by, their windows filled with the faces of people looking outward.

Lolly fought the urge to duck away from the outturned gazes, but of course they didn't know her or the little house behind her. To them she would resemble a woman out for a stroll when in fact she was a woman on a mission just concluded—reconnaissance of Dr. Hall's office—with confirmation that the office looked legitimate, like an unassuming place for seeking help.

Her winter coat now felt too warm for what would become a fifty-five-degree day. She unbuttoned her coat and brushed a wisp of damp hair from her neck. Her watch gave the time as 11:00. She was due at work by 12:00 and she was not about to develop a reputation for tardiness. From here on out her co-workers might study her a little harder to determine the accuracy of any rumors they heard about her, but she would provide no reason for them to think her lazy.

Fourteen

M onday morning found Lolly feeling all dragged out, as if instead of sleeping she'd spent the night trying to turn the clock back on how she'd arrived at the crossroads before her. The doctor's office had taken hold in her thoughts as a place where at one moment a nurse might discuss a coming childbirth with all its special preparations and attentions, and the next counsel a patient about how to end a pregnancy. She herself could never be such a nurse. In the first place, the studying meant stacks of textbooks and reams of tests. The exams alone could crush a person. But also, how could anyone do that kind of work and not absorb all the fear and grief and hope without becoming ... well, doomed in a way.

Standing naked before the half-mirror above the pine bureau, Lolly examined her body for signs of her newest secret. To her practiced eye she looked a tiny bit fuller through the breasts, a detail that no one else would notice. She hoped to keep it that way.

Dressed in her most casual clothes, she told Mrs. R. who, if it were possible, had grown even more solicitous, that she was going out for fresh air and errands.

"Fresh air. That's good," said Mrs. R.

Along the streets, some sort of flowering trees had burst into bloom. A type of plum maybe, abuzz with a few early bees out to sip nectar.

At the bridge where Lake Street spanned the Truckee, Lolly paused to consider the cottonwoods rooted fast to the bank as the nearby water rushed along. These specimens were not as huge as the California redwoods she'd seen in pictures, but their height suggested longevity, their trunks like craggy shields against the extremes of an open-air life.

Downstream from the bridge, the river swept north, past an enormous logjam of debris on the right, held fast by the flow of water. From that distance the heaped-up broken tree branches looked like the arms and legs of some giant race of bodyless people clinging to each other.

Along the block fronting the Polka Dot, a handful of Hawthorne trees looked thick with buds, lending a lighthearted air to the neighborhood of dormant yards and boxy houses.

"Hello," Lolly called as she stepped through the unlocked side door of the club.

"Over here," came Jackson's reply.

Lolly switched on a set of overhead lights and went to join him. Maybe he could lift the weight that had descended upon her.

"Hey," she said, stepping close. "What can I help with?"

Jackson turned toward her voice and shook his head. "I feel funny about you working for free. It's really my job."

"I can't just sit and watch," said Lolly.

"Most people could."

"Not me." She took the broom from his hand. "Besides, it'll go faster. Did you clean by the stage?" she asked.

"Yep." He left to bring back the mop and bucket. They worked in amiable silence until the floor was presentable. When they had put the mopping supplies away, they moved to the bar.

Lolly wet a rag for wiping the barstools. "Did you bring your guitar?" she asked.

"As promised. I'll break it out when we finish this."

Lolly nodded to herself, pleased. "I keep thinking you'd make a great jazz musician."

"That's not on my list."

Lolly scrubbed a little harder at a spot on one of the orange vinyl seats. "Why not? You're good, and it seems like you know as many songs as anyone."

"I don't know all the numbers that get played in a place like this. Those musicians are born to it. Most of 'em could play with just about anyone, even the big stars. Some of 'em play with the shows that come to town."

"But you could be that good, couldn't you?"

Jackson shook his head while he wiped a bottle of Dewar's Scotch and set it back behind the bar. "There's a difference. You don't have an ear for the difference between me and them. But it's nice of you to say."

Lolly didn't want to bring up Jackson's desire for some faraway place. She'd dealt with enough difficult news lately.

"Done," said Jackson, slapping his cleaning rag against the back counter. He felt his way to the sink and dropped it in. "Gimme yours and I'll leave it," he said to Lolly. "My Uncle, Big George, takes the rags home to wash."

"Do we need to put the chairs back around the tables?" asked Lolly.

"Damn, that's right, but easy does it."

Lolly moved to the closest table and lifted a chair from its place atop the woodgrain Formica. Setting it on the floor, she said, "I'm stronger than I look."

Jackson chuckled and crossed the room to the stage end, where he began returning chairs to their places. Eventually they met in the center.

"That's it," said Lolly at last.

"Good enough," said Jackson. "I'll get my guitar." He said it git-tar, with the accent up front. His worn black case sat on the lip of the elevated stage. "C'mon over here," he called to Lolly, who moved forward to join him. "Want a seat?" he asked, strumming a few chords. "I guess you have a request?"

"Oh," said Lolly, selecting a chair. It made perfect sense that he should think so. "I've been listening to a couple of records. One of them is by that Barney Kessel I mentioned."

He strummed some chords and adjusted two of the tuning knobs. "I can't play like him. But, ah, let's see. Here's a number recorded by a bunch of different cats. There's a guy named Lead Belly. You might've heard some other version." He launched into a slow number that built in intensity, his fingers moving deftly between chords. A fiercely beatific look came over his face.

Lolly had been trying to figure out why Jackson attracted her so. This was one reason. He held such talent inside him and shared it without boasting or expecting anything in return. His demeanor was the opposite of Russell's swagger and grandstanding ways. Not a bone in his body suggested that the world owed him anything just because he walked upright. And she would bet her paycheck that he'd never purposefully hurt a woman.

There was no amplifier so Lolly moved her chair closer to absorb the notes pouring from beneath his fingers. When he finished, she said, "Wow!" and sat a moment letting the reverberations continue in her mind. "What's it called?"

"'Rising Sun Blues.'"

"Will you play it again?"

Jackson cocked his head at her. "The same one? I know plenty others."

"I just want to hear that one again."

Jackson shook his head a little. "All right then." He waggled his fingers as if to prepare them for another assault on the strings and went after the song again. His intense expression and the flash of his hands drew Lolly in. Before long she had pulled her chair close enough to count the threads in the weave of his plaid shirt. Without planning to, she reached a hand out and laid it on the flat area below the strings. Jackson shifted slightly but he kept playing.

Her palm and fingers came alive to the guitar's vibrations. Even her arm. It was almost like being inside the music, or the music being inside her, the hearing and feeling and oneness with the notes. She wished she could sit there forever with the outside world held at a distance. When the song was done and the last note had echoed away, she sat speechless, as if drugged by her nearness to the making of music.

"You okay?" asked Jackson.

"Sure," she said at last. She needed to know why this music made her feel like it did. Thinking back to her waitressing days on the east side of Los Angeles, she had caught snatches of this sort of music mixed in with the popular radio hits. Not much, but a little. Now it seemed a symbol of all she'd been ignorant about, one more bit of her life bleached out by her years in the Oklahoma sun.

"What is it?" she asked.

"It's an old Jimmy Reed song. He wrote it."

"I mean, is that blues?"

"This one is, yeah."

"So that's the kind of music that I heard the night I came here? Was that what I heard?"

"Or you might have heard jazz. Any of those club musicians would know at least a little of everything. If it's new to you, you might not recognize that jazz comes from blues, which can have a certain chord progression. It might incorporate blues, or it can be more sophisticated, that's what some say, the arrangements more complicated, sometimes messier. Layers of sound, improvisation, riffs and like that."

"Does that make blues more basic?"

"That's right."

"Soulful."

He wagged his head. "That's one view. I guess I'd subscribe to that." He seemed done explaining, but Lolly wasn't sure she yet knew what it was about the music that made her not just listen, but feel it, too. With other kinds of songs, Dean Martin's for instance, you could sing along to the lyrics; the words mattered as much, or maybe more, than the music behind them. But with *this* music, the notes themselves, the way they drove toward a seamless whole seemed to transcend everything else. With Jackson's bluesy music in her head, not a single worry could take hold. Not Norma Jeane's fate, not Russell and his threats. None of her personal troubles.

Lolly had hungered to touch Jackson's guitar since the first time she'd seen him play it. The thing looked so simple, made of golden wood with a herringbone pattern around the border. It was probably like ten thousand others, but somehow it seemed a charmed object in his hands. "May I hold it?" she asked.

"The guitar? All right."

Lolly had moved her perch so close that Jackson just lifted the strap over his head and held the instrument out a little. "You right-handed?" he asked. "Just hold it like you saw me do."

"It's not as heavy as I thought," said Lolly. She slipped the strap over her own head and settled the instrument's body onto her lap. Up close, its wood was satiny smooth and a little warm from Jackson's body. She ran a hand over it. It seemed so beautiful it might of its own accord fill the air with some lush melody.

"Go ahead," said Jackson. "Make some sound."

Tentatively she stroked the strings. A wee twang issued and she almost laughed. "How do you make a real note?" she asked.

"You got to strum it, or pick at it with … intention."

"Don't I have to press the strings at the top?"

"Up along the frets, that's right." He stood and reached out to locate the guitar's neck. "Up top here, you got to press your fingertips. That makes the chords."

Lolly struggled a moment. "Mine won't reach around."

"Sure they will."

He pivoted around behind her chair. When he ran a hand across her shoulder to find his position, she held her breath.

"Hold still a minute," he said as he ran his left hand out along the neck of the guitar to grasp her wrist. "You got to shift your wrist," he said. "It feels wrong at first, but you got to wrap your fingers around to the top side."

Jackson's chin hovered just over Lolly's shoulder as he pressed her fingers against the strings. "That's what it takes, now give it a strum," he said. At the result, he said, "That's better."

Before she knew it, Jackson had reached around and cupped her right hand in his to help her strum. Though he was trying to explain proper technique, Lolly felt lost in the heat of his arms draped against hers. For a moment she thought their pulses rang the same, but of course that couldn't be so. No two hearts ever matched exactly.

Jackson's breath smelled of sugared coffee. "It takes some doing," he said. "Players build up calluses on their fret hand. Their playing hand too, or they use a pick. I do that some—Hey now!"

His exclamation snapped Lolly from her thoughts.

"You're wearing a ring on your wedding finger," he said.

Lolly shifted a little, but he held her hand fast, fingering her plain gold band before straightening and releasing his hold. She wanted the warmth of his body pressed once more against hers. In fact, she wanted to be held by a gentle man, a man who understood the need to stand still a moment. All the better if that man also understood the unspoken language of loss.

She stuttered, "I am," and wondered if the way her voice betrayed her was another sign of her need to cut ties with Russell, to relinquish her vows of *for better and for worse.* She had been holding tight to her search for Norma Jeane's final repose and the sense of freedom she felt in this mountain town. She had let Jackson think she was free to visit him here because she hadn't wanted to scare him off. Had he known she was married, he might have constructed barriers or pushed her away, which would have been the opposite of most men's actions, but of course he wasn't like most men. She said, "I meant to tell you but it never came up."

"I don't need no trouble with anyone's husband," he said. "I got enough to deal with."

"He won't be any trouble. He's not even here. We're not—well, I'm going to file for divorce, just as soon as I save enough money." There. She'd said it.

"That true?"

"Actually, I have a meeting with a lawyer today." A lawyer was not in her plans, but she could include a lawyer if that answered Jackson's concern. She wasn't ready to lose him when she'd only recently found him.

Jackson stood quiet a moment as if mulling over what she'd said. He couldn't see her hopeful expression or her body language.

"He's back in Oklahoma," she offered. "He wrote to say that he's done with me, with us." Almost true, that last part. Sensing Jackson's hesitation and added, "He wouldn't come here looking. He's not the type." She hoped that was true. She'd never known Russell to go out of his way to protect her, only for the purpose of asserting his manhood.

Jackson swayed a little, as if to the rhythm of an internal conversation that Lolly was not privileged to. At last said, "All right then. We'll play it like that. You want to try the guitar again?"

Lolly hadn't known she was holding her breath until at last she let it escape. "Just a little more, if you don't mind."

"I guess I don't," said Jackson, once more bending close and taking each of her hands in his. "Especially when you smell so good."

Lolly smiled to herself. His hands cradled hers, helping her set a few chords free in the empty room as her thoughts drifted into a fantasy of her making music while Jackson praised her attempt to enter his world. Fantasies. Like guitar lessons, always over too soon.

After exchanging pleasant farewells and exiting the Polka Dot, Lolly did as she'd promised, crossing through downtown to reach the area surrounding the courthouse where many small offices displayed signs for attorneys-at-law. Having dressed down a bit for janitorial work she felt a twinge of self-consciousness about stepping into any legal office, but she'd given Jackson her word.

One block southwest of the courthouse, she found the office of Clarence M. Wyre, Esquire, the middle doorway in a redbrick building full of offices and lunch spots. Gathering her resolve, she opened the office's glass doors and stepped inside where she approached a woman who sat typing at a mahogany reception desk. When the woman looked up, Lolly tried to stand a little taller. "Does Mr. Wyre represent divorces?" she asked the blonde.

The woman looked her over. "Of course," she said at last. "For a fee."

"How much would his fee be?"

"It depends on whether it's contested or not."

Lolly parsed the woman's words. Divorces surely qualified as contests, one person wanting what the other might not. In this case, Russell, in his final violent act, seemed to have reached the same conclusion, even if he'd done so by default. In fact, he had done her a favor of sorts, his actions releasing her from the need for further discussion. "There's no contest," she said, hoping she sounded certain.

"None?"

"He's not here," said Lolly, hoping that would suffice.

"And children?"

Lolly's hand went involuntarily to her waist, which she then tried to mask by smoothing her coat. "No. We have no children," she said.

The woman studied Lolly a moment as if assessing her truthfulness. "Okay, then," she said. "An uncontested divorce runs two hundred-fifty dollars, which includes an initial meeting, filing fees at court, and Mr. Wyre's appearance at the divorce hearing. A deposit of fifty percent is required at the time of the initial consultation. Children and property make all the difference. And also, whether the other party fights it. In that case there's more to take into account, including the likelihood of acrimonious debate. Shall I set an appointment for you?"

Lolly's thoughts stuttered at the notion of the money it took to undo a marital arrangement that had so inexpensively been set into motion, their simple "I do-s" spoken before a Los Angeles Justice of the Peace followed by two nights in a Sandman auto-court motel with a sea green pool and a coffee shop next door. She had accompanied Russell to Oklahoma, far from the California city that at the time had seemed so haunted by her childhood.

Now she supposed that Russell had not in fact gotten the wife he might have hoped for. He might have imagined he was marrying one of those sun-kissed California girls given to bikinis and Surf's Up, someone to show off back home. She might have been a disappointment.

"Why so much?" she asked.

"That's the minimum set by the state bar. The fees go up from there."

Lolly didn't have two hundred-fifty, not yet anyway. She said, "I'll have to call you when I know for sure."

"Fine," said the woman. She held out a business card, saying, "Mr. Wyre would be glad to meet with you when you're ready," and dismissed Lolly by returning to her typing.

Lolly ushered herself out into the waning sunlight, breathless from the thought of all the money it would take to sever her legal ties to Russell. While walking back to the boarding house, she mentally calculated what she'd earned through scrimping on meals and spending weekends breathing the fumes given off by permanent wave solution. Tucked in her top bureau drawer was a crumpled envelope holding sixty-two dollars. If she remained frugal and got lucky at the tables, in a week or two she might have enough to make a deposit with a divorce lawyer. Of course, she would need the other half eventually.

She walked along Virginia Street, crossing the bridge spanning the Truckee and passing opposite the Mapes, whose twelve floors of windows reflected the sun, now low in the sky. Brick and glass and not one balcony in sight for lounging upon in the glow of an afternoon. Or for stepping out into thin air.

Lolly had followed news reports about Norma Jeane's movies and multiple marriages. Soon Lolly herself would join that sisterhood of divorcees. Odd as it seemed now, before arriving in Reno she hadn't pictured herself divorced because she'd been taught that marriages were intended to last. The problem was, the vows never mentioned broken bones, split skin, or shattered trust.

Back at Mrs. Ruddle's, Lolly found another small package waiting for her on the kitchen table next to the sugar bowl. She put the teakettle on to boil while she peeled open the heavy white envelope, the kind used for fancy stationery or business correspondence. Inside she found a folding packet of picture postcards of the San Francisco Bay Area and coastline. Sea lions on the piers of a bayside wharf. Sailboats gliding under the magnificent arches of the Golden Gate Bridge. The Cliff House Restaurant looming tall above a stretch of beach dotted by summer sunbathers.

She recalled now that when she'd met Caldwell for that Basque dinner he'd asked if she'd ever spent time at a beach. She had not. Not everyone who lived in Los Angeles had the time and money to dally at the shore. In order to drive over for the day required a reliable car. In her third year of waitressing at Chicken Scratch, the breakfast and lunch place out on Foothill Boulevard, she had bought a decrepit

Buick which later Russell sold, saying his truck would better serve them in Gilleon. So much for the ocean.

With this newest gift and the others before it, Lolly felt a stab of pleasure not unlike what she had felt as a child scrawling words of encouragement and gratitude to GIs fighting oversees during World War II. That uptick in excitement at the potential for a connection with someone remote and largely unavailable. Fuel for daydreams. None of the soldiers had written back, and why would they? She was only a child and they were busy at matters of war. This was different, of course. This was no anonymous pen-pal because, for one thing, she was certain the sender was Caldwell, and for another, he kept omitting the part where he wrote anything at all. Which left a question about what sort of friends they were meant to be. In some ways he'd acted like a boss when she had not wanted him to, and in other ways he acted like a special friend acquired by accident who now elected to remain anonymous. The difference no longer seemed to matter.

Mrs. R came in and noticed the packet. "Another gift from your secret admirer?"

"Not secret," said Lolly.

"So, you know who it is?"

Lolly nodded.

"Someone from California? Or a Reno friend traveling there?"

Lolly thought a moment. There was no use guessing at the meaning of such gifts without letters to explain them. She shrugged in answer and said, "Someone I used to know."

Fifteen

On Tuesday, the day of her appointment at Dr. Hall's obstetrics office, Lolly walked to the Polka Dot in order to work for an hour or two alongside Jackson. Where at first he'd been a man of few words, of late he'd grown more talkative.

The shapes and textures of buildings and sidewalks between the boarding house and the nightclub had grown familiar. There came the sleepy morning sounds of a town most vibrant at night. As Lolly walked, her thoughts kept turning to what awaited her with the doctor that afternoon, but having resolved to remain stoical, she stuffed what lay before her into a mental cupboard. For the time being.

"Over here," said Jackson when Lolly pulled the side door of the Polka Dot shut as she stepped in. "There's no quit in you, is there?"

She flipped on the overhead lights. "Do you want me to quit?" Setting aside her tote bag, she unbuttoned the long-sleeved casual shirt she'd worn over the top of a nicer blouse.

Jackson grinned. "*I'm* sure not going to send you away."

His words warmed Lolly. She'd grown accustomed to Jackson's working style, to the way he navigated by feel and walked fencepost straight. She caught herself watching for the cock of his head that signaled a noise she hadn't noticed, the squeal of brakes out on the street, or the shout of children beyond the side door. And the way he held his hands still when talking.

She'd been wanting to ask him more about his desire to join Southern civil rights efforts. He clearly monitored what was happening to the Negro race in parts of the country reported as hazardous for protestors, sounding remarkably oblivious to the implications, or perhaps a better description was *accepting*, as if taking risks trumped the status quo. His attitude fed a worrisome knot inside her.

He told her, "All I got left to do is sweep. And my uncle said there's a broken glass from when they were closing up last night, somewhere up by the stage."

Lolly cleaned up the glass pieces before Jackson could pierce his hand again, afterwards handing off the broom and dustpan. He was halfway across the room, working his way around the tables when she said, "I've been thinking how it must be nice to work for your family's business."

"Hunh," came his reply.

"It seems like your relatives all look out for one another."

"What makes you think that?"

"Just an impression."

"Is that what your family's like?"

Lolly picked at a chip in her nail polish. "I don't mean every family's the same. Just that when a family runs a business, there are jobs for brothers and sisters, cousins too. That sort of thing." She had always thought of families as having an unspoken agreement about sticking together. Not that familial bonds didn't sometimes break. How well she knew.

Broom in hand, Jackson straightened. "Have you ever worked in a family business?"

"Well, no."

He leaned into the broom's handle and lifted his head as if gazing into the distance. "Then it probably sounds all smooth and slick, like everyone agrees all the time."

"I guess you're suggesting they don't."

"That's not how it works, not in our family anyways."

"Why not?"

"Only because everyone's got their own ideas about how things ought to run. But one person, maybe two, has the power to decide. Which means you can suggest all you want, point out a better way, bring ideas. But whoever's in charge remains in charge, you get what I mean?"

"I guess." Lolly thought a moment. "Is there fighting about how to run things?"

Jackson laughed. "You ever know a family who doesn't fight?"

Lolly thought back to Russell's family. He and his mother seldom disagreed, and Lolly had never seen Russell raise his voice to Katherine. She had never met Russell's father, who had died young. Before that, of course, her own family had been of the temporary, foster kind, not the sort that Jackson meant. She said, "I guess not."

Jackson had gone back to sweeping. "Isn't any family on earth doesn't fight. Doesn't matter if they come from the same blood, there's no single mind about everything."

Another thought that had been nudging Lolly rose up. "But you've got a sure thing here, don't you?"

Jackson fairly snorted as he speared the floor with his broom and continued moving around the tables. "You say that like working with family is some kind of cure for what ails you, but it's not. Let's change the subject." He thought a moment. "You like the movies? Did you see the one called *To Kill a Mockingbird.* I heard about it some when it came through the theaters."

"I don't think it even came near our Oklahoma town. Did you see it? Not *see*, I mean—"

"I know. Me and movies don't mix great because someone has to sit there and tell me what's happening which makes everyone hush us up. I can get someone to describe it afterwards, but it's not the same."

A few details from the entertainment news came to Lolly. "Gregory Peck. He played the leading man, um ..."

"Finch."

"That's it. A lawyer ..."

"In the south. Alabama or someplace. He defends a Negro against some white woman's charge of rape."

Rape. Wasn't that the way things often boiled down—to people hurting each other. "Did they make the book in Braille," she asked, "or doesn't that help?"

"I can read Braille some, but it's slow going." At that he declared his sweeping job done. "Can you see if I missed any big patches?" he asked Lolly.

"It's fine," said Lolly. Even if he had missed a spot, she would not be the one to find fault, not after what he'd said about the disagreeable side of his family's business. She proceeded to help him set the forty chairs or so back into place. He maneuvered around the tables like a deckhand on a boat.

"There," he said when they were done. "You want another guitar lesson? I brought it just in case."

"Through no fault of yours it would probably take me ten years to learn the basics," she said. "But if there's a record player, I brought music to play."

Jackson's face broke into a grin. "No kidding? What'd you bring?"

"It's a surprise."

He swung his body toward the stage. "All right then. When there's been music lessons, they might use a record player and leave it back of the curtain. It won't be fancy."

Lolly went up the steps at the side of the stage and pushed through the opening in the heavy black curtains at the rear, setting loose a light rain of dust. A moment later she came back out. "Are there lights for back here?" she called to Jackson.

"On the left side, near the front edge."

After Lolly had found the lights and rummaged around behind the curtain, she emerged with a small record player in a case. When she had it ready to run, she fetched her tote bag and pulled out one of the records that had come from San Francisco.

Jackson climbed the steps to the stage. He said, "That old player won't have good sound."

"That's okay." Lolly put the record on and set the needle in the groove. When she turned up the volume, out came the song she wanted to share.

"Mmm," said Jackson. "That's a nice sax solo. Let's see ..." He caressed his chin with one hand. "Is that Sarah Vaughan?"

Lolly clapped her hands with pleasure. "It's 'How High the Moon.'"

"I don't suppose he's on this one but a fellow named Joe Pass plays with her sometimes. Or used to. Italian guy. If you dig this kind of music then you know she's a powerhouse. She can really scat."

"She can what?"

Jackson chuckled. "Scat. Scatting. It's using your mouth like an instrument. 'Course some folks would point out that scat is another word for crap."

Lolly didn't know whether to laugh or act shocked. "I've been listening to it and I just can't imagine music getting any better, can you?"

Jackson cocked his head. "You giving up on Elvis?"

This time Lolly did laugh. "I don't think so. I just mean this is like nothing else. It's nothing like the music they have you playing in the Hideout."

"Oh, that. That's 50s popular music for the older set, but you could say it's all related because everything comes from what came before. Jazz comes from something else. Blues does too. Swing, big band, ballads. You name it, there's music that came before, and there will always be the next thing, and maybe it will seem new to lots of folks, but believe me, it will have roots that go way back." He tossed his head. "Do you buy your black and blue music at a local store?"

His question took a moment to process. She hadn't bought this music. "Black and blue?"

I just mean that she's black and singing the blues, and there's people in this town don't go for that type."

"You mean whites. There were whites that night when I came here with my friends."

"I'm just saying it's not all that common that folks make an effort to look for it and appreciate it, especially if it's not all smoothed out for dancing to."

It was fine by Lolly if Jackson thought her taste in music uncommon. In fact, he might mean it as a compliment. She asked, "Where'd you get all your knowledge of different kinds of music, and your own playing? It seems like it comes natural to you."

"My dad. He bought the records we had. He played too."

"You talk like he's gone."

"He's gone."

"What was his instrument?"

"Guitar. He played around Chicago, and around here."

"You miss him, don't you? I can tell from the way you talk."

Jackson just nodded.

"Does your mom play an instrument?"

"God, no. She hates it all. Hates the whole scene, how my dad knew so many people and how women seem to … um, never mind. Hey, let's hear what's on the B side. Turn it over, will you?"

Lolly did as he asked, announcing the title. "Misty. It says 'Recorded in New York City, 1958.'"

When the needle found the first groove and the music started up, Jackson said, "This one's got that big orchestra behind her. It's one of those smooth ones." He beckoned Lolly with his hand out. "Come here. I'll show you what this one's for."

Lolly threw a glance toward the side door, shut against everything that lay beyond the cinder block wall. She had pulled it shut as she came in, but it wasn't locked. Before she took Jackson's hand a thought crossed her mind about how what they were doing was risky business. Local signals made clear that public mixing for music was contained to jazz clubs. She and Jackson were in a jazz club with no public present, so she took a breath and settled her hand into Jackson's as he pulled her into a slow dance and fitted his body against hers. There was almost no getting closer than this. Almost.

He smelled strongly of man-heat and faintly of those peppermints he favored. The room was cool the way it always was, but his hands were hot and a bit damp, his right palm firm against her back and the other one cupping her right hand. Those hands of his, full of songs that rang of aching loss and deep desire.

A surge of adrenaline cleared Lolly's mind of all but the feel of her own ribs and breastbone, and her left arm draped around Jackson's shoulder. Though she'd wanted their time together to be nobody's business but theirs, she couldn't help recognizing the line they were crossing, her hand in his. This simple yielding.

The room fell away in her mind, replaced by a nightclub that wasn't just an empty plywood stage painted black with wing lights glaring down, but a jazzy place in a city that knew and appreciated such places for people getting together, a kind of Ellis Island of souls, each song rolling through the room, touching them all. Jackson would still be blind because, well, he would be, and unconcerned whether the woman in his arms was admired by others or dressed a certain way. He'd cast no sly glances around to see who was watching his footwork. In a place like that their dance would meet no objections.

This man, so adroit with guitars and music made small, almost tentative moves, barely leading; more a gentle rocking from side to side. For a moment Lolly thought that he could play his hands across her and make music, but, no. As much as she liked Jackson and his fine qualities and as dreamy as she found the music coming from the worn turntable, she folded her thoughts back into a more pragmatic form. This was just a song, just a dance. When the record ended, he asked her to start it one last time, which she did. When she stepped into his arms again, he said, "Now. Tell me about yourself. Maybe about that husband you say you're done with."

She told him about how Russell had come along in early 1957 when she'd been working at that diner in northeast Los Angeles. She'd felt stranded among what seemed like a million people, a swirl of humanity working on big plans of benefit to themselves, breaking into the movies and making it big or striking it rich. Russell wasn't the first wrong man she'd chosen, but what he had going for him was a suggestion of just how different his life was from the one she then inhabited. His distant hometown held a certain attraction, removed as it was from the city that represented all that had gone wrong for her to that point. She was ready to leave L.A. and Russell had seemed a reasonable alternative to the men she'd dated. Or to being alone. He seemed to offer a way to start the next phase of her life. She hadn't imagined the huge departure Gilleon would prove to be, how small-minded and gossipy. "He was a good kisser," she added, before realizing she'd said it out loud.

"That why you married him?" asked Jackson. "You marry the men you kiss?"

Lolly drew a breath. "I didn't say that."

"Good," said Jackson. He tightened his hold on her, which sent another jolt of electricity through her, and continued as if nothing had passed between them, whereas if anyone were to interpret her expression, they'd probably note her dazed look. Dazed and pleased, but nervous too, as if she'd broken some sort of rule. As if they both had. "You married him that year?" he asked.

"Yes."

He just shook his head.

"You disapprove?"

He seemed to hesitate. "That's not it. '57 was some kind of year for me too is all. Tell me more about your people."

"I told you I don't really have any."

"There's always someone."

Lolly thought a moment. She hadn't ever shared this kind of talk with her husband, nor with anyone else, but she was beginning to appreciate how Jackson would accept at face value whatever she said. Her memories fit into compartments, the satisfying ones separated from the harsh ones that included cold mornings without the heat on, and if you wet your bed you had to wash the sheets by hand in the lavatory sink, and then while they hung to dry you slept with no sheets. But what she told Jackson was all about a girl named Norma Jeane who back then was just a teenager and therefore still really a girl herself. Someone who used to sit raking her fingers through Lolly's unruly hair and plaiting it into thick braids. Always tender with the younger girls, Norma Jeane smelled of violets and White Rain shampoo. Since marrying Russell, Lolly often recalled what Norma Jeane had said. "I'm not going to settle for other people's dreams," she had told Lolly. "For what they say I should think or do.

I'm going to find my own way, whatever it takes."

Now Lolly fell silent, lost in thoughts of those earlier times, how she hadn't understood then the older girl's counsel about choosing a life's direction. At times she had tried to mine that advice to improve her own lot, but she had never been good at reversing course or countering other people's expectations. She regularly chose for herself what other people wanted or else removed herself from the conflict. Except today. Her time with Jackson was hers alone and no one else's. Suddenly she realized that they'd been rocking gently to the scratch of the needle on the record going around after the song had quit.

Jackson broke into Lolly's thoughts. "She was like your sister."

"That's how it felt."

He nodded. They were silent for a moment. Then he said, "I don't hear your kitchen timer ticking down but I suppose it's about to ring."

Lolly gasped. "My timer! I forgot to set it!" She shot a look at her watch then broke from Jackson's arms and scooped up the record, switching the player to OFF. "I've got to go," she cried as she grabbed her belongings. Without waiting for an answer she was out the door, hurrying toward downtown to hail a taxi that would speed her to meet with Dr. Hall, OB-Gyn.

At Lolly's request, the taxi driver let her out on Second Street, one block east and south of the obstetrics and gynecology office of Dr. Hall. A cold north wind had sprung up, but she hardly noticed as she fairly sprinted, arriving out of breath and slightly disheveled in the office's waiting room. She smoothed her hair with one hand and smiled sheepishly at the receptionist. "Golly, I'm late," she said, peeling off her outer work shirt. She stepped closer to the desk. "Am I too late?"

A woman in one of the cushioned chairs studiously turned the pages of a magazine and avoided Lolly's gaze. "Oh, I am," said Lolly to the receptionist, her legs going wobbly from the realization.

"Now, now," said the receptionist in a low voice. "These things happen. You're Missus ... Cooper? We did wait, but I'm sure you can understand, we eventually have to keep to our schedule." She nodded toward the woman with the magazine. "We recognize that our patients have busy schedules." The receptionist consulted her appointment book. "If you can wait a while, we might catch back up to an opening. It might take an hour or two, or I can give you another day and time."

If this woman only knew how hard it had been for Lolly to request this appointment, how she'd developed knots in her stomach about what she had to do, necessary as it was. If she chose to wait, she might sit for hours, dwelling on her decision while other women came and went. She couldn't do it.

"I'd better reschedule," she told the receptionist. She had brought this on herself, allowing her interlude with Jackson to interfere with her primary concern of her day. Somehow she had thought she could have them both—a life-affirming encounter with Jackson and a life-changing appointment. Instead, an extra thirty minutes with him had tipped her day over.

The receptionist said, "I've got another opening in ten days."

"Ten days? When I called for this one, you got me right in."

"There was a cancellation and you happened to call. We're a small staff in a busy office. I'm afraid it'll be ten days. Unless it's an emergency." The woman looked up from her scheduling chart. "Is it?"

Lolly was indeed distressed, but was having missed her appointment an actual emergency? She thought about the chain of days and weeks preceding this day and the deadline for setting into motion the decision she'd made. She had begun making choices instead of letting things happen to her and around her. This new delay was the cost of her having chosen to spend time with Jackson, and she would not equate her pleasant morning with an emergency.

She cast a glance at the woman waiting in the corner chair. You couldn't tell from the outside but she might also feel distressed; women in particular were good at holding things in. "I guess I don't need to throw a wrench into your day," she said, and accepted the future appointment.

Outside, the cold breeze filled the sky with thick clouds as Lolly headed on foot for the boarding house. It was only twelve blocks or so and she needed the slap of fresh air to counter the effects of flubbing her appointment. She followed Third to Washington, which led to Second Street. The wind grew brisker so she buttoned both of her shirts to the neck. She turned toward downtown, passing Hansen's Market, a few small bungalows and single-story buildings, a motor lodge, an auto repair business.

Within ten minutes she could make out the white cupolas of St. Thomas Aquinas Cathedral, its entrance practically at the sidewalk.

What had Mrs. R said about the place? It was a religious landmark built in 1907 by a Reverend Tubman. Lolly had smiled at Mrs. R's history lesson, but perched on the wooden pew of a Catholic church was where Lolly herself had learned to love the astonishing idea of God.

Once upon a time, with a child's delight, she had treasured the notion of all those saints championing every type of occupation, pursuit, and cause. She liked, too, how the statue of the Blessed Virgin seemed to counter the dramatic and shocking crucifix showing Christ nailed to the cross by his bloodied palms and feet. Mary had been a mother figure. There was the incense, which made her sneeze, and the priest's ornate vestments, and the services in Latin, that ancient, secretive language. There were rituals about kneeling, standing, and praying, and for how parishioners advanced up the aisle to partake of the Sacrament of Holy Communion. She had felt the great distance between her childish prayers and the worldliness of the priests who directed worship from an altar adorned with gold and silver objects, all of it as mysterious as a dream.

The cathedral's steps drew her up and in through copper-paneled doors where she stood just inside. What was she thinking? She hadn't been inside a Catholic church since Norma Jeane had left the orphanage. And she wasn't dressed appropriately for church, even on a weekday. On the plus side, her old friend had sampled Catholicism. It was the last Reno location Lolly knew to look for crumbs leading to Norma Jeane spirit.

The cathedral's inner doors led to a glowing nave beyond, where a woman who was leaving pointed at Lolly's uncovered head, prompting Lolly to pull a handkerchief from her tote and pin it atop her hair. Then her feet carried her into the nave. In the aisle she automatically genuflected, an old habit. Taking a seat in the closest pew, she sat with her hands in her lap.

Being inside a cathedral felt both blasphemous and hopeful, strange as that sounded. She had strikes against her dating way back, and with her current plans, more would be heaped upon her with no way to confess them. Still, the phrasing she had heard the older children practice came back to her, the words bubbling up from down the years: *Bless me Father for I have sinned.*

Sweet-sour words. Sweet with the memory of her brief time in the Church's embrace and sour with the knowledge that the Church, both the building and the people within it, was limited in its ability to protect parishioners from their own destructive behavior. Or from each other.

Having pinned her only hankie to her hair, she dabbed at her eyes with her shirtsleeve. This domed space of high walls colored-glass panels, and the Stations of the Cross, should feel like sanctuary. But Lolly could not shake the sense that evil could at any moment appear and take a seat in her pew.

She glanced to her right. Nobody. Her childhood fear of the orphanage man had sparked the distance she had put between herself and Catholicism. In those days she knelt as if practicing what the older children were learning, their mouths open and tongues ready to receive the Body of Christ, but she never progressed further than practice and imitation because that man also attended Mass, and he knew that she had seen him where he didn't belong, and that was the problem—the knowing. It was only during the years since that she began to realize that Norma Jeane, a teenager at the time, may not have objected entirely to what Lolly witnessed that night. In this sacred place especially, the memory of that long-ago night still haunted her.

Others might label her silly for fearing that one man. She was no longer a child and this was a different church and nearly empty to boot, just two worshipers kneeling among the pews, a lone woman dusting and polishing woodwork, and a bent figure lighting votive candles at the far right. Ridiculous to think the orphanage man might be in this very nave, or any nave in this state. But of course, *she* was here, which meant anyone could be.

Wresting her attention away from the others, Lolly began a silent rosary using the buttons on her shirt. *Hail Mary, full of grace. The Lord is with thee. Blessed art thou amongst women, and something something* ... So much for retaining all the details, but parts of the disused prayer flowed easily enough. She repeated its beginning a second time before a stocky white-haired man rose from a pew at the front and turned in Lolly's direction. An older man, so not the spitting image of the one she recalled, but those eyebrows! Even from this distance she could make out their shape, like clouds on a windy day. Her heart began to pound as if in answer to a warning. She rose abruptly with her tote and stumbled from her pew. Without a backward glance she fled through the grand entrance and down the steps into a frigid spring snowstorm blowing sideways.

At first she hurried blindly toward downtown, angling in the direction of the boarding house. So foolish to flee, but she couldn't help herself. She crossed at the corner nearest Paterson's and emerged near the Woolworth's to be battered anew by frozen flakes stinging her cheeks and sucking her breath away. She labored into the cold blast that seemed to tear at her double layer of shirts. The pins holding her hankie in place began to come loose so she tore them out, stuffing the hankie into her tote.

In desperation she stepped into the sheltering nook of a doorway and brought her tote to her chest. When the door swung open behind her, she stepped aside for a man coming out, who paused to adjust his fedora against the wind. He gave Lolly a crooked smile then stepped into the frenzy of whirling white. The door was caught open by the north wind, allowing Lolly to glance into the dark, warm interior. It was a bar.

The recognition struck up a longing for a salve for her battered thoughts. That old, calming fire. She mentally tallied the cash in her wallet and checked her watch. It was only 4:30. Maybe she'd order just one to temper the memory of that awful orphanage man.

At 8:00 p.m., Lolly jabbed her key at the lock in the front door of the boarding house. Her third try succeeded and she advanced on shaky steps into the front entry.

Mrs. Ruddle's head appeared in the kitchen doorway. "My word! I was worried about you out in this weather."

Lolly considered her landlady through bleary eyes. There would be no hiding her condition, but her burden of guilt and fear had abated. She took tentative steps forward as Mrs. R rushed forward to assist.

"Oh, hon." Mrs. R squinted at Lolly. "What's happened to you?"

"I didn't ... I didn't mean to," said Lolly. But in truth she had savored every sip of the lovely liquid that dulled memories and kept thoughts of her dwindling options at bay.

"Here. Let's go to the kitchen." Clucking in dismay, the landlady helped Lolly remove her damp outer shirt and don an old chenille robe. Soon Mrs. R was heating the potato soup left over from dinner.

"I've never seen you like this, and you in a delicate condition," said Mrs. R.

"I had a fright, and well ..."

The landlady shook her head in a way that suggested disapproval. All she said by way of admonishment was, "You've a baby to think of."

Little did Mrs. R know just how much thought Lolly gave to that subject each day. Try as she might to set her worries aside, she could not, not entirely. Not when she had failed at Dr. Hall's office. Not when her situation couldn't be solved by thinking, only by doing.

At Mrs. R's bidding Lolly drank a whole glass of water and ate a small bowl of soup. Once she was moderately revived, she brought up a subject that had dogged her while she sat in that bar drowning her sorrows. "Mrs. R.," she said. "You've kept a lot of old magazines, haven't you? Did you save Reno newspapers too?" Early on she had thought the woman's habit of saving stacks of printed goods somewhat eccentric. Now, though, she was hopeful that Mrs. R's hoard of papers and magazines would prove useful.

The woman wiped her hands on her apron. "Well, I don't save everything, and those magazines, even if they're out of date, they make good reading for my boarders."

"I'm hoping to find some news that's old by now. Do you remember anything important about 1957?"

"Fifty-seven? I'll say. That was the year of the gas explosion downtown. Bodies and burnt cars and a terrible mess. I've never seen anything like it. Why?"

Lolly shook her head to clear it further. "Someone mentioned a catastrophe that happened."

"That was something all right. I heard the noise from here. Of course, the authorities kept everyone away while they worked to put out fires and all. The newspaper printed a special section about it with a lot of photos. It was big news."

Lolly tipped the cracker crumbs from her saucer into the remaining soup in her bowl. "Would you have kept old clippings about it?"

"You're welcome to look, but can't it wait? You look whipped."

Lolly could probably lay her head upon the table and be dreaming in two minutes if not for the chance at information that illuminated Jackson's past, but she moved to the front room and dropped to the rug with her back against the couch, pulling the closest stack of reading materials toward her. None of it was in order. Soon she had found and bypassed newspapers documenting the floods of 1950 and

1955 with the Truckee River breaching its channel to consume First Street. Water had overrun the thresholds of businesses and casinos and turned cars into soggy parade floats. She also found special coverage of the flood that had inundated Reno on the first of February, 1963, just one day before her own arrival in town. By staying those first few nights at the Wagon Wheel auto motel, she'd missed seeing the crane lifting debris from downtown bridges and the water lapping at the Hotel Holiday parking lot. She had noticed sandbags in a few places, but by the time she'd found her way to the boarding house, most downtown streets had been swept clean.

Mrs. R's collection included special photo spreads showing various Nevada Day parades and Life magazine issues touting easily-installed home bomb shelters. There was a Time magazine cover showcasing JD Salinger's newest book, *Franny & Zooey*. Fifty minutes into her inspection, Lolly turned over a folded bunch of newsprint to discover the event that Jackson had referred to as *All hell exploded*. She'd never gotten around to asking more about what he had meant by that, but here was the evidence.

Reno's *Evening Gazette* of February 6, 1957, showed day-after photos of buildings in the area of the jewelry and loan shop, Paterson's men's store, and a whole block of Sierra Street reduced to rubble. With the headline, "Reno Starts Cleanup of Blast Debris," the special coverage included lists of those injured and hospitalized, those whose status was pending, and those killed in the blast. Among the dead: Mr. Jackson Mayberry, Sr., noted local musician and employee of the Paradise Club, crushed by a falling shop sign. Seriously injured but in stable condition at Saint Mary's Hospital was Jackson Mayberry, Jr., nineteen, a track and field scholarship recipient at the University of Nevada.

The explosion and ensuing fire had blown out the windows of more than one block and destroyed department stores, shoe shops, and an insurance company. The Elks Club too. The fire was billed as the worst in Reno's history, but the initial explosion had been the killer. That was the day Jackson lost his father and his own eyesight. Gone, and no goodbye.

If Lolly had once felt amused at her landlady's penchant for treasuring historical details and foisting them on others, she now felt only gratitude for the woman's good intentions toward posterity. The enormity of Jackson's loss bloomed in her mind. She knew what it was to feel reduced somehow by what she lived without: family ties, a circle of lifelong friends, success in school. He might not realize, but in a handful of ways not evident on the surface, he and she had plenty in common.

Sixteen

Anna Trimble, the new boarder, arrived while Lolly was at work. That evening, Lolly played just six hands of blackjack, breaking even before returning home to discover that Anna had already called it a night, no doubt under the influence of Mrs. R's maternal ministrations.

After her lackluster performance at blackjack, Lolly was looking forward to turning in too. First, though, she wanted to learn about the new boarder, so she agreed to a mug of warm milk, a few crackers, and a bit of conversation with Mrs. R.

"Trimble," said Lolly. "I thought you told me some other name."

"That fell through. The other gal changed her mind. Or decided to wait. Anna called on Monday, and now she's here."

Lolly was feeling a tad protective of her landlady, who had taken to feeding her without asking for extra fees. "What else do you know about her?"

"Just that she's unhappily married and looking to remedy the situation."

"Seems like divorce is a profitable business."

"Used to be booming, you know, a regular gold mine. But now it's just ... steady. Back in the thirties, that's when divorces became possible after six weeks of residency."

Lolly crunched through a saltine cracker. "I guess the city takes a cut."

"The courts, I suppose. That would be the county."

Lolly broke a second cracker in two. "This new boarder, she's from ... where?"

"Kansas City. Came on the Western Pacific. That's a good way to travel. Have you ever taken the train?"

"Me? No. I could have if I had gone north to Maynard, they have a depot. But traveling by bus costs less."

"Well, sure. But train travel, why that's practically like riding in your own private vehicle. Dining cars and club cars, and you can pay for a sleeping berth. They've got Negro porters."

Lolly wasn't sure how to respond. "Is that a problem?"

"Not at all. I understand there's a union of them, folks trained to provide first class service." She looked into the middle distance. "If I ever travel on a train I'm going to go first class. At least once."

Mrs. R sounded as if she could use an adventure. Lolly asked, "How long have you lived here?"

Mrs. R thought a moment. "Almost eighteen years." She sat up straighter. "Now, hon, you've got to eat if you're going to keep healthy."

Lolly had never even spent a decade at any one address, sometimes not even two whole years. The longest was her six years in Gilleon, if that meant anything. She felt as if she'd missed an important detail in her exchange with Mrs. R, though she wasn't sure what. A more troubling thought was that her landlady was counting on an outcome that Lolly herself was counting against. Mrs. R clearly expected Lolly to see this pregnancy through.

She touched her stomach with one hand and smiled apologetically. "I'm still off my feed," she said, glad that she could say that in truth. "But I could use some advice."

The older woman stopped puttering. "What is it, dear?"

"About the library that's south of downtown. Will they let me borrow a book?"

"Of course. This might still be a cow town in some ways, but we are civilized. It only takes a local address. You can use this one." Mrs. R pushed her glasses up to the bridge of her nose, a sure sign that she was about to impart a bit of history in response to Lolly's question. "Let me tell you how Reno got that library ..."

A little later, at her bedside, Lolly executed an expanded prayer. Her prayers had grown in the last week though her routine stayed the same—a long pull of bourbon, knees to the floor, head bowed. In recent days it seemed like there was more to say; either that or what she had previously left unsaid was finally churning up, like one of those lakes that turns over during freakish weather. Luckier people had someone to confide in, but not her. Who would understand her doubt and confusion, her crying in church, her trepidation about Mass? Norma Jeane might have. Would have. She, too, had lacked a confidante. You could pay professionals to listen, of course, but when you have no siblings, no mother, no kin to coach you during life's roller coaster ride, you can end up in deep water without a rudder. Back then, Norma Jeane had been Lolly's anchor, a real person on whose steadfastness Lolly had staked her peace of mind.

Of course, Lolly had not chosen Reno for its supply of rudders or anchors, though she had occasionally thought about Caldwell in those terms up until the day he'd left. He hadn't left *her* specifically, because they hadn't any declared intentions between them, but she couldn't help feeling that he had proved to be one more person not to count on. Sending anonymous records didn't count.

In the meantime, she would talk to God. Proof or not, she liked to imagine he was listening. She began with *Dear God, first of all, please bless Mrs. R because she is surely deserving. And look down with favor on Shirley and Doris in their new lives. Look after Jackson if you would. After what he's been through he could use some of your mercy.*

I'm a sinner, I know. Here, her mind wandered just enough to allow the thought that she should detest her sins regardless of any future salvation or punishment, those determinations being made after life ended. All manner of things could happen before then, reducing or compounding a person's standing in God's eyes. Not her time with Jackson, though, she wouldn't think of it. If they were both God's children, their guitar lessons and conversation, and even their slow dancing, could not be sinful, in spite of what others might say.

You are supposed to know what's in my heart, but I don't know how you can when I don't, not exactly. I know my child would be your child, too, but I've given this a lot of thought and I'm surer than ever that I'm not meant to be its mother.

In an echo of that night during which her fear of the orphanage man had trumped any thought of summoning help for Norma Jeane, Lolly's own newest concern, now roughly seven weeks gone and counting, had temporarily overtaken her search for a fitting heaven for her old friend's spirit. She continued, *I need a way out of this. If only you would show me a way, Amen.*

She took another swig of bourbon for good measure. When she climbed under the soft, flowered sheet and double layer of clean old quilts, she felt ripe for the deep sleep that her handy helper always delivered. Before drifting off, she realized that once again she had left Caldwell out of her prayers. Even though Caldwell's name belonged in a column of the unredeemed, he had been good to her in his own way. He wasn't on her prayer list, but she had not forgotten him.

It turned out that Anna Trimble was unlike any woman Lolly had ever known. The way she carried herself commanded attention, as did the clothing she wore, dresses and slacks cut from fine linen and wool. Silk too. Lolly could hardly take her eyes off the woman from the very moment they met. Anna seemed to invite consideration and made herself immediately at home in the boarding house. The first thing she asked was for Mrs. Ruddle to arrange a television repair man so that she could keep up with the nightly news and her favorites—*The Jack Paar Show*, for one, and *Route 66*. Mrs. Ruddle seemed smitten with Anna, promptly calling Barnes Television & Radio Repair to request a fix for the set that had sat largely unused since Shirley left.

"Don't you all keep up with what's happening around the country?" the redhead had asked over a welcoming dinner, fixed special even though it wasn't Sunday. Lolly had come straight home after work, arriving by 8:20 to a house scented with garlicky pot roast, twice-baked potatoes and creamed peas.

"There's the newspaper, twice a day," said Mrs. R, defensively.

"Of course, and that's as it should be. Mrs. Ruddle, this is the most delicious roast, I don't know how you do it. Will you please pass the horseradish?" Anna beamed her Pepsodent smile. She had insisted on delaying this special feast in order to share it with Lolly. The other days, though, she would take her evening meal at 6:00

They were ensconced at the formal dining table, Anna asking about the state of business in the fair city of Reno, how local government officials conducted themselves, and what did Mrs. R think about the mayors of Reno and its sister city, Sparks? Mrs. R was in her element, providing both bodily nourishment and a brief summary of Reno's founding in 1868 and that it was named to honor a Civil War general. Naturally, she provided her own perspectives on local cultural and political doings.

After they had all pushed their plates aside, Anna turned her chair to make eye contact with Lolly. "And how was your day? Tell me that you had an interesting day. All I did was contract with a divorce lawyer."

Lolly thought a moment. Her day had been remarkably like most since she'd arrived, except for ... "I borrowed a book from the library and then went to work. And now I'm home. That's pretty much it."

Anna ran a manicured hand through her bobbed locks. Lighting a cigarette, she said, "You're a reader. What title?"

Virtually the whole country had read the book that Lolly had only just now obtained. Her years in Gilleon had left her behind the times, but there was no harm in admitting it. She said, "The one they made into a movie—*To Kill a Mockingbird*."

A stream of smoke lifted above Anna toward the ceiling fixture. "If I remember right, that movie won an Academy Award. Supposedly Gregory Peck named it his favorite role."

"I saw it at the Crest Theater," said Mrs. R. "That lawyer character ..." Her face took on a look of concentration. "Atticus, isn't that an unusual name? I suppose it's common in the South. Anyway, you just knew he was in the right, though you have to admit that Negro was dangerous looking. A big man, and strong—uneducated, of course— the sort who could overpower a woman, even with a crippled hand." She gave a little shiver.

Anna was watching Mrs. R's performance with a slight smile. "I suppose they chose an imposing actor for the part so that he'd seem worrisome. Otherwise, the story is resolved too easily." She looked at Lolly. "Don't you think?"

Lolly shrugged. She did not know the movie nor the story, not yet. But the women's comments fascinated her. Would it trouble warm-hearted, generous Mrs. R or the newly-arrived Anna Trimble to know that Lolly had recently stepped into the arms of a coffee-colored man? For a slow dance, no less. In private. Hardly anything had happened, at least nothing that had led to anything, except she missed her appointment (and what a shame, that). The thing was, the facts of that morning's pleasantries were fairly tame, nothing to make a novel out of. Anything else was just her imagination, fleeting feelings she didn't fully understand.

When she glanced again at Anna, the woman was watching her. Disconcerted, Lolly said, "What?"

"Nothing." The woman smiled and stubbed out her cigarette. "Have you got it with you?

Lolly's first thought was of the record she and Jackson had danced to. Then she realized Anna meant her library book. She had been surprised by the book's size, much smaller than she imagined for the clamor and controversy it had created. She'd felt worldly simply toting it from the library and wasn't yet ready to relinquish her grip on it, not yet. She said, "It's upstairs, with my work things."

"Some other time then," said Anna, turning her attention to Mrs. R, who was setting a porcelain teapot on a pressed aluminum trivet, her bracelet jangling prettily. "Look at those charms," said Anna, reaching out to set them tinkling again.

Mrs. R turned her hand to and fro. "They're rather ancient, but I wear them when I'm dressing up a bit."

Anna fingered a silver starfish charm, then pointed to Mrs. R's palm. "What a long lifeline you have."

Mrs. R's face lit up. "Do you know palm reading? I've never had it done. Those parlors strike me as spooky, and wouldn't it feel odd to have a stranger staring at your hands? In fact, at the north end of town there's someone billing themselves as an 'ordained psychic,' and a Reverend Rosetta holding séances over on Marsh Avenue. I haven't ever been, but I always wondered ..."

"I'll take a look, if you want me to," said Anna. She pushed her ashtray aside and turned in Mrs. R's direction. "Now that I reside with you, I'm not exactly a stranger."

Mrs. R pulled her chair close and presented both of her palms to Anna. "Is this what you do, palm reading? You're so glamorous, I never would have guessed. Look at these poor hands of mine. I use lotion, of course, and rubber gloves when I can. But I always have my hands in water."

Chin on her fist, Lolly studied Anna as she drew a fingertip along Mrs. R's left palm and asked questions of the older woman. The new boarder put Lolly in mind of Maureen O'Hara, though with no sign of the temperamental characters the actress played in some of those John Wayne movies. She felt the pull of the woman's benevolent attention. Funny. Anna exuded a certain liveliness, or maybe flamboyance, the exact opposite of how Lolly saw herself, yet the two of them had one thing in common—they were both planning to leave behind their previous, married lives and move forward.

"I'd like to hear about your boarding house business," said Anna, switching to Mrs. R's right palm.

"You would?"

"I'm always interested in businesses that women own."

"Well then," said Mrs. R. She proceeded to explain about how Mr. Ruddle had been home on leave in 1944. She'd been almost an old maid, already twenty-five, and she hardly knew him before he asked for her hand in marriage. Though they were opposites, caught up in the whirlwind of their romance, she married him. The intimacy of Anna's touch must have opened up the private gates to the landlady's past because she told how she had received an overseas letter from David Ruddle with an envelope addressed to her enclosing a letter meant for some other woman he clearly adored. She'd hung on for months, especially as his Navy pay was coming to her, but their marriage had never felt right again once she knew the other woman's name. She and David had had no children else she would have planned to stay in her marriage. Before she had acted to divorce her husband, he was killed in action.

"And then what?" asked Anna.

"And then I bought this house and began taking in boarders. Turned out I was good at running the place and liked the girls who came through. Lots of them young like you, but some not so young. Some of them get divorced at the age I was newly married."

"Do movie stars stay here too?"

"Oh my, no. Those types go to divorce ranches just outside of town. Places where they can ride horses and sit at the pool, and for dinner it's fine dining, that sort of thing."

"Your cooking is plenty good, perfect for me," said Anna. "You can't help it that some people want fancy accommodations at a distance from prying eyes."

Mrs. R nodded. She didn't look distressed about the lack of Hollywood royalty. "There's enough divorces to go around. Why just in the last year or so, there's been dozens of famous ones in the news. Tony Curtis, Brigitte Bardot …"

"Marlon Brando," said Anna. "Johnny Weissmuller. I guess we're all the same when we want out of marriage."

Mrs. R looked at her palm again, "What do you see in my palm?"

"Of course this is not an exact science," said Anna.

"Please don't tell me anything bad is going to happen. I don't like bad news."

"This isn't predictions. That would be fortune telling. This is more a reflection of where you've been, or maybe how far you've come from wherever you started." She pointed to one of the lines. "This one, for instance, this is the 'life line,' and yours is curvy. That's supposed to indicate enthusiasm for life. And fortitude."

Mrs. R looked pleased. "I do stick with things."

Anna nodded. "And on your 'fate line,' this one here ... how this breaks up into separate, smaller lines, that's supposed to mean you've had many changes in your life due to events outside your control."

"Dear me. Stop right there. I'm getting breathless just hearing how accurate that is," said Mrs. R, pushing back her chair. "It's remarkably like having your mind read." She turned to Lolly. "Your turn."

Lolly looked at her own hands. Would they betray her secrets? She shook her head. "It's getting awfully late."

"It's just for a minute," said Mrs. R. "That way I get to watch. Then I'll do the dishes while you two get ready for bed or read or what have you."

Anna's expression seemed friendly and open, and Lolly didn't want to be a stick in the spokes of Mrs. R's dinner party so she moved to the landlady's chair and offered her palms to Anna. Trying to deflect attention from herself, she said, "You sound interested in what's going on around town."

"I might move here, afterwards." Anna ran one finger across Lolly's palm, imparting a current that both soothed and tickled.

"What would you do?" asked Mrs. R from her post behind Lolly's chair.

"Look for business opportunities, if there were any."

"What kind?"

"Oh, this or that. I'll just have to look around and see what's out there." Turning her attention back to Lolly, she said, "You're probably thinking about opportunities here too."

Lolly hadn't been, not exactly. She wasn't sure if this was the town for her, but Anna's words started her wondering if she ought to be planning a future. She hadn't another location in mind but other concerns kept her thoughts occupied.

As Anna pondered Lolly's hand, a shadow passed over her face, making Lolly's heart skip.

"What?" said Lolly. "What's wrong?"

"Nothing's wrong. Remember, this is supposed to correspond to how your life has been so far. This line represents your head, and the length of it suggests that you like physical achievements, maybe working with your hands."

That was close, actually. Lolly *was* good with her hands, if you counted waiting tables and fixing hair. "What else?" she asked.

"So ... this one's called your heart line, which points to matters of love. And there are these other lines that cross it."

Lolly had a sinking feeling. "Is that trouble?"

Anna seemed to be organizing her thoughts. She cupped Lolly's hand in her own and laid three fingers across Lolly's palm. "These divergent lines could mean different but related things. Emotional troubles or momentous decisions you've faced." She looked at Lolly. "Of course, like I said earlier, it's not an exact science."

Lolly felt herself holding her breath.

Anna continued. "I suspect that means you're like the rest of us." She gave a wry smile that included Mrs. R. "Not so lucky in love. At least not the first time, or in my case *times*."

Lolly let the thought roll over her. *Unlucky in love.* There was truth in that too, and she liked how it implied that it wasn't predestination, but simply poor luck in choosing. She could also grant the opposite—that Russell had been luckless in choosing her. If that were the case, maybe she had reason to be hopeful after all. If a person could attract luck, perhaps she could figure out how to attract the good kind.

Anna explained that by "times" she meant that she was planning to file for her third divorce, to which Mrs. R mentioned Elizabeth Taylor, which led to a conversation about the Hollywood lifestyle that almost begged a rotating cast of partners and a buffet of wild and sometimes lascivious behavior.

"I'll turn in," said Lolly at last. She felt tired enough to sleep, but wanted to crack open her library book.

Upstairs in her room, she held the book beneath the warm glow cast by her bureau light. Through its plastic library cover the plain red canvas binding looked particularly unremarkable. She had no idea what the title meant in relation to a story about a lawyer and a Negro defendant, but she liked the feel of it in her hands, not too large, not too small. Just right. She had worked her way through four of her secondhand books but this one was special, not because it had received so much acclaim, but because it seemed a door through which she might walk and thus find herself in a new place in relation to the larger world.

Opening the book, she found a quote attributed to Charles Lamb: "Lawyers, I suppose, were children once." And with that, she began the task of reading the first few pages.

Seventeen

The casinos considered Friday the start of the weekend, and Saturday the peak. Sunday evenings brought a winding down of action and free spending. Having figured out the pattern early in her tenure at the Paradise Club, Lolly felt an uptick in anticipation each time she set out for work on a Friday.

Mrs. R and Anna were deep in conversation when Lolly came downstairs at 10:00 a.m. to fix herself a cup of tea. The two were discussing how liberal the local divorce judges might prove. Or not. Up popped the name Barrett, and a figure of twenty thousand divorces granted.

"He must have set a record," said Anna.

"No doubt," said Mrs. R.

As Lolly headed for the stairs with her mug, the ladies had moved to discussing the cost of university classes. Lolly knew Mrs. R's fondness for the land grant institution standing solidly on an upslope just a few blocks north of downtown. She had recommended it to Lolly for summer picnics on the quadrangle and for the beauty of its redbrick buildings so like those of Ivy League colleges. As if Lolly would still be in town come summer. Such considerations required a future lasting longer than a quickie divorce and a recovery from her current delicate condition. Lolly smiled internally. Mrs. R deserved credit for the unflagging optimism she heaped upon everyone around her.

Lolly's shift at work dished up the usual action—customers, menus, water pitchers, and coffee refills. Karen seemed intent on avoiding Lolly's gaze. In response, Lolly took extra care with Karen's customers so they'd leave decent tips.

During her break, she worked her way through two more pages of Mockingbird (as she had come to think of it). The first page of the first chapter was numbered "9" and she felt a moment's pleasure at already being on page 13, where a character arrives and declares

straight out how he can read, saying, "You got anything needs readin'
I can do it …"

Lolly liked the sound of this boy Dill, but it was Scout who directed
her thoughts toward girls who weren't girly, who could be themselves
and say whatever they wanted and maybe even slug the mean boys.

Lolly had kept her routine of changing her blouse after her shift,
ordering a highball and listening to Jackson's music in the Hideout
before betting a few dollars on blackjack. By now she knew what kind
of lounge music to expect; the kind preferred by the owner. She was
there to support Jackson and his musicianship, and to sit in the same
room where his innate talent sprang from his golden guitar. In spite
of that, the lounge continued to feel empty without Caldwell inviting
himself to take a seat at her table. He'd been gone long enough, by her
estimation—ten or eleven days—that she had to concentrate in order
to conjure the details of him. There were his unusual sage-green eyes,
and how sharp he looked in a suit. His hands were long-fingered and
smooth. She smiled at the memory of those silly Grasshopper drinks
he'd bought her that first time. By default, she'd fallen into the role of
willing recipient of his largesse. She supposed now that his role had
been by default too—boss man, casino man, always on duty with
scarcely enough time for a life beyond work.

When Jackson's break came, Lolly went to the performance corner
to say hello. When she told him that she had another surprise to bring
to the Polka Dot, he cautioned that she couldn't count on meeting him
there on Monday.

"Why not?" asked Lolly.

"My uncle. He'll be down there working on some repairs to a place
in the floor where water leaked through."

"Tuesday then?"

"That might work, but if you see a car parked up close to the
building, better not come in."

Jackson was clearly taking care not to let his family know that she
was coming around. She was only visiting, their meetings weren't
dates, not even when he brought his guitar. Not even when she
brought a record. Technically, she was simply keeping him company
while he worked, and helping out too, but perhaps his family would
assume that she was making more of her visits than he. This was true,
but she just couldn't help herself. Jackson made her feel alive to all
kinds of possibilities. Still, there was nothing to do but heed his

warning.

Her recollection of Jackson's reticence to challenge his family on her behalf dampened her enjoyment of the Friday night revelry. From the bar she bought a fresh drink and crossed into the casino to work up enthusiasm for how the random numbers played out in blackjack. She'd brought twenty dollars with her, almost a third of the bus fare from Gilleon to Reno, or two weeks' worth of the kind of groceries she regularly bought, or a half-dozen home permanent kits. The thing was, the only time she'd seen people win big at the tables was when they bet more than a dollar or two. She hadn't yet felt brave enough to gamble big in order to win big, but tonight she needed her spirits buoyed. One more night of winning would give her enough money to pay the advance on her divorce.

Her favorite dealer was nowhere in sight, but Lolly chose an open spot at a table and sent a plea to a saint she concocted right on the spot—the patron saint of runaway wives. Better yet—a saint for the Jewish notion of lost souls. There were Catholic saints for pretty much every occasion and every type of troubled person, so why not? *Saint Norma, please let the cards fall my way.*

Just before midnight, Lolly arrived home by taxi to the boarding house. The front light cast the porch in a yellow glow and inside lights were ablaze behind Mrs. Ruddle's roller shades, which themselves were dressed with swags of sheer curtains.

"Hello," called Mrs. R from the kitchen as Lolly made her way in. "You're quite the socialite, out on the town. Even so, you're home before Anna."

Lolly peeked into the front room as she hung up her coat. Almost immediately there was the sound of a key in the door lock and in came a smiling Anna in a silk evening outfit.

"You're back," said Anna. "I was wondering if we'd have a chance to hear about your day."

"My day?" asked Lolly.

"Why not?"

"Oh, no reason. It was okay. I just now got home."

"From some fun and games?" asked Anna.

"Playing blackjack."

"You took them for some cash, I hope."

Lolly shook her head. "I tried, but all I won was ten dollars. That's almost like breaking even."

"You don't look very happy about it. When I break even, I count it as winning."

Lolly shrugged. What she needed were real winnings. "Were you gambling too?"

"I've been up the street having a cocktail at the Hotel Holiday. Do you know it?"

"I walk by it on my way to work."

"They've got a restaurant and lounge that overlook the river. It's not as glitzy as some, but I like it." Anna eyed Lolly for an instant then started toward the kitchen. "I take it that money is on your mind. Is it for your divorce?"

"Yes." Lolly wondered once more how it could cost so much to disentangle herself from that which had been so economical to initiate.

"Legalities," said Anna. "Let's have tea."

Mrs. R hovered like the good hostess of a cocktail party. "How about a snack, girls?" she asked.

"What have you got?" asked Anna.

"Cinnamon-raisin coffee cake."

Lolly had to smile. If Mrs. R had baked coffee cake, Anna had indeed earned the landlady's approval.

In the kitchen, Anna dug into the thick slice of cake that Mrs. R set in front of her and Lolly nibbled daintily at her own, which was smaller because Mrs. R was not one to waste food on someone who mostly pushed it around her plate.

"So," said Anna, picking up crumbs with a moistened fingertip, "you're gambling to win money. Does that mean you didn't arrive with your divorce all planned?"

Lolly paused. "That's right."

Anna nodded thoughtfully. "You wouldn't be the first one to decide after you got some distance from home. I take it you've found out how much divorces cost. Are you shocked?"

"That's one way to put it."

Anna looked to be doing the math in her head. "You've been in town how long?"

"Seven weeks in all."

"What's your job at the Paradise?"

"I'm a hostess in the coffee shop."

Mrs. Ruddle broke in. "She's been fixing hair in the kitchen here, too, when there's customers."

Anna ran her fork over her clean plate. "That's a talent. So, what fee did the lawyer quote you?"

"It was his receptionist, or maybe his secretary," said Lolly. "Two hundred and fifty, with half up front."

"But is your case complicated? Have you got a ranch to split, or four children at home, things like that?"

Lolly almost chuckled. "No. Not at all."

"Two-fifty," said Anna, "for not much work."

"That's what they told me at their office near the courthouse."

"Location might explain it." The redhead thought a moment. "You didn't give them any money yet?"

"No."

Anna squinted and cocked her head. "How would you feel about doing business with my lawyer, if he'd give you a better rate?"

"What do you mean?"

"A package deal," said Anna. "If I bring him a new customer, he doesn't even have to work for the referral. It would be like money walking in the door. You're sure you don't have any complications? Nothing to fight over."

Lolly's hand went involuntarily to her stomach, which had given a lurch.

Anna saw the motion. "Oh," she said. "Are you—you know ...?"

Reluctant to give up her secret, Lolly nodded.

"But he doesn't know it."

"And I'm not going to tell him."

"It's a complication." Anna bit her bottom lip. "But not if you don't tell your lawyer. Or the judge. In that case you need to make progress as soon as you can. If you want, I'll call Mr. Quick in the morning and ask if he can meet with us early next week. We can ask for a bargain."

"You're going to call him on the weekend?"

"He knows me from the last two times I lined his pockets. I have his number."

Lolly looked at Mrs. R.

The woman nodded, saying, "You do have doctor expenses to consider."

Lolly blinked. Mrs. R had no notion of the type of doctoring she had in mind.

Anna said, "The question is whether you want to meet with him. It's up to you."

Lolly's thoughts leapt to the words that had aligned her fate with Russell's. Her slow progress at accumulating cash was beginning to wear on her and Anna's was a reasonable offer. She nodded at Anna. "Yes. Yes, I do."

Eighteen

On Saturday, Lolly earned a few more dollars trimming the hair of one of the neighborhood ladies. Mrs. R hovered nearby, offering tea and a running commentary on the weather the activities of local ladies' service clubs—Minerva Club, Order of the Eastern Star, Emblem Club—and how Trinity Church's spring bazaar would outperform records set in previous years. It was a good thing that Mrs. R kept the conversation flowing; Lolly had only enough energy for the duty at hand.

That night, Jackson did not show for his Saturday performance in the Hideout. When Lolly asked Roger if he knew what had happened, all he said was, "He's out for tonight, that's all I heard."

The news peeled the luster from Lolly's evening. Not even the thought of winning a few precious dollars at blackjack could tempt her. And of course, there was no Caldwell either. She went home to read.

The next day was the same, with an extra jab of disappointment because the lounge was "dark" on Sundays—no performers. Though she ought to attempt to win more money, she knew it might backfire to gamble while dejected. Optimism was what attracted luck, so instead, she headed home to work through more pages of her library book.

On the table in the boarding house entryway, she found a small, fat envelope addressed to her. She carried it to the kitchen.

"Oh good, you found it," said Mrs. R, looking up from her magazine. "It came with a stack of circulars yesterday but I forgot to set it out for you." She gave a sly smile. "It's from your admirer, right?"

Lolly knew without opening it that inside would be a treat but no letter. No news, no questions, nothing to explain why he kept sending gifts. To keep her thoughts swinging back to him? His tactic was working. She'd never known such an odd arrangement. Other girls might have the fortitude to dispose of packages without so much as a peek at what they held, but not Lolly. She opened each one, and if pressed, would acknowledge how each gift brightened her day. Today she could use a boost.

She poured herself a cup of tea and carried her envelope to the table. In came Anna from the front room. "Did I hear the word *admirer*?"

Lolly smiled wryly. Not only a present, but an audience too. She didn't mind as long as the audience held only these two. She accepted a paring knife from Mrs. R and slit the envelope open.

"What do you suppose it will be this time?" said Mrs. R. "So far it's been records and postcards."

"Postcards?" asked Anna.

"Of San Francisco."

"What a city. Have you been there?" asked Anna.

"I haven't," said Lolly, extracting a packet of pink tissue paper. Within the layered tissue was a tangerine-colored pouch, silky to the touch. The two other women leaned closer as Lolly pulled opened its strings and tipped into her hand a single wavy pearl.

"Would you look at that," said Mrs. R.

"Mmm," said Anna.

"It looks like a pearl," said Lolly, "except for the shape."

"The fresh water type," said Anna. "They're kind of rare."

"What's a girl to do with that?" asked Mrs. R. "It's not even strung for a necklace."

"But it could be," said Anna.

Lolly just turned the pinkish-white, glowing object in her hand. She'd seen regular pearls before. Jackie Kennedy wore a string of perfect, white pearls. Other First Ladies, too, and actresses, and sometimes models in the fashion spreads of ladies' magazines, but she'd never seen any shaped like this. An unconscious smile formed on her face.

"Have you got a place to keep it?" asked Mrs. R. "A jewelry case, or ..."

"Not really." Since it wasn't actually jewelry and she didn't know what it meant, she would add it to the packet of San Francisco postcards and count it as a short-lived pleasure.

On Monday, Lolly woke with a nervous stomach. She had developed the habit of looking forward to spending a portion of her days off with

Jackson at the Polka Dot. Now she faced a delay, likely dictated by the caution he had counseled her to use in relation to his family.

Over the last few weeks, she had grown to think of her time with him as fated, that she had been meant to encounter him in the Hideout and befriend him, and he was meant to share his musical gifts with her. Through physical proximity they would enrich each other's lives.

Lolly did view her life as narrow, at least until now. Predictable days strung on a line. Nothing like the Mockingbird story she had carried down to the front room. Set in the 1930s, it told of Southern people unlike any she had known.

Why, in Mockingbird the children just took things into their own hands, even Scout, the daughter. *A girl!* If someone called Scout's father a rotten name, she would take a swing and knock that person hard. The characters in that family stood up for what they believed, even when they might be wrong, even when threatened or scared, or when someone might hurt them for it. She'd never known such brave people. Perry Mason was smart, but these people were brave, and in the case of the young ones, determined to figure out what they needed to make their way in the world.

The more she read, the more she thought about how she hardly ever acted with courage (maybe in leaving Gilleon, but then again, perhaps that was cowardice). It took no pluck to marry someone in order to escape a dead-end situation, and no smarts to think that the person you married might change your life for the better, take it in a new direction. She could see now that she herself had made no more headway in life than a butterfly caught in a windstorm. But she had intentions, for what that was worth.

The memory of a high school drawing class purled up around her. One assignment had been to render in charcoal an old pewter water pitcher set atop a stack of books. The teacher had instructed them to walk around the table that held the tableau, to consider all angles before taking up a station at an easel. That was, he had said, the only way to understand how the play of shadows and light changes what we see. Each observer's view is different, resulting in a different approach to representation. *That's what I need regarding Jackson*, she thought now. *A different approach to convincing him to stay put. A different argument for staying safe.*

With Anna away and Mrs. R puttering in the kitchen, the house was quiet. Lolly rose from her chair to fetch a fresh cup of tea, then returned to reading.

Reading had grown a sliver easier as she learned to pace the rate her eyes traveled, so her brain could keep up. She still sometimes struggled with the shifty nature of words, mentally sounding them out if they turned against her. But once they registered behind the curtain of her mind, they settled in place and stayed put.

By dinnertime Lolly had read more pages than on any other day of her life. She had made real progress. After Anna came through the front door, she finished the page she was on. Laying the book aside, she went to the kitchen.

"You looked so intent, I left you alone today," said Mrs. R, preparing to slice a steaming ham loaf she had pulled from the oven. "You will eat tonight, won't you? Look at Anna—she eats my cooking and her figure is fine."

Anna had one hip pressed against the counter, watching Mrs. R add pineapple rings to the serving platter. Anna said, "Oh, by the way, I settled on an appointment with Mr. Quick today. He'll see us tomorrow, mid-morning. That's one of your days off, right?"

Tomorrow—Tuesday—might represent Lolly's last chance to meet Jackson at the Polka Dot until her next set of days off. She weighed the pleasure of visiting Jackson with her great need for a bargain divorce. "Tomorrow's good," she said, as a thought arose about how she might contact Jackson. The other women began to talk about movies, Anna nodding at Mrs. R's remarks while her eyes were on Lolly.

Lolly had quit listening when the realization hit her that blind or not, wherever Jackson lived, he must have a telephone. She went to the kitchen drawer that held the Bell Telephone directory and carried the book to the front room. She found numerous Mayberrys, which was no help since none of them were for a Jackson Jr. Her disappointment only heightened her need to speak with him and the unfairness of the circumstances that held her at a distance. Even though she was distinctly herself and he was uniquely himself, she thought of them as a decent pair. Not a couple, exactly, but a set, like one of those mathematical sets from school, prime numbers or integers. Items that fell in together. If she remembered right, a set didn't have to be large; it could be two things alike.

So it was that Lolly formulated a plan for the following day. After joining Anna in meeting with Mr. Quick she would walk to the Paradise Club, and there she would tell yet another lie.

Mrs. R insisted on driving Anna and Lolly to the offices of Thomas L. Quick, Esquire, saying, "You should have a chauffeur, even if it's only me." She left them at the curb.

Inside the office, a pink-lipped receptionist fairly sang Anna's name in greeting. "Mrs. Trimble. So nice to see you again."

Anna inclined her head. "Miss Veronica, I've brought Mrs. Cooper."

"Let me show you in. Mr. Quick is ready for you."

They followed the receptionist through the carpeted reception area. Anna had offered to press Lolly's case with the lawyer, which was fine by Lolly because the only case she had to make was an admission of how strapped she was for funds.

Anna proved a formidable negotiator. First there was small talk, then a bit of banter, mostly on Mr. Quick's part. How good Anna looked—Mrs. Trimble, he called her—and how he just couldn't understand a man who couldn't keep a wife happy. Didn't a wife want a nice home and a few luxuries now and then? A bit of foreign travel, and on special occasions, a bauble set with diamonds? He seemed to speak as if he knew Anna's tastes, and maybe he did, considering she was obviously a repeat client. Or perhaps he knew enough about women to identify what it took to keep certain women content.

Lolly thought she saw in Anna's expression a marked lack of interest in Mr. Quick's small talk. She let the florid man ramble before reminding him that she'd brought him another customer. In fact, she'd decided that he might like to offer a special fee for Lolly's case because it could be brought before the court with minimal investment of time or effort.

"Now, now," he countered. "I would be remiss if I disregarded the bar association's requirement for a minimum fee of two-fifty. I don't set the rules, I just follow them. If a case is that simple, almost any attorney could prosecute it satisfactorily in court ..." At this he inclined his head toward Lolly, saying, "on behalf of this lovely lady." He gestured with pale hands. "From what you describe, Mrs. Cooper's case would not take an attorney of my experience to arrive at a fitting conclusion. No ma'am. Mrs. Cooper could retain almost anyone and get it done—" he snapped his fingers smartly— "like that."

"Why Mr. Quick," said Anna, lowering her voice and leaning toward the attorney's desk. "That's exactly the reason you could provide such an important service for a lesser fee. Because with your exceedingly fine talents applied in succinct fashion, the deed would be done. Yet another feather in your cap, even if a small one."

Mr. Quick's eyes widened a fraction as if he were at that moment registering the flattery within Anna's remarks, coupled with the suggestion that he *ought* to take Lolly's case. He said, "You would have me ignore the rules?"

"I did not discern that you were overly taxed by the rules when you and I last did business. I seem to recall one or two, shall we say, creative approaches to the complaint you helped me submit."

"My dear Mrs. Trimble. You know how I, ahh …" His thoughts seemed to catch up to his speech as his eyes remained locked on Anna's. "I do so appreciate you referring another client to my firm. This business is of course reliant upon satisfied clients and word-of-mouth. And then there are those repeat clients such as yourself." At this he gave Anna a nod before continuing. "But I am beginning to recall that I have an extremely busy court calendar this coming month. I sincerely doubt that I could fit another case in, no matter how uncomplicated, even for the sake of a valued client such as yourself."

Silence filled the room before Anna spoke again. "Mr. Quick, I was so hoping you could assist this friend of mine. Such a small task, a favor even, on my behalf. Let alone that a case so simple would sail even faster through the proceedings were you at its helm. I am sorry to hear that you are too busy for such endeavors."

The office was a comfortable temperature. Lolly and Anna were dressed in day suits and Mr. Quick wore a smartly tailored charcoal gray three-piece, but at this point his face grew pinker than it had previously been and his forehead began to glisten.

He looked to be digesting Anna's remarks in a manner to ease his mind, and failing as Anna continued. "I'm afraid that perhaps my own divorce will prove too taxing for your calendar, perhaps unnecessarily reducing the resources you so clearly rely upon and that are needed for more important cases." She glanced around as if just now coming to this perplexing realization. "Yes, I'm thinking that might be prudent. Perhaps I should withdraw and leave you to pursue those challenges which would not punish your calendar so remorselessly. I do know how the hours add up." She shook her head. "It's dreadful, really."

Mr. Quick's eyes widened perceptibly and his mouth opened and closed, then opened again before words came out. "I fear that I have given you the wrong impression entirely. I did not mean to imply that I could not take Mrs. Cooper's case *at all*—at some future time of course. I—I suppose I could find time for such a case. Yes."

He turned to Lolly. "Have you any children with your husband?"

Lolly felt hollow inside, as if a bystander at her own trial. She shook her head.

"No houses in dispute or other real property?"

"No property," said Lolly. Her holdings were meager. She had arrived at twenty-eight years of age without a tarpaper shack under her management. No mortgage, no automobile, not even a pot of geraniums to call her own.

Mr. Quick spread his hands as if making evident the reasoning behind his apparent about-face. "There, you see?" he said as he fussed with a bound calendar sitting atop his polished desk. "I'm sure we can find a slot. Let me just look before I confer with my secretary. Yes, yes. How about ... the latter part of April?" He looked from Anna to Lolly and back to Anna.

Anna tilted her head, then shook it gently.

"No?" he sputtered. "You're thinking about sooner?"

Anna nodded almost imperceptibly.

"Then let's look again." He asked, "Did you say, Mrs. Cooper, that you've already established residency?"

"She has," said Anna. "In fact, we're both residing in a boarding house just east of downtown."

Mr. Quick spent another moment consulting his calendar. He swallowed hard, then said to Lolly, "I take it then that you're quite ready to file papers and be heard in court?"

"Yes," said Lolly. She did not relish the prospect of working with this man, especially as he clearly preferred otherwise, but if Anna trusted him to handle her divorce, then she could too. At least hers should be a snap, and then she could move on.

"And then there's the fee," added Anna.

"Oh." Mr. Quick seemed to deflate at the mention of money. "What did you have in mind, my dear?"

"An affordable figure," prompted Anna.

"Of course." The man sat waiting.

"For such a simple case."

"As you mentioned."

"I'm thinking one hundred should cover it."

Mr. Quick nearly choked as he coughed. "Now, dear. Surely you don't believe I can cover the costs associated with even the simplest case for such a fee. Why, first we need a review of the facts, and then there are clerical services, and the filing fee, and an appearance before the judge."

Anna's eyes fastened on Lolly though her words addressed the attorney before them. "You are right once again. We absolutely must compromise. One-fifty, let's settle on that. Do you have a few more minutes in your schedule this morning? I believe we can dispense with the review right now if you have, say, fifteen minutes?"

"Whatever you think," said Lolly, looking from Anna to Mr. Quick and back again. Her own speech seemed to grow more formal under the influence of their respective gazes. "I only have errands to run downtown later."

"Of course. We won't be long. Mr. Quick, have you a pen? We'll be out of your hair as soon as you set these details to the page. I'm thinking you might give Mrs. Cooper my slot on your calendar for next week. My residency is incomplete and you and I can surely reschedule."

Mr. Quick blew out a breath and took up his pen.

Lolly provided the date of her marriage, her last permanent address, and the date in February when she'd arrived in Reno (just after the flood). She showed her Oklahoma driver's license and verified her birthdate and that of her husband. She provided Russell's last known address and the name of the Gilleon newspaper where a notice could be published. Anna extracted from the now-morose lawyer an agreement that Lolly could bring the fee as cash or a bank check to the consultation that would take place mere moments before her appearance in front of a judge. Just like that, Lolly, who had dodged her chance to refute Russell's threats, was halfway to divorcing him.

A half-hour later, Lolly stood before the door of the Paradise hiring office. She composed herself with what she hoped was a concerned but benign expression before stepping through to approach the closest worker, swallowing hard against the possibility of being found a fraud. "I'm hoping you can help me with a matter of family interest—for a Paradise employee."

A woman whose name badge read "Betty" considered Lolly neutrally.

"One of his relations, whom I know from my ... previous town, is trying to reach him but she hasn't had any luck. She's written to ask for my help, and so I promised I would search out his phone number. You know, to pass it along." Now that Lolly heard the story coming from her own mouth, it sounded feeble, but it was all she had come up with. Channeling Anna's purposeful posture, she held the woman's gaze and waited.

"Who is this employee?" asked Betty.

"Jackson Mayberry. He plays guitar on Fridays and Saturdays in the Hideout." She shrugged to suggest that she couldn't say whether it was worth Betty's bother; she was just the messenger.

"And the relative's name?"

Unprepared for such a query, Lolly gave the first name that came to mind. "Norma. Ah, Mayberry." A bit of extra baloney came to her. "A relation on his father's side." Suddenly the smallish office was too warm and she felt her color rise.

The woman seemed to relent. "Your name and work station?"

"Lolly—well, Luella Cooper. I work noon to eight in the coffee shop."

The woman nodded as she penciled on a notepad, giving Lolly hope that she was about to receive the very information she had come for.

"As I'm sure you can appreciate ... we have rules about sharing personal information." The woman gave her a pointed look. "I'll have to get back to you."

"Oh," said Lolly. "That would be terrific. I'm sure any help will be much appreciated. By the uh, by Norma."

Lolly turned and fled the office before she could foil her plan by speaking any more nonsense. Back downstairs she considered her surroundings. She was within a mile or so of the Polka Dot, which Jackson had warned her away from visiting when his uncle might make an appearance. The odds were that Jackson had finished his janitorial work by now and she'd encounter his uncle there. Or she might find the place cold and empty when what she wanted was

Jackson, warm-blooded and attentive to her explanation of how Mockingbird was opening her eyes to the world.

The Mockingbird novel seemed to be changing her with each page she read. She wanted to tell him how she could feel it. Tiny changes, yes. She was imagining how she could speak out against injustices to herself or others. The question was where she might put such improvements to work. She hadn't needed any of Scout's outspokenness during her search around Reno, a search feeling more futile as each day passed without definitive clues. And Caldwell, a person who had tested her patience and with whom she might employ Scout's tactics, was nowhere to be seen. Still, the story consumed her, held her fast through characters and circumstances entirely unrelated to her own.

The casino action surrounding Lolly came back into focus. Upstairs was the woman she had tried to induce into handing over Jackson's phone number. The woman would see through her lie or she wouldn't. Lolly would reach Jackson by telephone or she wouldn't. As she glanced around the casino, she realized that she had better apply herself to winning some cash. Caldwell had been right about how money made things happen. She needed money to address her own specific, pressing needs, and this place was brimming with the stuff.

Perching on a seat at a blackjack table, Lolly felt the heat inside her flare a shade brighter. *This* she was reasonably good at, the calm consideration of the high and low cards dealt after the shuffle, and the hands won and lost. Blackjack was half luck and half mathematics. That said, her process only worked because all cards dealt were eventually turned face up. She pulled out her wallet and considered the handful of fives and tens she had not yet transferred to her stash at the boarding house. Did she feel lucky? Not really. But perhaps she could beat the randomness of luck. Winning required watchfulness and patience, both of which she was good at. She settled more fully onto the tall-legged stool at the position known as "third base," the spot closest to the dealer's right hand and began to gamble with a purpose.

Nineteen

The next day found Lolly leaving on time for her morning appointment at the obstetrics office near the tracks that carried trains west through the Sierras, and in the opposite direction, out through a river canyon toward Utah and beyond. For an appointment that would require the removal of clothes, she wore her black work skirt and a long-sleeved cotton blouse topped by her overcoat, because even though the days were growing perceptibly longer, morning temperatures hovered in the forties until almost noon.

Exiting the boarding house, she walked a bit until she caught a Checker taxi on Center Street. The driver was friendly, predicting the imminent bloom of budding trees planted along the streets. "Crabapple," he said. "They need a spell of warm weather. A week's worth would do, never mind the spring freeze that sometimes comes round about now." He rolled down the window to flick his cigarette butt out then popped a piece of gum into his mouth. "Yessir. If you got other kinds of fruit trees, they can meet with trouble in spring, but those sour apple trees, they bloom no matter what. Might not bear fruit, but you get the prettiest look. I like spring, do you?"

Lolly missed the driver's question, her mind on the objective she'd set for herself. Her previous visit to this office had been a failure. The disarray of arriving late, her unplanned stop in the Catholic cathedral, the blurred hours in the neighborhood bar. She was determined this time to get the job done, so had called in sick to work from a public telephone and had brought all her saved cash. Back at the boarding house later, she could feign a mild case of flu for the rest of the day. Or a couple of days.

God, she hated this—the choosing between two wrongs and the telling of lies to do so. It felt like a negation of all the things she had ever done right. And what sorts of questions might Dr. Hall ask her? Would he need justification for special services related to ending a pregnancy? Would it matter that she was married, or about to be divorced? Would it matter that she'd left her husband and fled his

Oklahoma town? Did this doctor bestow his services differently to married women than the unmarried ones, divorced ones, young or old ones?

Lolly had arrived earlier than necessary so she stood in front of the house-shaped building shifting from one foot to the other, stomach in knots, waiting for a signal that the office would open. Soon a station wagon driven by the receptionist she'd seen last time pulled off the street and into a narrow parking slot alongside two other vehicles. The woman emerged, and, smoothing her skirt, went up the concrete steps to unlock the heavy front door. Lolly followed her through to the reception area.

"Mrs. Cooper?" asked the woman.

"I wanted to be on time," said Lolly.

"That's fine. I'm just opening up. Doctor is here, preparing for the day. His nurse too. They'll review the days' appointments before calling you in. If you'll take a seat, I'll bring you some paperwork to fill out, and there are plenty of magazines."

Lolly chose an upholstered wingback chair farthest from the front door. The office really did resemble a house, with hardwood floors covered by rugs, and arched, multi-paned casement windows facing the street. It occurred to her that even the lives of houses changed. The builder of this one had probably not meant it to serve as anything other than a house. But here it was, remade into a medical office for women patients in various states of womanhood, the hopeful, the elated, the worried.

A house made over into something else was not all that different from pickup trucks turned into campers, or wine barrels turned into planters for vegetables. Back in Gilleon, ranch families kept their rundown equipment, tractors, trucks, old school buses even, somewhere on their property. Whenever they needed spare parts, they pried them from their personal garden of derelicts. Few items were relegated to the trash heap; instead, they were repurposed to some other necessary end, a type of reinvention not unlike that which she herself was planning to undergo.

Her marriage, if not then completely busted, had been for the last two or three years limping along. Now, with Mr. Quick's assistance, she would be shed of Russell, who could do as he pleased, remain single or refashion himself as marriage material.

Just before the nurse called Lolly's name and led her to an

examination room, a roundly pregnant-looking woman arrived. She stepped up to the reception desk, causing Lolly to study again the magazine pages she'd been blindly turning. Someday, maybe, she herself would look as expectant as that woman. On purpose. Her hand went automatically to the waistband of her skirt. She didn't look pregnant yet. Her clothes still fit well enough, but by her calculation, she was almost two months along, and eventually there would be no way to keep the secret; she would run out of options for reinventing herself.

Not being certain how much her procedure would cost, Lolly had brought one hundred and fifty dollars with her, some of which had been earlier earmarked for her divorce. She had prepared for today by replaying potential scenarios in her head. She assumed her visit would include a heart-to-heart about her wishes, during which she would once more assert her determination to proceed. Conflicting thoughts tumbled through her—the need to retake control of her life, to do what was right for her but also the recognition that the choice she'd made was morally wrong, in opposition to Church teachings. How could something so wrong also seem right?

Before this moment she had sequestered thoughts about her medical condition where they wouldn't constantly intrude. Random facts broke through, but not enough to impede her work at the Paradise or dampen the time she spent with Jackson. If she had let it, the notion of pregnancy might have rendered her immobile. But she had decided not to give Russell that kind of power over her. He didn't deserve any more than he'd already exercised. When the nurse called Lolly and ushered her into the examination room, Lolly tasted panic. This was it. Would Dr. Hall deem her worthy of his services?

Now she found herself breathing too fast. She was here on a mission that she wouldn't discuss with coworkers, or Mrs. R or anyone she could think of. Norma Jeane, maybe, if they'd still been in touch. Putting on her coffee shop face, she decided that if the doctor was a stranger who wanted something she could give – in in this case information -- she could speak with him while not needing to know him better. Just an exchange, one she was grateful for, but still just an exchange.

What Lolly discovered was that the doctor wouldn't take her word for her condition. He required that she pee into a cup for a pregnancy test performed elsewhere on a rabbit. The results would come back in few days' time, a technicality since following his examination of her, Dr. Hall agreed with Lolly's assertion that she was pregnant.

She said, "So, what I'm after ... what I need ... is help, you know. To not be pregnant."

The doctor appeared to take stock of her. "And you thought I could do that?"

She swallowed hard. Did she have this all wrong? "I know someone who said maybe you could help. But she didn't say exactly those words. I just ..." Good God, had she presumed too much about the waitress at work and her slip of paper with Dr. Hall's name on it?

"I understand what you're asking for. Do you know such a thing can be dangerous?"

Lolly nodded, trying to keep her cool. Pretty much everyone had heard about women dying from this very thing. Even in America.

The doctor continued, "Some women choose to carry the developing fetus all the way to childbirth, and then if it's still not in their power to raise a child, there are adoption agencies. The Catholic Church, for one."

"No! I mean, no. I've thought a lot about it. I need to reverse this." Her emptiness in childhood was a memory carried in her body. Her arms remembered, her legs, her heart. In spite of the nuns' assertions that children were special to Jesus, her body knew, and her heart knew, that she was not cherished. She had been left behind by someone who chose to leave her behind. She would not *give away* a child.

"Husbands sometimes want a child born."

Lolly touched her wedding ring. She had been wearing it for protection against unwanted advances while at work or when relaxing with a drink in the Hideout, but it also represented her broken marriage to the man who had raped her. "He's far away. Now. It's not his to choose."

Dr. Hall nodded a bit as if coming to a conclusion. "I can tell you are determined. You seem to have made up your mind. But I don't offer the procedure you're asking for."

Stunned, Lolly said, "You mean I have this all wrong?"

"What you're saying you need is an 'assisted abortion.' Though I recognize that many women desire such, I don't perform that procedure. My practice provides general obstetrics and gynecology. There's a movement to make assisted abortion legal, but the machinery of that effort moves slowly. In the meantime ... I can refer to you a practitioner who is willing to take the risk."

Lolly knew that what she wanted was illegal, as most women knew, even those who'd never had to avail themselves of the procedure. Even those who had never been in desperate straits, or overwhelmed with a growing brood of children, or at risk medically, or a dozen other variations on the theme. She was beginning to feel the weight of the many hoops she'd already jumped through to get this far, which now seemed miles from her destination and only a step or two from where she had started.

"We'll call in the referral." He glanced at the nurse, who turned and left the room. "Nurse Wilken will set the appointment before you leave today. She'll write out the address for you. When you go, take the fee in cash. If you change your mind before then, you don't need to call them, simply don't show up. They will understand."

The whole affair sounded like it belonged to the dark arts of the Cold War between America and the USSR. People who knew people making arrangements that were financed with cash, only those people traded in secrets that could bring down governments. She said, "Thank you. It means a lot to me. I guess you hear that all the time."

Dr. Hall looked weary, as if the need to mix the business of birthing children with the business of circumventing their birth could grind a person to dust. Simply in making these referrals, Dr. Hall was putting his practice on the line. He said, "That's a typical sentiment."

"Some of the women you do this for, you're saving their lives." During the exam, he'd seen her scars and listened to how she had acquired them. To her great relief, he had not suggested she reconcile with Russell or justify herself further.

"You'll receive instructions from the other office, for afterwards," said Dr. Hall. "But then, at some point, you might want to consider birth control. You said you weren't using any, but options exist now."

"That was my husband's doing that I didn't use any."

"Then you were lucky for a long time, with whatever method you were using."

Lucky. She wouldn't have described herself as lucky, but now it seemed she had been. Had she stayed in Oklahoma, she probably would have found no doctor like this one. She said, "I don't think I need a prescription." It wasn't like she was planning an affair. Then for some reason she said, "Well, okay."

"Don't take these while you're pregnant," he said, pulling a pad of prescription forms from his white coat. As he was scribbling, the nurse, who had left the room, returned with a slip of paper on which she'd handwritten instructions for Lolly's appointment with the specialist and his fee—$225.

Lolly gasped. "So much?" A sum like that meant she would have been short on funds for her procedure had it occurred this very day.

"Afraid so," said the doctor. "But he's reputable. Knows what he's doing. You'll find everything sterile and medically sound."

"Can you take someone with you?" asked the nurse. "You shouldn't drive yourself home."

Lolly didn't have anyone she'd want to burden with her plans. Mrs. R, who didn't exactly seem the type to judge, was firmly Episcopalian, which made her practically Catholic, and so an unlikely co-conspirator. She couldn't very well ask such a personal favor of Anna, the worldliest person she knew, but also someone who was already acting as her divorce advocate. This was what happened when a person left one place for the next, and then the next. Had she been more settled in this town, she might have a few solid friends to rely upon. She told them, "I can take a taxi."

The doctor stood and the nurse reached for the door. Lolly's time was up.

After paying at the front desk for her examination, Lolly avoided the gaze of yet another patient seated in the waiting room. A brief glance told her that this one didn't look pregnant, which meant that from the outside, a casual observer wouldn't know if inside this fellow traveler lay contentedness or turmoil.

On Thursday evening, the restaurant manager brought Lolly a Paradise Club envelope, making her pulse jump. The manager paused as if to catch Lolly's reaction to what such a missive might mean, but Lolly nonchalantly slipped the envelope into the pocket of her uniform skirt and thanked him before turning away. Whatever this was—either a rejection of her request for Jackson's number, or an answer to her hopes—only her eyes would see it. Though she brought her racing thoughts under control, for the next two hours she kept patting her pocket as if to mollify the news held there.

When her shift ended, she went outside and stood in the glow of the closest overhead signs to peel open the envelope, warm from her body heat. Inside was a pink telephone message slip inked with the wording "J. Mayberry" and a telephone number starting with FA, the Fairview prefix. Relief washed over her. The hiring lady had granted her story enough credence to provide this information, a conclusion verified by the notation in the lower right-hand corner—"OK-BC." *Thanks, Betty,* she thought. *You're okay.*

Lolly hurried to a coin telephone booth near the Woolworth's store, a location not far from the Carnegie library where she'd borrowed Mockingbird. The booth's folding glass door squeaked in protest as she closed it behind her. With shaking fingers, she dropped a dime into the phone and made a silent wish for Jackson to answer as her call rang down the line. After five rings she began to fear the worst—a wrong number. Perhaps it was too late to call, or he'd gone for jazz at the Polka Dot (she had meant to go back there herself some evening). And then, a gift. The ringing stopped as the sound of an open line came on. Then a childish voice saying "Hello, hello?"

Taken aback, she quickly checked the message slip, which read FA-26771. Blinking against the booth's bright light she said, "I'm calling to speak with Jackson Mayberry."

From the other end came the sound of the phone banging against a hard surface and a small voice calling, "It's for you. A lady." And then there was a long pause, the sounds of Virginia Street traffic layered atop the static of the open phone line.

At last came the sound of the receiver knocking about again and then Jackson's resonant voice, a voice good for singing, if only he would. Lolly eased her grip on the receiver and said, "It's me. Lolly."

There was another pause as she waited, the glass box in which she stood a cold, cold place.

"That's you? Are you okay? How'd you—?" His voice sounded fine, with no trace of an illness that would have kept him from work.

"It's unexpected, I know. If I've caused a problem, I'm sorry. I didn't know you'd have children." Her heart sank at the mention of a detail about his life that she hadn't realized.

"Oh, them," said Jackson. "They belong to my mother's cousin. They come over sometimes when their mama gets called to work. Is anything wrong?"

They weren't his children? Thank God. When dialing she had feared the discovery of a wife. Jackson didn't wear a ring, and from their conversations she'd thought him a bachelor, but still, you never knew. She said, "Nothing's wrong. Just … just that I didn't make it on Tuesday because I went to a lawyer, and then you weren't at work, and I have something to share with you and I wanted to …" It felt silly now to try to explain how empty she'd felt at being thwarted in her weekly visit with him. How watching him work made her feel surer about herself. His straight stance in the face of obstacles, meeting challenges head-on or stepping aside as they rolled by. All of these feelings mixed up inside her, defying explanation, as did her feelings about his desire to exit the town she was only now settling into. She could not put voice to how a part of her hoped his intentions to leave town would … well, *fail* was not the right way to think of it; she would not wish him failure, just that those exact plans would not come to pass. If Jackson prevailed, she would be left adrift without one of the few people she had come to admire and rely upon.

Jackson spoke up. "It's good you didn't bother because Big George came two days in a row. I don't know why when there wasn't much to fix. Guess there's always next week."

Lolly's spirits rose at his willingness to think ahead. Even seven days hence counted as the future. But she had developed impressions about the Mockingbird story she wanted to share. Another week's delay was too much. She said, "Do you work other days at the Polka Dot? Do you work tomorrow?"

There was a pause, then Jackson said, "Hold on." His next words sounded distant, as if he'd turned away from the phone. "Hush. Hush up while I'm talking." When he came back on the line, he said, "Tomorrow? I guess so. Most weeks I work six or seven days down there. At night they jam or have lessons, or bands."

"Well, could we … could I … come by in the morning? Before my shift, is that okay?"

"Sure, I suppose. I'll start a little earlier. It's always the same routine, long as I get it done. 'Course you might want to watch for a car again."

Lolly felt a weight lift from her. Tomorrow would come and she would meet up with Jackson, and for now, that was all that mattered.

Twenty

L olly left the boarding house early after declining Mrs. R's entreaty regarding breakfast. Outside—a reversal of weather, winter reasserting itself. Snow flurries. A gusting breeze. Crazy.

The coast was clear at the Polka Dot. Lolly found the side door unlocked. She stepped in and scanned the gloom. "Hello," she called to Jackson.

"Over here," he said, though of course she had recognized his form.

She turned a bank of lights on and watched him work awhile. He declined to let her sweep or mop, but allowed her to return the upturned chairs to their places on the floor. She asked about his young cousins, technically cousins at some remove. He asked about her week, which she shared by describing the arrival of Anna Trimble. When she described Anna's negotiations with Mr. Quick, he said, "Sounds like a woman who knows what she wants."

Eventually Lolly brought out her library book. "I've been reading 'To Kill a Mockingbird.'"

"No kidding?"

"And I brought it. I thought you might want to, you know, hear parts of it."

"Sounds good. I could use a break," said Jackson, taking a seat and motioning Lolly to do the same. "I know the basics, but of course what I got was second-hand."

In an effort to work her way through it, Lolly had been skipping pages, looking for scenes portraying the lawyer and the accused man whose case he'd taken. She'd hit upon a passage that might help persuade Jackson to stay in Reno, and had practiced reading it. Now, she settled into her chair. "You know the story's about an accused Negro man and a white lawyer who takes his case. The Negro—his name is Tom—is accused of a crime he says he didn't do."

"Rape. But does the lawyer believe him?"

"It seems like he does. He's looking for clues to help defend Tom against the town's people. And their opinions. Then there's children, too. Atticus's daughter, who's telling the story, and her brother Jem. They take their father's side, of course, but then some other school kids turn on them."

Lolly turned to a page she had marked with a slip of paper. "The young ones, they have to defend their dad, you know, when the others call him names."

"Nigger lover," said Jackson.

Lolly recoiled. She'd seen that on the page but wouldn't have spoken those words aloud.

Into her silence, Jackson said, "That's the language, right? When'd you say this takes place?"

"The 1930s maybe. Seems like it."

"Hasn't nothing much changed, not down south."

"Well, there's some of that language spoken by hateful people. A lot of troubles are suggested, but you can feel the threat in the way people look at the children and talk about the lawyer, not to his face of course."

Jackson's posture grew rigid. "That's how it works. Sometimes to your face, sometimes behind your back."

Lolly paused. She hadn't meant to rile him, just demonstrate her interest in a story that she assumed would represent a subject close to his heart—the opportunity for justice. Jackson had shared his music; this was what she had to share. She turned to another bookmarked page she had practiced reading and tried for a different effect.

"Okay. So, here's another part where it's nighttime and the children go looking for their father, who turns out to be sitting in front of the jail where Tom's locked up inside. I'll read it to you, but don't laugh. I'm kind of slow."

Jackson settled back in his chair and hooked his thumbs into his pockets. "I haven't laughed at you yet."

Lolly took a deep breath and read in a halting voice.

In ones and twos, men got out of the cars. Shadows became substance as light revealed solid shapes moving toward the jail door. Atticus remained where he was. The men hid from view.

"He in there, Mr. Finch?" a man said.

"He is," we heard Atticus answer. "And he's asleep.

Don't wake him up."

In obedience to my father, there followed what I later realized was a sickeningly comic aspect of an unfunny situation: the men talked in near-whispers.

"You know what we want," another man said. "Get aside from the door, Mr. Finch."

"You can turn around and go home again, Walter," Atticus said pleasantly. "Heck Tate's around somewhere."

"The hell he is," said another man. "Heck's bunch's so deep in the woods they won't get out till morning.'"

At that point, Lolly stopped to let her breath catch up with the words she'd been reciting. She looked at Jackson, who was silent behind his dark glasses. "So," she said, "it was a mob of men trying to get at Tom. They were going to ... lynch him. They go away unhappy when the children interrupt and call out to the men, who they recognize."

There was a pause before Jackson said, "But they don't lynch him."

"No."

"So, the kids and the attorney, they saved him that time. Not later, no one could save him from the jury, that's what I heard. But just then at the jail, they made all the difference."

"That's right."

"See?" said Jackson. "That's what I'm talking about. Young kids, attorneys, regular people, anyone can set their minds to making a difference."

That's not what Lolly meant! She said, "It turns out they make a difference by *staying put*. They change things, just an inch, in their own town. Change happens slowly, but it happens."

Jackson tilted his head a fraction. "Where do you suppose that lawyer got his law training? Was there a law school in that town?"

Lolly thought a moment. "I'd say it was too small."

"No college or university." Stated like a given. "So, to make a difference in his own town that lawyer had to first go away, then come back and make a difference the way he knew how."

He had her there. "I ... okay, that's probably true," said Lolly. "But don't forget, this story is happening in the South, with good folks threatened, folks who are trying to do good. That's how people—innocent people—get killed. When they're trying to do good. This is just a story but I know that happens. There can be people who are trying to stick up for others, it's not even their fight, and they're the ones getting hurt."

"You know what they say—the tough things make you stronger if they don't kill you. Anyway, it *is* their fight. It's everyone's fight. It might not seem like that now because it looks like it's about Negro rights, but trust me, it's about rights for all people. For you too. And people have got to be willing to do their part."

"Even if they die?"

"That man Tom in the book, didn't he die?"

"They killed him."

He nodded and looked away, as if from behind his blacked-out glasses he could see into the distance. "It's got to be like this," he said. "There's always been kids standing up for what's right. Trying to desegregate schools and like that, but making a law is one thing, and taking that walk is another. If young kids can be that brave, so can the rest of us, we got to do our part too. Even when protesters went missing, the order down south gave way not one inch. Hell, there's been barely a budge in Reno, if you don't count the Harlem Club and this place. The New China Club, too. You know who Sammy Davis, Jr. is, that Puerto Rican singer?"

"From television."

"Right. So, if he comes to town to perform in a big club, you suppose he gets to stay like the white singers do in the hotel that's got the club?"

Lolly understood that if Jackson was asking, he already knew the answer.

He continued. "No Negroes are welcome in those places. They'd probably pay him good, but they don't want him in their restaurants or walking in their hotel hallways. His money, the cash they paid him, would be no good at the tables or in the bars. They'd escort him out of there faster than you could shake a stick."

Lolly's heart fell another notch. The more Jackson spoke about race, the more animated he grew, his hands shaping the air as he spoke. She said, "People are getting killed. You said so yourself. If you go, you might be next."

"I might."

"You don't sound bothered by it."

"Well, I am. But I'm more bothered by the idea of another fifty years of segregation and colored people being relegated to shit jobs—

pardon my language. I've got an uncle, for instance, who's a porter on the Great Northern Railroad. That's a serving job and they like Negroes for that kind of work. On the same train could he be a conductor? No. Could he be an engineer? There's never going to be a time when he could be anything but a porter unless a million of us protest Jim Crow attitudes everywhere we find them. Unless we march for the chance to make a decent life for ourselves, as decent as anyone else." He rubbed his face with his hands and adjusted his glasses. "Someday I'll find a way to get there. If I could just get close, I could be a part of it, but every damn thing gets in the way."

Lolly's argument had backfired. Not only that, but she herself might be one of those "damn things" getting in Jackson's way, doing her damnedest to convince him to deny his own dreams of doing the kind of good that he could envision as clear as day. She lacked his appetite to fight those who used violence against people who didn't fit their ideas of right and proper. She had already stood too close to that windmill with Russell, but she also knew the cost of looking away, of pretending that without much ado, everything would work out okay. Jesus. Jackson's battles were the sort she couldn't imagine fighting. She hadn't even fought her own yet.

Still, she couldn't shake her unease about some of the news stories she'd seen on television. "If you travel south and someone tries to hurt you," she said, "how will you protect yourself? Your cane?"

Jackson slid one hand into the front pocket of his black pants and brought out a slender silver knife. With the press of a button its flashing blade flew out. Lolly's breath caught. "Do you always carry that?" she asked, wide-eyed. "All the time? Even when you work?"

Jackson nodded. "Can't be too careful." He closed the switchblade and pocketed it.

Lolly's thoughts raced back to other knives. All knives were not the same, of course they weren't. But still, she wished Jackson, of all people, didn't need to carry one. He clearly intended to protect what little he had. He had a cause that meant more to him than any argument she could mount. He had dreams, and drive, and a knife. She knew what else he needed—for her to say the one thing that was useful to him instead of only to herself. It would mean giving up the connection they had built together out of conversation, music, and steady work, but she said it anyway. "How about taking a train? I came west on the bus but the tracks run through that same canyon.

There must be trains that can take a person anywhere."

Jackson gave a grunt. "I thought of that. But there's no way for me to buy a ticket without the whole world knowing. My family always knows where I am."

"They don't want you going?"

"My mom is the one holding everyone to it. Isn't one of them wants to end up on her wrong side."

Lolly was forming a picture of Jackson's many obstacles. "Did you ever try to get yourself a ticket?"

"What good would it do? I can't very well sneak away. Got to pack a bag, got to get to the station on time."

"What about the bus, or a taxi?"

"I had a bus driver go right past. And the taxis, some of them will pick you up, some won't. I don't ever risk a taxi for getting anywhere on time."

"Even if you dress nice?"

He just shrugged.

Lolly sensed Jackson slipping through her fingers but she held out hope that all he needed was to ask after the cost of tickets and the train routes. Maybe there would be sufficient satisfaction in taking that one step toward what he held in his imagination, for the time being. She said, "Do you want us to go together and ask about tickets?"

He sat up straighter. "You mean it?"

"Of course I mean it, but not today. I've got to get to work."

"Then when? How soon?"

Now he sounded like he could hardly wait to see her again, the way she had been feeling about him without reciprocation. She was stung by the obvious—that Jackson's desire to leave Reno was stronger than staying and being her friend. But still, this favor meant they would spend a bit extra time together. She said, "We could go tomorrow. I suppose trains run every day to a place like this."

"Tomorrow's good. I could skip the potluck and catch a ride here. Make like I got extra cleaning to do. Little George, he'll give me a ride to work." He shook his head. "But wait. I can't meet you there. I'm not good at walking all the way to downtown. It's too chancy to miss a turn."

"If I meet you here, we can walk together."

His face showed relief. "Man, that'd be a trick if I could get a ticket."

He held his hands out, palms up, and she moved closer to place her hands in his. He gave her hands a squeeze. "This means a lot to me," he said. "Even the attempt."

"I know," she said. "I know exactly what it means."

Twenty-one

That night Lolly headed home directly after her shift. She no longer had the heart to watch Jackson play his father's guitar in a lounge where he couldn't even stay to watch the next act. Also, there was the realization that he might soon leave Reno and she'd still be here.

The temperature felt near to freezing and clouds sat like a blanket drawn low across the valley, lit pink by the downtown lights. Lolly had never lived in a place where the clouds did that. Her breath rose in plumes as she walked the six blocks from the Paradise back to the boarding house, where Mrs. R greeted her with, "Good Lord, aren't you frozen? Come into the kitchen for a hot drink. I've got some nice navy bean soup, and there's cornbread with honey."

Lolly let Mrs. R take her coat and lead her into the warm kitchen where Anna was seated at the table with a cup of coffee and a magazine.

"We're kibitzing," said the redhead. "I always forget how cold it can get here, in March no less."

"We're having a coffee and brandy," said Mrs. R. "I hardly ever do, but Anna suggested it, and by golly, I had an old bottle of brandy still tucked in the back of a cupboard."

Lolly went to the counter and poured two fingers of Mrs. R's brandy into a mug and topped it off with coffee. Because her digestion was still persnickety, she'd eaten toast with jam at the coffee shop counter, but she now agreed to a bowl of soup to busy herself with.

"Long day?" asked Anna.

Lolly nodded.

"Seems like you're one busy lady. Seeing someone?"

Lolly took a sip from her mug. It had cooled just enough. She could sense Mrs. R listening as she rolled out cookie dough. Lolly answered, "We're not dating. Just friends."

"Someone from work?"

"You could say that."

Mrs. R broke in. "That casino boss? The one who took you to dinner?"

"Ah," said Anna, "a boss."

"Not a boss," said Lolly. "Not even close." She felt a twinge of regret that Campbell was no longer in the picture and then wondered why she felt that way. Maybe because they might have gotten to know each other if he hadn't left, and if she hadn't turned toward Jackson and ... clearly it was no use dwelling on a situation she couldn't change.

"Someone special then. To give you that faraway look." Anna seemed to be reading Lolly's thoughts without knowing how close *and* how far she was from guessing the truth. Lolly indeed knew someone special who might leave her in a heartbeat, and she used to know someone with, well, *potential*, who had disappeared. She shrugged. She wouldn't name names, but Anna's gaze was warm and Lolly felt she could safely offer, "A musician, actually, but it's not looking like it will work out, you know, in the end."

"I dated a musician for a while," said Anna. "He had great hands."

Mrs. R gave a snort as she worked at sealing a log of cookie dough in butcher paper.

"*What*?" said Anna with a grin. "He played piano."

The next morning, Lolly met Jackson in front of the Polka Dot. The sky hunched above the valley as if keeping watch over the snow it had deposited overnight. Jackson wore his work clothes topped with an overcoat. When Lolly remarked about his fedora, he said, "It was my father's. I wear it sometimes."

For thirty minutes they advanced slowly through the neighborhood leaving two sets of undulating tracks that turned to slush after they passed. Now and then, Jackson caught a toe on one of the uneven places in the sidewalk that his cane skimmed past. After his fourth half-stumble, Lolly stopped him.

"There's got to be a better way," she said. There was a bit of traffic on the street, but no taxis in sight. "We're still six blocks from the station."

"This is my reality. Everything goes slow."

"I hope you think it's worth it."

"Even trying is worth it."

"What if you trip over a broken piece of sidewalk?"

"Don't get hurt trying to catch me, just let me go. Falling won't kill me."

They moved ahead at a halting pace. Lolly couldn't think of a subject to talk about and Jackson seemed focused on keeping his balance. They walked in silence until with no preamble he said, "I'm not sure I've got it clear how you chose Reno. I mean lots of people go to Las Vegas for divorces."

Lolly hadn't told anyone, not even Mrs. R, what had propelled her to this place. She and Jackson had mainly talked about music and work, and his need to protest for Negro rights. She said, "It wasn't really divorce that brought me here. Not at first, even though that's what I'm working on now. I came because of ... well, that girl I told you about."

Right then, Jackson tipped off balance again. She automatically thrust her hand beneath his elbow and would have left it there for safety, but when he straightened he gave his arm a twitch, so she withdrew it. He said, "The one you were close to?"

Lolly's thoughts now leapt to girls and closeness and whether she might herself be carrying a girl, or that which might become a girl, if she let it. Once more she felt the clock ticking in the background of everything she did.

"You there?" he asked.

"What? Oh. The same one who was like a sister, for a while. You could say I'm looking for clues. She was working here, back in 1960. That sounds silly, I suppose. I've come three years too late. She's gone, but here I am anyway." The whole thing *did* sound silly in a way, if you didn't know the circumstances that had delayed her. Oklahoma and all that. She tried to make light of her timing. "And you thought *you* were slow."

When the drapery of clouds overhead began dropping snowflakes, turning the air white around them, Lolly pulled out a pleated rain bonnet and tied it over her hair. They walked on.

Jackson spoke at last. "So, it's probably not about her anymore if she's not here but you are."

Once again Lolly's thoughts reached for Norma Jeane. Shouldn't she have found traces of her friend around Reno? More than she had? If not in church teachings, then maybe along the downtown streets. The closest she'd come was that glorious Mapes view stretching out to the mountains and skyward.

It seemed now that her expectations could not be met by the reality around her. Plus, her own reality had changed dramatically. Like she had once told Caldwell—things were complicated.

She said, "We're at Fourth Street. Time to cross."

The green light changed before they reached the other side, the sparse traffic accommodating their pace. Lolly's thoughts circled back to Norma Jeane and what Rachel, the young Jewish wife, had told her. "Do you think people are truly gone when they pass on?" she asked Jackson.

"Are you asking if a soul stays behind when the body dies?"

"If a soul did stay, could another person feel it nearby? Would it feel like anything? Like love, maybe, or friendship?"

Jackson stopped in his tracks and turned toward Lolly, his expression unreadable. "I used to recite what I learned in childhood, about God and heaven and all. But when I lost my eyesight a lot of that left me, so I don't have any answers for anyone but me, and I'm not often sure about them."

Lolly was left musing, with no apt reply. She said, "The tracks are up ahead. That's the corner with the New China Club. Then it's half a block to the right."

Jackson began moving again. He said, "That club—that's Bill Fong's place. You ever go there?"

"No. I work until kind of late, and if I stay out, it's mostly in the Paradise."

"It's a nightclub. A mixed club. All kinds of people and good music."

"Like the Polka Dot?"

"Different. They got an International Night. You know, music from other places."

"Maybe I'll go sometime."

"Be sure to go with someone."

Lolly's feelings flared with hurt. He wasn't offering to escort her himself and she did not possess any other options. When she said, "I'm not dating anyone," her voice sounded angrier than she meant it to. "I went to your club and that worked fine."

"By yourself?"

"With friends."

"A group is fine. All I'm saying is don't go by yourself to any of these mixed places. They'll take it wrong."

Lolly wanted to protest but Jackson's comment rang with such authority that she walked on in silence. An hour in the slush and snow had brought them to the station entrance, where Jackson doffed his hat and knocked the snow from it and Lolly untied her pleated rain cap and did the same. Inside, they pulled off their gloves and stomped their shoes on the carpeted door mats.

The station air was thick with the odors of wool coats and damp leather shoes. Eight double benches set atop a checkered floor held people in various states of waiting or preparation. One man gripped a handful of red and yellow hothouse flowers. As Lolly directed Jackson through the center aisle littered with travel cases and tumbling children, the gazes of those without conversation or newspapers followed them.

The ticket counter was set into the east end of the waiting area under a ceiling hung with etched-glass light fixtures. Lolly and Jackson waited in a short line and when their turn came, stepped close. The counter agent spoke without looking up from rummaging in his cash drawer. He said, "What can I do for you?"

Jackson spoke. "I want to take the train to Alabama. Can I get there from here?"

The agent's attention leaped to Jackson, to Lolly, then back to Jackson. He said, "You want a big city, that's Montgomery. There's all kind of connections will get you *there*."

"My second choice is Mississippi; last is Washington."

"Washington state?"

"D.C."

The agent looked a little harder at Jackson. "That's a lot of choices. You shopping or you going to buy?"

Lolly bristled at the agent's words. What kind of question was that? What if they *were* just shopping for options? Wasn't it this man's job to help them?

Jackson kept a half-smile on his face as he answered. "I'm here to buy. I just need the amount."

"All right then," said the agent, pulling a set of timetables and charts from a heap near his elbow. With stained fingers, he grasped a pencil and mumbled as he began to list numbers on the scratchpad before him. "I've got routes through Kansas City, or Dallas. You folks got a preference?"

"Make it Kansas City," said Jackson.

"That'll take you through Salt Lake." He bent back over his charts. In another minute he looked up and pulled an adding machine toward him. With one stubby finger he stabbed its keys and rang up a total. "Get you to K.C. for $95.75 and Montgomery for another $85." He looked up from his figures. "Grand total—one-eighty and six bits, each."

Jackson's exhale could be heard above the station's sounds. He asked, "When does it go?"

Consulting his calendar, the man said, "I got one next Friday at three p.m."

Jackson nodded. "I'll take one ticket."

The man looked from Jackson to Lolly again. "Just one?"

"That's right," said Jackson.

"Well then I can't," said the clerk. He looked aggrieved about having tallied all the figures only to arrive at a sticking point.

"I have the money," said Jackson.

"It's not the money."

"Then what is it?"

"Aren't you carrying one of those blind canes?"

Jackson's cane was in his right hand, which was pressed against the front lip of the counter. He lifted it a bit to show he had it with him.

"Then that's the breaks. Company rules are: No tickets may be sold to solo travelers who can't take care of themselves. I sell you a ticket, I might get canned."

Jackson went silent but Lolly could not resist interjecting, "What about someone who works a job, two jobs, and gets around fine?" The agent couldn't know it, but she'd seen what a lot of people never would—what a reliable worker and employee Jackson was. Better than some who weren't blind. He navigated the Paradise, the alleys out back of it, managed to get around town, and hadn't he just walked all the way to the station in the snow? No one had carried him there. She would have misgivings about the type of violence he might encounter at his destination, but traveling by train would not undo him. She felt a further desire to protest rise up inside her, but Jackson's silence dampened her willingness to start an argument which might make him seem less than capable of making his own case.

The man looked as if he were done with the two of them. "I make no bones about how a person gets by on their own. I only do what I'm told, and I'm told I can't sell tickets to crippled people unless they've got someone to go with them. There are places where you've got to collect your luggage and change trains. Some connections have multiple terminals and travelers have to keep on time. Trains don't wait for anyone. You can see how that's a problem just waiting to happen."

Jackson shook his head as if hearing a familiar story. After a moment he turned away from the ticket window.

Beneath the cross-hatched ceiling and ornate lights, they took adjacent seats separated by curved armrests. Jackson wilted into his as if the day weighed more than it ought to. Lolly sat quiet for a few minutes, studying the floor. Jackson's shoes looked sodden; his trouser cuffs too. At last Lolly asked, "If you had bought a ticket today—say there weren't rules like that agent claims—and then you traveled to where people are hurting Negros and something awful happened to you, it would be my fault too for helping you. I would feel awful."

Jackson remained slumped a moment before he turned his face toward her and said, "I appreciate what you're saying, but it's not on you what happens to me. And it's not enough for me to talk about the way people disrespect Negroes and talk hate about them. I have to *do* something. I can't simply wait here for things to happen. I already spend a lot of my time waiting."

"You'll go to a dangerous place, even if you could get hurt, or killed?"

"It's like enlisting in the military. They don't only call people up, they've got people who volunteer. And why? Because they think it's right. The odds are usually lousy. Shitty in fact. But people volunteer. This isn't so different."

Lolly shook her head, though he couldn't see her. She thought about Russell, who took on rodeo broncs, which could hurt a person, but that wasn't the same. Russell's was a personal challenge, and he also wanted bragging rights. Jackson's endeavor was a true cause.

Jackson continued, "I'm not worth much to my people's cause in this town. This place will be one of the last to change. I could do more if I could just join up with others. Seems like that's going to be as hard as I thought."

The station clock chimed eleven as a loudspeaker called the

imminent arrival of a train from San Francisco and its departure for Salt Lake City in half an hour. Lolly gave a start and checked her watch. She said, "We'd better get you back, and I've got to go to work."

Jackson blew out a breath and rose to his feet.

The spring snowstorm had quit but what it left behind would quickly turn to slush. She said, "We'll never make it walking. We need a taxi." She led Jackson to the curb outside where four taxis sat idling. The closest driver rolled down his window. "Taxi, Miss? One or both of you?" he asked them.

"Both," said Lolly.

The driver paused a moment before getting out to open the front passenger door for her. She shook her head and pointed. "We'll ride in back."

When they were settled onto the wide seat, Lolly told the driver, "We're going two places."

"Where to first?"

Lolly turned to Jackson. "What's your address?"

"I've got some work to do at the club."

Lolly lowered her voice and leaned toward him. "*Your* address. You're soaking wet."

"I've got work," he said.

"At least go home and change your shoes. The left one's coming apart."

"Damn."

"Hey folks," said the driver. "We're wasting daylight."

"All right," said Jackson. "Park Street, two blocks east of the police station. Number twenty-six, dark green duplex with white trim."

"Then the Paradise Club," said Lolly, "Virginia Street entrance."

"I'll get you there," said the driver. He turned his radio to a big band program and pulled out from the curb.

Lolly felt the sting of Jackson's readiness to ride away from the friendship they'd been building toward something he couldn't even see. But she didn't like how the railroad was just plain wrong to put hurdles in the way of people who needed to travel. Certain people. Though Jackson would have to learn his way around the passenger cars and find his way to the lavatory, that didn't make him a troublemaker. He was adaptable and steady but they weren't going to give him a fair shake, which made her want to change the odds against him.

Lolly leaned toward Jackson and tried to speak beneath the Glenn Miller song playing on the radio. "How much money do you have?" she asked.

"Enough for what we were doing," said Jackson.

The driver, who had been slouched in his seat, straightened perceptibly.

"Give it to me."

Jackson swiveled slightly in her direction. "What for?"

"I've got a plan." When she caught the driver watching them in the rear-view mirror, he slid his gaze back to the road. She said to Jackson, "If you arrive with a ticket they'll have to let you board."

"I wouldn't be too sure."

"Once you've got a proper, legal ticket, what can they do? They won't know how you came by it. And if they fuss you can declare that your ... um, travel companion has already boarded. That they're waiting for you."

Jackson looked to be working his jaw. "Where'd you get an idea like that?" he asked. After a moment he said, "Think it'll work?"

"I figure what they don't know won't hurt them."

"And when there's no one saving me a seat?"

"Make up an excuse. Your friend has gone to use the lavatory, anything to delay until the train leaves. I don't suppose they'd want the fuss of throwing a blind man off the train with all those people watching. You might complain to City Hall or take your story to the newspapers."

"I'll be damned," Jackson said quietly. "You're full of surprises."

Lolly sat back, more pleased than when she'd shared the Mockingbird story. Still, the thought of what she'd just suggested made her stomach sink. Jackson was sure to end up far away from this taxi, this town, her.

When the driver turned east on Second Street, Lolly voiced that which had come to her earlier. "You'll need a reliable ride to the station. And maybe ... someone ought to travel with you. Not just for the train, but for whatever's waiting on the other end. I hate to say it but that agent was probably right about how tricky it could be to get around a big city, all those streets and buildings."

"Little George, maybe," said Jackson, "but we haven't ever talked about going away from here."

So, Little George was Jackson's choice on a moment's notice.

"Would he go with you?" she asked.

"Maybe, but it doesn't matter because I don't have that kind of cash and he's always broke. Your idea about *my* ticket, though, that might work." Jackson pulled his wallet from an inside coat pocket. Lolly counted silently as Jackson pulled bills out, fingering the turned down corners of them as he handed them over. When he stopped at a hundred and eighty, he had just three fives left.

On a whim, Lolly joked, "I think you've made me rich."

"Bet I haven't. That wouldn't be like you."

"I guess you do know me. Keep your fives. I've got the change."

"You sure?"

Lolly's next question was like asking for heartbreak. "When do you want to go?"

He looked away as if he was glancing out the window. "Right away, I suppose. I wouldn't want to give anyone the chance to stop me somehow."

Lolly wondered if he was thinking of her, or his mother. She said, "Can you walk away from your apartment?

"It's in my mother's name. All of it. I can send money later to cover the last of my bills."

"Then I'll go back to the station as soon as I can. Probably not this weekend, and I have court on Monday. But after that."

"You're really going through with court?"

"Didn't you believe me?"

"Sure." He reached for her hand and gave it a pat. "Good luck with that." Then he handed her another five. "For the taxi." When she tried to push the bill back at him, his expression grew solemn so she let the topic of taxi fare drop.

When he exited to the snowbound sidewalk, the taxi began to inch forward. "Wait a minute, will you?" said Lolly.

They waited until Jackson reached the right-hand doorway before Lolly gave the okay for the driver to proceed. Then she examined Jackson's money—three or four twenties, but mostly tens and fives. The ones were flat, fives were bent at the corners, tens were folded in half, and twenties were folded twice. His was a tactile approach to accounting, which made her think of squirreled money, the kind she had been putting aside for paying Anna's lawyer—that's how she thought of Mr. Quick, as Anna's, not hers—and for the procedure she had scheduled. *Procedure*, the most benign way of putting it.

Dr. Hall had said there was no way a pregnancy test would detect how far gone she was—six or seven weeks, or maybe eight. As long as it wasn't yet twelve, the end result would be the same.

Passages from her Catholic lessons rose up in her mind: Deliver us from the fires of hell, and another phrase about drawing all souls to heaven. *Dominus* and *spiritus*. Latin had always been beyond her. She preferred plain English, thank you, though obviously, the language of money was becoming more important.

Lolly tucked Jackson's cash into the zipped pocket of her tote. In contrast to Russell, Jackson trusted her, counting on her to help liberate him from a town that now represented an obstacle to his life's plan. Her offer to buy his ticket represented his best chance to reshape the trajectory of his life. She understood. Her own stash of money was earmarked for reshaping her own future. All that money for changing what sheer willpower could not. There wasn't a lot you could do without money. You could breathe, or maybe love someone.

The taxi let Lolly out along the same curb where she'd first seen Jackson wait for a ride. She paid the driver and added fifty cents for good measure. He seemed motivated by her largesse and came around to hold the car door for her, touching the brim of his plaid newsboy cap as he bid her good day.

With only ten minutes to spare, Lolly hurried to the alley entrance and made her way to the coffee shop. There she signaled the restaurant manager that she'd be back in a moment and went to stash her overshoes and coat where they would dry. Back at her post she folded her tote, which held the means for fulfilling Jackson's dream, and locked it in the cupboard beneath the hostess stand. As she pocketed the key, a middle-aged couple approached. Lolly put on her best smile and got to work.

In the lounge later, Lolly regretted having missed any of Jackson's previous performances. Now that he was bent on leaving, she would have few remaining opportunities to watch him or request a song, or even to just stand close. She ordered a bourbon and water and took a seat with the best vantage of the performance corner, trying to memorize the set of his jaw and the slight tilt of his head when he leaned into a song. She wondered if he'd take his guitar with him. People did that sometimes, carried not just memories with them, but objects from their past. Also, he might find work as a musician. That is if he made it through the first challenge he had set for himself—traveling to a distant place and arriving intact.

It was odd, how in knowing that Jackson meant to leave, she could feel herself conflicted over wanting to help him versus becoming the helper for his exit. She had feelings for him that she didn't know how to name.

For an hour she sat sipping cocktails that took the edge off the emptiness building inside her and wondered if Jackson could sense her keeping her distance. If he did, he didn't show it, which was good because she didn't want to breach the shield she'd been constructing against the day he would leave.

At the house, Lolly greeted Mrs. R, who offered her a cup of tea. When Lolly declined, saying she would turn in early, Mrs. R said, "I forgot to ask. Did you choose an obstetrician?"

Lolly's thoughts spun back to her conversation with Dr. Hall. She glanced down at her hands. "I saw a doctor last week."

"He'll probably recommend vitamins. There are certain kinds they'll want you to take. When do you go back?"

Lolly, flagging now, leaned against the counter with a hand to her temple. "Wednesday," she said automatically. An honest answer without giving away anything.

Mrs. R threw a glance at Anna, who returned a thoughtful look, saying, "A busy week. Anything else?"

Lolly's voice sounded weary, even to herself. "I need to say goodbye to someone who's leaving town."

The landlady nodded. "Is she going far? Or he?"

"East." She knew now which city she'd buy a train ticket for.

Anna asked, "To visit someone?"

"He's got, um, business there."

Anna asked, "Will you see him off?"

"I'm not sure."

"Is it the musician?"

Lolly nodded.

"Might make sense to play it down. People sometimes get the wrong idea, even if you have followed the process and have a divorce on the way," said Mrs. R.

"You might be tempted to join him," said Anna, startling Lolly. "People sometimes leap again too soon."

Lolly studied Anna through a mental haze. What was the woman thinking?

Anna tapped the tabletop with one manicured finger. "I only mean that leaping comes easy, once you find your legs."

Upstairs and kneeling beside her bed, Lolly felt momentarily at a loss. She had ramped up her prayers lately, primarily because she felt destined to collide with a mighty force. Her divorce was both difficult and necessary, a fact she accepted. It was the *other* decision for which prayer seemed requisite.

Some people she had known, devout people, asserted that a person should never pray for themselves, only on someone else's behalf. If that was the case, she'd been doing it wrong all this time. Of course there were others who could benefit. Jackson, for one. She did want him kept safe. If he was set on joining the machinery of protests and the battle for Negro rights, she wanted someone to keep him safe. God seemed the likely candidate but she hated to rely on a thing if it couldn't be counted on.

Another choice might be Saint Cecilia from Trinity Church. Should she appeal to the stained-glass Saint on behalf of a musician who as far as she could tell had never been Episcopalian? She herself wasn't Episcopalian either. Nor was she Catholic, in spite of the nuns' best efforts. Nor did she follow any of the religions her old friend had sampled. Maybe she was turning into Norma Jeane, a nomad in need of a way of believing that aligned with her personal situation.

It seemed obvious to ask a simple blessing for Mrs. R and Anna, who each grew dearer to her by the day, but there remained someone else. At the back of her mind sat Caldwell, the true disbeliever. She had the urge to ask a blessing for him, wherever he was and whoever he was with, but given his disbelief, that might be silly, or stupid—or maybe even sacrilegious. She wished that instead of cutting their exchange short, she had asked Caldwell for his views about a meaningful life. A good life. She could have asked, *If not God, then what?* If not a creator and all-knowing Father, then what could people believe in? Only themselves?

In light of the week to come, Lolly added a plea for guidance regarding the one challenge that might fundamentally change her ... into what, she couldn't say. Mostly she hoped to weather the coming week with her self-regard intact.

A short while later, Lolly woke with a start, on her knees, her face pressed into the quilt atop her bed. Her newest pint bottle of Old Grand-Dad had fallen from her hand and landed upright, not a drop spilled. She found its cap and spun it on, then tucked the bottle under her bed before she crawled in beneath the soft old quilts. Either prayers would work, or they wouldn't. All she could do now was sleep.

Twenty-two

S unday morning passed swiftly, with Lolly focused on a neighbor woman who had brought her young daughter for a trim. The day shone bright with a return to the warmth of spring and the suggestion of renewal, but Lolly would find no pleasure in this week until she kept her promises to herself and Jackson.

She had somehow spent a lot of precious years yielding to the losses in her life—an old friend now dead, and a marriage crumbling atop its wobbly foundation. Meantime, Jackson had been trying to gaze with blind eyes upon a future he believed in, one he could influence by heading for the action where clashing fists and marching feet rang as loudly as voices. He seemed oblivious to the perils that might await him elsewhere, but she knew that danger could as easily live at home as among strangers. Though she hadn't enough money to do so this moment, she had set her sights on purchasing two train tickets so that Jackson could travel with a companion. She wanted him safe, and to make that happen she needed to get her hands on more money.

In addition to dressing for work, she folded her good suit and her best shoes into her tote bag and swept her curls to the top of her head, spraying them into place with a bit of Final Net. A more formal hairdo that would serve her after work when she got down to a bit of risky business. From her hidden envelope of cash, she pulled four twenties. She knew of only one legitimate way to triple them in a hurry. It didn't always work, but when it did, it was out of this world.

After her shift, Lolly changed her clothes and walked the four blocks to the Mapes, a casino that was still on her mind. Stepping through the east entrance she realized that this was where she should have been gambling all along. Not because it was larger and ritzier than the Paradise, which it was. Nor because its clientele smiled wider, which they did. Not even because it was also home to a drug store, a boutique, and a radio station, but because when she crossed the casino's threshold, she could feel the spirit of Norma Jeane. The lush gold and red appointments, the gleaming chandeliers overhead, and the dealers in pressed white shirts and bolo ties held by silver slides set with turquoise. Every object, every person shone a degree brighter. Even the slot machines had better posture. At the coat room she relinquished her coat and tote bag.

"Wait," she said to the room's attendant. Retrieving her tote, she pulled out Jackson's wad of cash and tucked it into one of the snapped sections of her clutch. Not that the coat check girl would pocket a guest's fortune, but why tempt fate? With Lolly, Jackson's money was safe. She stepped to the bank of public payphones and called home to tell Mrs. R not to wait up.

"Are you all right?" asked Mrs. R. "Anything wrong?"

"Just staying out late," said Lolly.

"You haven't cancelled your court date tomorrow?"

"Not at all. I'll be there."

The casino was a living creature of many parts, table games in the center, slot machines around the perimeter, a bar at each end, and a coffee shop in one corner. Employees attended to the whims of customers while customers attended to their own pleasures. Far above the casino floor, the Sky Room looked out across the city lights. There would be no band on a Sunday night, but patrons could move seamlessly from its panoramic view to the mirrored elevators that delivered them back to earthbound rows of mechanized slots and felt-topped table games. A Life magazine photo once showed the film director John Huston playing craps while flanked by cast members of his Misfits film. Posed around the felted table, the crew wore harried looks, as if after a long day on the set it took a lot of energy to conjure up some fun.

Lolly knew nothing about the playing of craps or roulette, but she could add numbers with the best of them. She made her way to a blackjack table and paused to watch two gamblers. The dealer delivered red-and-white cards printed with the Mapes cowboy, whose chaps-clad legs formed a capital M. When the dealer had paid the man's winning hand and swept away the woman's bet, the woman looked up and caught Lolly's eye. Cigarette smoke curled genie-like above her head as she slid her ashtray to one side. "There's room for you," she said.

Lolly's gaze slipped to the woman's stacks of gaming chips and silver dollars. "Are you ahead?"

"I was up for a while, then down. Now I'm about even." The woman tipped her chin toward the dealer. "Franklin, here, is just back from his break. I'm hoping he'll deal me a reason to sit awhile longer."

The dealer gave a small smile and shuffled the deck a fourth time.

The woman sat erect on her tall-legged stool. No dainty gestures or attitude of apology for her choice of Sunday night entertainment. Recognizing the woman's determination, Lolly slid into the seat farthest from the column of smoke and pulled out a twenty. If she were to steer her own course through the events on the near horizon, she'd need the resolve to gamble with all the concentration she could muster. When the dealer offered her the deck to cut, she did so with a steady hand.

The game progressed and Lolly fell into the same patterns as the other players, rarely deviating from what was considered smart play. She took a break whenever Franklin took one, walking a slow circuit around the casino floor and at one point ascending to stroll past the mezzanine shops. Passing the elevator bank, she turned toward the ladies' lavatory and went in to stand before the mirror. Outwardly she looked the same, but now she felt different on the inside. The night's gambling had not sent up fireworks, but she had played more successfully than some. The man in the cowboy hat, for instance. He had called her "Ma'am" and tipped his hat as he took a seat between hers and another fellow's. Within a short time, the cowboy had run out of five-dollar chips. When he glanced for the final time at Lolly's small stacks of chips and silver, he shook his head. She knew what he meant. Some nights were not for winning.

As soon as she thought about *some nights*, her luck vanished, swallowing almost all her money in the next dozen hands. She'd been holding her own for about six hours but now, out of the eighty she'd brought, only five dollars remained. She sat before Franklin, knots forming in her stomach.

She had devised a three-part plan that, while expensive, felt right. #1 was her divorce, already secured with a bank draft that Mr. Quick would expect from her later this morning; #2, the purchase of an extra train ticket for Jackson; and lastly, $225 for her medical procedure. She needed to win a boat load of money or something would have to give.

Franklin gave her a contrite smile, as if he had siphoned the cash straight out of her hand. Lolly couldn't help but think that's what came of gambling. Not long after meeting her bartender friend Roger, she told him she hadn't anything to lose. By which she'd meant money, but now she truly had so much at stake. Things that money could buy, including Jackson's dream of being a catalyst for change, and freeing herself from the result of her rape by Russell.

With a deep breath Lolly opened her clutch to the section that held Jackson's money, just shy of two hundred dollars. *He wants this to work*, she told herself, swallowing hard. If he truly welcomed the physical risks necessary to enlarge his world, he might be willing to risk his savings too. *It's now or never*, she told herself. *Be brave.* Still, she felt a little dizzy at the prospect of jeopardizing Jackson's savings without even asking him.

"I need a few minutes," she told Franklin.

"Sure," he said. "I'm about to go on break. I'll tell them you'll be back."

Leaving three silver dollars to hold her place, Lolly rose and stood a moment, gathering equilibrium. A cocktail waitress in a spangled western costume (the same one who had come around hourly) appeared and offered drinks around.

"Water," said Lolly. "This time hold the bourbon."

The waitress noted Lolly's order as another dealer stepped in to take over Franklin's deck of cards.

By Lolly's calculations she had twenty minutes until Franklin returned to complete the last of his shift. Twenty minutes to change her luck.

She went straight away to the closest ladies' lavatory where she washed her hands and applied fresh lipstick. Her eyes ached from having spent hours studying cards after working a shift at the Paradise, which at this point had been yesterday. Red-rimmed eyes looked back at her from the mirror. A loser's eyes. She wished they weren't.

Returning to the casino, Lolly looked around. At just shy of 3:30 a.m. the place was nearly empty with the gamblers remaining either on winning streaks or possessed of an unerring faith in their ability to prevail. Winners and losers—two sides of the same coin, and all of them survivors. The coming hours held the start of a new work week for most people. Lolly was due in court at 11:00. If she left soon, she would have just enough time for a bath and a nap before preparing to meet Mr. Quick. But of course, if she left now she would leave a loser.

Lolly opened her clutch again and extracted Jackson's money. One hundred and eighty-five smackaroos. The money hadn't brought him much luck lately, unless befriending her counted for that. It was time to pay off his faith in her.

Bills in hand, Lolly made a circuit of the casino floor, stopping by every player of a slot machine, the three roulette players, and the ten others scattered among the four blackjack tables open in the wee hours. She greeted each and asked them to bestow good fortune by touching the wad of cash she held out to them.

Most accommodated her request. Two declined, casting sideways looks at her, and two asked her to return the favor for their pots of coins. She ended up back at Franklin's table a few minutes after he was back from his break.

The gentleman who had been at first base earlier was gone, but Lolly's silver dollars sat alongside a glass of ice water on a cocktail coaster. Franklin smiled as Lolly shifted everything to the next seat over.

"I've changed my luck," she said.

"That right?"

"Yep."

Lolly set one hundred dollars of Jackson's cash on the table top. "In for a dime, in for ... well, all in."

Franklin flattened out the bills before changing them for playing chips, which he slid to Lolly. Shuffling the cards with a riffle he said, "I shouldn't ask this, but are you sure?"

The refrain that came to Lolly just then was from a song lyric: *Luck be a lady tonight.* She nodded as she cut the deck. "Yes. I am."

At that, Lady Luck left to powder her nose. The cards got hot for a hand or two, then cold again. Strings of winning hands, strings of losers. Each time Lolly had two good hands in a row, her next hand went bust. Whoever had said that gambling was fun must have been off their rocker. Gambling out of necessity was agonizing, gut-wrenching work. Her scalp felt damp though it wasn't particularly warm where she sat.

Half of Jackson's hundred-dollar stake took a spin then ran right down the drain. Of their combined money she'd lost $125, and with it, her trustworthiness as a friend. Lolly, now the only player at the table, called a halt to the non-stop progression of hands. "I need to think," she told Franklin. He set the card deck before him, turned his empty palms up, then clasped his hands behind his back.

With her eyes closed and her head in her hands Lolly tried to calm her breathing. She had been so sure about the rightness of her plan. She knew better than to pray for luck at gambling. The one time she'd tried that it had backfired. If only she had someone looking out for her. Norma Jeane, for instance. Her old friend could be up there right now, watching over those left behind. *Norma Jeane. Norma Jeane.* A name that had added an extra glow to Reno.

Norma Jeane would not have given up on the plans she had made for her future. Lolly didn't want to give up either. She could do this. *She could.* And none of those five-dollar bets. She sat up straighter and pushed forty dollars of Jackson's onto the circle for wagers. "Franklin," she said. "It's you and me. I'm going to win again or go home broke."

He changed her cash to chips and shuffled the cards again. "That's a lot of pressure." His dark brown eyes looked worried. He glanced around as if checking for eavesdroppers. "You know, sometimes a person's got to call it a night."

"I believe in you," said Lolly.

"Please. Don't say that."

"Pretend this is a movie we're in, you and me. I'm the girl who's come to town desperate for some extra cash because ..." Here she looked past Franklin without truly seeing the gleam of polished fixtures and leather-bound tables. "Because someone she cares about has been jailed. Wrongly. And it's going to take big money to break him out." Warming up to the story, she cut the deck with a flourish. "She's down to the last of her money earned from being ... oh, a dance hall girl."

Franklin smiled now. "And the man. Is he an outlaw?"

"That's it. The people in the town think so, but that's a mistake too. He's not dangerous. He once saved the girl, so ..."

"So, she's going to bribe the sheriff."

"Right again. And you, Mister Dealer, are the key. If she goes broke, all is lost." Lolly looked him in the eye before checking the cards he'd dealt her. Jack of spades, nine of diamonds. Franklin had a ten showing. The odds were only fifty-fifty in her favor but it turned out he had to draw a card and that eight of clubs broke his hand. Just like that, Lolly had recouped all but ten dollars of Jackson's money.

Next she bet sixty dollars. Franklin, a gleam in his eye, picked up the story line. "I suppose the dance hall girl came west because someone jilted her."

"Actually, she's looking for her sister who is ..."

"Lost."

Lolly nodded as she checked her cards. They totaled fifteen against the queen Franklin had showing. There were too many face cards and tens left in the deck for her to risk calling for another card but she did anyway. Her luck held when Franklin dealt her a four and broke his own hand again.

With that win Lolly had recovered all of Jackson's cash and fifty of her own. *Norma Jeane*, she thought, *I'm running out of time.* With a deep breath she bet a cool one hundred dollars. "My last chance to make good."

Admiration in his eyes, Franklin dealt the cards in soft arcs. He said, "The man in jail. He loves the girl."

Lolly looked at her cards—a pair of kings. Her luck had changed for the better but she really needed to quit this game or arrive wrecked for her courthouse hearing. As it was, she would only get a few hours' sleep. Franklin's words sank in at last.

"No," she said. "He doesn't."

She took a sip of water and turned her kings face up and set another hundred out to cover splitting them into two hands.

"Wow," said Franklin. "Good luck."

Lolly licked her lips and signaled for one card. He dealt her a jack. "Want to split it again?"

Lolly paused, trying to mind-read the cards in his hands.

Into her silence he said, "I guess the dance hall girl, she must love the man who's in jail."

When his words sank in, Lolly realized that she didn't know the ending for her make-believe story. It seemed a signal that she should stop betting. "I'll stay on that. Hit this other one."

An eight. She rubbed her damp hands on her skirt and flashed a palm to signal that she was done taking cards. Now for Franklin's hand.

He turned up a ten to make a hard eighteen. His features relaxed as he paid her winning hand. Knocking his knuckles on the felt he said, "This other hand's a push." After a pause he asked, "Now are you ahead?"

"Yes, though not enough." There was no use trying to milk more profit from the cards. Not tonight. Lolly tipped Franklin with a ten-dollar chip and made to leave.

"I was rooting for you," he said.

Lolly smiled. "You were? I thought maybe you were rooting for the dance hall girl."

At the cashier's cage Lolly exchanged her silver and chips for paper money. She was sixty-five dollars to the good but by her estimate still a hundred dollars short of the total she needed. At least she had summoned Lady Luck back to her side.

Outside, Lolly changed into her walking shoes and pulled on her coat. The eastern sky was a blue-violet wash above the streets and buildings, the air crisp with cold. It was her last morning as a married woman. As she headed for the boarding house she rolled her soon-to-be-divorced status around in her head. Mrs. Russell Cooper would exist no more. In her place would stand a revised version of her old self. Her court petition included an official change of name from Luella to Lolly, the name Norma Jeane had given her that held all the right connotations. Of course, coming soon there would be other changes too.

Late morning found Lolly at the courthouse amid the clacking of heels on marble floors and hushed conversations all around. As she handed Mr. Quick the envelope holding the bank draft, he delivered the bad news—Lolly's hearing would be delayed. No telling how long, perhaps through the lunch hour and beyond.

He ushered her to one of the stiff-backed benches in the hallway nearest the courtroom of Judge Whitaker, who would hear her case. On the morning of their first meeting, when Anna negotiated their arrangement, the lawyer recited the types of charges one spouse could bring against the other. The list included impotency, adultery, willful desertion, conviction of a felony, extreme cruelty, and failure to provide. Plenty of choices, though none described the case in which the whole of a person's behavior is greater than the sum of its violent parts, or whether desertion applied to matters of the heart. "Just pick one," the lawyer had said. "They're not going to ask for pictures." Now he had to remind her which one she'd chosen. Extreme cruelty.

He said, "Mr. Cooper was not served with papers, which was as you anticipated. The Woods County sheriff tried but didn't find him at either of the addresses you provided. We ran a newspaper notice as required." He glanced down the wide hallway full of benches and people moving this way and that. "Have you heard from him? Did he contact you?"

Lolly's heart gave a thump. "No! I mean, not since that first letter. I thought the papers would get to him."

Mr. Quick frowned. "Of course, we hope they do. Notice from a court action can solicit a civil response, but sometimes the other party calls the plaintiff or shows up at court without giving notice."

Lolly flashed her gaze left and right. "You mean he might come without telling us?" Her thoughts reared up like wild horses and her mouth fell open. Would Russell appear now, at this eleventh hour? He always did like others to notice his entrance, but would he drive twelve hundred miles to recount his version of things? Her withholding of affection and her refusal of marital sex? Her homerun swing of the fireplace poker?

"Now, now," he said, "it's rare but it happens. Sometimes they even come to town and skulk around looking for the other party. Wives behave that way sometimes but it's more common with men. Especially the angry type." He looked at her quizzically.

Lolly glanced around nervously. She had put so many things behind her—the bus ride and her unease in the auto motel, Russell's report to the police, which had seemed like the last-ditch effort of a man who threw rocks from the shadows. Eventually, wrapped in the embrace of Mrs. R's hospitality, she had waltzed around town without concern for her own safety. And now Mr. Quick was suggesting otherwise. "I didn't—he didn't—I haven't seen him." Her pulse raced as her mind positioned Russell on the next bench over, ready to battle her in the courtroom. If somehow he convinced the judge—a male judge, of course—that *he* was the party wronged, the judge might not approve her divorce. The money she'd spent to get this far would be for naught, and perhaps the rest of her plans too.

Mr. Quick continued. "Like I said, it's rare, but I always ask." He folded his hands atop the leather briefcase on his lap and resettled his bulk on the bench.

With the sharp taste of fear on the back of her tongue, Lolly studied the people streaming past. When at last a bailiff called her case, her eyes were raw from too little sleep coupled with wide-eyed vigilance. Following her lawyer to the courtroom door, she glimpsed a man in a sweat-stained Stetson. Not Russell; he held himself differently, but Chester maybe, Russell's newest rodeo buddy? She tried to recall Chester's body type. Stocky? Lanky? She just wasn't sure, so she kept her gaze trained on the back of the stranger, but the man moved away, his boots striking time on the marble floor.

Lolly's heart echoed in her ears until Mr. Quick took her elbow and led her into the courtroom of polished paneling and a wooden rail dividing the judge's bench and counsel tables from the gallery. No audience, thank goodness; it seemed this judge heard cases in private.

They stood when the judge came in, all flowing robes and stern countenance. They sat again at his direction. From behind his elevated bench, the judge directed preliminary questions to Mr. Quick then asked for details about shared property and children and whether Lolly was sure her marriage was irreparable.

Mr. Quick gestured that Lolly should stand. When she did, her legs trembled but somehow managed to hold her up. She lifted her eyes to the judge looming above everything present—the court clerk, the court reporter, the empty peanut gallery. When his attention wandered, she sensed that his interest in her plea was cursory at best, which meant it was a mere formality that she must choose one complaint out of the many that described an unraveling marriage. No concern of his. Why would he care whether hers demonstrated unique details? It might only matter that she appeared in the presence of a lawyer and that her filing fees had been paid. She was probably just a case number in a long string of cases he'd hear this day. Suddenly, Lolly wanted to be more than that.

Her true complaint against Russell was recorded in words written on her mind's ledger, invisible to everyone but her. Standing before this judge on his perch, she wanted to speak the truth as she knew it and inhaled to begin. Mr. Quick drew a breath, too, as in preparation to interrupt her, so Lolly spoke quickly. "Your honor, it doesn't matter that I can check a box and be done with this because I want to say out loud what my husband did. You don't have 'invisible' on your list of reasons for granting a divorce. Or 'possession.' They're not illegal, but they're cruel."

Mr. Quick tugged at her sleeve but she ignored him a minute longer and went on to describe the way Russell had forced sex upon her, and another night chased her with the same intent, her use of the fireplace poker and the knife's flash of steel. Also, how she lay alone and injured, her stitches under cotton, waiting for the morning sun so she could flee. Speaking such words aloud, she wondered why she had not left Russell sooner.

When Lolly took a breath, the judge held up his hand, abruptly ending her account. He exchanged a look with Mr. Quick, who had counseled her to speak her prescribed lines and nothing more.

Mr. Quick stood to make a brief statement as Lolly retook her seat, blinking at how she'd broken ranks with her lawyer and defied his expectations; how speaking up made her feel more capable. Stronger. At the point where the judge declared Lolly's petition accepted, only twenty-five minutes had passed. Judge Whitaker banged his gavel and the deed was done.

Lolly followed Mr. Quick from the courtroom and down the stairs to the filing office, where a line had formed. When at last they reached the filing clerk, he handed over Lolly's petition and Lolly provided the boarding house address so that a copy of the final decree could reach her by mail.

Outside, cars rumbled along Virginia Street, oblivious to the relief of a woman standing alongside a portly lawyer, the two pausing very near to the exact spot shown in a scene in Norma Jeane's last movie, *The Misfits*. Norma Jeane had stood on these steps as she acted the part of a broken woman, or at least a woman with a broken marriage. Now Lolly stood on the same steps and felt a bit of something inside her loosen. There remained a residue of regret over having married a man she had mistakenly thought was right for her. And as always, that old guilt that followed her everywhere.

She took a deep breath. "I'm glad that's over," she told Mr. Quick. "Thank you." She took off her wedding band and slipped it into the pocket of her coat. It was a thin gold band, but her hand felt lighter at its absence.

The lawyer offered yet another lie in a string Lolly was party to. "A pleasure," he said before shaking her hand and descending to the sidewalk.

Lolly's watch read 3:00. Thoughts of Jackson and Russell were vying for space in her head when she noticed the sound of a church bell in the distance, tolling the hour, perhaps, or else a call to some religious offices known only to its members. The round, brassy tone sounded familiar. So much so that it seemed to be calling her name—*Lol-ly, Lol-ly, Lol-ly, Lol-ly*. She slung her tote over her shoulder to follow the sun-washed sidewalks to Sierra Street, then Rainbow, and at last to the church on Island Avenue.

As if to prove the good Father's assertion that Trinity welcomed all comers, Lolly found its wooden front doors unlocked. Inside, golden beams of light slanted through the nave from windows on the right, dust motes afloat in the wash of color. At the front, a man in a black shirt with white collar ambled toward the forward sanctuary without glancing around. Recognizing his slight stoop and silvery hair, Lolly knew why she had come. She had taken a leap by divorcing Russell and there was at least one more leap she needed to take.

 She waited while Father Gerard checked the drape of the embroidered cloth covering the high altar and inspected the candlesticks. He seemed so engrossed that she thought he might exit without speaking to her, so she advanced up the center aisle, calling "Father?"

No answer.

At her second call he turned. "Yes," he answered, moving toward her. "Good afternoon."

They met at the halfway point and stood side by side in the aisle. "I came in a while back," said Lolly, "and asked about the stained-glass windows."

The Father slid his eyeglasses up the bridge of his nose. "Of course. You thought them heavenly." He stood as if waiting for her to say more and Lolly wondered if she might be overstepping some unwritten boundary about pastor-citizen interactions. She didn't worship at this church and her one-and-only visit had been happenstance. Then again, he had invited her to return.

Into the pause created by her hesitation, he asked, "Did anything in particular bring you in today?"

Familiar concerns flooded Lolly's mind. Concerns she had never voiced. "So much has happened since I stopped in, and I have all kinds of questions. If it's no trouble, do you suppose we could visit?"

"Of course."

Though Lolly had recognized him without his robe and surplice, he retained a dignified, official bearing. For a fleeting moment she pictured him clothed like an ordinary man. She could imagine Methodist pastors as occasionally looking regular, while shoveling snow perhaps. Evangelicals, too, testifying on street corners in suits and ties. She was glad for the pastor's official air because she had official business to conduct with him. "Have I interrupted your day off?" she asked.

He gestured toward the closest empty pew. "I guess you could say I'm off duty, but that's really never the case. You're not interrupting, I assure you. It's a good view from the nave."

"A good view?"

He motioned to her to sit. "It's different from what one sees when looking out from the sanctuary platform. From there, one looks out and down toward the nave and the people arrayed in the pews. My number-one favorite is not in the front or even where we are now, but the very last pew because it takes in the whole view—the pulpit and choir, the altar, the worshipers, and it faces our sculpture of Christ."

Lolly considered their surroundings. "I never thought of that."

Father Gerard nodded once and folded his hands in his lap. "Enough about seating preferences. I suppose you have a different subject in mind."

Now that she sat so close to the person who might offer advice regarding her troubled thoughts, a zing of nervousness ran through her, but right behind it came a sensation of calm from mere proximity to this particular Father. Various thoughts jockeyed for position until at last she started with the immediate. "I was walking the opposite direction of home, and I didn't even know why until I got here. You know how that happens, you go along minding your own business, maybe you don't even have a destination, when suddenly you're standing in front of your favorite store window, or the house where a friend lives."

When Father Gerard nodded, Lolly continued. "I guess I knew I was headed this way but not why, until I saw you. I've been asking around about heaven."

"Go on."

"And there's more versions than you'd guess."

"Is that right? Personally, I like to leave guessing out of my thoughts about the hereafter. Did you come all this way to tell me that you've been asking around?"

"No. I came because I need to confess. I didn't get that far when I took catechism. All I did was practice." She knew she was rambling but she couldn't help herself. "It seemed that your church bell was calling me. Sounds silly, but it's true, and here I am and it's probably the wrong day."

Father Gerard took a breath. "Well, I hope you won't be too disappointed. If it's confession you've come for, we have nothing formal to offer. Some Episcopal churches have booths and all but we don't."

Lolly's heart sank. "You don't? When I came out of the courthouse I felt so free, but also sorry. About so many things. And when I came through these doors I just knew that I needed to confess my ... well, my divorce, for one."

"Your divorce."

"I know everyone says it, but I *had* to end it. Things happened between us that there was no going back to. I know we're all supposed to turn the other cheek, but the situation—our marriage—crossed way beyond what it should. I was out of cheeks, if that makes sense." They continued facing the organ and the multi-colored leaded windows. The lack of eye contact seemed to invite more revelation, so Lolly screwed up her confidence and continued. "When I was young, I learned how divorce is a sin, and I guess I believed that for years, but I can see now how it can save you from other types of trouble."

Somewhere down a hallway, a door slammed, which seemed to unspring one of Lolly's curls. As she reached up to re-pin it, she gasped. "I'm not covered!" Panic set in as she fumbled in her tote for a clean handkerchief. Father Gerard put a hand out to stop her. "It's all right," he said. "We're the only ones here."

When she asked, "For sure?" he nodded in answer. At that, her nerves unclenched. "The thing is," she said, "divorce was a problem for that friend of mine too. For one divorce you could maybe say enough rosaries, but what about the others? And there's a Jewish one in there too. What in the world do you do with that? Are there Jewish rosaries for their kind of divorce? And if you were Catholic—she was Catholic as a teenager—and later got a divorce, the Church would be displeased with your divorce, right? So, marrying a Jew after that might make you an adulterer, or—"

Norma Jeane's troubles had resurfaced so powerfully that now they seemed to fuse with Lolly's own. "Divorce isn't even the worst of it. Abortion. That would doom you." She looked at Father Gerard. "Wouldn't it?"

The pastor turned his gaze toward Lolly at last. "My dear, I can tell that all these matters regarding your friend, regarding life, weigh on you, but it is not my place to judge."

She blinked as his words sank in. "I'm sorry, what?"

"My job is not to judge others."

"Oh, but I thought—"

Father Gerard seemed to study the huge, carved figure of the risen Christ attached to the wall above the altar. "That's up to Our Father, not me."

Lolly blinked as she digested his words. "Even so, I know it's a sin. And I don't suppose God could be too pleased with people who make mistakes of faith. I thought it was supposed to be so clear, the differences between sin and right living and heaven and all, but it seems that no one agrees. I only found four versions of what comes next, but if you counted the ones I didn't check, there might be a dozen."

"An accurate perception. Do I detect in you some apprehension about the afterlife?"

"I'm worried for others, but for me too. I haven't gotten a straight answer out of anyone. Or … they're straight answers, but there aren't two that match. Everything I've learned since coming here throws mud on what I thought I knew."

"Contemplating heaven is as complicated as contemplating life, as complicated as the people who reach for it. The searchers, the certain few, the certain many. I cannot imagine that the searching displeases God."

"But if you were God, wouldn't you want all of your followers to march in the same direction? To get in line and … I don't know, believe the same thing?"

"But I am not God, not even close. As I said, that is not my role. I am simply someone who is willing to listen and guide, and offer hope."

Lolly corralled her thoughts. Even if Father Gerard was but a listener and not God's judge on Earth, she sensed that he would truly hear what she had to say and that her secret would be safe with him. She said, "There was an incident when I was younger, involving a man. I didn't understand what was happening at the time. Only afterwards I got to thinking that my friend and that man somehow knew each other. Maybe. But what he did with her was wrong, that much I know, because she was too young. And then I was wrong as well because I didn't tell anyone who could keep it from happening again to her, or to someone else."

The Father sat silent, so she continued. "When you make a mistake like that, it's always there, attached to you, and eventually the guilt changes everything inside you. It's hard to get anything else right. You can make mistakes for years. What I did ... what I didn't do but should have done ..." Her words trailed off as the memories pulled at her.

Father Gerard spoke at last. "How long has this been on your mind?"

"Twenty years, give or take."

"You must have been very young."

"She was years older but we were both children." She shook her head. "I was so unprepared. You don't imagine anything like that will ever happen to you, but it can. It does. And I never told her I was sorry for being so scared that I ran away instead of getting help for her, and I never properly—" she fairly choked on the words as they rose up inside her— "I never told her what I'd done. I never apologized."

"But she remained your friend all these years."

His observation brought Lolly back to the present. She had known Norma Jeane just those two years, and only in the way a child knows anyone. Through all the years since, she had clung to the notion of them as intimates, when in truth, any news regarding Norma Jeane had come to her through fan magazines and television news and movies. At one time, the two of them had had more in common than not, children cast adrift by other people's choices, but now, looking back, she realized that what they'd shared was a razor thin slice of time now past. The realization silenced her.

After a moment, Father Gerard said, "Have you prayed about all this?"

Lolly smiled weakly as she locked gazes with him. "Father, if my prayers were balloons, the sky would be full of them. I'm not short on prayers. The only thing I'm short on is answers. I guess I came here hoping you could help."

He rubbed his face. "It seems to me that you've been carrying these troubles around longer than a person should have to. Does it feel like that to you?"

"It feels like forever," said Lolly.

"I have an idea then, just a suggestion. Why don't you say one last prayer about your troubles, the ones that cause you such pain, then hand them over."

"I guess I don't understand."

He demonstrated with his hands. "Bundle them up, like so. Tell them farewell. Hand them to me and let them go."

Lolly's desire for relief had sprung upon her as soon as she had sighted Father Gerard near the altar. At that moment, a proper confession had seemed the only answer, but now he was offering a solution without pomp or ceremony. His suggestion sounded almost too easy given how long she had lived with the certainty that she might never be free of blame. Then again, if anyone knew the score, he ought to, so perhaps his idea would work. "Should I kneel?" she asked.

"Only if you feel compelled. Your intentions are what count."

Lolly folded her hands, a little damp from nervousness, and closed her eyes. Silently, she asked forgiveness for being a girl who didn't know any better not to abandon her friend to the orphanage man, and for becoming a woman who knew better most of the time but failed regularly anyway. At one point she prayed, *It wasn't Norma Jeane's fault. Some things you just can't avoid. You do them, and you know better, but they seem the only choice. A person breaking rules could be good on the inside. I hope that counts.*

Had this been a sanctioned confession, it would end with the detesting of sins and a promise to try to amend her life. But this was unofficial, so she offered, *I'll try to be better and sin less, but I'm sure if you know about the trouble I'm in, you know about the special doctor. For what I'm planning, I'm sorry. World without end, Amen.*

When she opened her eyes, Father Gerard cupped his warm, dry hands around hers and held them for a moment. Then he lifted his hands high into the air, opening them as if setting a bird free. "There," he said. "Given over to a mightier power."

At that, Lolly began to cry softly. For so long she had felt unqualified to seek official forgiveness when finding relief had turned out to be the simplest thing in the world. In the course of one hour, Father Gerard had sat beside her as if they were equals, and then he'd lifted more than half a lifetime of guilt from her. No darkened cubicle, no screen to separate them. No Our Fathers or Hail Marys.

Lolly dug in the pocket of her tote for a handkerchief. Out popped her one-and-only photograph of teenaged Norma Jeane, the one she always carried. "Oh," she said with a sniffle. "That's her." She passed the snapshot to Father Gerard.

"This is your childhood friend?"

Lolly dabbed at her eyes then blew her nose. "She was, before she moved away."

After glancing at the youthful inscription on the back he studied the black and white snapshot of the long-haired girl. "How old is she here?"

"Fourteen, before she left the orphanage."

"And at that time, you were ...?"

"Seven. A long time ago. Time that—oh golly—" Lolly stood abruptly and smoothed the wrinkles from her skirt. "I've kept you way too long."

The Father passed the photo back to Lolly. "I'm here because this is my calling. I'm glad you found your way here. If you don't mind seeing yourself out, I'll sit here a little longer."

"For the view."

He nodded.

Lolly looked at the likenesses of the two saints caught in colored glass and the words carved in mahogany along the railing across the front of the platform: *O Ye Children Of Men – Bless The Lord*. She shook Father Gerard's hand. "I don't know how to thank you properly, but I guess you know that you've changed things for me."

He gave her a small smile. "I am glad to be of help, but I would also credit your capacity to believe."

Lolly took her tote and stepped lightly down the center aisle's royal red carpet, feeling as if her divorce hearing and her time with Father Gerard had freed her to imagine a life less burdened than the one she'd lived for the last six and a half years with Russell, and the years before that, all the way back to that awful night in the children's home. Her search for a spiritual resting place for Norma Jeane now seemed both impossible and unnecessary. She had never viewed uncertainty as benign, but maybe in this case it could be. If she could trust what Father Gerard had left unspoken, there were questions you could never know answers to, and without such answers a person could still know peace.

Twenty-three

D usk was thick around her as Lolly returned to the boarding house. Though exhausted from a lack of sleep and court appearance, she felt lighter.

"You're back at last," said Mrs. R. "You were gone so long."

"It turns out that court can go off track by hours and even the lawyers can't control it. She slid onto a kitchen chair.

"Good grief. Was your petition granted?"

"Yes, thank goodness."

"Then we've reason to celebrate. Anna arrived a few minutes ago, suggesting that we all go out for dinner. I was going to fix stroganoff, but she convinced me I could use a break."

"Well, I—"

"You'll let us pay the tab, of course. It's tradition to celebrate, at least a little. You missed Shirley's dinner out, and Doris's too, but since you're off work tonight the timing is perfect." She patted her hands together as if to suggest the matter was settled.

"Couldn't we skip it? You've done so much for me already."

"Nonsense. You deserve a celebration as much as anyone. Anna's freshening up. You can do the same and we'll pick a place."

In truth, an early night in bed with her Mockingbird book appealed to Lolly but there wasn't a good way to decline Mrs. Ruddle's offer without seeming ungrateful. She needed no fortune teller to predict that in spite of all her landlady's encouragement, protection, and the securing of permanent wave customers, Lolly would soon disappoint her, in which case, she would do well to acquit herself gracefully this evening.

Anna came in wearing a pale green suit that set off her flame-colored hair. "Oh good, you're back," she said to Lolly. "How did things go?"

"Fine. I was a wreck but Mr. Quick took care of things."

"I'm glad you took my slot on the calendar. I've decided I wasn't ready for my preliminary hearing, the one that presages the fight to follow."

"That sounds different than mine. What's the preliminary part for?"

"It's the opening gambit. Where you try to get the judge on your side."

"Does that work?"

"Lawyers will tell you it does. They also expect you to pay well for it. But let's skip that for now and think about dinner."

Mrs. R chimed in. "Anna said she'd like to try Basque again."

"It's been a number of years," said Anna.

"I think we have choices," said Mrs. R. "There are oodles of Basques around. I dated one once."

"Oh?" said Anna.

"All I'll say about it is he had quite an accent. I had to concentrate to understand all those rolled Rs."

"Did he kiss you with an accent?" asked Anna.

Mrs. R chuckled. "None of your business. If you recall the restaurant over on Fourth, the other choice is Sarratea's on Virginia Street. Lolly's been to dinner there."

"Was it any good?"

"I didn't eat much, but it was fine," said Lolly. She wasn't about to divulge more about her dinner with Caldwell, an evening that was history now.

"Well, I vote for that," said Anna. "I hope they have steak, and bean soup."

As Lolly went to freshen up and change her suit jacket for a sweater, Mrs. R's voice followed her up the stairs. A reference to picon punch putting hair on your chest. When Anna's laughter rang out, Lolly smiled too.

The same neon sign greeted them at Sarratea's. As they stepped inside, Lolly's recollections of her dinner there with Caldwell rose like the tide. How the background noise had siphoned off when he leaned close to ask her questions, and how nervous she'd been as a married woman at dinner with a local man, which was silly now that she thought about it. Not a person in the place would have known who she was, and tonight would be no different. Of course, Caldwell might have been recognized by someone. He said he'd lived in the area for almost ten years. Across the distance of a few weeks, aided by her growing familiarity with her surroundings, she called up a bit of their exchange about his having San Francisco relatives—which accounted for the postmark on those packages—and her aversion to gambling when she couldn't afford to lose. Well, *that* had changed. When necessity met her poverty of funds, she had begun to pursue the green stuff that made the world go round.

And then there was that tiny bottle of perfume which had glowed with an exotic foreignness. She had taken to wearing a bit of it in the particular way recommended by a friendly Russian woman at work. According to the Russian, perfume was properly dabbed onto a cotton ball for tucking into one's bra where body heat would warm the scent. Cotton tucked into her bra had once meant an entirely different thing to her, but she liked the idea that only someone within intimate range should notice a woman's fragrance.

She had meant to make Caldwell's gift last longer, but its light musk and flowery notes had become a staple of each day that she left the boarding house. She hadn't saved it for special occasions because it had come into her possession on an ordinary day. The bottle now held one final drop, a reminder of when she'd been new to Reno and occasionally the object of Caldwell's attention before he went away without a backwards glance.

Lolly agreed to all the dishes Anna and Mrs. R proposed they order. At one point Anna announced, "It's good that we're not waiting for Lolly's decree, but celebrating her tonight because I'm not sure that I'll be around when her papers come through."

"What?" Lolly and Mrs. R said in unison.

"It seems that I may have been hasty. I've been speaking to Lawrence lately and he keeps trying to convince me to give our marriage another try."

"Oh my," said Mrs. R.

Anna nodded. "I know. I hadn't shared those details because, well frankly, I think better without pressure."

"But you talked like it was all over," said Lolly.

"*Kaput*," said Mrs. R.

"It seemed so, at the time."

"You said he was boring," said Mrs. R.

"Ordinary," said Lolly.

"Everything I loathe." said Anna. "And I meant those things. Plus, he married me for my money."

"Your money!" squealed Lolly.

"Why not? Marrying for money is an equal-opportunity vice. The truth is, I knew it and I married him anyway. But we've been talking—did I mention that he's got the nicest voice?—and now he's diminished my determination to divorce him by, oh, an inch or so." She held two fingers up to indicate the measurement. Lolly and Mrs. R sat blinking at Anna, who went on. "Don't tell me that you've never been wrong about how sure you were about a thing, absolutely convinced, and then another thing comes along and changes your mind."

"I believed you. You've been the surest person I know," said Lolly.

Anna chuckled. "I suppose it's all in the presentation." She held up a finger. "That's not to say that all of my marital troubles have reversed themselves. Not at all. Only that I'm inclined to give him some room to try again, to show me that he and I could be, just perhaps, more compatible."

"And here I just got my divorce," said Lolly.

"Were you having second thoughts too?" Mrs. R asked Lolly.

"No," said Lolly. "But divorce wasn't my reason for coming to Reno. I guess I knew where I was headed but the idea had to grow on me. Actually, I've been wondering why I stuck with my marriage for so long, why I couldn't see how our lives ran according to what he wanted. None of it was mine, really. I was just playing a part."

Anna nodded. "And so it goes. Anyway, what I meant to suggest was that Lawrence is coming to Reno for a bit and I thought we'd try separate rooms in the same hotel, to see how that works out. If neither of us picks a fight, we might take a room together." She smiled weakly. "No use rushing, we'll take it slow. And if we try but can't make a go of it, at least we're in the right town to finish it off." She looked at Mrs. R. "And I'll pay you to hold my room for me, in case ... well, you know."

Anna's declaration dumbfounded Lolly. The woman seemed to have everything going for her—looks, money, courage. For a while she had imagined that if she modeled herself after Anna, minus the multiple divorces, she might find a way around her troubles. Come to find out, Anna was as changeable as anyone.

"Enough about me," said Anna. "Let's toast the new Lolly."

When Lolly's fresh cocktail arrived, Anna filled Mrs. R's glass to the rim from the table's carafe of hearty red wine. "Here's a

Scandinavian toast," she said, clinking glasses with the others. "Long life. Friendship. *Skol*."

"*Skol*," the other two responded, and Lolly thought how in a long life there would be few things that totally escaped the effects of history, specifically a person's personal history. But as Father Gerard had demonstrated, the *weight* of history could be lightened some through the relinquishing of guilt, and fear. If a person could ease burdens as heavy as those, they might feel braver about what came next.

The next day found Lolly dressed in her nicest slacks and her best blouse, wearing the last drop of her French perfume. In the kitchen, she accepted a baking soda biscuit and a cup of tea from Mrs. R.

"How are you this morning?" asked the landlady. "I feel like I drank too much red wine last night. That's what I get for trying to keep up with Anna."

"You drove us home okay."

"That's good, but I'm really too old to feel like this. You look like you're dressed for leaving the house, not for lying about reading a book or painting your nails. Don't you want a day off to recover from your court hearing?"

"I've given my word to take care of something."

Mrs. R clucked her tongue. "You are one busy girl. I guess you'll have to rest later."

Lolly headed south toward California Avenue where a special purchase awaited her attention. Her route took her along the block lorded over by the Mapes, magnificent even in daylight. She had no business going inside, wasn't even dressed for such a place. Still, on the walkway near its First Street entrance she wavered. This was a place where money flowed like blood. She knew that blood money could change a life, and how the lack of it could do the same.

She was tempted to step inside to have a look at its glamor and shine. She hadn't had her fill of luck lately, only a nibble here and there. Though she'd come away yesterday morning with Jackson's bankroll intact and hers a tiny bit fatter, she hadn't exactly struck it rich, at least not enough for the costly purchases on her list. A nice big chunk of luck would solve a lot of things right about now.

Just inside the double glass doors she peeled out of her coat. None of the blackjack dealers in sight looked familiar. Had it been midnight she might have found Franklin again, but instead she stepped closer to watch a table being dealt by a woman wearing the nametag "Georgia."

Along came a cocktail waitress. "Care for a drink?" she asked.

"I'm not even gambling."

"House rules. You might be between games."

Lolly asked for a glass of milk, something easy on her stomach.

"You want a shot in that?"

"You mean booze?"

"Some people like it with bourbon or Kahlua. They say the flavors go together."

Lolly thought about how she'd switched from cocktails to water after losing her own savings and before her battle to recover her own bankroll and Jackson's. Through the euphoria and exhaustion of that long night she'd eventually risen whole, but the thought of how the booze had not helped, had probably tainted her self-control, soured the memory. "Never mind," she told the waitress. "I'd better not." There might be other chances. Maybe. All it would take was one more lucky night to enlarge her bankroll and solve a few problems. Of course, you had to be in a town like this for that kind of possibility.

It was warm enough to walk coatless down Virginia Street. In a half-mile she arrived at the bookstore on California Avenue. Good news. The Braille version of Mockingbird she had ordered by telephone was in. She paid for it and tucked it into her tote, then headed back toward downtown.

She dawdled as she walked along, checking store windows and even detouring over to the pawn shop where she'd purchased her pocket books. There she stood gazing at the window display of clocks without really seeing it. Her plan for the day was to help Jackson fulfill his goal of a stealthy exit. He'd be on his way to fulfilling if not his dream, at least his goal. She herself had never found a real, true purpose. Norma Jeane had dreamt one up and eventually made it big, but not Lolly. If she were braver, she might go with Jackson and find a place within the larger cause he spoke of, but she couldn't imagine leaving a place like Reno and heading for a city where you might stand in the wrong protest line or eat at the wrong counter and get yourself beaten, or jailed, or killed. Even white people. Even women. She pictured the South as a place where Negroes would never enjoy even the few liberties available to them in Reno. She had lived in

Oklahoma, and that was almost as southern as states like Mississippi and Alabama.

At Woolworth's she went in for a tube of Revlon's Peach Parfait lipstick then stayed for a snack at the coffee shop counter, where she ordered a slice of coffee cake and the glass of milk she'd been hankering for. In an effort to delay what was yet to come, she lingered as long as she reasonably could until the place was bustling with customers waiting for seats. She paid her tab and left.

Ambling up Virginia Street, she paused to admire window displays of jewelry, stationery, and ladies' wear. Just before the Reno arch she passed the Ground Cow Restaurant where she'd dined with Caldwell that one time. For twenty feet on either side of its doors the air was thick with aromas of greasy string fries and grilled beef. At Commercial she turned right where there were more business signs and doorways to spend a few moments admiring.

Her feet moved her forward while her mind churned with the same old concerns. Jackson was willing to travel alone but she wanted better for him. A safer scenario. He was bound to find trouble if he went alone to one of those violent places he spoke of. The more Lolly dwelled on it the likelier it seemed he would end up hurt. Almost a certainty. She could change the outcome, perhaps, by arranging travel for a companion. The question was, who could serve as companion? Could *she*? She feared the violence that he almost welcomed for how necessary it seemed. Direct violence, purple-faced people spitting and swearing and threatening, some of them kicking and slashing the protestors. The violence itself was an obstacle for her. But also, much as she hated to admit it, there was the reality that Jackson had not invited her along.

There was another option which she quickly dismissed. She could give him back his money and explain how he'd gotten his hopes up for nothing. That she wasn't the ally and friend he'd taken her for, which would mean declaring herself the opposite of how she wanted him to view her.

Despite her delaying tactics, Lolly arrived at the entrance to the rail station where it was time to keep her word. Hoping it would lend a touch of clarity to her thoughts, she took a deep breath of clean air, cold and sharp, before pushing in through the double glass doors and passing among the clots of travelers with suitcases and children in tow.

Behind the opening in the grating above the ticket counter stood the agent who had declined Jackson's request on Saturday. Facing him again had not been part of her plan. He might not recognize her, but if he did, she wanted him to think only of people traveling in pairs.

"Yes, Miss?" he asked.

She thought about what the agent had said about blind people traveling alone, how dangerous it could be. She couldn't let Jackson travel alone into danger. Two cross-country rail tickets seemed more necessary than one ticket for Jackson and one medical procedure for her. Her insides did a little flip.

"Miss?"

Lolly shook her head to clear her thoughts and brought her hand to her waist. She had a week or two to address her secret. "Two tickets, please, to Washington D.C."

There. She had done it. Not Jackson's first choice, but still on his list. A city where Negroes were said to be generally more welcome than in the deep South. He would hopefully find less turmoil there.

The Capital," he said with an appraising look. "That's a fair piece to travel. You want the one that leaves on Thursday?"

What Lolly wanted was to go back to a day with Jackson when he took up his golden guitar and played songs that made her feel alive. Or else to stand still until the world caught up with what she wanted for him, and for her. She couldn't change the present moment any more than she could replay her own mistakes and give them a different outcome. She licked her lips and tried to channel Anna. "Thursday will be fine. Can you tell me when it will get there?"

The agent began sifting through a book of tables and schedules. "Should get you there by Sunday morning. I've got first class or coach."

"Better make it coach." She stood silent while the agent calculated the fare, muttering slightly as he punched numbers into his adding machine. When he looked up, Lolly steeled herself for the total.

"Two hundred five each. Four hundred ten for the two of them. That's connecting through Chicago. The most direct route." He glanced at Lolly's left hand. "There's a sleeping car," he said, "with berths set aside for women and children. Unless you're berthing with someone."

Lolly kept her gaze steady and resisted the urge to touch her unadorned ring finger. She had given no thought to the configuration of passenger trains, but of course such long-distance travel meant that trains rolled all night long. She told him, "If that's extra, then skip the berth."

As the agent made out the tickets, she dug into her tote bag. Early on she had kept Jackson's money separate, but in the wee hours of Monday morning his savings had passed into the Mapes' possession then back into her own hands. Jackson would not have been allowed to gamble in the Mapes, to wager his own money or win on his own behalf, so she had won a bit of someone else's money to spend on him. The thought brought a smile to her face.

"Two by rail," said the agent, taking Lolly's money, "for Thursday, ten o'clock. It won't pull out early but you'll want to be here by nine because there's no assigned seats in coach cars." He handed her two heavy paper tickets meant to carry people a long, long way.

"I forgot to ask," said Lolly. "If these don't get used, then what?"

The agent gestured with an ink-stained hand. "A problem comes up, bring them back to change for a different week. Or, a different destination. We can refund, too, but it gets made out as a counter check to take to the bank."

Lolly took the tickets to an open bench seat where she pulled out her gift for Jackson. The bookstore clerk had cut the string for her and now she thumbed open the brown wrapping from a thickly bound Braille version of Mockingbird. Its paper jacket showed a rusty red background behind a tree in silhouette, upon whose branches glowed a few green leaves. She opened the book to a random page and ran her fingers across the rectangular cells of raised dots. With this, the tables were turned. While Jackson could not have read a solitary word of her library version, her hand was blind to this Braille. For once, though, she could imagine his way of beholding a story.

She tucked the tickets into the book and the book into her tote; the wrapper went into the closest bin. Shrugging into her coat again, she went out into an afternoon breeze smelling of alpine lakes and shadowed forests of aspen and pines on the verge of waking, or so she imagined. At the corner where Commercial met Center Street, she hailed a passing taxi to take her to 26 Park Street.

Though Lolly had kept her promise to herself and the one to Jackson, the looming loss of him felt like an ache. A part of her wanted to rush directly to him with the evidence of how she'd made good on her word but another part wanted to formulate a new and convincing argument against his plans. Not that the rationale she'd tried thus far had altered one iota of his own hoped-for plan. She just wasn't yet ready to give up.

As the taxi rolled past the police station Lolly said, "Don't turn yet. Drive a little farther then come back around."

"Whatever you say," said the driver. "It's your dime, and that makes you the boss."

Twenty-four

L olly's taxi pulled up in front of Jackson's duplex at 3:45. Her thoughts had not cohered into a new argument to use on Jackson, but she had delayed long enough to allow for his arrival home from working at the Polka Dot.

"You want me to wait?" asked the driver.

"No thanks, I'm fine."

Taking her payment, he said, "No offense, but we just came by police headquarters, in case you need 'em."

She gave him a hard look. "Are there many reports of trouble just two blocks from the police?"

He glanced away sheepishly. "All I'm sayin' is you look kind of proper. There's dive bars to the east and those can attract criminal types. I'd hate to hear later that some fare of mine got robbed after I left her."

For a moment Lolly wondered whether the driver might be fishing for the nature of her business in a low-rent neighborhood just a hundred steps from the station house, but she knew now that Reno accepted, perhaps even welcomed, individuals who defied convention. According to Mrs. R, early settlers endured tremendous hardships while crossing Nevada's eastern mountains before braving the belly of the state. Pioneers they were, and migrants, criminals and farmers, treasure seekers and people hungry for a fresh start. Lolly was no better or worse than those who came to this place empty-handed or burdened by secrets. Everyone had secrets. The key was to figure out which secrets bled danger, or, like Father Gerard had shown her, which had outlived their power to haunt. She had certainly learned a thing or two about unconventional behavior these last few weeks. She said, "I'll be fine," and paid the man.

She stepped out and waited until the taxi pulled away before she turned toward Jackson's duplex. She felt for the Braille book then fingered the wedding band in her coat pocket as she recalled the blackjack dealer's suggestion about how the outlaw loved the dance hall girl. He didn't, and she knew it. He was simply the sun casting fire and light on an earthbound creature. The sun kept its eye on its work, never reaching for the flowers it showered with light, even when they reached for it. Still, it was hard to let go of the sun.

Shouldering her bag, she mounted the steps and rapped on the right-hand door. Nothing. She rang the bell and waited. From inside came the garble of a television. She pictured a blind man feeling about for his cane, but no one answered.

She rapped harder, the hollow sound drifting past her toward the street. This time she heard scuffling sounds just beyond the door before it scraped open an inch to reveal two pair of eyes in small dark faces. Lolly was taken aback by the sight of children until she realized they were likely his nephews. *Of course.* She waggled her tote. "I have a delivery for your uncle. Is he here?"

The door opened wider. "I'll take it," said the taller of the two. He held out his hand.

"I'd like to give it to him myself."

The boys studied her a moment before the taller child shoved the other one aside and closed the door with a resounding thud. More muffled sounds came from inside and Lolly found herself looking left across the shared front porch to assess whether the ruckus had roused the curiosity of a duplex neighbor. It hadn't yet.

Eventually, small hands appeared at the curtains in the front window and the same two boys peered out as the door scraped open again. Jackson stood in the opening, bare-chested, his arms like bundled ropes. With the corner of a striped towel, he swiped at a line of shaving cream rimming his jaw. Lolly drank in the sight of him.

"Yes?" said Jackson in Lolly's general direction.

It was the first time she'd seen his face and the scars near his eyes ordinarily obscured by his dark glasses. His pupils looked like misted windows, letting no light in and none out. She said, "It's me, Lolly. I guess I've come at a bad time."

"They said 'a delivery lady' and I couldn't think who.'

"S.P. ticket service."

"I like the sound of that. You want to come in?"

Lolly did want to see how Jackson lived, but she pointed out that he already had guests.

"Oh, yeah," he said, as if suddenly remembering. He turned toward the room behind him. "Hey boys," he called out. "Go on home.

I've got to go soon anyway."

"Aw, we wasn't in the way," said the smaller one.

"It's no use arguing," said Jackson.

"But she's got somethin' for you and we wanna see it."

"That's none of your business." With his free hand he beckoned them to him. Dutifully they stepped into range. "Did you leave any Army men out?"

"No," said the taller boy.

The smaller boy punched the first one in the arm. "Ow!" came the reply. "Okay, I'll check." He disappeared from view and soon came back. "They're under the table now," he said.

"Better be," said Jackson, reaching to gather both boys to him before saying, "Get on, and straight home."

Lolly stepped aside so they could push past onto the stoop. Two steps down to the sidewalk and they were away, running a footrace toward Kuenzli Street. "How far do they have to go?" she asked.

"Just to the apartments around the corner," he said. "It's kind of crowded over there. I figure this place gives them a break."

"I can tell you care about them."

He held the door open for her. "C'mon in. You might watch out for Army men."

Inside, Lolly tore her gaze from Jackson long enough to absorb how his front room was lit by two floor lamps and a television whose bright screen showed nothing but squiggly lines accompanied by cartoon babble. An adjacent dining space held an old oak table with three chairs pulled up around it and a pile of action figures beneath. Everything worn but serviceable, and not a woman's touch anywhere. The aroma of fried hot dogs reached her and Lolly found herself wondering if Jackson cooked—surely those boys wouldn't—and how that worked for someone blind. By feel, maybe, using great care.

She hung her coat on a hook by the door and set her things on an end table positioned near the sofa.

"All I've got to offer is orange pop," said Jackson. "Or coffee. I can make some."

"Nothing, thanks. I just came from the train depot and I thought I'd better reach you straight away." Though the sight of a shirtless Jackson muddled Lolly's senses, speaking those words reinforced her desire for keeping open the subject of his leaving. Even if he wouldn't choose her to accompany him, or couldn't, he could choose to stay put in Reno. He could work for change in his own town. From what he'd said, *someone* needed to.

He spoke in her direction. "Sorry to make you wait, but I should put myself together. Be back soon as I can." His upright, rolling gait carried him to a doorway opposite, where he disappeared from sight.

After a bit he returned, dressed in the kind of black shirt he wore when performing at the Paradise, all traces of shaving cream gone but still no sunglasses. Lolly was at last glimpsing the private side of his public guise.

Perched on a cushion of the room's nubby orange davenport, Lolly marshaled her thoughts. "The train goes Thursday at ten. They start boarding at nine."

"Man, that's great." He lifted his face as if hearing the call of his future. "Not too many people would have come up with the plan you did, but you were bold. That's one of your strengths."

Lolly glowed at the compliment. "I went for my divorce." Another promise kept.

"That right?"

"Yesterday. It's strange. You think about it and worry about it and then when it comes it's like being knocked in the head by an invisible anvil. The judge is scary, sitting up high, and they don't even want you to tell your story. Just 'Yes, your honor and no, your honor.' Of course, it was coming for a long time and it shouldn't have felt so sudden, but it did."

"It's official then?"

"Well, my lawyer said it's not official until the decree comes, which can take a few days."

"But your part's done."

"As far as I know. Supposedly, they file away all those records at the courthouse and keep them forever. He called them permanent records of impermanent lives."

"Hunh. So, you're free to do just about anything. What's your plan from here?"

He was asking the very question on Lolly's mind. What was she meant to do next? Mrs. R's last two boarders had returned to where they'd come from, but for her, Gilleon had fallen off her list and southern California held no attraction. All those tall buildings, the scramble of traffic, and that Hollywood effect. No offense to Norma Jeane, but Lolly wanted nothing to do with all that posturing and paste wax. She could stay put, or she could go just about anywhere. To the nation's capital, for instance, a foggy, amorphous option that seemed weighted toward the impossible side of the scale. Of course, she was still pregnant, which limited her options. She said, "I still think someone ought to travel with you."

Jackson stood a little straighter. "I appreciate your view on that, but there isn't anyone else who can go."

"No one?"

"I did talk to Little George. Did you mean Little George?"

Lolly wasn't sure how to answer. The second ticket was real, of course, but it also felt symbolic, as if for anyone who needed a way to reach the next place they were going.

Jackson asked, "Who else did you think could go?"

"At one point I thought ... but then ..."

"I wasn't thinking that—"

"It's okay." Lolly took a breath. "I know that I don't have the same dreams as you."

"You mean the dream of being judged for what's inside?"

"Oh, well sure."

"Or making something of myself to be proud of?"

"That too."

Jackson raised his hands. "So we do want the same things, but maybe my dreams are farther down the highway than yours."

His risky plan for reaching for his dreams pierced Lolly again. She studied him to see if his expression revealed something different than his words, but it didn't. "You see, that's what's got me—What I mean is, are you one hundred-percent sure about going off across the country?"

"I thought you understood that."

"What about your music?" A thin argument.

"A half-dozen others in this town have more talent in their pinkies than I'll ever have, and there's no future in playing the Hideout."

"Somewhere else then."

Jackson's smile was wry. "I wasn't ever going to be a full-time musician. That was my father's calling. I only play to earn a paycheck, such as it is, and my relatives pitch in to keep me afloat. This place, for instance." He waved a hand in the air. "It's my mother's, in her name."

"You'd be leaving your nephews and all your Reno relatives."

One side of his mouth drew down. "They'll do like other families; they'll adjust. What I'd like is for them to think, someday, that I had a part in what happens beyond the door that's closed right now but needs to be opened. Right now it's only a crack you can hardly see a sliver of light through. Someone's got to put their shoulder against it and push. I'd like them to think I tried."

Lolly felt the rightness of his logic as her last-grasp thought tumbled from her mouth. "Your mother, though. She's already lost your father, and now you."

Jackson's face went tight. His tone changed too. "She lost my father, which is why she keeps me under her thumb. But I lost more than my father. I lost my eyesight, and my plans, such as they were, the kind of plans a Negro's allowed. Before I went blind, I was already less of a man because of being Negro." He began shifting his weight from one foot to the other. "You might not know this. It's been a decade since the Supreme Court ruled, but just this last year the governor of Mississippi was still refusing to integrate schools. He called it genocide to let Negro students into white classrooms. *Genocide!*

"In his capital city, they've got an armored tank with machine guns. And trucks with cages to hold the Negroes they're going to throw in the pokey. And attack dogs. And spies so that they know when the protests are planned for. Black people can't even vote without a fight. Right here in America."

Lolly sat speechless as more words poured out of him.

"Being a Negro means you're less employable, less valuable, less paid, you got less future. Your color's the first strike against getting ahead. Try adding that you're blind. With that combination you got next to nothing plus you got less future than those Negroes who can see." He pointed in Lolly's direction. "You," he said, "cannot know what that's like. It's all good and well to sympathize—" He jabbed at his temple— "and appreciate the low position and struggles of your fellow man. But anyone who's not me, they can't know. There is no way for them to know."

Lolly felt battered by the anger behind his words. "I hear what you're saying. That a person has to strive for a better life. I have to strive too. I have burdens and setbacks. That sounds like a defense but I'm trying to understand. All I know is that when things look bleak, that's when we shouldn't give up hope. Every night I pray—"

"Praying hasn't helped a lick. God did not stand down the Little Rock protestors from spitting on those school children. He is not going to stop the lynching or the police dogs. It's *people* doing these things to each other, harming each other, so it's *people* who have to stop the injustice and make change happen."

"But—"

"Where was God when my father took me downtown on some crap errand for Old Man Byrne right as the buildings blew apart?" He jabbed a finger at his blind eyes. "This damage. It's His handiwork too."

Lolly's heart gave a lurch. "It is not!"

"Isn't it? In my mother's church, God's hand is everywhere. In the actions of the smallest child, in a bird's flight from the nest. Guiding me when I play guitar."

Lolly jumped to her feet. "I read about that explosion. It was just a fluke. Only bad luck that you were downtown, you and all the rest. Your father died, I know that, and that's where you were injured." Stepping forward she took hold of his arm. "You can't blame God for bad luck. Every single person knows bad luck and troubles. All of us."

Jackson pulled his arm from her grasp. "Maybe divorcing your husband sorrows you. Maybe so, but when it's over there will be some other man, someone to go to the clubs with and out dancing with. But you will not be less of a person for what has happened to you."

Lolly's ire flared. "That's what you think?" she said. "That because I'm free to eat where I want and go into businesses around town, that I'm somehow untouched by pain? You can't see it, nobody looking with only their eyes can see it, because it's not only on the outside. All of *your* hurt isn't on the outside. Plenty of it's *inside* too. The same as mine."

Hastily, she pulled open the buttons of her blouse, one shank of thread giving way entirely. She wrenched the garment from her shoulders, pulled her bra down to her waist, and stood bare chested before him. Her heart was firing on extra cylinders as she grabbed his hand and pulled him a half-step toward her. He tilted then righted himself as she pressed his palm to the raised scars that striped her right breast.

Mouth falling open, Jackson flinched at touching her flesh. "Wh-what?" he stuttered as he tried to free his hand from hers.

Lolly held tight and turned his hand over so that the smoother side might discern the differing textures. "Scars," she said. "External and internal. So you see, I'm damaged goods too."

His voice went hoarse as the fight left him. "How—?"

Lolly guided his hand to the stripe of belly skin above her waistband. "And pregnant. I didn't ask for it, and I don't blame God. I blame my *ex*. It *is* people who do the hurting."

Jackson stood frozen while Lolly watched emotions play across his face. A moment passed before he said, "You've got troubles. I understand." He nodded. "You deserve better." When he pulled her tight to him, she felt the import of her secret scars fade away. Then he kissed her. With relief, she savored the taste of his peppermint mouth.

Almost immediately Jackson stiffened, but Lolly held him firm, her head filling with images of the afternoon they had danced to the Sara Vaughan record in the empty jazz club. The array of tables and chairs, the stage curtains pulled back, the one set of stage lights making shadows of their movements as he rocked her gently to the lushness of that misty melody. The sweet memory obscured the sound of footsteps on Jackson's front stoop.

Then reality overtook memory as the door opened and Ruby Truth Mayberry stormed in, fury in a flowered house dress.

Twenty-five

From Mrs. Mayberry's mouth came shrieks and angry words—"slut," "hussy," and something about slumming—as Jackson shouted in protest. Lolly scrambled to pull her clothes together and seize her coat from near the door.

The Braille book fell to the floor as she scooped her tote from the end table and pushed out through the open front door. On the front walk, she buttoned her blouse and shimmied into her coat. Two autos swerved as she cut across Second Street, the sound of their horns lost among her racing thoughts and the loop of Mrs. Mayberry's shouts laced with Lolly's dismay at inciting such wrath. What had she been thinking? That her need for him was greater than his desire to break free? That her presence would not encumber his passage toward a different, larger life elsewhere? She had fallen under the spell of his innate humanity, her head full of notions about how the world *should* work, not how it *did* work. She had meant to make things easier for Jackson but instead had made a mess of things.

It was going-home time for the eight-to-five crowd, the sun nearly gone. Lolly, overheated and breathless, hurried past businesses closing up and restaurants open for business, arriving back in the familiar territory of the Holiday Hotel and the Lake Street bridge. When she came to a halt, she was on the bank above the river, among giant cottonwoods that towered over the darkly silvered motion twenty feet below. The air smelled of wet earth and the sharp new green of willows. From under the bridge, a bat broke free to circle twice before disappearing upstream.

Lolly loosened her coat as she contemplated the gleam that carried away everything delivered into its embrace. Some of Jackson's praise came to her—about her bold ideas, her willingness to bend the rules for good (this from a man who would throw himself at the wolves to further his cause). Though he seemed to believe that she was made of stronger stuff than she knew, he was probably lost to her now. She'd come full circle to being alone again. At least she had the memory of his arms around her and his kiss. She still had Mrs. R, who knew the pain of love and the business of boarders, and there was Anna, experienced in the boomerang nature of togetherness. And her link to Norma Jeane, who had outwardly seemed blessed while she searched for something to fill her soul. Each of them advanced one or more steps only to fall back now and then. Forward, back.

Only the water moved just one way. Forward.

Lolly turned to set her tote bag on a boulder when suddenly she was half-sliding down the steep bank, bushes snagging her coat sleeves and stinging her hands, young shoots and twigs breaking beneath her grasp.

Momentum carried her into the shallows' edge, where she grabbed a fistful of willows and hung on tight with stones slippery beneath her feet. Overhead, another bat wheeled and turned as the meltwater slowed time to a trickle and stripped breath from her lungs. For a strange, desperate moment she replayed how her arrival had brought Mrs. Mayberry into Jackson's duplex where the means of his escape lay tucked within the pages of Mockingbird. She'd helped open the door to his future but her presence had also beckoned the hornets. Had she ruined his chance to recast his life in a different city? She hoped not. She had only meant to protect a heart embittered by the country's racial divide while bent on facing down a biased status quo.

She brought one hand to her waist and said a little prayer, which brought Father Gerard to mind. He counseled trust in a higher power and the release of letting go. What would he say about the river that washed earth and stones? Did the river trust a higher power? Was this its way of letting go? Feeling blurry, she released her hold on the willows and stepped into the icy rush where with a cry she lost her footing. Her knees buckled and her legs scraped a boulder as the dark swirl swallowed her shoes.

Wait! she thought, *not like this!* She paddled her hands toward the shore, but the current won, pulling her downstream. As coherence thinned, one last memory floated past—a quote from page 136 of the Rowe typing book. "In this world, it is not what we take up, but what we give up, that makes us rich ... Henry Russell Beecher."

Then everything went black.

Twenty-six

T here came a hazy, haloed light, just like in the movies. Lolly moved toward it in her mind. She was somewhere special.

And then a voice, indistinct. *Could it be? Norma Jeane?*

Lolly waited but no one appeared. There was nothing she could identify as love, or a spirit. No golden streets, no gates of pearl. She began to think she'd misunderstood. Neither heaven nor hell contained only light and murmuring voices; nothing in those early lessons described murmurs.

She bid goodbye to the light and drifted away.

Twenty-seven

O nce again, the light, and this time a voice calling from a
distance, calling, "Mrs. Cooper," as if it hadn't gotten word that
Lolly had left that name behind. *Divor* ... she thought, trying to
correct the distant voice.

"Look," said a different voice. "She's waking." And then there were
white-clad shapes hunched over her.

"Saint?" squeaked Lolly.

One shape formed into a nurse as the other turned away and
disappeared. "No, dear. They brought you here."

"Wha?"

"That's right. You're at Washoe Medical Center. How are you
feeling?"

"Hap?"

"You're happy? Oh, you mean 'What happened?' Mercy! They
pulled you from the Truckee where you were pinned against the old
railroad pilings. They got to you fast." She reached for Lolly's wrist
and stood silent. After a moment, she said, "You'll feel groggy as your
body flushes out the sedation. You should rest."

When the nurse left her bedside, Lolly sank back into dreamless
slumber.

The next thirty-six hours delivered a blur of nurses monitoring
vital signs, removing her catheter, and assisting her to the lavatory.
When she surfaced, time lay fog-like across jumbled thoughts about
the Paradise and the jangly spurs Russell wore when he rode rodeo,
Jackson's guitar and those peppermints he favored. Everything
through a murk except the water's icy grip, a recollection clear as air.

Dear Mrs. R appeared and remained by her bedside,
administering the broth and clear liquids brought in by a young
woman dressed in stripes. Then, early Thursday morning, the nurse
and doctor came in together and made to send Mrs. R away so they
could speak privately with Lolly.

"Let her stay, please." Lolly smiled wanly at her landlady. "There isn't anything she can't know."

The doctor considered Mrs. R then turned again toward Lolly. "Mrs. Cooper, this is a delicate matter, but we have some unfortunate news. You experienced a miscarriage in the emergency room."

Mrs. R sucked in a breath as Lolly brought her hands to her face. A dozen thoughts took flight. The weeks of worry, the fear of being pinned forever to Russell, her evenings gambling for the money to end his hold on her, the longing for clarity and purpose. Searching and avoiding and reaching. Her discovery of the bold, mouthy girl in Mockingbird. And then, at the river, what felt like ghostly hands guiding her into its shadows and light. "Dear God," she said at last.

The doctor asked, "Did you know?"

"I prayed," said Lolly. After a pause she added, "Not for—Well, maybe ... It was so cold." She shook her head. Had she known the river might kill her, or save her? What she knew no longer seemed to matter. What mattered was the high desert light slanting in through the window beyond the doctor's left shoulder, the crisp white sheets under her palms, and the pillow behind her head. The ceiling's grainy texture and that tiny tea-colored stain in its far corner. Ordinary details only available to someone miraculously alive.

"Is there someone we should call? Your husband perhaps?"

Lolly laced her fingers together. "There's no husband. He left me weeks ago."

The nurse's gaze flicked to the stripe of pale skin circling Lolly's ring finger, a remnant of her marriage past, as Lolly wondered if what she'd just said was correct. It was, partly. He had left her emotionally and injured her physically. Switching gears she asked, "Will I be ... *okay?*"

The doctor chimed in. "You were in the water nearly ten minutes. Doesn't sound like long but the body's systems shut down to protect its internal organs and brain. That same response slows bruising. Your X-rays show no broken bones. There's a bandage on your back over a deep scratch. Besides today's visible bruising, more discoloration from deep contusions may appear over the next few days. You'll be sore where you made contact with objects, but it's not the same as what we see with auto accidents. There is quite a bit we don't know about the hypothermic process, but in this case, we can hope you'll experience no lasting damage."

Lolly now recalled how the current rammed her against a pile of logs and debris, the feel of wooden arms plucking at her, scraping her, holding her head just above the water line. Before long there were human arms, someone in the water beside her, reaching for her, hoisting her up onto the bank. Her thoughts had been sludge. "I'm lucky," she said, thinking about the river's danger, and its mercy.

"We all think so," said the nurse. "Your friend here has indicated that you room with her and will do so after your discharge, which we're planning for tomorrow if you continue to improve."

The doctor halted the conversation to listen to Lolly's lungs and scribble on a chart, which he handed to the nurse before he left.

When he had gone, the nurse continued. "Many people don't understand how slippery the river's bank can be. One minute you're on solid ground, the next, you've lost your footing. The Truckee looks modest but it can be treacherous, February's flood notwithstanding. Don't feel too bad. Even longtime locals underestimate it." She nodded briefly. "Oh—there's been someone asking about you the last couple of days. We haven't shared any information because he looks kind of rough."

An image of Jackson appeared in Lolly's mind. The day of her visit to his duplex apartment and his mother's riotous arrival now seemed a lifetime ago; the second time in as many months that she'd fled an angry storm. She had helped Jackson plan to leave his family without their knowledge, maybe without even a goodbye. The hardest kind of leaving. Had he had a change of heart?

The nurse looked at the notes in her hand. "A Mr. Benjamin Caldwell," she said. "Do you know him?"

Lolly's thoughts ground to a halt and changed course. At her delayed response, the nurse added, "If he's unwelcome, we can send him away."

So, it wasn't Jackson, who had for a time filled an empty place inside her. Her thoughts wheeled round to Caldwell, who had previously seemed a solid (if sometimes intrusive) presence. His name revived her disappointment at his unannounced departure, but she couldn't deny her pleasure at receiving the gifts he had sent.

It seemed now that she had lost track of certain details about Caldwell. She recalled his generosity in the Hideout lounge and how he leaned in as he listened. He had been a good listener. Other impressions hovered just out of reach and there arose a question that she needn't ask the nurse because only one person would have the answer. How had Caldwell known where to find her?

To the nurse Lolly said, "I'm at a loss about Mr. Caldwell being here."

The nurse checked her chart. "There's a note about him showing up early Wednesday but since you were under observation they sent him away. He's been here off and on. They wouldn't provide him with your room number."

"I'll see him, but first I need a few minutes."

As the nurse left, Lolly turned to Mrs. R. "I don't understand how he knew to come here."

"Anna recognized your coat and your tote bag too. She was taking some small items to the Holiday Hotel, where she and Lawrence are getting rooms. You know, that temporary togetherness she mentioned. I guess she was nearby and heard people shouting from the bridge. She said she told the newspaper man—amazing how they end up at every catastrophe—that the unidentified woman who had slipped down the bank into the river had better remain unidentified or he'd have certain people to answer to. You know Anna. She gets her way." She studied Lolly's reaction. "I was stunned, of course, but when I gathered my wits, I called the Paradise. I didn't know what kind of shape you were in but I didn't want you to lose your job because of not letting them know that something had come up. I telephoned for the restaurant manager, but the operator took the message. I promise you I didn't give any details."

Lolly fingered the buttons of the quilted bed jacket Mrs. R had brought her. "You probably saved my job but there's still something I can't put my finger on."

Mrs. R spoke again. "Well, I can leave you to talk with your ... gentleman."

"Please stay," said Lolly. "He's a friend from work. One of the bosses. But I'd better know, is my face all bruised? I haven't had a good look."

"There are purple marks by your left ear. If he is a gentleman, he won't mention them."

Before Mrs. R could ask more questions there was a knock on the door; it swung slowly open. From the doorway Caldwell studied Lolly as she studied him. His navy-blue suit looked a size too large and stubble darkened his face. His first words were, "I checked Saint Mary's but they swore you weren't there. I got the staff to confirm that you were here, but not which room." His hands hung limp at his sides, as if he didn't know where to put them.

Lolly motioned toward Mrs. R. "This is Mrs. Ruddle. It's her boarding house where I live."

Caldwell finally reacted to the other woman. "Ben Caldwell," he said, stepping forward to shake her hand. "It's a pleasure to meet you."

"Likewise."

"Do you want to sit?" asked Lolly.

"There was a message from work saying that a medical situation would keep you out for a time, but no timeframe."

Lolly couldn't put her finger on what sounded strange about that. She asked, "But why would you check the hospitals?"

"It just felt wrong. You never miss work and I needed to know that you were okay. Are you okay?" Caldwell's eyes held worry and he looked more miserable than Lolly felt just then.

She turned his words over in her mind and found that his concern warmed her. "Things were rocky for a while, but it seems like they're going to work out."

"It was nice of you to make such an effort for an employee," said Mrs. Ruddle.

"Yes—well, I—" He brought a hand to his whiskered face. "I must look a mess. I should go and clean up." He turned toward Lolly. "Can I bring you anything, a magazine or a book? I don't suppose you want chocolates?"

Chocolates? Lolly couldn't remember the last time anyone had offered her sweets, but at this moment she had more serious business in mind. "None of that," she said, "but they want me to stay one more night and I could stand to write a letter."

Mrs. R and Caldwell answered at the same time— "I have notepaper at the house" —and— "Armanko's will have stationery."

Lolly said to Caldwell, "If you could find some that's not too girly." Now that she was free of Russell, she could tell him off.

Caldwell broke into her thoughts. "You're not wearing your ring."

Lolly looked at her bare hand. "It's in the river."

His look lightened. "Oh, then you must be divorced. They say that's what the ladies do but I haven't ever seen it." He smoothed his rumpled suit coat with his hands and nodded to both women. "If you don't mind the wait, I'll be back in an hour."

As he went out, a hospital volunteer delivered a vase of peach, yellow, and white roses that glowed like a sunrise.

Mrs. R handed Lolly the attached card which Lolly read aloud. "A Bouquet of Get Well Wishes From the Paradise Club."

"Since when does a casino send roses?" asked Mrs. R. "Carnations maybe, or lilies."

Lolly smiled. "Since managers do as they please." Then she made a special request of Mrs. R. "Not that you haven't done me twenty favors just this week."

"Hon," said Mrs. R, "I'm just glad you're still here to need one more."

Caldwell, clean-shaven and wearing a fresh-looking suit, returned an hour later to the hospital room where Lolly was tucked into bed, damp hair knotted over one shoulder.

Mrs. Ruddle made ready to leave. "I'll go now," she said to Lolly. "There's a new boarder coming tomorrow at noon, but I'll fetch you home if you'll have them call when you're ready."

"Let me bring her, won't you?" said Caldwell. "I'd like to."

At Lolly's nod, Mrs. R said, "The patient agrees." She made it to the doorway before turning back. "You're the secret admirer who sent those packets of music, aren't you?"

Caldwell met her eye. "How do you figure?"

Mrs. R answered as she went out. "While you were gone for writing paper, she wanted her hair washed."

At Lolly's praise for the flowers, Caldwell gave an abbreviated bow. He pulled the bedside chair closer and presented her with a slim box of cream-colored paper and the pen from his inside jacket pocket. Lolly asked for the bed tray and prepared to set down the words she had formulated, but try as she might, with him watching, she was at a loss for how to start. At her squirming and delays, Caldwell asked what was wrong.

She paused before answering. There were so many things he didn't know about her. She didn't know him all that well either, but in spite of certain obstacles, he persisted in expressing an interest in her. That ought to count for something. She decided to be honest. If it scared him off, so be it. "I'm no good at spelling, never have been."

"You and a million others."

"It's one way of not being as smart as other people."

"There are all kinds of smart."

"I'd like to think so, but sometimes you have to get the words right."

"Then I'll help you, if you let me."

Lolly demurred. "It doesn't feel right that I'm telling off my *ex* with the help of another man."

"I'm not exactly *the other man*." Caldwell paused and looked away before he continued. "It seemed like there was already someone else."

Lolly did not confirm or deny. Instead, she said, "That makes me want to ask why you sent gifts but no letter. Not even a note. At least my husband wrote five whole lines."

"Good ones?"

"Not especially."

Caldwell cleared his throat. "I didn't write because you made it clear that you were married." He looked thoughtful as he continued. "I didn't want to only be—" He shrugged. "I was being cautious. Not my usual approach."

Lolly recalled how his stealthy exit had stung her. "Is it your usual way to leave without a word?"

"I had to. No time to spare."

"That's what everyone says—*I had to*."

Caldwell's expression grew sober. "It was one of those things you can't plan for. I packed a bag and thought I might not make it in time. But my mother lingered at the end, very ill. I buried her this last Saturday."

She took a breath. "Oh dear, that's so sad. Were you close?"

"Not really. To be honest, she wasn't mother material and I wasn't a very good son."

Now Lolly wondered what she'd been doing on Saturday as Caldwell buried his mother. She couldn't recall exactly. Playing blackjack, maybe, so she could afford the special doctor, which might have proved right as rain, or else another mistake. The only thing she knew for sure was that everything preceding this day was now history. One of the believers she had spoken with described the finality of every moment's passing. Not a one could ever be recovered. That's how all the previous weeks felt to her now. She'd been present for each and every moment, but each of them was now only memory. She said, "I didn't know. I'm sorry for you, even if …"

Caldwell looked lost in thought, so Lolly waited. Then she said,

"Your father? Brothers or sisters?"

Caldwell shook his head.

They fell to silence. After a moment Lolly said, "When I was a girl, I invented parents for myself because I didn't know who my people were. It's hard, you know? You imagine what life could be like. You daydream about someone coming through the door to take you away, someone who's been waiting for a girl like you, faults and all." She looked at her hands. "You get used to it, not having family. Other people come along, and there's work to keep you busy. You probably know what I mean. It turns out you have to claim the people you care about and hope they feel the same."

Caldwell seemed to be listening but sat silent until Lolly asked if he would miss his mother.

He said, "I suppose so, eventually. I didn't know her all that well."

"You didn't?" It seemed to Lolly that not having parents at all formed the primary reason for not knowing them. If you had parents, you couldn't help but know them.

"She sang in the clubs—San Francisco has dozens of them—gone late in the afternoon and often all night. Spent what little money we had on costumes and records."

After a moment Lolly said, "Those records you sent to me, were they hers?"

Caldwell nodded. After a moment Lolly asked, "So, you're from San Francisco. Will you be going back?"

His eyes crinkled at the corners. "I left the big city long ago. I have plenty of reasons to stay put here."

"Your job."

He caught her gaze and held it. "That's one thing."

They talked until Lolly's dinner tray came, this time with beef stew. Caldwell stayed until the nurse arrived to announce the end of visiting hours. He would head next to the Paradise. "To preview the new musician for the lounge."

Lolly took a moment to digest the news. "For the Hideout?"

"To replace that guitar player. Mayberry."

"Did he quit?"

"Sounds like it. They've booked another opener." He held her gaze a moment. "Didn't you know?"

"I—" Lolly shook her head. "No."

"Well, now that I'm back, they've got me running again, so I'll check out the new guy."

"They rely on you for just about everything, at least it seems that way."

"I guess I'm still the protégé."

Lolly realized with a start that Caldwell was describing one of those hairline cracks that Jackson had mentioned, the smallest opportunity regarding the club's policies about race and other matters ... that a person might put their shoulder to and push. She said, "That means you could change some things."

"You mean operations?"

"Who gets hired, what types of customers are allowed."

"That's decided at the top, or near the top."

"You're near the top."

He nodded. "You sound like you've got something on your mind."

"It seems to me certain procedures could work better, you know, for keeping up with the times. The Paradise could take the lead instead of following the other casinos." With those words, Lolly detected the gleam of a future that held meaning beyond waitressing, or trimming hair, or shift work.

A nurse passing by leaned in through the doorway to crook a finger at Caldwell. He stood, saying, "The old man is pretty set in his ways. But then again, he talks about businesses needing to evolve or else fail. Oh—you didn't get your letter written."

"I'll work on it tonight. There's no use pretending I can suddenly spell."

At the doorway Caldwell said, "I'll come about ten tomorrow. We can go when you feel ready."

"Did they tell you what kind of instrument the new musician plays?"

"One of those electric keyboards. It'll still be music the old man likes. Why?"

Lolly reached for a sheet of writing paper and picked up Caldwell's pen. "I'm learning to be curious about music, and other things."

The next morning, after a hospital breakfast of hot cakes and oatmeal, Lolly donned slacks and a pair of Mrs. R's boots, a half-size too large. She covered her bruised arms with one of Mrs. R's blouses and a jacket.

It had snowed a half-inch overnight, just enough to sugar-frost the landscape. Shortly after eleven with Caldwell at her side, a nurse wheeled Lolly to the auto entrance where Caldwell's sedan waited. After taking from him the bouquet, she noted the morning paper folded next to the driver's seat.

"I've kind of lost track of the headlines these last few days," said Lolly, as they pulled away from the circular drive.

"I only caught today's. Gray Reid's is remodeling. The new Harrah's has announced plans for a hotel tower. And there's a demonstration planned for the Capital Mall in D.C. A big Negro march."

So, Jackson's train tickets might work out after all. She allowed herself to imagine that he was this very moment bound for events that would animate his life. He *would* find his way into the thick of things, upright as ever while marching toward his own goal. *Godspeed.*

She dabbed a finger at the moisture in her eyes as the question that had been nagging her finally formed. "I'm trying to figure out— People call in sick all the time. If Mrs. Ruddle left a message for the restaurant manager, how would you get the news all the way over in San Francisco?"

Caldwell let out a breath. "Because they thought I would want to know."

"Is that part of your job too?"

He looked at his hands on the wheel. "Not exactly. The restaurant handles its own scheduling, but Ginny—the swing shift operator— nothing gets by her. She called and gave me the message, because ... I don't know. Somehow, she *knew*." He shrugged as if in awe of women's intuition but kept his eyes on the road. "Where to first?"

"I'd like to leave these flowers at Trinity Church. They were a lovely gesture but—no hard feelings—they're sort of overwhelming."

Caldwell steered for Island Avenue. "They're from the Paradise, the whole crew."

"And I appreciate them, but they're a little too grand."

At the church, the side lawn held a skiff of snow but the walkways and steps were only damp. Caldwell carried the heavy vase and flowers while Lolly used the handrail to mount the stairs. Stopping to catch her breath at the top, she said, "I can take that from here, but I'm sure you'd be welcome inside."

"I don't mind waiting out here."

"They don't bite, you know. Church people."

He smiled and studied her a moment. Then he motioned for her to lead the way.

Inside, Lolly gestured for Caldwell to set the bouquet on the vestibule table. She detached the gift card which Mrs. R had stuck back on its plastic stem. On a whim she turned it over. A penciled notation on the back read "OK, BC." The inscription seemed oddly familiar, but her mind was already admiring the way the church's dark paneling glowed in the morning light. She went through the door to the nave and glanced around. Its arched ceiling truly did look like the upturned hull of a boat meant for sailing a star-filled sky.

The clergyman coming down a side aisle was Father Gerard, so Lolly moved toward him. They spoke for a few minutes before she pulled a cream-colored envelope from her jacket pocket and handed it to him. They exchanged a few more words, then she returned to the vestibule where Caldwell stood waiting, hands at his sides. His hands weren't like Jackson's coffee-colored hands, callused and full of the blues, but they were good hands, she could tell.

"Where next," he said. "The post office?"

Writing the letter to Russell had clarified for Lolly that he and she could both be right and both be wrong. The same as when attempting to decipher notions about heaven, your perspective would depend on where you stood. She said, "I decided not to mail all that hurt and blame. I needed to write it out but I've let it go."

Caldwell seemed unfazed by her reversal. He moved to the door leading out as Lolly turned to the church's guest book resting beside the vase of roses. She was beginning to understand just how far she'd traveled a road alongside people who had taught her a certain kind of courage. She couldn't replicate Jackson's direct confrontation of dangerous, hateful people, but in learning to stand her ground instead of fleeing trouble, she might fashion a future that suited her instead of suiting others. With Caldwell's pen, she signed her new old name from before Russell, before Jackson, and before Caldwell and the Paradise: Lolly Marie Graham.

Gently, she extracted a single white rose from the bouquet that was already sweetening the air around it. A flower in memory of an old friend gone to a place that Lolly could not know, would not know for a long time, if such a place was even knowable. She returned the pen to Caldwell then followed him out onto the church's upper landing.

The Truckee River's channel was just across the street, edged in snow and visible from where they stood. Lolly studied the shifting shadows and light that to the uninitiated made the river look as if it rolled benignly in place, when in fact it traveled without cease. This brought to mind her own movements from the L.A. orphanage to foster homes, to restaurant work, to Gilleon, and finally to Reno where she had failed at her original goal, instead focusing on survival. Yet instead of feeling guilt like she might have in the past, she felt only gratitude, which seemed necessary and right.

She said, "Watching the river, you would swear it stays the same, but it's the same as someone told me about time. Every instant, it's brand new."

"This time of year, it runs high and it's mostly snowmelt," said Caldwell, "so cold it can kill."

She watched the water a moment longer. "I believe that," she said, "but I also know it can sometimes save."

He turned to stare at her, but she only smiled. "I'll tell you about it," she said. "Some other time."

With that, she descended to the sidewalk. Let the river continue its never-ending journey, constantly leaving this town for the next one. She wasn't a river, so she could stay put. She had some living to do on solid ground.

~*~

Author's Notes

This book project was such a labor of love. I began researching the facts that support it way back before the Covid pandemic, and such is the passage of time that I can only hope that the scribbled notes I kept are complete about sources for information and people who read early versions of Lolly's story. I am enormously grateful for the kind attentions and assistance of: critique partners and authors themselves, Lisa Mortara (who also provided guidance about Catholicism of the 1960s) and Bill Kuechler, and thoughtful critiquers Kate LaRue and Anne Buckley. Early readers included Grace Caudill, CJ Waldren, Pam Alvey, Carolyn Hendrickson, Alexandria King, Gina Akao, and Christine Rost.

Local music guru Steve Funk gave me the blues in the most helpful way; I benefited from the newspaper columns of local writers and historians Bob Chez, Neal Cobb, Guy Rocha, Mel Shields, Karl Breckenridge, and Patty Cafferata; Trinity Episcopal Church's Mac Wieland and Father Seville admitted me to their universe and invited me to soak up the beauty of their worship space; Kathy Berry's 2012 community college class addressing Ghosts and Spirits provided food for thought, as did the OLLI lecture of Sacramento entertainment critic Mel Shields.

Historian and University of Nevada, Reno, special collections expert Mella Harmon answered questions about Reno's divorce trade of yore and provided access to historical photos and records; old friend and historian Kim Henrick introduced me to Mella Harmon and separately to longtime musician and guitar collector Jim Geil, who schooled me about guitars (Kim knows the best people)

A tip of my hat to the helpful staff members of the Nevada Historical Society and the Washoe County and University of Nevada, Reno, libraries. I found quiet and solace among the pines at Bill and Sue Z's mountain home, and a lesson in Nevada's mid-century neon signs from Will Durham's collection exhibited at the Nevada Museum of Art in Reno. And thanks to a variety of churches and synagogues that allowed public access to their places of worship.

I cannot imagine using only a smart phone or laptop to properly research settings, language, cultures, and music for the writing of a novel. Those tools are grand, but it takes a world of sources and sometimes years of gathering and absorbing impressions, parallel stories, and purposeful information as background for my own stories. I thank all of the human sources listed above and above all, my partner in serious stuff and shenanigans, Jim Riley.

And you, dear reader, deserve thanks for being a reader of books. Authors and writers always hope to attract folks like you. May there always be books that need readers and readers who need books.

I invite you to turn the page in order to sample *Yellow Moon Rising*, my Depression-era suspense story that stars a Lakota ranch hand and healer being tracked by a Union Pacific Railroad detective as she chases her murderous uncle.

Sample: *Yellow Moon Rising (Western Suspense)*

Kansas City, Missouri
1936

Stopping before the entrance of Conboie Undertaking, Raylene smoothed her rumpled brown dress, the most appropriate garment to be had on short notice before viewing the body of her *até*. Her father. The nearby secondhand store had charged her twenty-five cents for the too-large, slightly wrinkled garment, but included a newsboy cap for ten cents more.

She could make out the bank clock on the building at the corner, which read 10:00 straight up. There was no sign of her sister Annie, who must have received a similar letter about their father's death with its invitation to this place today.

Where was that sister of hers, simply tardy or already inside? Before proceeding, they should speak about what Thomas's death meant to the family. They should be together in this. Raylene glanced at the foot traffic around the soup kitchen a few doors up but caught no sign of Annie, which made her wonder how long an undertaker would wait for an Indian's relatives to arrive. Probably not long. She counted out two more minutes, then stepped through the undertaker's door, travel bundle in hand, and advanced slowly through the vestibule's low light.

Of the two men at the far end of the small parlor, one advanced down the center aisle to meet her, saying, "Good morning. I'm Gerald Lambert, Mr. Conboie's assistant." His gaze flicked down her odd costume to her worn western boots and back to her face. "Are you Miss ... ah, Yellow Moon?"

"Little Moon," said Raylene.

"But you've come regarding Thomas Yellow Moon."

Raylene glanced around. Still no Annie. "Your letter left little travel time. Almost two days by train."

"I understand."

She set her bundled jacket on the closest chair, one of many arrayed in rows, and asked, "What can you tell me about my father's death?"

The assistant lifted a hand to his sternum. "What can *I* tell you?"

"Was it a robbery, or a raid of some kind? Your letter said an apparent fight at his saloon." On her journey south to Missouri with the countryside rolling past her train window, she had pondered who would fight with Thomas. If not the police, perhaps the husband of a lover or a disgruntled loser from one of his backroom card games. More importantly — to whom would her father *lose* a fight?

"The language in that letter was provided by authorities. They haven't mentioned a suspect, if that's what you mean." He fidgeted under her gaze.

She decided that her sister, not known for punctuality, was somehow delayed. Raylene would report to her later. "I guess I should see him."

As the assistant led her up the aisle, the second man stepped forward with a sober air. In one hand he held a dark blue purse by its handle. "Excuse me, Miss. I am John Murphy of the Union Pacific Railroad. I understand this is a dark time for you and I would not trample your feelings, but I'd like to ask a couple of questions about your sister Annie. I brought her purse."

Raylene considered this man, whose spectacles and carefully pressed suit suggested a no-nonsense type. "What do you mean, you brought her purse? Why would you have her purse?"

"The police gave me leave to bring Miss Moon's purse when I came to ask if you knew the whereabouts of some jewelry in her possession."

The railroad man might as well have been speaking a foreign language. Raylene was there to see her father's body, not to listen to nonsense about a purse purported to be Annie's. "Please explain yourself."

"I'm working a case regarding some missing jewelry that involves your sister."

"Has she filed a claim with your railroad?"

Mr. Lambert broke in. "Did you not receive our letter about Annie Moon?"

"I received only the one about my father. The reason I've come."

The assistant cleared his throat. "The first letter we posted to you gave news of your sister's passing. You should have received it before the one about your father."

As Raylene's thoughts went spinning, she steadied herself with one hand on the back of the nearest chair. Was it possible for not only her father to be dead, but Annie too? Her sister, her *chuwé*, who had slept beside her in childhood and protected her on the schoolyard. Dead? An impossibility, yet here were respectable-looking men telling her just that as they watched for her response. Not a woman to dissolve from emotion, she inhaled slowly and asked, "When did this happen?"

"We received Miss Moon's body two days before your father's. The authorities obtained your postal address for us."

Raylene's mind wanted to reject the possibility that Annie was dead, yet why would these men fabricate such a story? She drew another silent breath before speaking. "There was no letter about Annie. What was the cause?"

"Natural, according to police,'" said Mr. Lambert.

"So, I'll be viewing her body as well?"

"Well, no. We buried her on Wednesday."

"Why her but not my father?"

The assistant licked his lips. "There must have been instructions and payment."

"But I have only just arrived."

"When Mr. Conboie says bury someone, we do it, but we waited regarding the, ah, gentleman."

"Who paid to bury my sister?"

Mr. Lambert lifted his shoulders as if to suggest ignorance.

"Then I'll ask Mr. Conboie."

"You may do just that, but you'll have to wait 'til he gets back from Denver. Business, you know."

Raylene studied the assistant and decided he was determined to keep her at a distance from any pertinent details. She didn't know why this would be, but he seemed to be in charge of this place so she said, "I will see the body you have not buried."

John Murphy broke in. "Miss — about the missing jewelry …"

Raylene took the purse he held out to her. "Is my sister implicated in a crime?"

The railroad man straightened. "I've only come to ask questions."

She wondered if this stranger suspected Annie of theft when Annie was no thief. "Can *you* tell me about my sister's death?"

His eyeglasses gleamed in the low light. "I cannot, but I do know that your sister's landlady is holding other possessions for you, should you want."

He did not seem an aggressive sort, nor a salesman trying to get into her pocket, but clearly, he wanted information she could not provide. She said, "I cannot help you and you cannot help me, so I would like to finish what I came for."

Mr. Murphy stepped aside as the assistant motioned toward an opening toward the front of the seating space, saying, "This way."

He strode forward and turned left, but a closed door off to the right caught Raylene's attention. She moved to it and found that the office within was unoccupied, so she spun toward a short hallway beyond and opened the first door she reached, which held stainless steel tables and countertops arrayed with chrome basins, glass jars, coiled tubes.

Mr. Lambert arrived beside her in a huff. "Miss Moon, this room is off limits!"

"You buried Miss Moon. I am Miss Little Moon."

"Fine, but I insist you return to the parlor. Or else."

"Or else what?"

"Or I will be forced to call authorities."

She said, "I would like to ask Mr. Conboie about my sister's burial."

Mr. Lambert drew himself up. "You are trespassing in this hallway."

She glanced into the gloom. "There might be other rooms to check."

His shout nearly deafened her. "Mr. Murphy! Call the police!"

Raylene blinked at him and pointed back in the direction of the office. "You could call them yourself. I saw a telephone."

"Oh, no no no." He narrowed his eyes. "I'm not falling for that. If I step away, you will do as you please."

Raylene had made her point. She did not know the likelihood of finding Mr. Conboie on the premises and an interview with police would not further her cause. She shook her head and retreated toward the parlor, leaving Mr. Lambert to latch the embalming room door. The railroad man stood in the same place as minutes prior.

"Mr. Murphy?" said the assistant.

"Had I imagined you in mortal danger," said the Union Pacific man, "I would have summoned authorities or aided you myself. *Were* you?"

The assistant only frowned in reply, then motioned to Raylene that she should lead the way to the open chamber opposite, which was lit by the glow of small electric sconces. She did so, stopping before a rolling cart that held a wooden coffin exuding the aroma of fresh-cut pine. Mr. Lambert lifted the coffin's lid and backed away.

Sorrow that had traveled a long road bubbled up inside Raylene at the sight of Thomas buttoned neatly into a plain cotton shirt and clean, worn trousers. The sight of him solid but dead seemed unreal, yet she stood now before his silent body. The deep lines of his face looked soft, his scarred hands, perfectly still. She remembered back to her childhood when he had seemed so tall and true. He was a natural on a horse, sometimes buying and selling them. He had not been tender or gentle, was occasionally gruff and a bit distant, but she had always known she had a father. *Annie,* she thought now. *Here is Ate´. You should be here with me, but you are not. Why is it that you are not?*

When the assistant interrupted her reverie, she swallowed her grief before he could perceive it. He said, "Of course, there's no good time to offer this, but should you desire more formal attire for your father, I can arrange it. A suit perhaps, or else something less plain in the way of a casket?"

Raylene had the remainder of Raul's cash — a dollar and change — that her rail ticket had not consumed. Had she arrived with a pocket full of money, would she now spend it on a fancy casket to drop into a hole in the ground? The ground cared not whether it received the dead in painted, pillowed boxes or atop pyres of sagebrush and willow. Eyes on the body before her, she said, "I doubt you bury the dead without a box."

"The coroner pays for these plain ones, but when we locate family members, they quite often prefer something more memorable. We have nice caskets to show you."

Raylene ignored the assistant and gazed upon her father's corpse, its face aged by the life he had fashioned for himself and Annie in a city where they didn't belong and would never be fully accepted. In another time, his body would have been remanded back to the earth in ashes, back to ravens and wolves, to sun and wind and rain. But he was here now, in the city he had chosen, and she was without the means to reverse what others had set into motion.

Leaning in, she inhaled the odors of embalming fluid and laundry powder. Not a hint remained of the honest sweat of a day shoeing horses in the sun, or repairing tools, or driving wagons, or even his work in the saloon. *Father, why you?*

She ran her forefinger into a slit in the front of his fresh-washed shirt and felt the crude stitchwork that had sewn together a slash in his torso. So — the fight had involved a knife. That explained the cuts on his left hand.

She paused. Death was a regular part of life on the prairie and on the reservations. Animals died and people perished. Sometimes one killed the other, or the weather did, or misfortune. She was not a stranger to death, but death in a city seemed a different creature. Once more she imagined various possibilities: a thief had gone for the cash drawer, or Thomas had crossed somebody, a supplier perhaps. Or a drunk, having spent his rent money, had picked a fight.

Each awful option seemed plausible, but the evidence before her suggested far worse. No one robbing a saloon used a knife because saloon-keepers often kept pistols or long guns. And as wily as gamblers could be, they were unlikely to best a man who had handled knives since his youth. Though her expression gave nothing away, a rising anger joined the sorrow that had taken root within her, bringing her as close to fury as she had ever felt. She knew of only one person clever enough and quick enough to kill Thomas, but *he* wouldn't, would he?

Yellow Moon Rising and its sequel (Yellow Moon Justice) are available through most book retailers and in e-book form on Amazon.com

The author thanks cultural consultants Danialle Rose, of the Cheyenne River Sioux, and Thomas Ghost Dog, of the Oglala Nation, for their invaluable insights regarding culture, history, and language; and Thomas for granting permission to use his hometown of Manderson, South Dakota, nearby to which his grandfather William Ghost Dog sponsored the first rodeo held on Pine Ridge Reservation land.